Silas glanced over at TJ, his heart breaking a little with worry over her.

"I can't help but be concerned. That last letter..."

What he wanted to say was "we have to find True Fan before True Fan finds you," but he held his tongue. She was already scared enough. She didn't need him sharing his instincts or experience with her.

Unfortunately, those instincts and his experience on the job told him that True Fan would be making good on those threats—and soon.

As he pulled up in front of her house, he turned to her and reached for her hand. "Do me a favor, okay?" She nodded, seeming surprised by how serious he'd become. "Don't go anywhere alone. Take one of your sisters if you insist on going out. Especially don't go chasing True Fan. Wait for me. I'm not sure how long my business is going to take me, but—"

"You don't have to worry about me. I'll be fine."

How many times had he heard those words? "That's what they all say." He felt her shudder. "Just do it for me."

B.J. Daniels is a *New York Times* and *USA TODAY* bestselling author. She wrote her first book after a career as an award-winning newspaper journalist and author of thirty-seven published short stories. She lives in Montana with her husband, Parker, and three springer spaniels. When not writing, she quilts, boats and plays tennis. Contact her at bjdaniels.com, on Facebook or on Twitter, @bjdanielsauthor.

Books by B.J. Daniels

Harlequin Intrigue

Whitehorse, Montana: The Clementine Sisters

Hard Rustler
Rogue Gunslinger

The Montana Cahills

Cowboy's Redemption

Whitehorse, Montana: The McGraw Kidnapping

Dark Horse
Dead Ringer
Rough Rider

HQN Books

The Montana Cahills

Renegade's Pride
Outlaw's Honor
Hero's Return
Rancher's Dream

Visit the Author Profile page
at Harlequin.com for more titles.

B.J. DANIELS

NEW YORK TIMES AND USA TODAY
BESTSELLING AUTHOR

ROGUE GUNSLINGER
&
HUNTING DOWN
THE HORSEMAN

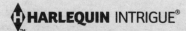

ISBN-13: 978-1-335-54272-4

Rogue Gunslinger & Hunting Down the Horseman

Copyright © 2018 by Harlequin Books S.A.

The publisher acknowledges the copyright holder of the individual works as follows:

Rogue Gunslinger
Copyright © 2018 by Barbara Heinlein

Hunting Down the Horseman
Copyright © 2009 by Barbara Heinlein

This edition published by arrangement with Harlequin Books S.A.

For questions and comments about the quality of this book, please contact us at CustomerService@Harlequin.com.

® and TM are trademarks of Harlequin Enterprises Limited or its corporate affiliates. Trademarks indicated with ® are registered in the United States Patent and Trademark Office, the Canadian Intellectual Property Office and in other countries.

Printed in U.S.A.

HARLEQUIN®
www.Harlequin.com

CONTENTS

This book is for Gale Simonson,
part of the Simonson duo, who keeps our lives
interesting in the Quilting by the Border group.
You are always like a breath of fresh air.
Thanks for keeping me smiling.

ROGUE GUNSLINGER

Chapter One

The old antique Royal typewriter clacked with each angry stroke of the keys. Shaking fingers pounded out livid words onto the old discolored paper. As the fury built, the fingers moved faster and faster until the keys all tangled together in a metal knot that lay suspended over the paper.

With a curse of frustration, the metal arms were tugged apart and the sound of the typewriter resumed in the small room. Angry words burst across the page, some letters darker than others as the keystrokes hit like a hammer. Other letters appeared lighter, some dropping down a half line as the fingers slipped from the worn keys. A bell sounded at the end of each line as the carriage was returned with a clang, until the paper was ripped from the typewriter.

Read in a cold, dark rage, the paper was folded hurriedly, the edges uneven, and stuffed into the envelope already addressed in the black typewritten letters:

Author TJ St. Clair
Whitehorse, Montana

The stamp slapped on, the envelope sealed, the fingers still shaking with expectation for when the novelist opened it. The fan rose and smiled. Wouldn't Ms. St. Clair, aka Tessa Jane Clementine, love this one.

TJ ST. CLAIR hated conference calls. Especially this conference call.

"I know it's tough with your book coming out before Christmas," said Rachel, the marketing coordinator, the woman's voice sounding hollow on speakerphone in TJ's small New York City apartment.

"But I don't have to tell you how important it is to do as much promo as you can this week to get those sales where you want them," Sherry from Publicity and Events added.

TJ held her head and said nothing for a moment. "I'm going home for the holidays to be with my sisters, who I haven't seen in months." She started to say she knew how important promoting her book was, but in truth she often questioned if a lot of the events really made that much difference—let alone all the social media. If readers spent as much time as TJ had to on social media, she questioned how they could have time to read books.

"It's the threatening letters you've been getting, isn't it?" her agent Clara said.

She glanced toward the window, hating to admit that the letters had more than spooked her. "That is definitely part of it. They have been getting more… detailed and more threatening."

"I'm so sorry, TJ," Clara said and everyone added in words of sympathy.

"You've spoken to the police?" her editor, Dan French, asked.

"There is nothing they can do until…until the fan acts on the threats. That's another reason I want to go to Montana."

For a few beats there was silence. "All right. I can speak to Marketing," Dan said. "We'll do what we can from this end."

"I hate to request this, but is there any chance you could do a couple of book signings while you're at home before Christmas, right before the book comes out?" Rachel asked. "I wouldn't push, but TJ, we hate to see you lose the momentum you've picked up with your last book."

"That would be at least something," Dan agreed.

"If you don't make the list, it won't be the end of the world," her editor added. "But we'd hoped to see you advance up the list with this one. I love this book. I think it's the best one you've ever written."

The first week a book came out was the most important and they all knew it. If she didn't make the list—the *New York Times* list—it would mean losing the bonus she usually got for ranking in the top ten. It would also hurt her on her next contract, not to mention the publisher might back off on promotional money for her.

"We don't mean to pressure you," Dan said. "But I'm sure if the police thought this fan was really dangerous—"

"I think going to Montana is smart," her agent cut in. "You'll be safe there with your family over the holidays. We can regroup when you get back."

She rubbed her temples. "I could do one book signing in my hometown since there is only one bookstore there. Whitehorse is tiny and in the middle of nowhere. The roads can be closed off and on this time of year, so there won't be much of a turnout though."

"Isn't the *Billings Gazette* doing a story on you as well?" Trish from Marketing asked.

"Yes." She groaned inwardly, having forgotten she'd agreed to that months ago.

"That will have to do, then," her agent said, coming to her defense. "Her next book will be out in the spring. Let's plan on doing something special for that."

"We have ads coming out in six major magazines as well as a social media blitz for this one," Rachel said. "You should be fine. You have a lot of loyal fans who've been waiting patiently for this book. Your presales are good."

"Are you all right with this?" her agent asked.

She nodded and then realized she had to speak. Her throat was dry, her stomach roiling. Just the thought of any kind of public event had her terrified. But before she could answer, the call was over. Everyone wished each other a happy and safe holiday and hung up, except for her agent.

"Are you sure you're okay?"

"I will be once I get home," she told her and herself. She couldn't wait to get on the plane. She hadn't been back to Montana for years except for her grandmother's funeral.

"Keep in touch. And if you need anything…"

TJ smiled. She loved her agent. "I know. Thank you." She disconnected. Every book release she worried it wouldn't make the list or wouldn't be high enough on the list—which meant better than the last book had done. Not this time.

"You have bigger things to worry about at the moment," she said to herself as she walked to her apartment window and looked out.

I know where you live. You think you can sit in your big-city apartment and ignore me? Think again.

That ominous threat was added at the bottom of the last written attack she'd received from True Fan. What was different this time was that her fan had included a photograph taken from the outside of her New York City apartment. She'd recognized the curtains covering the window of her third-floor unit. There'd been a light behind them, which meant she'd been home when her "fan" had taken the photo from the sidewalk outside.

It was recent too. One of the wings of Mrs. Gunderson's Christmas angel was in the photograph. Her elderly neighbor had put it up only two days ago. TJ had helped her.

Just the thought of how recent the photo had been taken made her shudder. She glanced at her phone. Her flight was still hours away but she preferred sitting at the airport surrounded by security screened people to staying another minute in this apartment.

Sticking her phone into a side pocket of her purse, she grabbed the handle of her suitcase and headed for the door.

Nowadays she always checked the hallway before she left her apartment. She did this time as well. It was empty. She could hear holiday music playing in one of the apartments down the hall. The song brought tears to her eyes. She was a mess, way too emotional to spend the holidays with her sisters—especially since the three of them had been estranged for months.

She hesitated. Maybe she should change her flight. Go to some warm resort. But just the thought turned her stomach. She was going back to Whitehorse. Going home for Christmas.

She rolled her suitcase down to the elevator and pushed the button.

When it clanged its way up from what sounded like the basement, she waited for the door to open. If anyone she didn't recognize happened to be on the elevator, she would make an excuse about forgetting something she needed in her apartment and turn back until the elevator left again.

She knew it was silly, but she couldn't help it. No one was taking the threats seriously. But she had watched the tone of the letters degenerate into angry, hateful words that were more than threatening. This person wasn't done with her. Far from it. She couldn't shake the feeling that her "True Fan" was coming for her.

The elevator stopped and the door began to open. Empty. She let out the breath she'd been holding. Stepping in, she pulled her suitcase close and pushed the button for the ground floor.

The fan writing her the threatening letters could be anyone. That was what was so frightening. It could even be someone who lived in this apartment complex. Or someone she'd met at a conference. She met so many fans, she couldn't possibly remember them all. It embarrassed her when they complimented her books. She wanted to hug them all. She doubted she would ever get used to this. Writing had been her dream since she was a girl. Getting published? Well, that was like a miracle to her. She couldn't believe her good luck.

Until she'd begun getting the letters from her True Fan.

Outside the apartment building, the sidewalk was filled with people hurrying past. Shoppers laden with packages, others rushing off to work... The city was bustling more than usual. She glanced at the faces of people as they passed, not sure what she was looking for. Would she recognize her rabid fan if she saw him or her?

She couldn't help studying their faces, looking for one that might be familiar. She didn't even know if her "fan" was male or female. She also didn't know if the person was watching her right now.

After a while, everyone began to look familiar to her. If anyone made eye contact, she quickly dropped her gaze as she made her way to the curb to signal for a cab. She wrote about crazed homicidal people. Wouldn't she recognize something in True Fan's eyes that would give the person away?

With a screech of brakes, a yellow cab came to a stop on the other side of the street. The driver motioned for her to hurry. But a large delivery truck was coming too fast for her to cross before it passed.

She felt something hit her in the back. Letting out a cry, she found herself falling into the street in front of the large speeding truck.

Chapter Two

It happened so fast. One minute she was standing on the curb waiting for the large delivery truck to pass before crossing the street to the waiting taxi.

The next she was falling forward into the street and the truck bearing down on her. Her arms windmilled as she tried to catch herself, but there was nothing to grab. She could hear the deafening roar of the truck's engine, smelled diesel fuel turning the air gray and closed her eyes as she realized she was about to die.

The hand that closed over her arm was large and viselike. One minute she was falling headlong into the street in front of the truck and the next she was snatched from the crushing metal bumper as the truck roared on past.

Pulled by the hand gripping her arm, her body whipped back. She slammed into something so solid it could have been a lamppost. She turned just quickly enough that her face came in contact with the chest of a large male body as she tried to get her feet under her. He steadied her for a moment before the fingers on her arm released.

She looked up in time to see the man who'd saved her turn and walk away as if rescuing women was something he did every day. Trembling all over, she was still reeling from her near death.

"Wait!" she called after him. He'd just saved her life. But if he'd heard her, he didn't turn. All she got was a brief glimpse of granite features, collar-length dark, curly hair beneath a baseball cap above wide shoulders clad in a tan suede sheepskin coat before he disappeared into the crowd.

She turned to find her suitcase and purse had fallen to the ground at the edge of the curb. Still shaken, she reached for them. The taxi that had stopped for her was long gone. No one seemed to have noticed what had almost happened to her.

Why had the man taken off the way he had? A Good Samaritan who didn't like taking credit for his deeds? Or, she thought with a shudder, the person who'd pushed her in front of the speeding truck—and then saved her.

Was it possible the man had been her True Fan?

She remembered being hit from behind and then the viselike grip of his large hand as his fingers bit into her arm. He hadn't even taken the time to see if she was all right. A shudder rattled through her. Had this been a warning?

A cab pulled to a stop in front of her. Tears burned her eyes as she stepped toward it. After all this time of being away, she couldn't wait to go home to Whitehorse.

SILAS WALKER SWORE. He'd lost the man he'd been following in the crowd of Christmas shoppers. Now he leaned against the front of a building, watching the street. His leg hurt like hell. He realized he was limping badly and cursed. If it wasn't for his injury, he wouldn't have lost the man.

Or if he hadn't stopped just long enough to grab that woman who'd been jostled by the crowd and almost fallen in front of a delivery truck. He shook his head. She should have known better than to stand that close to the street, especially with the sidewalk this crowded. He hated to think what could have happened if he hadn't been right behind her.

His cell phone vibrated. He checked the screen. A text from his boss that he wanted to see him ASAP. That couldn't be good. He quickly texted back that he was on his way.

One look at the way he was limping and he knew exactly what his boss was going to say. He'd come back to work too soon. That he knew his boss was right didn't make it any easier to accept.

But after today, after messing up an easy tail, Silas had to accept that he wasn't up to the job yet. That alone would force him to lay off his leg for a while. Just over the holidays, not that he was happy about it.

A taxi pulled past. He spotted the woman in the back seat. She wore a bright red long coat with a multicolored scarf—the same woman he'd grabbed out of the way of the truck.

But that wasn't the surprising part. He recognized her. He'd studied that face on the back cover of her book more times than he wanted to admit. He couldn't believe his luck. TJ St. Clair. The thriller writer. Her photo hadn't done her justice.

As the taxi drove on past, he realized she was probably headed for the airport given that he now recalled seeing a suitcase next to her. Somewhere for the holidays?

Smiling, he told himself she might be headed home to Montana. If he was right... Well, what were the chances they might cross paths again?

TJ HAD WONDERED what it would be like seeing her sisters again. The last time they'd been together they'd argued. Well, that is, she and Chloe had argued with their younger sister Annabelle over their grandmother's house.

Grandmother Frannie Clementine had died a few months ago. In her will, she'd left everything she had— basically her house in Whitehorse—to Annabelle.

"Did you know she was going to do that?" they'd demanded.

"No, I swear I didn't," Annabelle had said on the phone since she hadn't attended the funeral or seen the will.

"Why would she do that?" Chloe had demanded.

"I have no idea," their sister had said. "Except... well, I always got the impression that she liked me the best." She'd tried to pass that off as a joke, but they'd all hung up angry.

Now as TJ stepped off the plane, she felt bad about the argument. The house had turned out to be a whole lot of work—and had held some surprises that neither TJ nor Chloe would have wanted to handle. It had been clear why Grandma Frannie had left the house to Annabelle, who they all agreed was more like Frannie than either TJ or Chloe.

The Billings, Montana, airport was small by most airport standards and sat on rimrocks overlooking the state's largest city. She hadn't gone far when she saw her sisters waving at her from the bottom of the escalator.

TJ couldn't help but grin. They were both wearing elf hats. She groaned. "This has to have been Annabelle's idea," she said under her breath. But the sight of them in those hats had definitely broken the ice.

She laughed as she reached them, hugging one and then the other. As she pulled back, she felt such a surge of love for her sisters that it brought tears to her eyes.

"We didn't want you to feel left out," Annabelle said, and whipped an elf hat from her bag and settled it on TJ's blonde head. She grinned and put her arm around them. "We look like triplets."

"Heaven forbid," Chloe said.

"I'm starving," Annabelle said, surprising no one. Since she'd quit modeling for a living, she was always hungry. "Ray J's barbecue when we get home, eat here or just get snacks like we used to for the ride home?"

"Snacks!" TJ and Chloe said together.

"Did I mention I bought your favorite bottles of wine?" Annabelle asked. "Or we can go out and party tonight."

TJ and Chloe groaned in unison and then laughed. It felt good being around them again, TJ thought, and felt her eyes burn again with tears. Coming home for the holidays had been the right choice. She realized this was the best she'd felt in a very long time.

Annabelle chattered as they walked through the terminal toward the exit. TJ half listened, thankful that the trouble between them had blown over. They were all three back in Montana just like when they were growing up. They were sisters and she couldn't have been more delighted to be with them, even though people stared.

She laughed. She'd forgotten they were all now

wearing elf hats. For a few minutes, she'd completely forgotten her near-death experience this morning in the city and True Fan's threats.

But as she and her sisters passed a group waiting in one of the departure lines, she saw a woman raise her phone and take a photo of the three of them. Glancing back, TJ saw the woman quickly begin texting someone.

Chapter Three

"Wow," Chloe cried from the front seat of the SUV as she showed TJ her phone. "It's already all over social media." There was the photograph of the three of them in their elf hats. Just as she'd feared, the woman had recognized her, tagging the photo with her pen name. "Ah the life of the rich and famous."

TJ groaned. "Now everyone will know that I've come home to Whitehorse for Christmas."

"It isn't like it was a secret, right?" Annabelle asked as she drove. "Everyone knows you're from White-horse, Montana. Not much of a leap that you would be going home for Christmas." She glanced in the rear-view mirror. "Seriously, is it a problem?"

"No," TJ lied. "It's fine. Sometimes it would be nice to be anonymous though, but I don't have to tell you about that."

Annabelle sighed. "Yep, but when now faced with being anonymous the rest of my life… Well, it's an adjustment. I have to admit, it was fun seeing my photo on the front of magazines—even if it was a doctored photo of me. Nothing is all that real with modeling."

"So you're not going back to it?" Chloe asked their

baby sister. "You're just going to marry Dawson Rogers, become a ranchwoman—"

"And live happily ever after," Annabelle said with a giggle. "Yep, that's the plan."

They began discussing people they knew in Whitehorse and how things had or hadn't changed.

TJ only half listened to their conversation. She hadn't told either sister about the threatening letters—let alone what had happened in the city only hours ago. The more she'd thought about it on the plane ride back to Montana, the more unsure she was that she'd been pushed in front of that truck. Could it have been an accident? Or had it been deliberate? Either way, if that man hadn't grabbed her...

She shivered and looked out at the snowy landscape. If that man was her True Fan, he'd been watching her apartment. When the light had gone off in her living room, he would have known she would be coming downstairs. Or he might have been a stranger passing by.

TJ shook her head, determined not to think about it. She was safe now. At least for a while.

"So we're talking wedding bells," Chloe was saying.

"Wait, I must have missed something," TJ said, sitting forward to hear. "You and Dawson? When?"

"We haven't set a date yet. I know it's quick, but I would love a Christmas wedding, something small and intimate," Annabelle said, sounding dreamy. Both Chloe and TJ groaned and then laughed.

"Love," Chloe said with a shake of her head.

"Actually," TJ said, settling back into her seat, "I always thought you and Dawson were a good match."

They talked about weddings, growing up in Whitehorse, people they knew who'd left—and those who had stayed. The time passed quickly on the drive to their hometown.

As they pulled up in front of the house they'd grown up in after their parents had died, Annabelle cut the engine. Conversation died. They all looked in the direction of Grandmother Frannie's house. Even though Frannie had left the house to Annabelle, TJ would always think of it as their grandmother's. None of them spoke. The only sound was the tick, tick, tick as the motor cooled.

"Are you two all right?" Annabelle asked.

TJ hadn't realized it when they'd met her at the airport, but Chloe had flown in only thirty minutes before she had. Which meant that like her, she hadn't been to the house where they were raised since the funeral.

"It's like it was when we were kids," Annabelle said, as if trying to reassure them.

From the back seat, TJ glanced at her sister in the rearview mirror. All three of them knew the house would never be like that again. Not after their grandmother's secrets had been unearthed, so to speak.

"If you don't want to stay here, we can go out to Dawson's ranch," Annabelle said. "We have a standing invitation."

TJ smiled at that, seeing how happy her sister was to be back together with her high school sweetheart. "I'm good with staying in the house."

"Of course you are," Chloe said. "You write murder mysteries." She sighed. "I am good with staying here too. I think it's what Grandmother would have wanted. But it's still weird. I can't believe the secrets our grandmother kept from us."

TJ chuckled. Frannie had been a tiny, sweet little woman who everyone said wouldn't hurt a fly. "Seems all those wild stories we thought she made up to entertain us had some truth in them."

"Imagine if she hadn't toned them down to PG," Annabelle said.

They all laughed and opened their car doors, the earlier tension gone. Getting the luggage out, they made their way up the shoveled path through the deep snow. *Christmas in Whitehorse*, TJ thought. The last time she'd left here, she'd been pretty sure she'd never be back. But as she breathed in the icy evening air, she knew she was exactly where she wanted to be right now.

Annabelle scooped up a handful of snow in her mitten and tossed it into the air over them before running toward the door, fearing payback. Both TJ and Chloe let out cries as ice crystals glittered in the silver evening before covering them from head to toe.

TJ shook the light snow from her long blond hair and laughed. It was good to see Annabelle like this. It had been a long time. Now, she was again that adventurous young girl who'd gotten stuck in the neighbor boy's tree house.

"I thought you'd want your old rooms," Annabelle was saying as they crossed the porch and she unlocked the door.

TJ hadn't known what to expect as the door swung open. Her grandmother had been a hoarder in her old age. The last time she'd seen this place—when she and Chloe had come up for the funeral—it had been so full of newspapers, magazines, knickknacks, old furniture and so much junk there were only paths through the house. Little had they known what was buried in there.

She stopped in the doorway, dumbstruck. The junk was gone. The walls were painted a nice pale gray, and the place looked warm and welcoming, complete with new furniture.

"Annabelle, you shouldn't have gone to so much trouble. We aren't staying that long," TJ said, shocked.

"It wasn't all me. Willie insisted on helping and I wasn't about to say no," Annabelle said. "You remember Dawson's mom. When she takes on a project… You have to see the kitchen. Dawson completely remodeled it."

TJ could only nod and follow her sister into the kitchen where their grandmother used to attempt to cook. She stopped in the doorway. This was the room where Annabelle had discovered her grandmother's biggest secret. It looked like any other kitchen in an older remodeled house.

"Remember the cookie jar where Frannie kept her grocery money?" her sister was saying. "I saved it."

Chloe had stepped in and was looking around, wide-eyed. "It's amazing." She met TJ's gaze. "Ghosts?"

"Gone," Annabelle said, and crossed her heart with her index finger. "No ghosts."

TJ thought ghosts were the least of her problems. "Did Willie help you with our rooms as well?"

"She did. Come on, I'll show you." Annabelle ran up the stairs. TJ and Chloe followed, whispering among themselves.

"She did a great job," Chloe was saying. "Remember what it was like?"

"Unfortunately, I do," TJ said. "Like a horror story."

"Or a thriller," Chloe whispered back. "Like the kind you write."

TJ didn't need the reminder.

Annabelle had stopped at Chloe's old room. They joined her. The room had been painted her favorite color, pale purple, and decorated to fit their investigative reporter sister's style.

"You do realize that this visit is temporary, right?" TJ asked. Annabelle didn't seem to hear her. Stepping down the hall, TJ stopped at a room she knew at once was hers. It was painted a pale yellow. A quilt of yellow-and-blue fabric lay on the antique white iron bed. There was a small white desk and chair to one side of the bed with a lamp and spot for her laptop. On the wall above it was a framed collage of her book covers.

"Do you like it?" Annabelle said behind her, sounding anxious.

"Oh, Annabelle." She turned to hug her sister, hoping to hide her discomfort. The last thing she wanted to see were her book covers right now. They reminded her of the threats from her True Fan, who had found fault with all of her latest plots—and even her covers.

"It's perfect."

Her sister seemed to relax. "Is this going to be all right?" she asked.

"It is, Belle," she said using a nickname for her littlest sister that she hadn't used in years. "I'm glad you kept Frannie's house."

"It was Dawson's idea. He bought it for a rental but he thought it would be nice for us to have it for when the two of you visit. After we're married, we'll build a house with guest rooms for you and Chloe when you come home. Then we'll either rent this house or sell it. But I like the idea of keeping it. At least for a while."

She loved her sister's enthusiasm, but she couldn't imagine visiting Whitehorse often. So she said nothing, just smiled and hugged her again.

Chloe came out of her room holding a framed photo of the three of them.

"Check this out," she said, wiping tears as she showed TJ a photo of them when they were girls. "We were so cute."

"We are still cute," Annabelle said. "Let's go to Ray J's and get some barbecue. Then I'm thinking we should go to the Mint and celebrate."

"Whoa," Chloe said. "Barbecue, yes. Our old bar, no." She looked to TJ to back her up.

"How about we come back here, open the wine and make it a fairly early night," TJ said. "At least for today. It's been kind of a long day. But could we stop by the bookstore before it closes on the way to supper? I need to see if they have everything they need for my book signing."

"You're doing a book signing this close to Christmas?" Chloe said.

"Don't ask."

THE BOOKSTORE WAS actually a gift shop that carried her books because she was considered a local author. TJ stopped inside the door. It had been so long since she'd had her very first signing here. She remembered her excitement from the acceptance of her book to actually seeing her words in print. She'd been over the moon. She hadn't been able to quit staring at her book. The memory made her smile. Her dream had come true.

Her first book signing under this roof had been good. She'd known most everyone who'd waited in line to talk to her, wish her well, say they knew her when, and then get their book signed.

TJ hung on to that feeling for a moment before stepping in to look for the owner. Her sisters scattered throughout the store, oohing and aahing over this or that as she made her way to the books.

There were a dozen piled up next to an older image of her along with some articles about her on poster board. She'd been interviewed so many times and freely told stories about her life, her dreams, her process.

She couldn't help but grimace at the memory of the tongue-lashing the New York City police officer had given her when she'd taken the threatening letters in to him.

"Look, there's nothing we can do," the cop said. "These aren't the first threats you've gotten, nor will they be the last. You writers," he said with a shake of his head. "I checked out your web page, your social media. Your whole life, everything about you from what you ate for dinner last night to your favorite color, is out there for public consumption. You put your life out there to promote yourself and your books. So..." He shrugged. "What do you expect?"

Not seeing the owner, TJ stepped away from the book display and the poster of her as she heard more people come into the store on a gust of cold air. She hadn't gone far when she heard a deep male voice ask if they had TJ St. Clair's latest book.

She turned and froze. The man was a good six foot five, shoulders as wide as an ax handle and arms bulg-

ing with muscle. But it was the dark curly hair at his
collar, the baseball cap and the sheepskin coat that
sliced into her heart like a knife.

The owner of the store was telling him about the
book signing the following day and how TJ had grown
up right here in Whitehorse. "Here, you'll want a bookmark. The signing is at 10 a.m. Best come early because it will fill up fast. Tessa Jane hasn't done a
signing here in years so we're all very excited."

"Yes, I don't want to miss that," he said, his voice
a low rumble.

TJ felt glued to the floor. This was the man who'd
pulled her back from the speeding truck—and possibly
pushed her to start with—early this morning in New
York City and was now here in Whitehorse? Even as
she told herself it couldn't possibly be the same man,
she knew in her heart it was. The only way he could
have gotten here this quickly was if he'd already had a
flight out of the city. As if he'd already known where
she was going.

Just then he turned and she saw the dark beard on
his granite jaw. A pair of piercing blue eyes pinned her
to the spot. What she saw, what she felt, it came in a
jumble of emotions so strong and unsettling that she
turned and ran.

Chapter Four

TJ stumbled blindly out the door and around the corner. She leaned against the brick wall and tried to catch her breath. Her life felt out of control. *She* felt out of control. She'd never had a reaction like that and now, shivering out in the cold, she wondered what had possessed her.

She couldn't even explain her response to the man. What had she sensed that had her running out into the cold? She shivered, hugging herself as she thought of those blue eyes and the look in them. It was as if he could see into her soul. She knew that was pure foolishness, but how else could she explain her reaction?

"What in the world!" cried her sister Annabelle as she found her leaning against the outside of the building. Chloe came running up a moment later. "What happened?"

TJ couldn't speak. She shook her head and fought tears. But it was useless. She began to cry, letting out all the frustration and fear that she'd been holding in the past six months.

Her sisters rushed to her, drawing her to them as they exchanged looks of concern. "Let's get her over to the coffee shop," she heard Annabelle say.

TJ tried to pull herself together. At the sound of a truck engine, she looked up. To her horror, she saw that it was the man she'd just seen in the gift store driving by slowly. She couldn't see those blue eyes, but she could feel them on her.

"Who is that man?" TJ asked on a ragged breath before the truck disappeared down the street.

Her sisters turned to look.

"I saw him in the gift shop." Chloe shook her head. "I have never seen him before that," she said with a shrug.

TJ had expected Annabelle to say the same thing and was surprised when her sister said, "The mountain man?"

"You know him?" TJ asked as the pickup continued down the street. The truck, she saw with surprise, had a local license plate on it. How was that possible? It was the same man she'd seen in New York City earlier today. But how could that be? She was losing her mind.

"His name is Silas Walker. He moved here about six months ago," Annabelle was saying. *He'd moved here six months ago?* That was about the time TJ started getting the letters from True Fan. "He keeps to himself. Has a place in the Little Rockies."

"You can bet he's running from something," Chloe said. "Probably has a rap sheet as long as his muscled arm."

"Do you always have to be so suspicious?" Annabelle said with a sigh.

"Seriously, he's either a criminal or an ex-cop."

"One extreme or the other?" Annabelle grumbled. "Sweetie," she said, turning back to TJ. "You're shivering. Let's get you into the coffee shop."

It wasn't until they were seated, cups of hot coffee in their hands, that her sisters asked what was going on.

She wished she knew. Fearing that she was letting her paranoia get to her, she didn't know what to say.

"TJ?" Chloe prompted.

"She's finally getting some color back into her face," Annabelle said. "Just give her a minute."

She took a sip of the hot coffee. It burned all the way down, but began to warm her ice-cold center.

"Tell us what's going on," Chloe said. "Tessa Jane, you looked like you saw a ghost back there. Do you know that man?"

Looking up at them, she knew she couldn't keep it from them any longer.

It all came pouring out about the fan that at first was so complimentary but soon became more critical, making suggestions that when she didn't take them became angry.

"Who do you think it is? Probably some aspiring writer with too many rejections who's angry at you because you got published and she didn't?" Annabelle asked.

"Or maybe another writer who's jealous of your success?" Chloe added.

TJ shook her head. "That's just it. I have no idea. It could be just a reader who doesn't like the direction my books have taken. I'm not even sure if it is a man or a woman. I'm not the first writer to run into this problem. Readers bond with an author. They have expectations when they pick up one of your books. If you don't meet those expectations…"

"What? They threaten to kill you?" Chloe cried. "Have you gone to the police?"

She told them what had happened. "The officer was

right. My entire life is out there in the cloud. When I was starting out, I hadn't realized that everything I said to the press or online would be available online forever. At first I was just so excited to be published. I never dreamed…" She shook her head.

"I can't believe the police blame you," Chloe said.

Annabelle agreed. "Though I have to admit, it goes with the business. I ran into this with modeling. Once you're out there, you become public property."

"That's ridiculous," Chloe said.

"Don't tell me that you haven't run into this as a reporter," TJ said.

"People storming in angry about something I've written? Of course," Chloe said. "It's part of the job. You can't please everyone. But if you're being threatened…"

"What are you going to do?" Annabelle asked.

She shook her head. "The police officer I talked to said I should ride it out. That the fan would get tired of harassing me. But I'm worried with this new book that True Fan isn't going to like it at all. After seeing that man…"

"You think it's him, your True Fan," Chloe said. "The one who looks like a mountain man?"

TJ sighed and told them what had happened only that morning on the street in front of her apartment. "He saved me, but did he? I felt someone push me in front of that truck. If he hadn't grabbed me…" She saw her sisters exchange a doubtful look. "I know it doesn't seem likely that they are the same person, but…" She halted for a moment. "I swear it's the same man. I… feel it."

"Okay, it's a stretch," Chloe said. "But I suppose

it's possible. You were in New York this morning and now you're here. Why couldn't it be the same for him?"

"He could have even been on the same flight," Annabelle said. "You flew first class, right? He probably flew coach. And since you didn't have any luggage to claim…"

"Okay, it's not that much of a coincidence if he is the same man," Chloe said. "It doesn't make him True Fan though."

"Right, it isn't like he followed you here," Annabelle said. "He's been living here for the past six months."

"Six months," TJ said in a whisper. "That's how long I've been getting the letters from True Fan."

SILAS DROVE TOWARD the Little Rockies, anxious to get to his cabin. As he drove, he contemplated what had happened back at the gift shop. It didn't make a lot of sense and he was a man who prided himself on making sense out of situations.

At least he'd been right about one thing. TJ St. Clair had been headed home for the holidays. When he'd realized that, he'd been looking forward to meeting her. But after what had happened back there…

She'd run out of the shop in tears. Because of him? Or someone else she saw in the store? Odd behavior. He considered that it might have something to do with what had happened this morning in New York. A scare like that would make anyone jumpy. He frowned to himself, wondering again about her near accident this morning.

Was she merely jostled? Had someone purposely pushed her?

He shook his head, reprimanding himself for not leaving his job behind along with the suspicions that went with it. He was in Montana now. He'd bought this place outside of Whitehorse in the Little Rockies so he could get away from his stressful, dangerous, always unpredictable job.

Here, he did so much physical labor that all of that ugliness was forgotten—at least for a while. Here, he'd put that world as far away from him as he could.

And yet you still read thrillers. Not just anyone's. You read her books.

He laughed as he drove toward the mountains. That's because she was the reason he'd moved here. After reading TJ's books, he'd been curious about Montana, curious about the wild prairie, the endless sky, the wide-open places that she talked about in her books. Once he saw the area, he was hooked. She had always mentioned the Little Rockies so of course that's where he went when he was looking for land. While he loved the prairie, he also wanted a hideaway like the lawless days when Kid Curry and Butch Cassidy and the Sundance Kid roamed this area.

He'd bought into the mystique because of TJ St. Clair and because of her books, but he'd never dreamed he'd get a chance to meet her here in her home state. Which was why he couldn't miss her book signing tomorrow. He knew even before he turned onto the snow-packed road that led up into the mountains to his cabin that nothing was going to keep him away. He realized that he'd been wanting to meet her for far too long.

TJ LISTENED TO her sisters chatting, knowing they were trying to get her mind off True Fan and her book signing tomorrow. She smiled and nodded and added a word or two when required as she tried to enjoy her barbecued pulled pork. It was delicious and she was hungry after a long day with little real food.

But she couldn't keep her mind off the man she'd seen at the gift shop. The mountain man. Her True Fan?

She thought back to the first letter. It had been so complimentary. The writer had loved the book, sounding surprised as if not a thriller reader. She tried to reconcile that first letter with the more recent bitter, hateful ones she'd been getting. She couldn't square them anymore than she could the man she'd seen first in New York and now in her local gift shop asking about her book.

The first letter had been like so many of the others that she had hardly noticed it.

"You really need to hire someone to answer these," her friend Mica had said when she'd seen the stack TJ had been working her way through on that day six months ago.

"I've thought about it, but I'd rather not answer them than have someone else do it for me. I know that sounds crazy."

"No, I get it." Mica had opened a couple of the letters and begun to read them. "Aww, these are so sweet. They love you. This one is from a woman who is almost ninety. She wants you to write faster." Her friend had laughed. "Oh and this one is long." She'd watched Mica skim it. "Good heavens, do people often tell you their entire life histories?"

TJ had nodded. "They want to share their lives with me because they feel they know me from my books. You can see why I try to answer as many of the fan letters as I can. Unfortunately I can't answer them all. I just hope they understand."

After her friend left, TJ had answered as many of

the letters as she'd had time for since she had a book deadline looming. She *always* had a deadline looming.

That part she didn't mind. She loved writing the stories. It was the other things that ate up her time that she hated. There were always art forms that needed to be filled out describing her story, her characters, suggesting scenes for the cover.

Then there were the many edits and proposals that needed to be written. Add to that the blogs and promotion requests. It was a wonder she ever had time to write the books.

She had been thinking about that when she'd picked up one more fan letter to possibly answer. The first thing she had noticed was that there was no return address on the envelope. She hadn't thought too much about it since often the readers would put their addresses inside their letters.

Slicing open the envelope, she'd pulled out the folded unlined discolored paper. She remembered holding it up to the light, wondering how old it was to have turned this color. The letter had been typed on what appeared to be a manual typewriter. TJ had an old heavy Royal she'd picked up and kept in her office only as decoration. She'd always been impressed that Ernest Hemingway had written on a manual typewriter, since she doubted she would be writing books if it weren't for the ease of computers.

Dear Ms. St. Clair

I've never written an author before. I guess there is a first time for everything.

I recently checked out your first book from the local library. It was quite pleasurable to read.

You clearly have talent. I was surprised when I started reading and couldn't put it down. I definitely enjoyed your descriptions of Montana and the country around your "fictitious" small town.

I'm actually looking forward to your next book,

Your True Fan so far

TJ had laughed. The reader certainly hadn't thought he or she was going to like it. It had pleased her that her True Fan had been surprised and willing to try another one of her books. Maybe next time the person would purchase one rather than wait to get it at the library.

She had looked to see if there was a name or an address. Apparently the reader didn't require an answer. She'd tossed the letter in the trash since long ago she'd given up keeping all the fan mail. She'd thought nothing more of it.

That, she realized now, had been her first mistake. There might have been fingerprints on that first letter before things went south.

Chapter Five

"I want to read the letters you got from this so-called fan of yours," Chloe said once they were back at the house and alone. Their sister had gone to see her fiancé, Dawson Rogers, promising to come back before all the wine was gone. "Something tells me they are much more threatening than what you told Annabelle."

"I didn't bring them with me," TJ said. "I didn't even save the first few." But she remembered them and often saw them in her sleep, waking in a cold sweat, her heart pounding.

Dear Ms. St. Clair
I was so disappointed with your last book. To think a tree was killed to make the paper that book was printed on... You should be ashamed.

I expect each book to be better than the last. I don't think that's unreasonable. In my last letter, I made some suggestions as far as the plot and character development.

Clearly, you dismissed those suggestions. Maybe you think you know more about writing than I do. Since my opinion doesn't count, you

won't be surprised to hear that I don't trust you
as a narrator.

I'm your only honest fan. If this is the way
you treat a true fan, I hate to think how you treat
your other readers.

You have really let me down. We might have
to do something about that, don't you think?
Your only True Fan

She'd thought that would be the last time she'd hear
from that reader. She didn't remember a suggestion
for a book that True Fan had claimed to have sent her.
Readers often thought she should do books about vari-
ous secondary characters from her novels. One even
suggested getting a woman out of the criminally insane
ward of a hospital so she could find her true love. What
readers didn't seem to realize was that those decisions
weren't always up to her—even if she was inclined to
do a certain character's story.

She'd thrown True Fan's letter away—just as she had
the first one—and moved on to a letter by a woman
who would love a signed book sent to her sister for her
birthday. Her sister loved TJ's books and was laid up
after a car wreck. The sister's name was Rickey. The
reader had said that the sister was a huge fan.

TJ had picked up one of her books and signed it:
*Rickey, Happy Birthday. Hope you're well soon, Best,
TJ St. Clair.*

She put it with the letter in the pile to be mailed,
only vaguely remembering that it went to a post office
box in Laramie, Wyoming.

After that, she'd gone back to writing her book and
forgotten both letters.

That had been her second mistake, though she'd had no way of knowing it at the time. It wasn't until she received the next letter from True Fan:

Dear TJ St. Clair
You really aren't as bright or as talented as I first thought. Actually, I'm amazed you make any money at this. A person you don't know from Adam tells you a hard-luck story and you send them a book? You are so gullible. But "Rickey" thanks you. Tee Hee. I'm feeling so much better and I like having a book that you touched.

Unfortunately, your books are getting worse. I didn't think that was possible. I told you what to do, but you just keep ignoring me. Because you think you're so much smarter than me, more talented? You keep making this mistake and we'll see who is smarter.
Your True Fan until The End

"Believe me," TJ told her sister now. "I've read them numerous times. I can't tell if they are from a man or a woman. They could be from *anyone*. Anyone who owns an old manual typewriter."

"Well, they have you running scared, so you must believe the threats are real," her sister said.

"The last one promised that True Fan would be seeing me soon and unless I apologized for ignoring the advice the person had been giving me, I was going to die like one of the characters in my book," TJ said. "True Fan said I could pick which character and which death and kill myself because it would be less pain-

ful than if a fan had to stop me from writing by killing me."

Chloe shivered. "That sounds like more than a
threat. The police didn't take that seriously?"

TJ poured herself a glass of wine, her hands shaking. "Even if True Fan had said he or she was going
to kill me, there is no return address. The postmarks
have been from all over the country. Where would
they begin looking for this person? We don't know if
it's a man or woman. So until True Fan actually makes
good on these threats…" She got to her feet. "I hate
talking about this."

"This man we saw earlier, you realize it's a long
shot that he's the same one from New York, but I could
do some checking. Annabelle said his name is Silas
Walker." She ran upstairs, returned with her laptop
and began to tap on the keys.

TJ was thinking how nice it was to have an investigative reporter in the family when Chloe let out a sharp
breath and looked up. "What?"

"He was one of New York's finest, but left a year
ago after being caught in some kind of internal sting
investigation."

"What kind of investigation?" TJ asked around the
lump in her throat.

Chloe shook her head. "Dirty cops. He apparently
was never arrested. All they said was misconduct that
betrayed the public's trust. That could be anything from
lying to cheating on overtime or much worse. Here's
the kicker: he was rehired a month later but then quit."
She looked up from her computer. "This guy could be
dangerous."

"What guy could be dangerous?" Annabelle asked

as she came through the front door on a gust of winter wind. TJ and Chloe shared a look. "Are you talking about the Mountain Man?"

"He's an ex-cop who was fired at one point," Chloe said. "I was saying he could be dangerous."

"Why was he fired?" their sister asked as she shrugged out of her coat, hung it up and joined them. She poured herself a glass of wine. Her cheeks were already flushed. From the cold? Or from her visit with Dawson Rogers?

"Let's not talk about this," TJ said. "Tell us about you and Dawson."

Annabelle shook her head. "If you really think this man is dangerous then you need to cancel your book signing tomorrow."

"Bad idea," Chloe said. "She'll be perfectly safe at the gift shop with us and half the town there. This is her chance to find out if he's this True Fan who's been sending her the threatening letters."

"You really think it's him?" Annabelle asked.

"First I'm shoved from behind in front of a speeding delivery truck, he saves me, then shows up in White-horse and I find out that he moved here six months ago—about the same time I started getting the threatening letters. What are the chances that he's *not* True Fan?" She shuddered at the memory of those blue eyes. She'd felt strangely drawn to him at the same time she'd felt afraid.

"What does she do if he *does* show up at the book signing tomorrow?" Annabelle demanded of Chloe. "Just ask him if he's her True Fan?"

Chloe groaned. "She'll play it cool. We'll be there. If he is this crazed fan, he won't do anything at the signing, but he might say something that gives him away. Once we know for sure then we go to the sheriff."

"TJ play it cool?" her youngest sister said with a laugh. "No offense, but if today was any indication—"

"I can do it." TJ nodded with more enthusiasm than she felt. She had to. This had to end because she couldn't take anymore. If it didn't, she feared True Fan would end it the way the letters had promised. "Maybe he won't even show."

"I wouldn't hold my breath," Chloe said. "If it's him, he'll want to get as close to you as he can. He's been taunting you. Now he'll want you to know just how close he is."

As if TJ didn't already know the psychology behind a person like this. She wrote about them all the time. If this man was her True Fan, he didn't just want her to know how close he was. He wanted her to know how easy it would be for him to get to her. For the past six months, this had been leading up to the moment when she faced her killer—just like in one of her books.

Chapter Six

When TJ woke the next morning, she was shocked to see how late it was. She hurriedly showered and dressed. When she came downstairs, dressed for her signing, Annabelle handed her a cup of coffee and a donut.

She took the coffee, declined the donut and watched as Annabelle ate it.

"I love not being a model anymore," her sister said, smiling with a little sugar glaze on her lips before she licked it away.

TJ couldn't help smiling as well. Her sister looked great, not skinny and pale like she had when she'd been a top model. "I need to get to my signing."

"We're going with you," Chloe said, coming out of the kitchen. "Are you nervous?"

What did she think? She'd never been good at book signings. Probably because she'd never wanted the attention. She'd only wanted to write the stories that were in her head. Little had she known the rest that was required of a published author. TJ knew she was naive to think that she could simply lock herself away in a room somewhere and do what she loved.

When her editor had told her that she needed to

be more of a presence on social media, she'd actually thought about quitting the publishing business.

But she couldn't quit writing. When she'd take a break, the longest she could go was three days before she started writing in her sleep. The characters would start talking and she'd have to get their stories out. She loved that part.

TJ remembered how surprised she'd been when she found out that not everyone had stories going in their heads. She'd asked the person, "Well, then what do you think about when you're in the shower or driving?" The answer had been, "I've never thought about it. Something I'm sure, but not stories."

It had also surprised her when other writers had told her that their characters didn't talk to them. Well, hers certainly did. Soon the ones from her next book would be nagging at her to begin writing again.

"Come on," Chloe said, "or we're going to be late."

TJ wished they could just get into Annabelle's SUV—she'd traded her sports car for something more practical for Montana—and hit the road. She thought she could and not look back at this point in her life.

There was already a line at the gift shop when they arrived. TJ couldn't help looking for the mountain man, but with a sigh of relief, she didn't see him. Maybe after yesterday, he wouldn't show up.

"Park in the back," she'd instructed her sister.

"You aren't getting cold feet, are you?" Chloe asked.

"I always do but nothing like I have right now." They entered the back door. TJ dropped off her coat and purse in the stockroom and took a moment to compose herself. *You've done this dozens of other times. You can do this.*

But none of the other times were like this.

Stepping out of the back, she headed for the table that had been set up for her along with a chair and a huge stack of her books. The owner hustled over to see if she needed water, coffee, anything at all.

"A bottle of water would be wonderful," TJ said, her throat already dry as she felt eyes on her from the line of people waiting a few yards away. She tried to smile as she slid into the chair and picked up one of the pens the store owner had thoughtfully left for her.

"Here's your water," said a familiar voice.

TJ turned to see a dark-haired woman her age. "Joyce?" She couldn't help her surprise. She hadn't seen Joyce Mason since high school. Joyce had been voted the girl most likely to end up behind bars. It had been a play on words, since Joyce had been wild—and also a drinker who was known to make out with guys in the alley behind the Mint Bar.

"You work here now?" TJ asked, feeling the need to say something into the silence. Joyce was thinner than in high school, but wore the same shag hairdo and pretty much the same expression, one of boredom. The only thing different was that she sported a few more tattoos.

"Does it surprise you that I read?" Joyce asked.

"No." She let out a nervous laugh. "As a writer, I'm delighted."

"Yes, we all know you're a writer." Joyce put down the bottle of water and walked off.

TJ was still reeling a little from Joyce's attitude when she heard a squeal and looked up to see another familiar face. Dorothy "Dot" Crest came running up to her all smiles.

"I can't believe it!" Dot cried. "I just had to say hi. I'll get in line," she assured the waiting crowd. "I definitely want one of your books. I've read them all." She leaned closer. "They are so scary and yet I can't put them down." She laughed. "This is so exciting."

With that she rushed back toward the end of the line. As she did, she said hello to people she knew. Dot knew almost everyone it seemed.

"Ready?" the owner asked, coming up to tell her again how delighted they were to have her here.

Was she ready? She felt off-balance and the signing hadn't even begun. Normally, TJ was more organized. She'd barely remembered to grab a few bookmarks as they'd left the house. She hadn't even thought about a pen. That showed just how nervous she was.

She smiled up at the first woman in line. She looked familiar, but for a moment TJ couldn't come up with her name. That was the problem at book signings. The names of people she knew even really well would slip her mind.

"Just sign it to me," a person would say.

She often used the trick, "Would you mind spelling your name for me?"

That didn't always work. One woman who was so excited, telling everyone how long she'd known TJ, made her draw a blank. When she'd asked her to spell her name, the woman recoiled and said, "It's Pat."

TJ had been so embarrassed, but there hadn't been time to explain how often her mind went blank at these events, even with the names of her closest friends. So she never saw Pat again.

Now the older woman with the dyed-brown hair

standing in front of the desk said, "You probably don't remember me."

For a moment, TJ didn't. She looked familiar. Really familiar, but...

"I'm not surprised given how much you didn't pay attention in class."

Bingo. "Of course I remember you, Mrs. Brown. I had you for English in high school." Annabelle had told her that the woman had only recently retired after having a minor stroke. "Would you like me to sign this to you?" she asked her former teacher.

"Of course. But you probably don't know my first name. It's Ester."

She signed the book, stuck in a bookmark and handed it to the older woman.

Ester Brown hesitated. "Just the other day I told my husband I wasn't the least bit surprised when I heard you were writing books." She hugged the book to her. "You were never at a loss for words in my class." With that she turned and walked away.

TJ frowned. Hadn't Annabelle told her that Mrs. Brown's husband had died?

One after another new and old readers stepped up and TJ signed their books, visited and moved on to the next one. She was surprised how many people had turned out. But the last time she had signed a book in her hometown had been her first one years ago.

"Hi, TJ," said one of the men from the line. She'd seen him, but hadn't paid much attention. She was looking for the mountain man. But if Silas Walker was planning to attend the signing, he hadn't shown so far, and another five minutes and she would be done. The line had dwindled, she realized with relief.

Her hand hurt from signing books and smiling and trying to remember faces she hadn't seen in years.

Now as she looked at this man, his name suddenly came to her. "Tommy Harwood."

"Tom," he corrected. He seemed surprised that she remembered him. He'd been one of those on the fringe. He'd been an average student, an outsider. He'd been invisible—just like TJ. While her sisters had been popular, TJ was a dreamer who preferred to be off by herself with her head in a book.

Now Tommy was getting a little bald. From the jacket he was wearing, she saw that he worked at the local auto shop.

"Do you want it signed to you?" she asked as she opened a book and lifted her pen expectantly.

"Sure, as long as it's to Tom."

She nodded and signed *To Tom, Enjoy, TJ St. Clair.* It was the best she could do given that she didn't think she'd spoken more than a dozen words to Tommy over the years. No matter what Mrs. Brown said, she wasn't the talkative one in English class. TJ realized she must have her confused with Annabelle. Great.

"Are you in town long?" Tommy asked quietly.

"Just for the holidays." She handed him the book.

He continued to stare at her. "You're probably busy, but if you ever want to get a cup of coffee…"

"Thank you. That's sounds nice. I'll let you know."

He nodded. "I should let you get to your other fans."

She watched him walk away for a moment, trying to shake off the odd feeling he'd given her.

"I love your books," a woman said as she quickly took Tommy's place and it continued.

As the line dwindled, she began to relax. She loved

her readers and was reminded of the time before her first sale. She'd been writing short stories. That's when she'd gotten her very first fan letter. The magazine reader had said she should be writing books. She'd framed that first letter and put in on her wall. It had given her hope each time she looked at it during the writing of her first book.

She could smile at the memory. There'd been so many days when she didn't think she could finish an entire book. It had felt overwhelming. Add to that the fear that it wasn't good enough, that everyone would hate it, that it would be rejected.

And it was. Her first book was still in the bottom of her closet where it would remain, never to be published. But that first book had given her hope not only that she could finish a book, but also that she could write a better one.

And she had. A book a year for the past seven years, all of them published, each doing better than the last. She remembered the thrill of her fourth book making the *New York Times* list.

She'd heard of authors who'd treated themselves with trips to Europe or purchased new cars after making the list. She'd gone for a walk, grinning the whole way, and on impulse had treated herself to a hot fudge sundae. It was as decadent as she ever got. Restraint in everything, that was TJ St. Clair, aka Tessa Jane Clementine. Those words could have been stitched and hung on her wall.

She'd always been like that. Holding back, never letting herself go. It drove her sister Annabelle crazy.

"Don't you ever just want to let loose? Do something crazy? Take a chance?"

"I might want to, but I don't," had been her answer. The truth was she'd never been brave or daring. That huge hot fudge sundae? It had made her sick and had been a good reminder of why she used restraint in all things.

No, her heroine in her books, Constance Ryan, was the one who did crazy, brave and daring things. Constance loved defying the odds. And for so long, TJ had loved writing about her—living through her.

As she finished signing a young woman's book, TJ saw him. The mountain man, Silas Walker, had just come in the door and was headed her way.

Chapter Seven

Silas was a little concerned about what kind of reception he might get. Because of his size and the way he looked, especially during his time in Montana when he was "roughin' it," he tended to scare little children. Lately he'd been working undercover, so his beard was longer than usual. He'd let his hair grow as well.

But the woman who wrote these murder mysteries? Come on, TJ didn't scare that easily, did she?

He guessed he was about to find out as he headed for the table where she had just finished signing a book. There were still several books left, he noticed with relief. He'd run late today because of the snowstorm in the mountains last night. He'd barely been able to get his pickup out. But he wasn't about to miss purchasing a signed book from TJ St. Clair today.

When she spotted him approaching, he had to admit, she looked like a deer in headlights. It perplexed him. She couldn't possibly have thought that he was the one who pushed her into the street yesterday. He'd been the one who'd saved her.

"Hello," he said as he reached the table. "I can't tell you how excited I am that I didn't miss your signing." His gaze locked with hers and he was shocked to see that her eyes weren't blue, but a languid sea green that took his breath away for a moment. Her blond hair framed a face that he'd memorized, since he'd looked at the black-and-white photograph on the cover jacket so many times.

She'd intrigued him from the first time he'd picked up one of her books. He normally didn't read thrillers. Hell, his life was one. No, he couldn't remember what had possessed him.

He'd opened one of her books to the first page and started reading. Before he knew it, he was on page 30. By then, he was hooked and knew he wasn't walking out of that bookstore without that book.

It wasn't until he'd finished it that he saw TJ's photo. He'd actually thought the book had been written by a man. He remembered smiling. He liked surprises and this woman had surprised him and intrigued him.

Now he watched her pick up one of the hardcover books at her elbow and open it with trembling fingers. That he made her nervous surprised him even given the way she'd acted yesterday. In her books, the characters were so gutsy. He liked to believe that TJ possessed— if not all of her character Constance's gutsiness—then at least some of it. The last thing he'd expected to see in her eyes was fear.

"Who would you like me to sign it to?" she asked, her voice breaking.

He knelt down, realizing he was towering over her, although he suspected that wasn't the problem. "Silas." He spelled his name and watched her write it out in her neat penmanship. "I can't tell you what a thrill this is. From the first time I picked up one of your books, I wanted to meet the woman behind them."

He saw her pen falter on the page. Those sea green eyes came up to meet his. He smiled and saw her shiver. She quickly looked down and hurriedly signed "Enjoy" and her name. Well, not her name exactly. TJ St. Clair he'd learned was her pen name. Her legal name was Tessa Jane Clementine.

She handed him the book. "I hope you like it." Her voice was throaty, almost a whisper.

He saw that there was no one behind him since he'd caught her at the end of the signing. "I have enjoyed your books so much. I just had to tell you that." He started to rise, but stopped. "I know this is probably out of line, but is there some reason I make you so nervous?"

She parted her lips as if to speak. She had a great mouth, he noticed. She quickly closed it for a moment before she spoke. "Is there a reason you should make me nervous?"

"Not that I know of," he said. "When I saw that you were going to be signing books here, I had hoped..." He shook his head. "You probably don't accept dates from your readers. I don't blame you. It's just that reading your books...well, I feel I know you. That must sound crazy. But you're why I ended up building a cabin here." He shrugged. "I'm sorry, you're probably anxious to leave." He smiled as he rose. "Maybe we'll see each other around town. Thank you so much for this," he said, looking down at the book in his hands. "I'll treasure it." He met her gaze. "It was wonderful meeting you."

TJ SAT STUNNED as she watched Silas Walker stride over to the checkout counter and pay for his book.

She kept thinking about his intense blue eyes and his disarming smile. He knew that he made her nervous. Had he been enjoying that, or was he trying to make her less nervous?

"Well," Chloe whispered as she rushed over to her. "Is it him?"

For a moment she couldn't speak. "I have no idea. Apparently, he was going to ask me out but changed his mind."

Annabelle appeared to hear the last part. She let out a laugh. *"So he just wanted a date?"*

"He gave you no indication that he might be True Fan?" Chloe demanded.

"None." And yet… She remembered the way he'd looked into her eyes. What had he been looking for? She shuddered and let out a sigh. "I am so glad this book signing is over."

"He was at your table for quite a while," Chloe said, not letting it go. "What else did he say?"

"I don't know," TJ said. "My brain was on spin cycle. He said he felt as if he knew me from my books and that was probably crazy. Oh, and that I was the reason he built a cabin here. That is, my books were."

Annabelle's eyes went wide. "That doesn't sound good, but you don't live here anymore. You live in New York City, so…"

"He didn't mention saving your life in the city yesterday morning?" Chloe asked.

"No," TJ said with a shake of her head. "I should have asked him but my suspicions all seemed so ludicrous at the time. He kept looking at me as if…" She shook her head. As if he really just wanted to ask her out? Or something else? She had no idea.

"You knew your True Fan could be charming, right?" Chloe asked. "Maybe you should have accepted the date."

"No!" Annabelle cried. "What if he is...True Fan?"

"Well, he changed his mind about asking me out, so the point is moot," she pointed out. "Tommy Harwood asked me out though." Her sisters gave her a blank look, which confirmed that Tommy had gone through high school as invisible as she had been.

When she described him, Chloe said, "I do remember him vaguely."

"Kind of getting bald guy with the little potbelly?" Annabelle asked.

"That's him. He works at the auto shop."

They both quickly lost interest in him.

"I saw Dot. She hasn't changed a bit," Chloe said.

"Joyce Mason apparently works here," TJ said, keeping her voice down. She thought Joyce might be hiding nearby listening. "She was a little strange."

Chloe put an arm around her as she got to her feet to leave. "You survived it."

She smiled. She had. But she was no closer to finding out if one of the people who'd come through the line was True Fan.

"I say we go have some lunch," Annabelle said.

"It's that or head straight to the Mint Bar," Chloe said. "Up to you, Tessa Jane."

"Didn't someone say food?" Annabelle asked innocently. "I'm starved."

Chloe looked to TJ and said, "Food. I've never seen you this thin."

"Yes, we'll get you some good Montana eats and

fatten you right up," Annabelle agreed. "How about some chicken-fried steak?"

TJ felt her stomach roil at the thought. "Yum."

Her sisters laughed as they headed out the door. It was a wonderful sound that felt like a much-needed salve. She told herself that her True Fan hadn't been in Whitehorse today, hadn't come through the line, hadn't gone home with her latest book.

And yet she couldn't help but think about each and every one of the people who'd come through the line, including the young woman who'd been right before Silas Walker. TJ had been distracted, but now that she remembered…

"I signed a book for Nellie Doll," she said as they started up the street.

Chloe stopped, coming up short. "Lanell? I didn't see her in the line."

"She sent her niece to get it for her," TJ said. "The niece had me sign it 'to Nellie, just like old times.'"

"That is kind of creepy, isn't it?" Chloe said. "You and Nellie weren't friends."

"No," TJ said. "Far from it." She tried to shake off the memory.

"You aren't thinking that Nellie…" Annabelle was walking backward in front of them, looking from TJ to Chloe and back again.

"That she's True Fan?" Chloe shook her head. "Anyway, didn't you say that the letters had been sent from all over the country? I'm betting Nellie's never been out of the county."

TJ nodded, remembering the girl Nellie had been in high school. She couldn't imagine that she'd want to drop so much money on a hardcover book, especially TJ's.

She tried not to think about True Fan. She had so many amazing readers. Why did one fan have to spoil it? What bothered her was that she really didn't know whether True Fan was a man or a woman. She'd had several women murderers in her books. In fact, in the book she'd just signed, the antagonist was a woman.

Chapter Eight

TJ woke with a headache after a night of weird dreams. She took a couple of OTC painkiller tablets after her shower. She was not looking forward to her interview with a reporter from the *Billings Gazette* later this morning.

As she dressed, she could hear her sisters already downstairs in the kitchen. Opening her bedroom door, she followed the rich, wonderful scent of coffee down the stairs.

She couldn't help smiling to herself. There was something so comforting about being back in this house with her sisters. Just the sound of them lightened her step as well as her heart. As she walked into the kitchen, she headed straight for the cupboard where she knew she would find a mug.

"Good morning!" Annabelle called from the table, where she and Chloe were already sitting with their coffee. "It's a beautiful day."

TJ blinked as she looked outside to see the sun shining on the new snow, making it glitter blindingly. "Were you always this cheerful in the morning?" she asked her as she took a seat at the table.

"Don't you hate morning people?" Chloe said, and grinned, since she was one as well.

"I thought we'd get a Christmas tree today," Annabelle said with unusual jubilance. "Willie saved some of Grandma Frannie's ornaments from the trip to the dump. We could decorate the tree later, and I need to do some Christmas shopping."

TJ could see what her sister was trying to do—get her mind off True Fan and yesterday's book signing.

"Is there a place to buy a tree in town?" Chloe asked.

"Don't be silly," Annabelle said with a laugh. "We're going to take a picnic lunch and go up into the mountains and cut one. I found an ax in the garage."

"Ax?" Chloe cried.

"The Little Rockies?" TJ said, and both sisters turned to look at her.

"Why do I detect a strange excitement in those three words?" Chloe asked. "You aren't thinking what I think you're thinking."

"Of course not," TJ said. "It's just been so long since I've been up there." Both sisters were studying her. "Come on, he isn't True Fan."

"He said you were the reason he moved here," Chloe reminded her.

"Yes, but a lot of my readers say they feel as if they're in Montana when they read one of my books and they can't wait to visit," she pointed out. "It's not that unusual."

"This one *moved* here," Chloe said.

"So you really don't think he's the one?" Annabelle asked suspiciously.

"He did nothing to indicate that he was anything more than a normal fan," TJ said truthfully. "So," she said, getting to her feet. "I'll pack the lunch. Let's go to the mountains and get a tree." She started at the knock on the door.

"I wonder who that is," Annabelle said as she went to answer.

TJ heard her laugh. "You're delivering mail door-to-door now?"

As she stepped out of the kitchen, TJ saw the woman hand her sister a letter. "You got mail," the woman said with a laugh as she looked past Annabelle to TJ. "Fan mail. Our own famous author. I tell people I know you—well, know that you used to live here—and they don't believe me."

All TJ could do was nod and smile as her heart sank. She felt all the color leave her face as Annabelle thanked the woman and closed the door.

"Carol from the post office," her sister was saying. "She said this came for you yesterday and since you don't have a post office box, she decided to drop it by. How's that for service? TJ?" Annabelle had seen that she'd gone pale.

Chloe took the envelope from Annabelle by the corner. "I'm sure there aren't any prints, but..." She held it out to TJ.

She didn't reach for it. Even from where she stood, she could see the typewritten address. Any other city and the letter would have ended up in a dead file because it had no return address and was addressed only to TJ St. Clair, Whitehorse, Montana. Another joy of living in a small Montana town.

"Aren't you going to open it?" Annabelle asked.

TJ couldn't find the words to speak.

"I'll open it," Chloe said, and walked into the

kitchen to get a sharp knife. She carefully opened the letter, using the point of the knife to unfold the discolored paper.

How had the fan known she would be here? TJ groaned inwardly. Her fan knew she was in Whitehorse. Of course her fan knew; she'd just had a book signing. Not to mention she'd been recognized at the airport. That person had put it up on social media. Everyone in the world with a smartphone knew she was in Whitehorse—especially True Fan.

"The writer mailed it to you in Whitehorse, Montana," Chloe said. "So True Fan knew you were here. Only in a small town like this would you have gotten it," she said, voicing what TJ had just been thinking.

"Remember when we first came to live with Grandma Frannie?" Annabelle asked. "Frannie said Whitehorse wasn't the end of the earth, but it was damned close. She said on a dark night you could see the fires of hell." She laughed but quickly stopped when she saw that she wasn't helping lighten the mood.

"Wait a minute," Chloe said. "This letter was mailed *before* you got here. Whoever sent it knew you were coming here. Either that or figured it would be forwarded to you."

TJ couldn't wrap her head around that. She felt as if someone was always watching her, trying to figure out what she would do next. "How bad is it?" she asked from the kitchen doorway.

Chloe turned to look at her. Annabelle was standing off to the side, hugging herself as if she didn't want to know what the letter said any more than TJ did.

"Read it to me," she said, not wanting to touch it.

Dear Tessa Jane,

I would love to see the expression on your face right now. You really think you can get away from me? I told you, I'm your True Fan until the end. Now that I have your latest book, I hope you won't disappoint me again. I'm not sure I can take any more disappointment from you. I'm not sure what I'll do.

I thought I could help you, make you a better writer. But you've continued to ignore me as if you think I have no value. That hurts me deeply. I'm not sure I can let you go on writing these books.

The only way you can save yourself is if you made up for it in this recent book. Let's both hope that you do.

Still your True Fan until The End

"What is this person talking about?" Chloe asked as she finished reading.

TJ couldn't speak for a moment. The letters had started out being addressed to Ms. St. Clair. Then TJ. Now Tessa Jane. Each growing more familiar.

"TJ, what is it this person wants you to do?" Annabelle asked, worry in her voice.

She sighed. "One of the main characters told a lie but went unpunished."

"So punish the character," Annabelle said. "It's got to be more than that."

"True Fan also wants the lead character to fall for—"

"Durango," Chloe said with a curse.

She looked at her sister. "You read my books?" This day was just filled with surprises.

"Guilty. I hate to ask since it's going to spoil your latest book for me, but Constance doesn't end up with Durango?"

TJ shook her head. "Durango dies in this book."

SILAS HAD WOOD to chop and bring into the cabin. On the way home from town he'd heard that another storm was coming in. He'd bought groceries before leaving Whitehorse since he could be snowed in for a few days with the blizzard that was reportedly coming. As long as he had plenty of firewood, he would be fine.

But when he'd reached home, the one thing he wanted to do more than anything else was start TJ's book. Her books aside, he now couldn't get the woman herself off his mind. When he'd looked into those amazing sea green eyes… He'd started to ask her out even though it was clear that he made her nervous. But just the thought of having a chance to talk to her about books, writing… Not that he hadn't noticed how attractive she was. He shook himself. He had wood to chop.

After unloading everything from town, he made short work of getting enough wood in for the next few days. The first few snowflakes drifted down as he started to carry in the last load of split logs. He stopped for a moment to look up at the heavens. Snowflakes whirled down from a white, low sky. The air was cold and crisp and smelled of the tall pines that surrounded him and his cabin.

But it was the utter silence that captivated him. He'd never known such quiet after living in the city all his life except for his stint in the army overseas. His close friends thought he was crazy for coming here.

"Why the middle of nowhere in Montana?" one friend had asked.

"It's because of that writer he likes," another friend joked. "TJ St. Clair. How'd this guy talk you into something so crazy?"

Silas had let his friends think that the books were written by a man. He'd thought so himself at first, so why not? "I liked the way the writer described the area. It's exactly like in the books."

"Just be glad he's not doing this because of some woman," his friend said.

"That's the worst," the other agreed. "We'd know for sure that he's lost his mind."

They'd all laughed, Silas the heartiest.

TJ MET THE reporter at the Great Northern. She'd suggested it because she knew they would be able to find a quiet corner in the dining room to talk. After ordering coffee, the reporter began to ask her questions.

She'd done dozens of interviews since publishing her first book. Reporters asked many of the same questions. Where do you get your ideas? Everywhere. She'd spent years being a wallflower and watching people. She was fascinated by what made each one tick. The good, the bad, the truly ugly all made for great characters.

What inspired you to write this book? She'd seen a news story on television and while her story had taken a different twist, it had been the starting point.

TJ answered one question after another, adding examples and little asides, all the time her mind on the mountain man, Silas Walker.

Finally the reporter asked her what she knew now

that she wished she'd known when she started. How hard it is.

"This is the hardest work I've ever done," TJ said truthfully. "It isn't an eight-to-five job where you go home at night and forget it until the next day. There's no Thank God It's Friday. No paid vacation and sick leave. Once I start a book, those characters are with me until I finish their story. They wake me up in the middle of the night. They nag me until I finish the book."

"So one of the fallacies is that you have all this time on your hands because you don't have to punch a time clock," the reporter said.

TJ laughed and nodded. "Everyone dreams of staying home, working in their pajamas, not having a boss looking over your shoulder. It's a little more complicated than that. It's a lot of long hours at a computer."

She was glad when the interview was over and she could walk back to the house where her sisters were eagerly waiting. By then, snow had begun to fall. The flakes were huge and drifted on the breeze.

"Did you know it was supposed to snow?" Chloe asked later as Annabelle slowed the SUV to make the turn at the tiny town of Zortman stuck in the side of the Little Rockies. Zortman had a bar-café, post office, church and a small building used as a jail.

Huge flakes drifted down from the dull white sky to stick on the windshield. The SUV's wipers were having a hard time keeping up. Several inches of snow had already fallen on the road. Their tracks were the only ones so far on the road south.

TJ could see patches of dark green through the falling snow as they approached the Little Rockies. The mountains rose from the prairie in steep rock cliffs and pine-covered slopes.

Before the town of Zortman, set back against the cliffs, Annabelle turned off on a road that passed the cemetery and some summer campsites. As the road climbed deeper into the mountains, the snow seemed to fall harder.

They had gotten bundled up, determined to get rid of the pall that had fallen over them after the latest letter from True Fan. Annabelle had thrown the ax into the back of the SUV along with some rope to tie the tree on the top—once they found it.

"I'll park up here and then we can get out and walk," Annabelle announced. "I'm sure we'll find the perfect tree."

Chloe groaned as she looked out the window. "I know it's beautiful, but I don't like this. What if we get stuck?"

"It's not that far of a walk into Zortman," Annabelle said as she kept driving up the narrow, snowy road through the dense pines. "Also there are cabins up here. I'm sure we can find someone to help us."

Chloe made a skeptical sound and turned up the radio as a Christmas song came on. She began to sing along, with Annabelle joining in. TJ didn't feel like singing. She'd seen a newer mailbox back on the county road. S. Walker. Silas Walker's cabin must be up this way.

She hadn't wanted to worry her sisters, but there was something about the man. So much so that she had to know if he was True Fan. This latest letter made her even more suspicious that it had to be him. The postmark on the letter had been Whitehorse.

"So True Fan knows someone in all these places where the letters have been mailed," Chloe had said back at the house before they'd left. "She or he gets friends to mail them, saying it's a game she/he is playing with you."

"You're saying True Fan knows someone in Whitehorse who mailed the letter?" Annabelle had said. "But wouldn't that person know TJ?"

"Not necessarily," Chloe had said, and had shot her sister a look.

"Stop trying to make me feel better," TJ had said. The owner of the gift shop had called her Tessa Jane, the name everyone in Whitehorse had known her by. And now her True Fan was also calling her by that name after meeting her at the book signing? Or had True Fan known her real name all along since it was right at the front of the book under copyright?

She knew he could have found out her name in any number of places, but that True Fan was now using it…

Annabelle pulled out in a wide spot and cut the engine and radio. The silence was as deep as the snow around them. "Ready?"

They tugged on coats, snow-pants, boots, hats and mittens and disembarked with Annabelle toting the ax. At first they walked up the road but quickly realized they would have to separate and go into the woods to find a tree.

"Remember no taller than eight feet," Annabelle warned them. "Trees always look smaller out here."

"You'd think she'd been doing this her whole life," Chloe commented to TJ before they split up. "One trip to get a tree with Dawson and now she's an expert."

Growing up, their grandmother had had a fake tree, one of the first ones they'd come out with.

TJ stepped off the road into the trees and then waited until her sisters disappeared into the woods before she dropped back down on the snow-covered dirt road. She could see older tire tracks now filling with snow from where someone had driven in here earlier. She followed the tire tracks in the deep snow, determined to find Silas Walker's cabin.

Walking through the falling snow had a dizzying effect on her after a while. It was like being inside a snow globe. She stopped to look back and saw how quickly her tracks were filling in.

TJ had no idea how far she'd gone when she noticed fresh tracks had turned up an even more narrow snowy road that led up the mountain. There were no new tire tracks on the road she'd been following. If Silas Walker had driven back in to his cabin after the signing then there was a good chance these tracks were his.

She decided to follow the tracks in the hope of coming across his cabin. Following the tire tracks, she hadn't gone far when she caught the smell of wood smoke on the air. She kept going through the falling snow, losing track of time and distance.

After continuing to climb up the road deeper into the mountains, she stopped to catch her breath and considered turning back. But she'd gone too far to do that. She told herself that if she didn't come across the cabin soon, she would.

She wasn't worried, but when she looked back, she saw that her boot tracks had filled in. All around her was nothing but white. The snowflakes were falling much harder now. She could barely see the road ahead through the snow. She felt a chill and realized how crazy this had been.

Just a little farther, she told herself, and was almost ready to give up when she spotted smoke rising up out of the trees in the distance. Hurrying now, she headed toward it. Annabelle had said that there were several cabins up here. She told herself that this one had be Silas Walker's. There'd only been one set of tracks this far into the mountains and most of the cabins up here only were used in the summer.

As she drew closer, she saw the truck he'd been driving parked next to the small log cabin. Wet and cold, she hesitated. She knew she should get back to her sisters. They would be worried about her.

From the side of the cabin Silas Walker stepped out carrying a huge armload of firewood, startling her. As if sensing her, he looked up. Surprise registered on his face, then another emotion.

TJ spun around and tried to run back the way she'd come. Her boots slipped on the icy road beneath the snow. She went down hard. Her left leg twisted under her as her boot heel caught on the ice. She let out a cry of pain. Struggling to get up in the deep snow, she realized her ankle was hurt badly. She dropped back to the ground, grimacing in pain, suddenly terrified because she wasn't going far on this ankle.

When she was suddenly lifted off the ground, she screamed. She struggled, but Silas had her in a bear hug and this man was way too large and strong for her to overpower him. Her scream was suddenly cut off by a large gloved hand over her mouth.

"Stop struggling, you're only going to hurt yourself

worse," he said next to her ear. "I'm going to set you down on your good leg. Okay?"

She sucked in air through her nose and stopped fighting him to nod.

The moment he set her down, she slugged him in the stomach. It was like hitting a block wall and turning, she tried to run and immediately collapsed on her bad ankle.

He was on her again, covering her mouth as she began screaming in both pain and terror. "One of us is crazy. Since it's not me," he said, "we're taking this inside the cabin where it's warm." He tossed her over one broad shoulder and turned them both toward the cabin.

She screamed and pounded his back, but it had no effect as he strode up the porch steps of the cabin, shoved open the door and stepped inside. Swinging her off his shoulder, he dropped her unceremoniously into a large overstuffed chair.

Immediately she tried to get up, letting out a cry as she put pressure on her hurt ankle. Not that she was going anywhere even if she hadn't twisted it. He dropped a hand to her shoulder and held her in place as he kicked the door shut. It was warm inside the cabin and at the smell of something cooking her stomach growled, although she hardly noticed.

"What are you doing out in a blizzard?" he demanded, towering over her. He smelled of freshly cut pine. There was a maleness about him that was intimidating and at the same time intoxicating, even if he was her demented True Fan. She thought of a mountain lion on the prowl and felt like a small rabbit wanting to run for its life.

"You have to let me go!"

He held up his hands. "Not until you tell me what's going on. What are you doing here, TJ?"

So he had recognized her, even bundled up with her hat covering half of her face.

"I was out looking for a Christmas tree. I got turned around." She started to push out of the chair but he held up his hand.

"Hold on. Looking for a Christmas tree? And you just happened to stumble onto my cabin? Tell me you didn't come up here by yourself."

"I didn't. I came with my sisters. They'll be looking for me. That's why I have to go. They'll be worried."

But even as she said it, she knew they wouldn't be able to find her. They thought she'd come up here to find a Christmas tree. They would be looking for her closer to where Annabelle had parked the SUV. By now they could have a tree and be loading it.

She imagined them calling her name, joking around until they started to get worried when she hadn't appeared. Would they try to track her? As hard as it was snowing right now, her tracks would have filled in. They'd never be able to find her.

What had she been thinking? She hadn't. She'd acted on instinct and this is where it had led her.

She tried to get up again. He didn't push her back down, but he did move to crouch down in front of her. "TJ, you're a terrible liar, no offense. What are you really doing here?"

If only she knew. It wasn't as if she'd had a plan. She'd wanted to find his cabin. She'd wanted to spy on him. She'd wanted to learn more about him because she believed he was True Fan? Or because of that exhilarating and yet confusing mixture of strong feelings she'd had the first time she'd laid eyes on him?

What she hadn't wanted to do was get caught and end up trapped in his cabin with him. It galled her what she'd done, since there was no way she would have let the heroine in her books do something this stupid.

Past him, she could see just how small the cabin was. It was only one room with a fireplace, a very small kitchen area, the chair she was sitting in and a bed. Next to the bed was a makeshift desk. It was what she saw on it that stopped her heart.

Sitting on the desk was a large old manual typewriter.

Chapter Nine

TJ felt her eyes widen in alarm. Silas had seen her look in the direction of the typewriter. Now he was frowning at her in a way that turned her blood to slush.

She thought of all the books she'd written where the heroine escaped by hitting the villain with a makeshift weapon. Or catching him off guard and kicking him in his private parts before bolting for the door.

While there was a floor lamp next to the chair, she couldn't imagine how she could grab it, swing it and hit him hard enough to get away. That was if she could walk on her ankle—let alone run.

But given no other option—she sat up a little. He was crouched directly in front of her. She'd barely kicked out with her good leg when he grabbed it, stopping her foot before it could reach its mark.

"That only works in your books," he said, his voice deep and rough. "Most of the time, it only makes the bad guy more angry. Let's quit playing around. Tell me what's going on."

"I know who you are." She hated that she sounded near tears. "You're my True Fan."

He frowned again. "Yes, I'm a fan of your books but…"

She felt fear give away to anger. "You've been sending me the letters!"

"Letters?" he repeated.

"Don't deny it. I know it was you who pushed me in front of the truck in New York yesterday morning."

He rocked back on his haunches. "Whoa. Yes, I was there, luckily for you. I didn't realize that you even saw me. Only I didn't push you," he said, enunciating each word. "I was the one who *saved* you before you became roadkill."

"Right, you just *happened* to be walking past."

"No, as a matter of fact, I was following someone." He made a face as if he saw what she was thinking. "It wasn't *you*. I was on a stakeout."

"I know you're not a cop anymore because you got fired."

"Did some research on me, did you?" He grinned. "I'm flattered. But don't believe everything you read in the paper. Anyway, I work for a private investigative business now. Or I did. I just took a leave of absence. Or did you already know that as well? And, sorry, but I haven't been writing you any letters."

"You've been taunting me for months. Admit it. I just got your latest threatening letter today."

"You've got the wrong guy."

"Really? Next you're going to tell me that you just happen to have a manual typewriter like the letters have all been written on," she said, jabbing a finger in its direction. She saw his sheepish look. "That's what I thought."

"You have it all wrong," he said, getting to his feet. "If you must know, I've been trying to write a book." He shrugged, looking embarrassed. "I use a manual up here because the power goes out more than it's on this time of year. I read that you write every day so I've been trying to do that." He moved to the woodstove. "You inspired me to at least try. Unfortunately, I don't have your talent."

She watched him throw another log into the woodstove. Did he really think she believed him? "I need to go. My sisters will be looking for me."

He turned to look at her. "Have you checked out the weather outside?"

She hadn't, but she did so now. The wind had picked up, whirling snow in a blinding white that covered everything. Worse, the visibility was only a few yards. She'd grown up in this county. She knew how easy it was to get lost. Ranchers often tied a rope from the house to the barn so they didn't wander off track and freeze to death.

"Once the storm stops, I can try to get us out of here in my pickup," he was saying. "But the truth is, I barely made it back earlier with a load of wood I cut from that beetle kill area by the road. I shouldn't have to tell you how slick that road into the cabin is. By the way, how is your ankle?"

"It's fine." She started to get up. He didn't move to stop her. But as she put pressure on her twisted ankle, she winced in pain. Who was she kidding? She wasn't going anywhere on that leg even if she could find her way back. She dropped into the chair and dug out her cell phone.

"Good luck with that," he said as he watched her. "I've never been able to get much coverage in a storm. Sometimes a text will go through."

TJ saw that he was right. She only had two bars. She

bit her lower lip, fighting back tears as her call didn't go through. Her sisters would be frantic.

She sent a text. At Walker's cabin until storm lets up. It was the best she could do since the text appeared to have gone through.

Raising her gaze, she realized that at least Annabelle and Chloe were together. While she was the one in real trouble.

"Look, maybe we could start over," Silas said, seeing how upset she was. "We're stuck here until the storm stops. By then, your sisters will have Search and Rescue looking for you. In the meantime, I've got some beef stew and some homemade bread I baked in the woodstove yesterday. It was my first attempt so I'm not making any promises."

She swallowed and looked out at the storm before turning back to him.

"Are you all right?" he asked quietly.

"I shouldn't have come here."

No, she shouldn't have. "Hey, you thought I was this person who's been writing you threatening letters. Actually, I'm relieved. I couldn't understand your reaction to me at the gift shop or at your signing. I didn't think I was that scary." Still she said nothing. "You really think someone pushed you yesterday in New York."

"I know someone did. I was shoved in front of that truck."

She was looking at him as if she wasn't convinced it hadn't been him. He could see now where she might have gotten that idea. He should have stuck around and talked to her. But he would have lost the person he was tailing. As it was, he did anyway.

"That was pretty gutsy of you to come looking for me the way you did. Given you thought I was the person who was writing you threatening letters let alone suspecting I pushed you in front of a truck. Probably not your best plan. Good thing I'm not that person."

"Good thing," she said, a little sarcastically. "Otherwise I would be trapped here with someone who wants to hurt me."

He rubbed his whiskered jaw. "How can I prove to you that I'm not this fan you say has been taunting you?" He stepped over to the typewriter. "Truth is, I admire the devil out of you. You're why I wanted to write my own book. I thought it would be easy." He laughed, picked up a handful of typewritten pages and came back over to where she was sitting.

To his surprise, she seemed to flinch at the sight of the paper. "Don't worry, I wasn't going to ask you to read it." He realized that she was staring at the paper as if...as if what?

She snatched a sheet from his hand. "Where did you get this?" she said, holding up the paper. His expression must have conveyed his total confusion. "Copy paper is usually white or some color. This is discolored. There even appear to be watermarks on some of it as if—"

"As if it was stored in a basement for years?" he asked. "I bought it at a garage sale in town last summer."

"*Whose* garage sale?" She sounded as if she didn't believe him. But then again, she hadn't believed anything he'd said.

"How should I know whose garage sale? Remember? I'm new here." He could see that she was still expecting more of an answer. "It was some elderly woman. Her house was for sale. Apparently she'd had boxes of the stuff in her basement for a while. She was practically giving it away."

"Why would she have boxes of it in her basement?"

"I have no idea. Wait. I might have overheard someone say she used to have a business in town that sold office products. Is it really that important to you? I bought one of the boxes filled with reams of paper. You're welcome to—"

"The person who has been sending me the threatening letters typed them on a manual typewriter like the one you have on paper exactly like this." She held up the sheet, her eyes glittering with tears. "Still going to tell me that you aren't True Fan?"

SILAS HELD UP both hands. "Maybe, since we have a little time now that we're snowed in, I can convince you of my innocence. In the meantime, why don't you get out of those wet outer clothes?" he suggested. "By the way, if you have to use the facilities, there's only an outhouse in the back. It's a short walk, but if you can't make it out there with your ankle, I'll be happy to help you."

TJ wished he hadn't mentioned it because now she felt the need to go. She pushed to her feet, grimacing as she put weight on her ankle. Silas was at her side in two long strides.

"Lean on me," he suggested as he walked her to the back door off the kitchen. As he opened the door, a gust of wind showered them both with snow crystals. They stepped out into winter, Silas closing the door behind them.

He was right. It was a short walk and he'd shoveled

earlier. But the snow had filled in the path. Tucking their heads into their coats they made their way to the outhouse.

"Sorry. It's pretty primitive. No hurry," he said as he opened the door and let her limp inside. "I'll wait at the back door of the cabin. I'll come help when I see you."

She closed the door. It was freezing in the one-hole outhouse. She couldn't remember the last time she'd used one. Drawing down her pants was no easy job as bundled up as she was. As she lowered herself to the wood seat she was sure her behind would freeze to it.

No hurry, Silas had said, but she hurried, anxious to get her pants pulled back up to get heat to return to her backside. Shivering, she opened the outhouse door. Good to his word, he came charging out.

As they made their way to the back door of the cabin, TJ saw that the storm had only worsened. She thought of her sisters and felt horrible for taking off the way she had. She just hoped they were smart enough not to be out looking for her in this. Hopefully Chloe had gotten the message she'd sent.

Back inside, Silas led her to the sink and provided her with soap and warm water that he'd heated on the woodstove in a large kettle. She washed her hands, dried them on the towel he handed her and let him lead her over to the chair again. While he busied himself at the stove, she got out of her wet boots, coat and ski pants. Down to a sweater and jeans and socks, she shivered in the chair until Silas brought her over a quilt to wrap up in. She watched him take her wet things and hang them up on hooks by the door, telling herself he had to be True Fan, and yet...

As she watched him, she told herself that a man

who was this thoughtful couldn't possibly have written those vile things about her. But like her other readers, he probably thought he knew her, thought he knew what was best for her.

The man unsettled her no matter who he was. She reconciled that strange feeling she'd had at the gift shop when their gazes had met. She'd seen…darkness. Something dangerous. Something violent. She tried to shake off the memory. Where had those feelings come from? Worse, because she still felt them, why were they so strong?

She tried not to flinch as Silas pulled up a stool that had been by the fire and sat down in front of her, his expression somber. "How serious were these threats against you?"

TJ debated how much to tell him. If he was True Fan, then he already knew, so what was his game? And if he wasn't? "One of them suggested I should kill myself and do the reading world a favor. Another said I should die like one of my villains in my books. The latest one just indicated that the letter writer couldn't let me keep writing these books, that this would have to end."

He shook his head. "How did this all get started?"

"Why the interest?"

He smiled. "Believe it or not, I'm still a lawman at heart. I like catching the bad guys. But I also admire you and enjoy your books. Since we're going to be here until the storm passes… Maybe I can be of assistance."

TJ couldn't help being skeptical. It came with her personality. Maybe that was why she wrote what she did. She didn't trust what was behind a smile or kind words. Grandma Frannie used to tell her to lighten up. Like that was possible.

More to the point, she wasn't sure what to make of Silas Walker. All the evidence pointed to him being True Fan. So was this just him still taunting her?

Looking into his blue eyes, she thought she saw genuine concern. She felt confused, thrown off balance by the man. She remembered how easily he had thrown her over his shoulder and carried her into the house. If he was True Fan...

"It started like any other letter from a fan," she told him, gauging his expression as she talked. She told him about the first few letters from the person who called him or herself True Fan's being complimentary, all the time studying his face, looking for...looking for a lie in all that blue. But she saw nothing but sympathy and a growing anger at True Fan.

When she finished he got up from the stool without a word and moved to the woodstove. He seemed to be thinking as he stirred the stew.

She studied his broad back, wondering why he'd been fired from the police department. "Well?" she prodded.

He stirred the stew for a minute or two before he turned back to her. "If you really were purposely pushed into the traffic yesterday, then we would have to assume your True Fan either lived in New York or just happened to be there yesterday. But if you're right about the paper True Fan is using to write the letters on coming from the same place as I got mine, then..."

She nodded, her heart pounding. Was this where he told her it had been him all along? "True Fan had to have gone to the same garage sale you did. Someone with connections to both New York City and Whitehorse since True Fan also took a photograph of my apartment," she reminded him.

He raised his gaze to hers. "A fan anywhere in the country could have had a friend in New York snap a photo of your apartment. Also, your near accident yesterday could have been just that. I think your True Fan is right here in Montana."

"Right where you just happened to be. Right where you just happened to be passing by yesterday."

He mugged a face at her. "The reason it's called a coincidence is because they do exist. I had no idea the woman I grabbed to keep her from falling in front of a delivery truck yesterday was you." He crossed his heart with the index finger of his left hand.

"You're left-handed." The words were out before she could stop them.

He looked confused again for a moment before he smiled. "I forgot. Your heroine Constance Ryan always falls for left-handed men. I'm betting there were a couple of left-handed boyfriends in your past." He turned back to the stove.

He'd be wrong about that. There had been one though—Marc. He'd been left-handed and one of the mistakes she'd made when she'd first started writing was that she'd made her heroine in her ongoing series too much like herself. *Write what you know*, she'd always been told. She didn't know anyone as well as she knew herself.

But while Constance Ryan always fell for left-handed men, she was the woman TJ wished she was. Unfortunately the similarities were obvious to anyone who knew her. Constance was a blonde with aquamarine-blue eyes, five foot six, curvy. A woman who loved spicy food and drank her coffee black and by the gallon.

But that was where the similarities stopped. Constance was daring. As a private investigator, she took on cases that others had turned down. She was smart and determined. Even after almost getting killed in every book, she still came back for more.

Constance also loved men—and men loved her. She always ended up curled up in bed with some handsome man. She wasn't one to stay long with any of them. Constance Ryan lived her life the way TJ wished she could.

But TJ was too much of a prude who'd hardly dated, even at college. Also she believed in happy-ever-after—even if her alter ego didn't. She didn't want a string of men. She just wanted that one man who would make her heart pound.

Like this man was doing right now. Only was it fear? Or something just as dangerous, given the two of them were alone, snowed-in deep in the mountains?

"I CAN SEE why you thought I was writing the threatening letters to you," Silas said after dishing them both up bowls of hot beef stew with a side of his homemade bread slathered in butter.

He'd pushed his stool over against the wall and leaned against it as he ate. He was glad to see that TJ seemed to have relaxed a little. Outside, the blizzard was still raging. He'd built the cabin to withstand the winter cold so it was cozy inside, but he could hear the wind and see snow piling up at the windows. He wondered if the snow would be too deep to drive out once the storm stopped.

"I've been thinking how to go about finding this fan

of yours," he said between bites. Because he'd realized he had to help her whether she wanted it or not. The only way to prove to her that he wasn't True Fan was to find the culprit. Also, finding the nasty letter writer with TJ definitely had its appeal. He'd never dreamed he would get a chance to even have a cup of coffee with her—let alone spend time in his cabin with her.

"I can't wait to hear your plan." She'd stopped, her spoon in midair, to look at him. He could see she was still suspicious. He didn't blame her. Given the evidence against him, he would have thought the same thing she did.

"It seems simple to me. It all comes down to the old discolored copy paper. Anyone can shoot a photograph of the outside of your apartment—"

"How would they know where I lived unless they had contacts…say, inside the police department?"

He smiled at that as he watched her take a bite of the stew. He could see that she liked it, which made him a lot happier than it should have. Pride cometh before the fall, his father used to say. "You like the bread?"

"You really baked this in that woodstove?" she asked skeptically.

"I did. See that iron box on the top? It's an oven. This is my first attempt. I'll get better."

"It's very good. I've never attempted bread—even in a real oven."

He smiled, warmed by her compliment more than by the stew. He took a couple more bites before he said, "As to the question of how to find out where you lived…all anyone had to do was follow you home from a book signing. How many have you done in New York and gone straight home afterward?"

She didn't answer, his point taken.

"As for the push, there were so many people rushing around with Christmas shopping. I got jostled myself just moments before that. I didn't see anyone push you but I was in a tight crowd of people who were forced to the curb. I just caught you falling out of the corner of my eye, but there were people in front of me, including a woman with a huge shopping bag who could have hit you."

He watched her lick her lips after taking a bite of the bread covered with real butter. No butter substitute in his kitchen, ever. He could tell she was considering his theory.

"So let's say True Fan knows someone in New York who could have followed me from a book signing and taken a photo of my apartment from the street."

"Or she could have even hired someone to do it," he added, thinking about the private investigative business he'd been working for since leaving the police department. It was amazing to him what people would pay to learn.

TJ nodded, no doubt thinking of Constance, the heroine in her books. "So then it would just come down to the copy paper you both purchased at a garage sale last summer in Whitehorse?"

"August. I also bought this stool there."

Her gaze darkened to deep sea green. "So it's someone who lives in Whitehorse." She shivered and for the first time, he thought she might actually be considering that it wasn't him.

"I'd suspect it's someone who knows you and has reason to be jealous of your success," he said. "Maybe an old rival? An old boyfriend? Maybe even a former friend."

Chapter Ten

"I still can't believe you really made this bread," TJ said as she accepted another piece. Her walk to find his cabin had left her famished.

He grinned, obviously pleased. "For my first time, I think I got lucky, huh."

"It's delicious and so is the stew," TJ said, feeling conflicted. Could she trust this man? Sometimes the way he looked at her with those potent blue eyes, it made her squirm uncomfortably. It was when she glimpsed a dangerous edge to him that she had her doubts. She tried not to think about the predicament she was in—trapped in a cabin in a blizzard in the mountains with a man she didn't trust.

Common sense told her he had to be True Fan.

But after seven books, she knew from experience that the villain often proved to be the person you least expected—not the obvious one. Of course, that was fiction and this felt more like any real life she'd lived so far.

There was something so charming about Silas because of his easygoing manner. And that he was a little domesticated made him even more appealing. He seemed almost shy around her. She saw none of the anger that had practically dripped from True Fan's threatening letters.

After months of running scared she wasn't sure she could trust her instincts, though. Look where they'd brought her.

As she finished her stew and bread she noticed it had gotten dark, although it was hard to tell how late it was since the thick-falling snow still made it fairly light out. She pulled out her phone, hoping for a response from one of her sisters, but there was nothing. She looked at the time and realized with a start that she would be spending the night in this cabin with this man. Her heart began to pound a little harder.

Silas rose to his feet, stepping to her to take her bowl and spoon. "Don't worry," he said as if reading her mind. "You can have the bed when you get tired. I have a sleeping bag I'll drag out. I've curled up in front of the fire on the rug more times than I can remember when I was building this place. The bed came later."

He moved to the makeshift kitchen. Earlier, he'd refilled the kettle on the stove. Now she watched him wash up their dishes in a pan in the sink. He was so self-sufficient. Handsome too in a rough, untamed way that both intrigued her and scared her.

"Don't you get lonely out here?" she asked, wondering if there was a woman in his life back in New York.

"Just the opposite," he said without turning around. "I come here for the peace and quiet. Listen." He stopped what he was doing to half turn to look at her.

She heard nothing but the pop and hiss of the fire in the woodstove.

"Not one siren to be heard. No traffic. No honking taxis. No loud music from the apartment next door."

He let out a sigh. "This is why I love this place. Sometimes I just have to get away from all the racket. Here I get up when I feel like it, I go to bed when I'm tired. I spend my days working on the cabin, cutting wood for the stove, cooking my own meals. When I'm not working, I'm reading. Or attempting to write," he said with a chuckle as he went back to his dishes.

"I had forgotten what it was like living in Montana," TJ had to admit.

"That's right, you grew up in Whitehorse."

She nodded, remembering sledding and ice-skating in the winter, tubing the river in the summer. She'd forgotten what small-town living was like, the slower pace, the unlimited space, the quiet. "I hadn't realized that I missed it."

He turned then to look at her as he dried his big hands on a dish towel. "You must enjoy the glamour and excitement of New York City though. Isn't that why you live there? You can write anywhere."

"I did enjoy the city, especially at first. It felt as if it was where I needed to be to have the career I wanted."

"But now?"

She shook her head. "I hate it. True Fan has ruined the city for me. I don't feel safe there anymore." She let out a bitter laugh. "I don't feel safe anywhere."

He put down the dish towel carefully and turned to lean back against the kitchen counter. "I'm so sorry about that. It's another reason we have to find this person and put a stop to it. I would imagine it's also been hard for you to write."

She looked away. "You have no idea. Or maybe you do."

Silas cocked his head. "I know you still don't trust

that I'm not this person. That's okay. You have to be skeptical to write the books you do—and to be safe. But I promise you I'm going to find True Fan even if you don't want to help me." He pushed off the counter. "Hot chocolate or tea?"

"Tea."

TJ watched him put a smaller kettle on the stove and prepare two cups with tea bags. "I'd like to read some of your book."

He froze for a moment before turning. "You're going to laugh, but right now I'm more terrified than when I'm facing down a junkie with a gun."

"If you don't want me to…"

"Oh, that's just it. The thought of you reading anything I've written both excites and terrifies me. Didn't you feel that way?"

She smiled, nodding. "I remember the first time I took a writing class. I just wanted the instructor to tell me I could do this."

"Did the instructor?"

"No. Looking back, the woman didn't know anything more than I did about how to have a writing career, even though she'd sold a couple of books. I don't think she wanted to get my hopes up since by then she knew how hard it was."

"Well, you don't have to worry about that with me. I enjoy writing, so I'll keep at it hoping I get better no matter what you say. But I really would appreciate your opinion."

Crossing to the typewriter, he reached beside it and picked up a few pages.

"Give me the first chapter," she said. Aspiring writers always wanted to show her their favorite chapter in the middle, not realizing an editor would never read that chapter if they couldn't get past the first one.

He brought over a dozen sheets of paper. She noticed the way he held them in those large hands, like he was carrying a bird with a broken wing.

"You don't have to read the whole chapter," he said, carefully handing her the pages.

The first thing she noticed was that the pages had been typed with a new ribbon. There were none of the light and dark letters like on True Fan's.

Silas stood over her for a moment, then quickly moved away to take his coat from the hook by the door. "I'm going to bring more wood in from the porch," he said. "I suspect the temperature is going to drop tonight. I'll have to keep the stove going." With that, he went out the door on a gust of cold, snowy wind.

For a moment, TJ watched the snowflakes that had swept in melt on the wood floor. Then she turned to the pages of his book and began to read.

SILAS STOOD OUT on the porch in the blizzard smiling like a fool. TJ St. Clair was reading his book. He felt his stomach roil. What if it stunk as badly as he feared it did? What if she told him to use it to start his next woodstove fire? Or maybe worse, he thought, what if she told him it wasn't bad? That it was good enough that he should keep at it? That he had promise?

He wasn't sure which was his greatest fear—fear of failure or of success. They scared him in ways his job never had—even when he'd recently been shot. He rubbed his thigh unconsciously, realizing that his limp had been hardly noticeable. Or maybe he'd tried harder for it not to show around TJ.

Silas felt a shudder when he thought of her True Fan. How dangerous was this person? Would they really go through with their threats if pushed too far? More than ever, he was determined to find the person and put an end to all this.

The wind whipped snow into his face and down his neck. He shivered and hurriedly grabbed an armload of split firewood to take back inside. By now, TJ would have read far enough that she'd have an opinion. Feeling as if he was about to step in front of a firing squad, he told himself he could take whatever she had to offer, and pushed open the door to the cabin.

At first he didn't see her. The chair was empty and for one heart-stopping moment, he thought she had taken off out the back door. But as his gaze shifted, he saw her standing on one foot by the woodstove. She had the small kettle handle in one hand and was pouring boiling water in each of his mismatched mugs.

He dropped the load of wood in the bin near the stove and tried to slow his pulse. "You shouldn't be on your ankle."

"I hopped over. The kettle was boiling." She studied him. "You thought I'd left."

"I thought I was going to have to try to find you out in that storm. I wasn't looking forward to it."

She nodded. "That's the only reason?"

"Maybe I like your company." He could tell that wasn't what she meant at all. She thought he'd lured her here and that he was never going to let her leave. "Here, let me finish the tea." He helped her over to the chair and she dropped into it. "Are you warm enough?"

She nodded and seemed to watch him as he went back to the stove, returning with her cup of tea.

"I'd ask if you want sugar…"

"Constance Ryan takes sugar in her coffee, not me," she said, taking the mug of tea. "We aren't our characters."

"Aren't we? I knew you took your coffee black. Wasn't sure about tea." He thought of his own protagonist in the book he'd started. It was him and it wasn't. But still there was so much of him in his words that he felt vulnerable, something he'd seldom felt even on duty as a cop.

TJ sipped her tea as he hung up his coat and walked back to the counter to pick up his mug.

"I hate to even ask," he said, seeing his chapter lying on the footstool near the chair. He couldn't tell if she'd read any of it, let alone the whole chapter.

TJ NOTICED THE way the large mug disappeared in his hands. Silas seemed so gentle and yet she'd seen the way his muscles had bulged when he'd carried in the wood. For a man his size, he moved with a grace that again reminded her of a mountain lion.

"You have talent, but I don't have to tell you that," she said as she picked up the chapter from the stool and he moved to it to sit down. "I was drawn right into your story. I wanted to read more." He was cyeing her as if he was waiting for a "but." "You've had other people read some of your book, right? I'm sure they've told you…"

He shook his head. "You're the first and only."

She couldn't help being surprised. "Then you really didn't know."

"I'm trying to decide if you're just being nice."

"I'm not. The one thing I learned a long time ago

was that people who tell you you're better than you are are of no help. You need real criticism if you're going to get better, and I believe we have to continue to strive to do so."

He seemed to let out a breath before taking a sip of his tea. "Like I said, I enjoy writing so I'll keep going, but I'm overjoyed to hear it's okay."

"It's more than okay," she said. "I won't promise you that you can have a career writing. Just being good isn't enough. It takes determination and some luck."

"I have the determination. I'm not so sure about the luck." He smiled. "But I feel lucky right now. It's nice to have company."

They drank their tea in the comfort of the cabin as the storm raged on outside. The stove popped and crackled. Silas got up to throw more wood on the fire, then turned and looked at her shyly. "You wouldn't be interested in playing some cards, would you?"

She laughed. "What did you have in mind?"

"I don't even care. Crazy eights. Old maid. Five-card stud. I love to play cards and I'm sick of solitaire."

"My sisters and I used to play all the time. Do people still play with actual cards now that they have virtual games?"

"I have no idea," he said as he brought over a deck of worn cards. From a space behind her chair, he pulled out a small folding table. "You can even beat me. That's how desperate I am," he said with a laugh.

TJ snuggled into the chair. She hadn't played cards in years. She watched Silas shuffle the deck and realized she was beginning to trust him. She hoped that wouldn't be her last mistake.

Chapter Eleven

They played cards until after midnight. Silas couldn't recall a time he'd had more fun. TJ was an excellent player no matter what game they played. She challenged him. He couldn't remember the last woman who'd done that. She'd relaxed during their games and he'd gotten to see the woman behind the best seller.

She was fun and funny, sharp-witted. He liked her, and not just because she thought he had talent.

It wasn't until the last game that she began to look nervous again. He put the cards away and went to the built-in drawers on the other side of the bed. Pulling out one of his T-shirts, he held it up.

"I think this will cover everything but your toes if you're interested in wearing it to sleep in," he said. "I'll go out and get some more wood and give you a chance to change. Or you can sleep in your clothes. Whatever you prefer." He put the T-shirt down on the bed. "You need to go out back first?"

She shook her head. They'd made several trips out to the bathroom earlier during their card games.

"Sorry, I don't have a spare toothbrush. Wasn't expecting company, but there is toothpaste and water by the sink. Let me know if there is anything else you need." He headed for his coat by the door.

Once outside, he killed time thinking about True Fan. If it hadn't been for this crazed reader, he might never have gotten this close to TJ. That was a thought he wasn't about to share. He also tried not imagining her in his T-shirt. The thought made him grin and ache at the same time.

It had been so long since he'd been truly interested in a woman. He blamed it on everything that had been going on in his life. But he knew that had only been part of it. He'd missed the companionship. Hell, he'd missed the sex. And just thinking of TJ wearing his T-shirt... He shook off the thought.

If he wanted this to go any further, he'd best take it slow. The woman was beyond skittish. She was running scared. Not just that. She still didn't trust him. He hoped to fix that.

He warned himself that she'd be gone as soon as the storm quit. That's if her sisters didn't show up with the National Guard and probably half the county's lawmen before the night was over. Otherwise, he would get her out of the mountains in the morning one way or another.

The thought that he might not see her again was almost physically painful. He'd been captivated by her since her first book. Now that he'd gotten to spend this time with her, well, he didn't want it to end.

That alone surprised him. He dated in New York, but usually he was fine only seeing a woman a time or two. He didn't feel that way about TJ—even if he hadn't been worried about her.

Loading up another armful of wood, he tapped at the

door. Hearing nothing, he stepped in. She was tucked in bed, the down comforter up to her chin. She looked so damned cute in his bed. He quickly closed the door on a blast of snow and wind and, turning his back to her, dumped the wood and took off his coat.

Seeing her in his bed made him ache. It also threw him a little off-balance. He felt both protective and attracted to this woman. Just the thought of kissing her... "Have everything you need?" he asked, his voice sounded strange to his ears.

She nodded and watched him with just her eyes as he went to the area by the bed, opened a cabinet and pulled out his sleeping bag.

Rolling it out on the rug in front of the fire, he turned out the lights and lay down on top of it. A moment later, she tossed him a pillow from the bed.

"Thanks," he said into the quiet darkness. The storm had let up a little. He felt like he did when he was a kid at a sleepover. He didn't want to sleep. He wanted to talk about all the things that interested him, from life on other planets, to Big Foot's possible existence, to what TJ's favorite Christmas gift of all time was.

"Do you remember lying in bed waiting for Santa?" she asked from the darkness.

He chuckled. "I do. I never wanted to close my eyes. I was afraid I'd miss it."

"I hated it when I found out he wasn't real."

"He's not?" The fire crackled and after a few moments, he realized that she'd gone to sleep.

TJ woke to find the cabin empty. The bedroll and pillow were no longer on the floor in front of the wood-stove. And while a fire was going, Silas was nowhere to be seen. Sitting up, she saw that the pillow she'd tossed him was lying next to her on the bed. His bed-roll had apparently been put away.

Had he only gone to the outhouse and would be back any minute?

She heard something outside. For a moment she thought it was his heavy tread on the porch, but soon realized it was him trying to start his pickup. She threw back the covers and got up. Her ankle was better, only tender to the touch and black and blue along one side.

Silas had been right about his T-shirt. It fell to her ankles. As she slipped it off, she sniffed it as if she thought it might contain his scent. She held it for a moment, feeling like a teenage girl again, before tossing it on the bed and quickly pulling on the clothes she'd worn. She'd moved to the chair and was putting on her socks when she heard him come up the porch stairs and into the cabin.

"Good morning!" he greeted her, brushing snow off his coat and stomping it from his boots before stepping in on the rug. "Truck's cleared off and the motor turned right over after a few tries. If I have to, I can chain up all four tires to get us out of here. I wasn't sure how much of a hurry you're in to get home."

Last night she'd been champing at the bit. This morning, she hated to leave this cabin. Hated to leave Silas. Which was why she needed to, even if she wasn't worried that her sisters would be frantic.

She glanced around the cabin. "I can go when-ever you're ready. I appreciate your taking me back to town."

"Not a problem. I've enjoyed having you here. But

I'm not much of a host if I don't offer you breakfast," he said.

She was tempted. The warmth of this cabin, the scent of homemade bread, the good-natured, handsome man standing in the doorway. At that moment, she desperately wanted Silas Walker to be anything but True Fan.

"Thank you, but I really should get back. My sisters will be worried even after the text." Actually, more worried after the text.

He nodded, not looking any more anxious to leave than she was. "I'll be in the pickup. Come out when you're ready." He turned then and disappeared back outside.

TJ stepped to the hooks by the door, pulled down her coat, tugged on her snow-pants and boots. She took one last look around the cabin, thinking she might never see it again. Out of the corner of her eye she saw the typewriter. Curiosity killed the cat and every B movie heroine who decided to see what the noise was in the basement. Still, she moved to the typewriter and shuffled through the papers. Just pages of his book. She checked the trash can next to it. No partial letters written in too much haste.

Silas Walker wasn't True Fan. But Silas wouldn't be living out here in the woods unless he was running from something. She hated that she was thinking like her sister Chloe, the investigative reporter. But something had to explain those glimpses of darkness she'd seen in his blue eyes.

Walking out of the cabin, she limped her way through the deep snow to the pickup, where he was waiting behind the wheel. He leaned over the seat, pushed open the passenger side door and held it for her to get in.

"Shoot, I forgot about your ankle," he said. "I should have offered to help you."

"It's better, but thank you. Are you always so cheerful in the morning?" she asked.

"Do I detect that you aren't?" he asked with a laugh as he shifted the pickup into low gear. "Cross your fingers."

They chugged up the hill, the back of the pickup sliding a few times before they reached the road she'd come down earlier. There was no sign that anyone had been down the road last night.

"Okay," Silas said with a sigh of relief. "That was the worst of it. At least I hope so."

The sun topped the pines, making the fresh snow sparkle so bright that it was blinding. "It's so beautiful," she breathed. "I'd forgotten days like this."

He glanced over at her, but said nothing as he quickly turned back to his driving. The pickup bucked and slid and chugged until they reached an even wider snowy dirt road and finally the plowed, though snow-packed highway.

Silas patted the dash and said, "I knew you could do it, Gertrude."

"Gertrude?" she asked with a laugh. She was relieved they'd gotten out of the mountains without any trouble. She was also relieved that the easiness between them had returned.

"Be careful," Silas joked. "Don't insult her."

"I wouldn't dream of it," TJ said.

"Old Gert here reminds me of Constance."

She lifted a brow as she looked over at him. "Your

truck reminds you of the heroine in my books?" She couldn't help feeling a little offended, since she and Constance had a lot in common. No man had ever compared her to a pickup.

"Both Gert and Connie are dependable. They're up for anything when you need them. They both have their own kind of charm."

TJ smiled. "Well, when you put it that way…"

He chuckled and drove, looking comfortable behind the wheel even though the highway was slick and the landscape so white that it was hard to tell where the two-lane began and ended.

Normally, TJ would have been nervous about going off the road and ending up in a snowbank. But there was something about Silas that was a lot like his truck.

Chapter Twelve

"I don't know how to thank you," TJ said when Silas pulled up in front of the house. "It was interesting and…fun."

He grinned. "Glad to hear it. I was delighted for the company. It was nice visiting with you. But I hope we see each other soon." He jumped out to open her door. "I meant what I said about helping find that fan of yours. If I can figure out which house I went to for that garage sale and what happened to the woman who sold me the paper, do you want to go with me to talk to her?"

She couldn't help her smile. "I do."

He nodded, his smile broadening. "Then I'll let you know."

"Thank you." She gave him a nod and a wave as she started for the house. She heard him close her door, go around and climb behind the wheel. As he pulled away behind her, she hoped she wasn't wrong about the man. His words had made her all warm inside. Not to mention what happened when she'd looked into those blue eyes.

He was the kind of man a woman could fall hard for. Which made her all the more leery. There was a reason Constance never gave away her heart in the books. Her creator had given her heart away once, only to have it broken badly. To say they were both gun-shy was to put it mildly.

She'd barely reached the porch when her sisters came rushing out, both talking at once.

As Silas drove away, a sheriff's patrol car pulled up out front. TJ and her sisters turned to see Sheriff Mc-Call Crawford climb out.

"Are you all right?" Annabelle whispered.

"I'm fine. What is the sheriff doing here?" she whispered back.

"Chloe called her."

Of course she did. TJ sighed under her breath. "Did you get a tree?"

Annabelle smiled. "Of course. We're putting it up later."

The three waited until Sheriff Crawford joined them before going inside. Chloe, who clearly had taken charge, ushered them all into the kitchen.

"I see you made it home safe and sound," the sheriff said to TJ.

"I'm sorry my sister got you over here," she said. "I'm fine."

"She was trapped in the woods in a blizzard with Silas Walker," Chloe said, as if TJ had to be reminded. "I asked the sheriff here because I want to know more about this man who had my sister, especially since he'd been fired from the police force."

McCall smiled and declined the coffee Annabelle offered her. The two were on a first name basis after what Annabelle had found in the house last month.

"I could use a cup," TJ said as they all sat down.

"Silas bought some land in the Little Rockies about six months ago," the sheriff said once they were settled in. "I believe he built a cabin." McCall looked to TJ, who nodded. "Yes, he was fired from the New York City police force as part of an internal sting operation." Chloe looked at TJ as if to say "See?"

"But Silas was innocent. He was working undercover on behalf of the department to root out the dirty cops."

"That sounds dangerous," Chloe said.

All TJ could think about was the man who'd served her homemade bread and stew he'd made himself. The man who wrote beautiful words, deep with meaning. A man with many talents.

McCall continued. "He was offered his job back, but he declined because a cop who testifies against his own isn't necessarily welcomed back with open arms. There was an attempt on his life. He was shot. He is now employed part-time by another former police officer who started his own private investigative business."

TJ realized that she hadn't been the only one limping. But Silas had been trying hard not to show it.

"Have you met him?" Chloe asked McCall, clearly still skeptical.

"I have," the sheriff said. "I found him to be quite delightful." She looked to TJ, who nodded before picking up her coffee cup. She could feel both of her sisters watching her intently.

"I hope that answers any concerns you have about the man. But your sister told me that you've been getting threatening letters from one of your fans," the sheriff said, meeting TJ's gaze.

She nodded. "I was worried Silas might be the fan."

"But you're not now?" McCall asked.

"No, I'm not." After hearing what the sheriff had to say, she realized she could trust her instincts about Silas. Her new instincts that told her he wasn't True Fan. Not that he wasn't dangerous to her. Just the thought of him made her heart beat a little faster.

"Well if you need anything, you know where my office is," McCall said as she got to her feet.

TJ said she did and was glad when Chloe walked the sheriff to the door.

"Well?" Annabelle said the moment their older sister was out of earshot. "What happened?"

"Nothing happened."

Annabelle rolled her eyes. "How did you end up at his cabin?"

Chloe had returned after seeing the sheriff out. "Yes, how did that happen?"

TJ recounted seeing the mailbox by the road and wandering back into the woods, curious about him. "I didn't realize how far I'd gone and the blizzard was getting worse. I fell and twisted my ankle. Fortunately, he helped me into this cabin. By then it was snowing too hard to drive out so he suggested I stay the night."

"Why do I suspect there is more to the story?" Annabelle asked.

"He was very nice, charming actually, and he fed me homemade stew and bread that he'd made and we played cards until it got late."

Her sisters exchanged a look. "Have you forgotten that you thought he was True Fan?" Chloe demanded.

"No," TJ said. "And at first I thought he was. But none of that matters now. You heard the sheriff. There is nothing to worry about with him." They both looked at her as if they weren't convinced. "Isn't it possible that he's just a nice man who still wants to help me?"

"What does that mean?" Chloe asked.

"He's determined to help me find True Fan," she said with a shrug.

"Seriously?" Annabelle asked, eyes widening. "He is awfully good-looking if you like that big, muscled, chisel-jaw kind of man."

"I would be very careful," Chloe said. "Even if he isn't True Fan, this man could still be dangerous."

"You mean dangerous to someone as naive as me?" TJ said, bristling because she'd figured that out all on her own—but wasn't about to admit it.

Her sister seemed to take her time answering as if taking care with her words. "You haven't dated since Marc. That's all I'm saying."

She wanted to argue that Chloe had no idea how many men she'd dated, since they didn't live in the same city. But she saved her breath. Her sister was right. She hadn't dated since Marc. He'd been her college boyfriend. Her first. Her last. Their senior year at university, he'd gotten a job with a defense contractor working in high-risk countries.

The plan had been that she would kick-start her writing career and they would get married after he had an adventure and made a lot of money. She hadn't liked the plan, but Marc had been so excited, saying he needed to live a little dangerously before he could settle down. He'd been killed in Iraq when the company office where he worked was bombed.

"I'm only saying that I don't think you want another man who lives that close to the edge," Chloe said quietly.

TJ felt tears burn her eyes. Her sister was right. Silas Walker had gone into a dangerous profession and even volunteered to go undercover to weed out dirty cops. Just as Marc had felt the need for adventure in danger zones in the world.

"Don't worry," she said, more to herself than to her sisters. "I won't make the same mistake again."

A knock at the door relieved the tension in the kitchen. "I'll get it," Annabelle said, jumping to her feet.

TJ stayed where she was. She couldn't help thinking about how gentle and caring Silas had been. And yet from the first she'd sensed that darkness, that violence, that menace. Was she doomed to be attracted to men who liked to risk their lives?

Annabelle returned on a gust of cold air. TJ had her back to the door but she saw from Chloe's expression that something was wrong.

"Who was that at the door?" Chloe asked.

"It was Carol again from the post office," Annabelle said.

TJ didn't need to turn around. She knew without seeing the letter in her sister's hand. True Fan had sent her another threat.

SILAS DROVE AROUND Whitehorse street by street, looking for the house where he'd picked up the reams of paper at the garage sale. Whitehorse was only ten blocks square so it didn't take long to find the house where he remembered stopping at the garage sale.

He pulled up out front, got out and started toward the front door. As he did, he saw a front curtain twitch. A moment later, he knocked at the door and waited. He knocked again.

A small elderly woman opened the door a crack. "Yes?" she asked.

"Hello." He smiled, but she still looked wary. He couldn't remember the woman who had sold him the reams of papers, but he was pretty sure it wasn't this one. The house had been for sale because the owner was moving into the rest home as he recalled.

"Who is it, Mother?" said a younger voice from behind the woman.

"I don't know."

The door opened wider as another hand appeared on the edge of it.

"Can I help you?" asked a woman a good thirty years younger.

"I was looking for the woman who used to live in this house," Silas said. "She had a garage sale here last summer?"

The younger of the two nodded. "Melinda Holmes. She moved into the rest home." She pointed down the street.

"Thank you." He started to turn away.

"You bought something at her garage sale?" the woman asked, clearly curious why he would be looking for Melinda Holmes about dealing with an item from last summer's garage sale.

"Reams of paper," he said, turning back.

"Oh." She looked disappointed. Had she been hoping for a chest with a secret in it? Or something of more value that he might have wanted to return? Whatever she'd been hoping for, those hopes dashed, she closed the door.

Glancing at his cell phone, he saw that it was still early. He drove over to the house where he'd dropped off TJ earlier. Getting out, he walked to the door, wondering what kind of reception he would get not only from her, but also from her sisters.

He climbed the stairs to the porch and knocked. The young woman who opened the door was blonde and blue-eyed. There was just enough resemblance that he knew she was one of TJ's sisters.

"Hi," he said, and smiled. "I was hoping to see—" Just then another sister appeared, followed by the one he'd come for. His smile broadened as TJ came into view.

"Silas," she said, sounding a little breathless as if she'd just raced down from upstairs. There was an awkward moment where they all stood there looking at him. The sisters were definitely giving him the once-over.

"Please, come in," TJ said, shooing her sisters aside. He wiped his feet and, removing his Stetson, stepped into the house. "I don't think you've met my sisters. This is Chloe, who's an investigative reporter, and Annabelle, who is—"

"Just Annabelle now," the young woman said.

"I was going to say, just nosy," TJ finished.

All three were beautiful alone, but together they made quite a sight.

"This is Silas Walker," TJ said almost shyly.

He nodded to the other two women. "Nice to meet you."

"Can we offer you some coffee?" Annabelle asked.

"Thanks, but I'm fine. I just came by to tell your sister…" his gaze went to TJ "…that I found that house we talked about. The owner is in the local rest home. Melinda Holmes. Do you know her?"

"She should, since you used to steal the apples out of her tree on the way home from school," Annabelle said with a laugh. "I wonder if she'll remember you."

"Isn't that the woman who beat you with the broom as you were climbing her fence?" Chloe asked.

"Ah, the memories," TJ said as she reached for her coat. "I'd love to stay and reminisce but I have to find True Fan."

"If you haven't already found him," Chloe said under her breath.

Silas merely smiled, said how nice it was to meet them and TJ closed the door behind them. He saw that she'd showered and changed into jeans, boots and a sweater under her coat. Her blond hair was brushed and now floated like a golden cloud around her shoulders.

"I apologize for my sisters," she said. "They're... protective."

He chuckled. "You should be thankful for that." Glancing over at her, he grinned. "You really did steal apples from this woman we're going to see?"

"Let's hope the reason she's in the rest home is because she has forgotten the past," TJ joked.

"Not too far into the past though," he said as he opened the passenger side of his pickup. "We need to know who all she sold paper to."

THE REST HOME sat on a hill overlooking Whitehorse and the Milk River drainage. The valley was covered in trees that seemed to follow the river northward. Silas parked and started to get out, when she stopped him.

"I got another letter."

"Let's see it." He heard the fear in her voice, but when he turned to look at her, she looked deceptively calm. However, as she opened her purse and removed the envelope, he saw that her fingers were trembling.

Silas carefully opened the envelope and pulled out

the letter, trying not to touch it more than necessary. He wondered if TJ had taken the same precautions or if all three of the sisters had manhandled it. Not that he thought there would be fingerprints on it. With all the crime shows on television now, only a fool would send an anonymous threatening letter and leave behind evidence of the sender.

> Tessa Jane,
> I had such expectations for you and your books. I am sick over what has become of you—let alone what you have dragged your characters through. I knew you would corrupt Constance. For a while, she was the best of you.
> Not anymore. That she could kill Durango... That YOU could kill him. He was the good in Constance. How could you not see that? You took a beautiful thing and ruined it.
> I told you I was your only True Fan until the end. Well, I'm afraid this has to end. I can't let you write another book. I'm sorry, but you've abused your talent, and for what? Fame? Fortune?
> You've been playing God with your characters—and your readers.
> It's time to pay the piper.

SILAS FELT FURY roiling up deep inside him. Who was this crazy person? And more important, just how dangerous was True Fan?

He looked over at TJ. She'd gone pale, as if remembering each word of the letter as he was reading it. He told himself it didn't matter how crazy this person was or if they were serious about their threats of violence;

they had to be stopped. He could tell that TJ was terrified. He couldn't imagine what it must be like for her to try to write another book with this hanging over her.

"All right if I keep this for now?" he asked as he carefully put the letter back into the envelope. She nodded as if she wanted nothing to do with it. "When is your next book due?"

"Four months from now. And no, I have nothing done on it," she said. "I might have to buy back the contract—if my publisher will let me."

He swore under his breath. "Let's hope Melinda Holmes has some answers for us," he said as he opened his door.

TJ HAD FELT sick to her stomach since opening the letter from True Fan. But having Silas helping her made her feel stronger as they entered the rest home. She'd been surprised that he'd moved so quickly on this. She hadn't expected him to go in search of the garage sale house so fast.

But she was thankful that he had and that he was taking the threats seriously. Once inside the rest home they were directed to Melinda Holmes's room. Unfortunately it was empty. A passing nurse told them to try the dining room.

They found her sitting by the window staring out at the winter day. TJ barely remembered her from the broom-swinging woman who'd pounded her backside as she scrambled over the wooden fence behind the Holmeses' house.

"Mrs. Holmes?" Silas asked. No reaction. "Mrs. Holmes?" he said a little louder.

The elderly gray-haired woman turned from the

window. "I'm not deaf," she snapped, her narrowed gaze going from Silas to TJ. "I know you," she said in a hoarse voice as her gaze bored into TJ. "You're one of those wild Clementine girls. You've been in my apples again, haven't you?"

"You grow the best apples in the valley," she said as she took a seat next to her. "This is my friend Silas."

Melinda's gaze shifted to him. "You stealing my apples too?"

"No, ma'am. I wouldn't do that."

His answer seemed to satisfy her. "So what do you want, then?"

"You're the woman who used to own the store here in town that sold paper supplies, right?" Silas said.

"That was years ago."

"I bought some reams of paper from you at your garage sale last summer."

She looked from him to TJ as if to say, "So?"

"Do you remember who all you sold the paper to?" he finished.

She looked suspicious. "Why? There wasn't a thing wrong with that paper. Might have been a little discolored, that's all. Some of it got wet, but it dried out just fine."

"It was great paper. In fact," Silas continued, "I'd like to see if I can find more of it. I thought some of the people who bought it might make me a deal."

Melinda Holmes seemed to appreciate a man who liked a good deal. "A lot of people were at that garage sale. You expect me to remember after all this time?" She huffed at that. "There was that one woman from the school. She bought a few reams. Probably all gone now since she said she was going to give it to the school district to use."

"You don't remember her name?" TJ asked.

"Never knew it," she snapped without looking at her. Her face was set in a grim line and for a moment TJ thought that was all they were going to get.

"Then there was Nellie," the elderly woman said as if there hadn't been a break in the conversation. "She bought my bowl set. It had belonged to my mother." The woman bit her lower lip for a moment looking as if she might cry, before she said, "And there was that maddening Dot." She shook her head. "That woman has always annoyed me since she was a child. And that one fella... Sulky and kind of creepy as a boy—you know who I'm talking about," she said, turning to TJ. "He used to follow you girls home every day from school. He seemed to favor you."

"Tommy Harwood." TJ had known who she was referring to right away even though she hadn't realized that he'd followed them every day from school. She'd only caught him at it a few times.

"That's all I can remember," Melinda said, clearly finished with them. She turned back to the window.

TJ and Silas rose and left. "For someone with a bad memory she did well, I'd say," he said with a laugh. "You know these people she was talking about?" She nodded as they climbed into the pickup. "Could one of them be True Fan? Maybe this creepy kid who used to follow you home?"

"Maybe. I think I heard he lives by the railroad tracks on the way out of town," she said. "But he wouldn't be home now. He works at the auto shop. But Nellie should be home. Do you want to try her?"

Lanell "Nellie" Doll answered the door, opening it only a few inches. Still TJ saw enough of the inside to see that the woman's mother, who she lived with, was much like TJ's own grandmother—a hoarder.

"What are you doing here?" Nellie asked suspiciously.

"I stopped by to make sure you got the book I signed for you," TJ said.

"I did." She looked at Silas, clearly still waiting for an explanation.

"That wasn't the only reason we stopped by," Silas said. "Last summer I bought some paper at a garage sale from Mrs. Holmes. She thought you might have bought some as well and might have some extra still."

"Paper?"

"Mrs. Holmes sold it by the ream."

"If I bought some, I can't remember," Nellie said. "I probably used it up by now."

"I'm sorry, I should have introduced my friend," TJ said. "This is Silas Walker. He's a writer. Along with inexpensive paper, he was looking for a good manual typewriter."

"And Mrs. Holmes thought I might have that as well?" Nellie asked, sounding indignant. "That old woman should mind her own business."

"If you do have either, I would be happy to buy them," Silas put in.

Nellie was shaking her head. "I don't have any paper or a typewriter to sell. I'm busy so if that's all…"

"Have you started reading my book?" TJ asked before Nellie could close the door in her face. She was odd and secretive enough that she could definitely be True Fan. Not to mention unfriendly.

Nellie rolled her eyes with an impatient sigh. "If you must know, I don't care for your books. But my niece knows that we went to school together. Yesterday was my birthday so she thought it would make a nice gift to have you sign it for me."

"I see," TJ said, trying not to laugh. This was too funny. She loved the woman's honesty. "So you didn't read at least the first one I wrote, out of curiosity?"

"I couldn't get through it. But I never was much of a reader."

TJ could hear the drone of the television in the background and recognized the sound of a daytime drama. They were keeping Nellie from her "soaps."

"We're sorry to have bothered you," TJ said and Nellie quickly closed the door.

"Well, that was fun," Silas said as they climbed into the pickup.

TJ chuckled. "Wasn't it though."

"You went to school with her?"

"We weren't friends," she said unnecessarily.

He laughed. "I would have never guessed."

"I think we can scratch her off our list," she said.

"I don't know about that. She definitely has some hostility issues."

TJ looked out the window at the town where she'd grown up. "Some of the people I went to school with thought I was stuck-up. Annabelle was stuck-up, but me?" She shook her head. "I was shy. Introverted. I've always had stories going in my head, which were more interesting to me than school. I remember being called on by the teacher and not having a clue what she'd been talking about. I'm sure the teacher and the other students thought I was slow if not stupid. My teachers used to tell my grandmother that I didn't apply myself."

"Me, I actually didn't apply myself." He shrugged and started the pickup. "Dot next?"

"Dorothy Crest? It seems unlikely that it would be her, but I guess that's the point. Whoever True Fan is, it's someone who is hiding behind anonymity."

"True Fan is probably capable of putting on a good front to your face. The fact that he or she doesn't sign his or her name makes me think that True Fan is a coward and probably not dangerous—at least face-to-face. But if they undermine your writing then they have to be dealt with."

She smiled over at him. "Then by all means let's go see Dot." She put in a call to Annabelle, who informed her that Dot had bought her parents' house and now lived in it with her husband, Roger. With Roger at work, TJ figured they would find her alone. She was right.

Dot came to the door in an apron, throwing it open, all smiles when she saw them. "Come in! This is such a treat. A real live famous author in my home."

TJ introduced Silas.

"You write as well? Wonderful. You'll have to tell me the title of your latest book so I can pick it up. I love to read when I have time, which isn't often keeping up this house, you know."

She led them through the living room, pointing out that she had all of TJ's books on a special shelf of their own. The house was immaculate even though Dot kept apologizing for the mess.

In the roomy farm-style kitchen, she offered them cookies straight from the oven and coffee, saying that the coffee was always on at her house.

TJ took a warm chocolate chip cookie and listened while Silas visited with Dot. He asked about the paper she'd bought at the garage sale last summer, adding, "I think that's where I saw you before." He told her he'd been using his to write a novel on.

"I gave mine to the grandchildren. They love to draw and go through so much paper."

TJ was glancing around the kitchen when Dot said, "You've never seen my house. Would you like a tour?"

"I'd love one," she said, and got to her feet. The rest of the house was just as spotless as what TJ had already seen. In what appeared to be a den, she saw a laptop, but no typewriter.

"I'm halfway through your new book. I had to quit because I wasn't going to get my work done." Dot shook her head. "But I didn't want to put it down. I'm in awe of the way you make our little town come alive."

"You do know that the books aren't about White-horse," TJ said.

"Of course." She gave TJ a wink.

"They're supposed to be any small town in Montana."

Dot either ignored her or didn't hear her. "I'm so glad you stopped by with your friend. I'd seen him around but I had no idea he was a writer."

TJ found it amusing that when locals called him a mountain man they were a little leery of him. But now that they would soon know he was a writer, his mountain man appearance would be accepted as just the way writers were.

They found Silas sitting where they'd left him in the kitchen, but TJ had the feeling that he'd looked around the lower floor while they'd been gone.

They thanked Dot and left, but only at her insistence that Silas take a few cookies for later.

"It's her," he joked as they drove away. "All that cheerfulness has got to be hiding something."

TJ chuckled. "I had the same thought," she said as she settled back against the seat. The sun shone in the pickup's side window. She felt warm and content and realized she hadn't felt like this in months—except in this man's presence.

"Any other leads we should follow up, or should we have lunch?" he asked.

"You probably have other things you need to do," TJ said.

"The sooner we find this creep, the better," he said.

But as he drove down the main drag of Whitehorse, she saw him suddenly look in the direction of a man crossing the street ahead of them—and freeze for a moment.

"Silas?"

He didn't answer.

"Is everything all right?" she asked, fearing what now had him looking like a man who'd seen a ghost.

He seemed to come out of his fugue state as the vehicle in front of them that had been waiting to turn finally moved. The man who'd crossed the street was now nowhere to be seen. He appeared to have stepped into the Mint Bar. "Sorry, I just thought I saw... Never mind. It wasn't who I thought it was."

But she caught him looking back at the bar and later watching his rearview mirror as if he thought they might have been followed. Whoever he'd thought the man was, his reaction had been powerful. Silas was still spooked and she had a feeling he didn't scare easily.

Chapter Thirteen

Silas glanced at his phone and groaned inwardly. He was still shaken. The last thing he wanted to do was cancel out on TJ. But right now he had to take care of some business—and quickly.

"I'm sorry. There's something I need to see about right away," he said to her. "Can I take a rain check on lunch? I'll call you later."

"You don't need to go see this Tom Harwood with me. I appreciate you finding the house where you got the paper. I can take it from here."

That's what worried him. "I don't like you doing this on your own. I'll take care of my business, then check with you later, if that's okay."

"Of course. But are you sure everything is all right?" she asked, looking worried. She'd seen his reaction to the man crossing the street. He felt bad enough that the man might have seen him—and TJ. He didn't want her dragged into his dirty business.

"I'm fine. We'll talk later," he said, smiling over at her. He must not have been as convincing as he'd hoped, because she still looked worried.

"I need to go Christmas shopping with my sisters,

so please, take care of whatever you need to, and don't worry about me."

He glanced over at her, his heart breaking a little with worry over her. "I can't help but be concerned. That last letter…" What he wanted to say was, "We have to find True Fan before True Fan finds you," but he held his tongue. She was already scared enough. She didn't need him sharing his instincts or experience with her.

Unfortunately, those instincts and his experience on the job told him that True Fan would be making good on those threats—and soon.

As he pulled up in front of her house, he turned to her and reached for her hand. "Do me a favor, okay?" She nodded, seeming surprised by how serious he'd become. "Don't go anywhere alone. Take one of your sisters if you insist on going out. Especially don't go chasing True Fan. Wait for me. I'm not sure how long my business is going to take me but—"

"You don't have to worry about me. I'll be fine."

How many times had he heard those words? "That's what they all say." He felt her shudder. "Just do it for me."

TJ FELT HER throat constrict. Silas was so worried about her that it gave her a chill. "I will. But promise me something," she heard herself say. "Be careful. I don't know what this business is you have to take care of, but I'm betting it's dangerous from your reaction back there."

He said nothing for a moment, just squeezed her hand. "I'll call you later."

She nodded as he let go of her hand. For a moment she was afraid to leave him. But he reached over and opened her door and all she could do was look at him for a moment before climbing out. It felt so strange to feel this close to someone she'd met only hours before. She was making her way toward the house when she heard him drive away. There was an urgency about his leaving that made it all the more frightening.

What kind of trouble was Silas in? Something to do with his former job? Or something to do with his more recent one as a private investigator? She knew so little about him and yet she felt she knew him. Just the first chapter of his novel had made her feel closer to him. She could understand why readers thought they knew her and feared some of them did.

Her heart ached as she turned to watch his pickup disappear around a corner.

"Well?" Chloe said from the open doorway.

"Is that what you're going to say to me every time I return to the house?" TJ demanded as she stepped past her and into the warmth of the living room.

"It is if every time you leave it's with that man," her sister said.

Annabelle called from the kitchen that she'd made sloppy joes for lunch and TJ was just in time. Taking off her coat and dropping it on a chair in the living room, she followed the sweet, temping scent into the kitchen.

"I haven't had sloppy joes since I left Whitehorse," TJ said as she helped set the table. Chloe was standing in the doorway, arms crossed, looking upset. That was the problem with mystery writers and investigative reporters, TJ thought. *We see things other people miss.* Chloe knew there was more to Silas. She'd seen the darkness, the danger.

"Silas found the house where he bought reams of paper last summer at a garage sale," she said as she took a seat at the table. Annabelle brought over the dish of sloppy joes and put it on the table before taking a seat. Chloe joined them, though with some reluctance.

"The paper is the same paper True Fan uses to write me letters," TJ said. "Or at least it looks to be the same. So we asked who'd bought some of it at the garage sale last summer."

"And?" Chloe said. She hadn't touched her lunch yet.

"She gave us a few names. Dot, Nellie Doll, someone from the school and Tommy Harwood were the ones she could remember. She said Tommy used to follow us home from school all the time." She turned to Chloe. "Do you remember that?"

Her sister nodded. "He had a crush on you." She frowned. "Wasn't he at the signing?"

"He was." TJ took a bite of her lunch. "Annabelle, this is delicious. I didn't realize how hungry I was."

"So did you talk to the others?" Chloe asked.

"We didn't get a chance to talk to more than Nellie and Dot," she said, not looking up from her meal. "Silas had some business he had to take care of. He's going to call later." She lifted her gaze to meet Chloe's dark blue one. "He isn't True Fan."

"No, but he certainly has taken an interest in finding this person, hasn't he?"

TJ shrugged. "Maybe he's more interested in me."

Annabelle's eyes went wide. "So something *did* happen at the cabin. Did he...kiss you?"

TJ laughed. "No, and nothing else happened either. He was a perfect gentleman." She saw that Chloe felt that proved her point that Silas was in this just for the excitement. For the possible danger. That he was like Marc.

"So are we going Christmas shopping this afternoon?" she asked, hoping to change the subject.

"I thought we'd walk since it is such a nice day," Annabelle said. "I want to find something for Dawson. I need your opinion. I found a shirt down at Family Matters. But is a shirt too unexciting for our first Christmas together—well, first this time around?" she added with a giggle.

It was impossible not to smile at their sister's happiness. Even Chloe, whose brow had been knitted with worry, broke into a smile.

"I'll have to see this shirt," Chloe said, and finally began to eat her lunch.

TJ tried to relax. She hadn't told them about Silas's reaction earlier or her fears. She'd gotten close to this man so quickly. That alone should have been a red flag. That Silas was in some sort of trouble seemed more than likely. He'd tried to play it down, but she'd seen how scared he'd been. What did it take to scare a man like him?

She tried to put him out of her mind. It hadn't been that hard with other men she'd met and even dated. But Silas... There was something special about him. And yet, Chloe's fear that he was too much like Marc kept nagging at her. She couldn't go through that again. Her heart couldn't take it.

"YOU'RE SURE IT was him?"

Silas held the phone more tightly in his hand. "Not positive. I only got a glimpse of him."

"Okay," said his friend and employer at the PI

agency Cal Barnum. "First things first, I'll see if he's still out here in New York. This town you're in, it's small, right?"

"It doesn't even have a stoplight."

"So there is little chance he just happens to be there?"

"None. If he's here, then he's come for me."

"Maybe you should make yourself scarce," Cal suggested.

Any other time, Silas would have taken that advice. "It isn't that simple right now. I'm helping a friend with a problem she has."

"A friend? A new *female* friend, I take it?"

"She's in trouble. I can't just drop it."

"Okay, so how long before DeAngelo finds you?"

Silas pulled off his Stetson and raked a hand through his hair. He'd figured out how small towns worked pretty quickly after moving here. People weren't suspicious. They were annoyingly helpful. Looking for someone? Hell, they'd draw DeAngelo a map to his cabin.

"I'm going to have to find *him*," he said.

Cal swore. "I'm sorry. You knew it was just a matter of time. From the start, you'd been suspicious of that crazy bastard Nathan DeAngelo."

Silas and Nathan had been thrown together as partners when Silas had started with the force. Nathan had been there for a while and had promised to teach him the ropes. It hadn't taken any time at all to see that his partner liked cutting corners.

"I'd hoped he'd have the sense to let it go," Cal was saying.

"That isn't his way." He put his hat back on, his mind already working. He had little choice. He'd have to run DeAngelo to ground—or wait at the cabin for the man to come gunning for him. Silas had never been good at waiting.

"Let me know if you hear anything I should know," he said to Cal.

"Keep in touch and…good luck."

It was going to take more than luck. He knew DeAngelo well. He'd helped bring the man down for his crimes. But when it came to hard time, the man had slipped the noose. Too many friends in high places. Too much dirt out there that DeAngelo was holding over even those in the judicial system.

So where to begin looking for the man? Although that wasn't the main question on his mind. *What are you going to do when you find him?*

TJ TRIED NOT to worry about Silas as she and her sisters walked uptown. Annabelle was right. It was a beautiful December day, the sun shining, the new snow so pure white and sparkling. Christmas decorations adorned all the houses they passed and each of the stores along the main drag of Whitehorse.

"We should drive down to Billings," Chloe said, not as enamored with the small Western town as her sisters.

"This is so much better than the rat race in the largest city in Montana," Annabelle said, and laughed because all three of them lived in cities that made Billings seem small.

"Okay, come see this shirt I found for Dawson," she said, dragging them into the clothing store.

TJ spotted her former high school English teacher looking at scarves and quickly stepped behind the racks of clothing to escape. By now Ester would have finished the book. TJ didn't want to discuss the theme or her mistakes in grammar. Ester was one of those teachers who couldn't help wanting to continue to teach even in retirement.

Annabelle held up the shirt she'd picked out. "What do you think?"

It was a blue checked Western shirt. "It looks just like him," TJ said.

"I'd just buy him a rope. He's going to need it, married to you," Chloe joked. TJ was glad to see that her older sister had quit worrying about her for the moment.

"What does that mean?" Annabelle demanded. "That he'll want to hang himself or that he'll have to hog-tie me to keep me on the ranch?"

"I hadn't thought of either of those, but you have a point," Chloe said. "Buy the shirt. He won't care. He adores you and anything you give him, he'll love it."

Annabelle still looked skeptical. She shifted her gaze to TJ who smiled and nodded. "What he really wants for Christmas is you."

"I need to go down to the gift shop," Chloe said after Annabelle bought the shirt and had it wrapped and they exited the store. Annabelle said she wanted to look in the gift shop as well.

TJ had no desire to go into a place that sold her books for fear of running into someone who wanted to talk about the latest one. She knew killing off Durango was going to cause some readers to be upset. But she had to take the books where they led her.

Also, she had no desire to see Joyce Mason again. She considered her for a moment as True Fan and couldn't imagine the woman going to the trouble to write her the threatening letters. Joyce was more of an in-your-face kind of person.

"I'm going to duck into the coffee shop," TJ said. "Why don't you meet me there when you're through?" They agreed and parted. She breathed in the winter day, her thoughts instantly returning to Silas. Worrying about him, she didn't even notice a figure step out of the alley until she was grabbed.

A hoarse voice whispered, "Don't scream. It's just me, your biggest fan."

Chapter Fourteen

Silas drove down the main drag, parking next to the city park. Whitehorse had been one of those spots along the railroad that had grown into a town. Because of that the unmanned depot sat beyond the small park on the other side of the tracks.

His senses were on alert as he got out of his truck and checked the street. With all the shoppers, the small town was bustling. DeAngelo couldn't have picked a better time. The rest of the year a large, dark-haired burly man wearing city clothes would have stood out from the locals and been easier to spot.

DeAngelo always wore expensive slacks and polished black shoes. He was obsessed with shoes and many times couldn't stop himself from stopping in the middle of the sidewalk to wipe away a spot on the leather.

Silas had been expecting him to show up for over a year. He'd thought it would be outside his apartment in New York City. Or maybe even *inside* his apartment. He'd been rigging his doors all these months, so sure that it was only a matter of time before they came face-to-face.

When that happened, he'd always told himself that he would have only a matter of seconds to make his move. In truth, he would probably not have any time at all. DeAngelo knew him too well. Also there was nothing to say that hadn't already been said in court. From the witness stand, DeAngelo had mouthed "You're a dead man" the last time he'd seen him.

But after a year had passed with DeAngelo back on the streets, Silas had thought maybe the man had wised up. Maybe even a little time behind bars had taught him that he didn't want a repeat appearance.

Silas should have known better.

And now DeAngelo had not only shown up in Montana, but also at the worst possible time. Now Silas had met TJ and promised to help her. Lately, he'd even let himself think he might have a chance at settling down, having a home, a family. He desperately wanted this chance to get to know Tessa Jane. He'd actually been thinking that he might have a future.

Now those thoughts mocked him. As long as there were DeAngelos in the world, he would never find peace, let alone chance falling for someone and starting a family.

He waited for a car to pass, then ran across the street to the last place he'd seen his former partner. Pushing open the door to the Mint Bar, he stepped into the warm beer-scented darkness.

TJ SCREAMED AND kicked as she tried to free herself from the person who'd grabbed her. The toe of her boot came in contact with bone.

"Damn, you didn't have to kick me."

She spun around to come face-to-face with Tommy Harwood. The scream died in her throat as she saw him rubbing at his shin as if she'd nearly broken his leg.

"You can't just grab someone like that," she said, furious with him for scaring her the way he had.

"I just wanted to get your attention."

Well, he'd done that.

He quit rubbing his leg and looked embarrassed. "I thought... I thought you might want to have a cup of coffee with me."

She'd been headed for the coffee shop, she reminded herself. Also, hadn't she wanted to quiz Tommy about the ream of paper he'd bought? "I'll buy," she said. "For kicking you."

Grudgingly he agreed.

"You're not working today?" she asked after they'd ordered two black coffees and taken them to a table by the window.

"Got off early."

She realized that this could be the longest coffee date she'd ever had if the conversation was anything like this. She decided to get right to it. "I meant to ask you about some paper you bought last summer at a garage sale."

He seemed surprised by the question, but answered anyway. "At Melinda Holmes's house."

"So you remember." When he said no more and looked away, she said, "Do you own an old manual typewriter?"

He looked up then, his dark eyes boring into her. "Is that really what you want to talk about?"

"I'm looking for one to buy," she said.

"And you thought I'd have one?" He shook his head. "Why wouldn't you go out with me in high school?"

Seriously? "High school? Is that what you want to talk about?"

"Yes. You knew I had a crush on you. You weren't

even famous then. You weren't even *popular*. So why not go out with me?"

He wanted to be honest? Fine. "Since apparently you followed me home every day after school you would know that I didn't date much. Also it was creepy, you always looking at me the way you did, not to mention the only time you asked me out was in the middle of Biology class. You expected me to say yes in front of everyone?"

"That wasn't my best moment, I'll admit, but you still could have said something after that."

"I wasn't interested. But I wasn't interested in anyone else either."

"You went out with Darwin."

"That was his junior prom. I double-dated with my sister Chloe. She forced me to go." TJ remembered the scratchy dress, the uncomfortable high heels, the whole awkward night right up and through Darwin's sloppy kiss. The memory made her shudder. "It was a mistake. One I wasn't about to repeat."

"So you were shy and awkward. So was I. You didn't even give me a chance."

"Tommy—"

"Tom."

"That is all history. I can't undo any of it. If I could, I would never have gone out with Darwin, all right?"

"But you might have gone out with me?"

She picked up her coffee cup. "So you don't have an old manual typewriter?"

"What if I do?" he asked challengingly.

"Then I'd like to see it."

THE BAR WAS dim enough that he had to walk halfway in to see everyone inside. He told himself that he'd recognize DeAngelo without any trouble. He was wrong. The man who turned around on his bar stool had changed. His dark hair had receded. His face was gaunt and pale, and he'd clearly lost weight. He didn't look healthy, let alone strong and dangerous.

"Took you long enough," DeAngelo said. "I see you got rid of your date," he said, looking past him. "So have a seat. You can buy," he said, patting the empty bar stool next to him. "We need to talk."

The last thing Silas wanted to do was have a drink with his former NYPD partner. From the beginning they were too different. Silas went by the book. DeAngelo never met a rule he didn't want to break. But even so, Silas had never dreamed just how crooked the man had become before it was over.

"We have something to discuss?" he asked without moving.

His former partner chuckled. "You were always as stubborn as a brick. Sit down. If I was here to…" he lowered his voice even though there was no one sitting close by "…kill you, you'd already be dead and we both know it."

That, Silas thought with a grimace, was true. He knew firsthand how dangerous this man was. A part of him was thankful that DeAngelo wanted only to talk. Silas had become complacent. Up here away from the city, he'd become too comfortable. He'd let his guard down. Given that DeAngelo was here, Silas knew he should be dead. So why hadn't his former partner made his move?

Sliding onto the bar stool, he nodded to the bartender that he'd take the same thing his "friend" was having. A few minutes later, two beers were plunked down in front of them.

"I've never seen you drink beer," Silas commented. "You always went for the hard stuff."

"Maybe I've changed."

He wouldn't bet the farm on that, but he said nothing as he took a swig of his beer from the bottle. "What are you doing here, Nathan?"

TOMMY HAD WANTED her to ride in his car with him, but TJ had insisted on meeting him at his house. She let him think she had her own car. She also let him know that she had to tell her sisters where she was going since she was supposed to be shopping with them.

"Whatever," was all he said as he headed for his pickup parked across the street.

TJ waited until he drove away before she started to go down to the gift shop to tell her sisters where she was going. It was the smart thing to do. If Tommy was True Fan, she had no business being alone with him, period—let alone being with him alone and with no one knowing where she'd gone. So she was glad when the first sister she came across was Annabelle.

"I'm running over to Tommy Harwood's," she said, making it sound casual. "I'll be back soon. Shall we meet up before supper, maybe go have a steak or something?"

"Dawson's mom invited us out, remember?" Annabelle said. "You remember Willie and she wanted to see you."

"Okay. I won't be long. I have my cell." With that she left Annabelle looking at jewelry, knowing she could be there for a while.

The walk to Tommy's house was only four blocks down the side road that followed the tracks out of town toward Glasgow. Back when the towns along this stretch of new rails were being named, whoever was in charge got tired of coming up with ideas and simply spun a globe and randomly picked. It was why there were towns with names like Malta, Zurich, Havre and Glasgow.

Tommy's car was parked in front of a small neat white house. She tapped at the front door and it opened almost as if he'd been watching out the window for her.

"You *walked*?" He sounded appalled that she'd done that after turning down a ride with him.

"I decided to leave the car for my sisters. Anyway, it's such a nice day, I wanted to walk."

He shook his head and turned back into the house. She followed. The place was as neat inside as it had been outside. She wondered if there'd been a woman in his life at some point. Hadn't Annabelle told her that he'd lived with his mother for years until her death?

"Can I get you something to drink or eat?" he asked as she closed the door behind her.

She turned and seeing how nervous he was, instantly became more nervous herself. Coming here had probably been a mistake. Knowing Annabelle she might not even remember where her sister said she was going.

"I just came to see the typewriter," she said, trying not to be rude, but not wanting him to get the wrong impression. "It's a gift for my sister Chloe."

"Yes, the typewriter," he said glumly. "It's in here." He led the way through the house. She found herself looking for possible weapons she could use against the man if needed. Tommy wasn't large but he looked strong. Definitely stronger than she was.

He'd reached the kitchen. She saw stairs that went down into the basement but had already decided she wasn't going down there. He could bring the typewriter up if that's where he kept it. She was beginning to doubt he even owned one and was beginning to suspect this had been a ruse to get her into his house. But if that was the case, then at least he wasn't True Fan.

"There it is," he said, not going near the basement stairs.

She looked to where he was pointing and saw an old manual Royal sitting on the floor in front of a door to the screened-in back porch.

"I use it for a doorstop. It weighs a ton," he said.

She stepped over to gaze down at the machine. It had an old, worn-out ribbon in it, but from the dust on the key arms it appeared it hadn't been used in years. "This is the only one you have?"

He gave her a disbelieving look. "You didn't come here to buy a typewriter. I know. I read your book."

That stopped her cold. She held her breath, always wary when this was the way someone began a conversation with her. *I read your book.* Sometimes that was all they said. But she had a feeling Tommy had a lot more to say.

Chapter Fifteen

"Look," Nathan DeAngelo said after taking a long gulp of his beer. Silas could tell it wasn't his first. "I don't blame you for what you did. I knew the kind of guy you were from the start. A Goody Two-shoes." He held up his hand before Silas could say what he was thinking. "Don't get me wrong. You did what you thought you had to do bringing us all down. But some of the guys aren't as…forgiving."

"This isn't news," Silas said, already bored with this conversation. He took a drink of his beer, wondering what had really brought his old partner all the way to Montana. Not to tell him something he already knew.

"I've moved on," DeAngelo continued. "I've got a pretty good gig going with a security company." He shrugged. "Keeps me out of trouble. The thing is, you taught us all an important lesson. We're not going to make the same mistakes again. We're not going to get our hands caught in the cookie jar again. That's why the guys all chipped in to hire a hit man to take you out. No way to trace it back to them."

Silas looked over at him and saw that he was serious. "And you came all this way to warn me."

"Like I said, I'm more forgiving." His gaze softened. "You and I were partners. The others can't believe you'd turn in your own partner. But I knew you would. I even suspected you were coming after us."

He shook his head. "I don't get it."

DeAngelo shrugged and drained his beer before pushing to his feet. "I can't explain it myself. Maybe I'm getting soft." He did look like he was. The security job obviously wasn't keeping him in as good of shape as the police department had. Or maybe he couldn't get his hands on the kind of drugs he'd had on the streets.

"Like you said, you could have killed me yourself and been on the next plane out of here. Why hire someone?"

"A professional seemed the way to go. Also we have something on the assassin so less chance of any blowback, you know what I mean?"

He did. "When?"

His former partner laughed. "Now what would be the fun of me telling you that?" He patted Silas on the shoulder. "Thanks for the beer. Almost like old times."

"One more thing," he said. "Did you chip in for the hit man as well?"

DeAngelo laughed and raked a hand through his thinning hair. "You know I did. Don't want them gunning for me next. It's bad enough that I didn't get the amount of time a lot of them did. And before you ask, no. No one knows I came up here to warn you. I know it's crazy, but I guess it's my way of saying I'm sorry. If you hadn't been so damned straitlaced we could have been great friends."

"I wasn't straitlaced. I just wasn't a dirty cop."

DeAngelo's smile blinked out, just like the light

in his dark eyes. "See, you have to go and ruin a nice moment. Good luck." With that the man turned and walked away.

"I'M SORRY, BUT I don't have any idea what you're referring to," TJ said, just wanting to leave this house and Tommy. "You read my book and you know what?"

"Durango. I know why you killed him."

She hated to ask, but saw no way not to. "Why?"

"Because he wasn't the kind of man you wanted anymore."

"Tommy—"

"Tom."

"I'm not Constance. Durango died because he got cocky. He felt invincible. He forgot he was mortal." Also because Constance needed to move on from him. She needed another hero, maybe one not as flawed as Durango. Or maybe more flawed. She wouldn't know until she wrote the book.

"He was Marc, the guy you were engaged to in college," Tommy said.

She felt her face burn with irritation and embarrassment. That was one of the problems with a small town. People knew way too much of your business even after you left. Anger overtook her embarrassment. She didn't have to explain her actions to anyone, especially Tommy.

"I really don't want to talk to you about this," she said, and looked at her watch. Her sisters should be through shopping by now, or at least interested in eating.

"It's fine if you don't want to admit it," he said. "But if you ever quit making the same mistakes with men…"

She stared at him. True Fan told her how to write. Tommy was telling her how to run her love life? "Who are you to tell me who I should be with?" she demanded angrily.

"Just the man who's watched you make the same mistakes since you were a girl," he said, apparently unperturbed by her angry outburst.

"I can see myself out," she said, and spun on her heel, stomping out of the house. The walk back into town did her good, even though the temperature had dropped. The air smelled as if snow was imminent. She'd heard that yet another storm was coming in. Winter in Montana, she thought, and pulled her coat tighter around her.

She was almost back when a horn honked right behind her. She jumped, having not heard a vehicle approach. Turning, she told herself that if it was Tommy she would kick in one of his door panels.

But as the car pulled alongside, she saw it was her former English teacher Ester Brown. Great, she thought, as Ester whirred down her passenger side window.

"Why don't you get in," she said in a tone that made it clear it wasn't a question but an order. "It's too dangerous to walk along this road."

TJ bristled. A few too many people had been telling her what to do. She wasn't one of this woman's students anymore.

"Thanks, but no thanks. I want to walk so I'll take my chances getting run down on the road." She turned and stalked off, keeping to the edge of the road facing traffic so the elderly woman didn't mow her down on principle.

She heard Ester mumble, "Always was too stubborn for her own good," before she hit the gas and took off with the chirp of the tires.

Fortunately, town was only a short walk. She found her sisters coming out of the drugstore, both carrying an assortment of packages. They really had been Christmas shopping. She realized that she should be doing some of her own. But she couldn't get into a holiday mood—not with True Fan so close by.

"Where have you been?" Chloe asked with her usual suspicion.

"Didn't Annabelle tell you?"

Annabelle, who had been looking into one of her bags she was carrying, looked up at the sound of her name.

"You didn't tell Chloe where I'd gone?" TJ chastised. What if Tommy had been True Fan? What if she was bound and gagged in his basement?

"Oops, sorry." Annabelle turned to Chloe. "She went to Tommy Harwood's house."

"Not all that helpful now, sis," TJ said.

"Why in the world would you do that?" Chloe cried.

"I thought he might be True Fan," she said, suddenly tired. She watched Ester Brown drive by, glaring at her as she passed and turned away from the street. She was reminded of all the reasons she'd left here, threatening never to come back. "Tommy gave me a lecture on my mistakes when it comes to the men I choose."

Both of her sisters lifted brows at that.

"I'm starved," Annabelle said quickly to change the subject before they got into an argument on the street. "Let's go to the Great Northern and have some lunch."

TJ looked up the street and saw Silas coming out of the Mint Bar. He spotted her and stopped. He'd been headed toward his pickup parked across the street when he saw her. Now he stood as if unsure what to do.

"You guys go on ahead. I'm tired and not hungry

right now. I think I'm going to walk home." She headed toward Silas, ignoring Chloe's comment that for the first time Tommy Harwood might actually know what he was talking about.

JUST THE SIGHT of TJ stopped Silas in his tracks. His spirits instantly lifted and just as quickly dropped. Nathan DeAngelo was a lot of things, a liar among them. But this time, Silas believed the man. He'd found over the years that there really was often some misguided honor among thieves. He also knew how much Nathan had hoped that Silas would adopt his way of thinking when it came to following the letter of the law.

"Hi," TJ said as she approached. She was frowning.

He realized that she'd seen him come out of the bar. She'd also seen his reaction earlier when he'd spotted DeAngelo crossing the street to the bar. She was too sharp not to have put it together.

As he looked into her beautiful face, he knew he had to keep his distance from her. It was bad enough that Nathan had seen him with TJ. He couldn't have his enemies using her against him. And at the same time, he couldn't just dump her unceremoniously.

The thought surprised him since it wasn't like they were a couple. But he'd promised to help her find True Fan and the one thing he'd lived by all his life was making good on his promises. He also couldn't put her in any more danger than he had and yet, seeing her, all he wanted to do was take her somewhere, just the two of them. He felt torn. While he shouldn't be with her right now, he also couldn't explain himself on the busy street.

A snowflake drifted down, followed by another large lacy one. His breath came out frosty white as he stepped to her. "Is there somewhere we can go and talk?" he asked. "Alone?"

She nodded and let him take her arm as they crossed the street to his pickup. Once inside, he started the engine, waiting for the heater to warm up enough to chase off the frosty chill in the cab. TJ hadn't said anything since climbing into the passenger seat. Outside, snow began to fall in a blur of white.

"I could take you to one of my favorite places outside of town," she said, breaking the quiet.

He looked over at her, telling himself all the reasons this was a bad idea and yet unable to simply walk away from her. The heater began to warm, clearing off the frost on the windshield enough that he would be able to see to drive.

Shifting the pickup into gear, he pulled out and followed her directions as they left town and headed northeast. Neither of them spoke as he drove. Snow blew across the highway. He recalled someone telling him they were called snow-snakes. It had a hypnotizing effect. He had to concentrate to keep the pickup on the highway as both the snow on the ground and the now falling snowflakes whipped around the truck.

They'd gone out of town some miles before she told him to turn. He checked his rearview mirror, not for the first time. He didn't believe they'd been followed. That was the problem with a small town. There was no reason to follow them. All the killer had to do was wait. It would be easy to find Silas's cabin. This was the kind of job even an amateur should be able to handle.

The road TJ had him turn onto went from snow-packed pavement to deeper snow-covered gravel before she told him to turn once more. He could see an expanse of flat white through the falling snow. As they neared it, he realized it was a frozen-over lake. He saw picnic tables covered with snow under the trees along the edge of the lake and pulled down into one of the campsites.

This one was somewhat sheltered by the trees. He left the engine running, knowing how quickly the cab would get cold without the heater, and watched the snow whirling around them. He liked the intimate feeling. He could almost pretend that they were the only two people on earth in the warm cocoon of the pickup's cab.

"You're in some kind of trouble, aren't you?" TJ said after a few moments.

He glanced over at her and simply nodded. "I can't let you get dragged into it so I'm going to have to stay away from you for a while."

"What if that isn't what I want?" she asked, her voice breaking.

He met her gaze. His blue eyes shone. "It is the last thing I want. I know I promised to help you find True Fan—"

"Is that the only reason?"

"I think you know better than that." He let out a frustrated sigh and reached over to brush a lock of her hair back from her face.

TJ CLOSED HER eyes at the warm caress of his fingertips on her cheek.

"Tessa Jane." He said her name like a curse, his voice thick with emotion. "All I can think about is you. You've completely captivated me."

She opened her eyes and met his blue gaze. Without another word, he reached for her, drawing her across the bench seat of the pickup. She felt a burst of pleasure expand inside her as he wrapped her in his strong arms and kissed her. His mouth was warm and sweet on hers.

"I've been wanting to do that since the first time I saw you," he said pulling back to look into her face.

She kissed him in response, weaving her fingers through the curls at his nape, breathing in the male scent of him. Desire sparked into a blaze inside her. She didn't care what Tommy or her sisters said. Silas was all man and more enticing than any she'd ever met. She felt safe in his strong arms and desperately wanted to lose herself in him.

He kissed her again, this time slowly, expertly. He deepened the kiss as he slid out from under the steering wheel to pull her onto his lap. She pushed aside his coat and opened the buttons on his shirt until she could press her palms to his rock-solid chest. She felt him shudder, desire a blowtorch in all that blue. Heat pulsed through her to her center.

Silas unzipped her coat and found his way to her bare breast. She arched against him as he thumbed the already hard nipple to an aching point. His hand slipped into her jeans and panties. He found the spot and she knew this had been building for some time because she cried out as the release came almost immediately.

He drew her to him, holding her as she felt the waves of release ebb through her, leaving her feeling weak. She started to reach for him, but he stopped her and kissed her tenderly. "I hadn't meant for it to go this far. The first time I make love to you, I don't want it to be in the front seat of my pickup. I want to take this up sometime soon." He touched her cheek, his fingertips warm, his gaze filled with desire. He groaned and pulled back his hand. "We should get going."

She fixed her clothing, zipping her coat. Even with the heater going, the windows had fogged over. This was so not like her. She barely knew this man. This was the kind of thing that Constance would do. For some reason that made her smile to herself.

Silas slid back over under the wheel and turned up the heat. "I'm not going to be able to see you for a while." He glanced over at her.

"You're not going to tell me what kind of trouble you're in."

He shook his head as he reached over and caressed her shoulder for a moment. "I can't tell you how much I hate this. But while I'm worried about you and True Fan, being around me right now is more dangerous."

"I'm getting it narrowed down. I talked to Tommy Harwood today." She shook her head at the memory. Wouldn't Tommy love to know about this? She felt her face heat and looked out at the lake for a moment. "It's not him. I've reached a dead end."

"I thought by following the paper trail we might find this creep. I'm sorry. The paper didn't lead us anywhere."

She agreed. "Too many people could have gotten some of that paper even if they hadn't bought it at the garage sale. But I think you're right. True Fan is a coward." She turned toward Silas. "So take care of your trouble and don't worry about me."

"That won't be easy," he said as he removed his hand from her shoulder and got the truck going. She heard the worry in his voice and knew that whatever trouble he was in, it was serious.

Chapter Sixteen

Silas dropped her off at her house after another kiss. TJ could tell that he hadn't wanted to let her go any more than she had wanted to leave him. Their feelings for each other had happened so quickly, it scared her. But it also excited her. For the first time in her life, she was being adventurous. It felt good.

She thought about his kisses. It felt wonderful.

"I don't know when I'll see you again," he said, his voice rough with emotion. "But know that you won't be far from my mind."

She'd wanted to ask him how dangerous this trouble was, but in her heart she knew. She'd seen how scared he'd been when he'd recognized the man crossing the street earlier. Someone from his past? Someone he'd helped put in jail? Whoever it was, the man was dangerous.

Her heart ached. She and Silas had just found each other and now... Both of them had someone who was clearly threatening to hurt them and it had thrown them together. Earlier, at the lake, that feeling of impending doom had pushed them together faster than either of them had wanted.

But there was no denying the chemistry between

them. They'd bonded at the cabin. She thought of their card games late at night with a blizzard howling outside the cabin and hugged that memory to her, afraid she might never see Silas alive again.

"This is about those cops you put in prison, isn't it?" she asked.

He looked at her. She could see him fighting not telling her the truth. "Was that man in town to kill you?"

"No. Warn me."

Her chest felt as if an elephant had settled on it. "Can you go to the sheriff?"

He shook his head. "I have to take care of it myself."

"Oh, Silas."

He touched her cheek again. "I need you to be careful."

"You too." They locked gazes for a long moment before he reached over and opened her door. There was nothing more either of them could say.

She watched him drive away before making her way up the porch steps and into the house. Her sisters were in the living room. They'd opened a bottle of wine. Both looked up expectantly at her as she came in and hung up her coat.

"Oh no, you didn't," Chloe said.

TJ turned, feeling her face heat even as she denied it. "We kissed and made out some…"

Her sister groaned.

"Oh let her have some fun," Annabelle said.

As TJ joined them and poured herself a glass of wine, she found herself near tears with worry. "I like him."

"We can see that," Chloe said.

"You should invite him to the Christmas dance at

the old gym," Annabelle suggested. "Everyone in town will be there. Dawson and I are going." She grinned, hugging herself.

"The two of you are killing me," Chloe said.

"Isn't there someone you were interested in at the newspaper?" Annabelle asked.

Their sister shrugged. "I dated some, but no, I've never met The One."

"How do you know?" Annabelle said, turning in her chair as she warmed to the subject. "Look at Dawson and me. I left him even when he bought a ring and asked me to marry him. I thought he'd never forgive me. He said I broke his heart." Her voice cracked with emotion and tears flooded her blue eyes. "But we found our way back to each other. What about your old boyfriend, Justin Calhoun?"

Chloe shifted uncomfortably in her seat. "He wasn't my boyfriend exactly. Anyway, that ship sailed a long time ago. Didn't he marry…what was her name?"

"Nicole Kent," Annabelle said. "But he didn't marry her. They were engaged—at least according to Nici—but they broke up. She married someone else, got divorced. She lives here with a couple of her sisters and their kids."

"You've certainly gotten caught up on local gossip," TJ said, and took a sip of her wine. "Didn't Tommy live with his mother for a long time?"

Annabelle laughed. "As a matter of fact, he did. She died a few years ago and he sold her house and bought that one out by the tracks."

TJ looked over at Chloe. She seemed to be lost in thought. Justin? The two of them had seemed perfect for each other but Chloe had been on her way to college so nothing had come of it. But TJ had always wondered if Nicole Kent hadn't been the reason the two hadn't seen each other after that. She remembered the girl and felt a shiver. That one had always been trouble.

They all jumped at a knock on the door. Exchanging looks, TJ got up this time to answer it.

"You really should get a post office box," Carol said as she handed her the letter that had come for her. "You're going to get me fired."

"Thanks for bringing it by, but if anymore come—"

"Don't worry. I'll see that you get them." Carol turned on the step and, the bells she was wearing jingling, took off toward her vehicle. Carol always wore bells at work this time of year.

TJ looked down at the letter in her hand and realized her hand was shaking.

"Here, let me open that," Chloe said, taking the letter from her as TJ stepped back inside. She tore it open and pulled out the sheet, discolored like all the others.

This time True Fan didn't even bother with her name.

I told myself not to take it personally. But you have ignored everything I've told you. You seem to think you're so much smarter than me. You don't need my help. You never have.

All my attempts to make your books better have been ignored. You find me to be nothing more than a pest you can't seem to get rid of. Well, that will soon be over. I've tried to let it go. But in good conscience I can't let you go on the way you are.

I don't think of myself as a violent person. But someone needs to stop you. This time you've gone too far. I guess I'm going to have to do it myself since you didn't take my advice. You could have done the world a favor by taking your own life, but why would you listen to me now? I'm going to have to take care of this myself. There is apparently no one else.

There was no True Fan to the end. The letter just ended.

Chloe threw it down in disgust. "This person is crazy. I think it's time to take it to the sheriff." She got to her feet. "Do you have the other letters that have come since we've been here?"

TJ nodded. There was a chilling violence to the letter, as if the person had reached some breaking point. She hugged herself as her big sister made the call.

Annabelle took the empty wine bottle and glasses into the kitchen. She'd finished washing the glasses when there was a knock at the door.

THERE'D BEEN FEW times in Silas Walker's life that he hadn't known what to do. He prided himself on making quick decisions, the kind that had saved his life more than once. But right now he felt adrift. He had no idea who had been sent to kill him—not that it would make much of a difference if he did.

He'd like to think that DeAngelo had exaggerated about just how professional this hit man was. He hoped for an amateur. Or at least someone who would give him a fighting chance by being just bumbling enough to give him a slight edge.

As he drove through the falling snow back toward the cabin, he considered his options. He could return to New York City. Or he could take his chances at the cabin. He couldn't get TJ off his mind. Right now, the last thing he needed was his mind on anything but staying alive.

Earlier, he and TJ had come close to making love in his pickup. He'd wanted her more than he'd wanted to stay alive at that moment. To find someone like her now, now when his life was on the line, seemed too cruel a cosmic joke. It made him more determined to come out of this kickin'.

He stopped at the turnoff where he still had good cell phone coverage and called his friend and boss. "I just had a visit from my former NYPD partner. My buddies hired a hit man to take me out."

Cal swore. "How can I help?"

"I thought there might be something on the street. I'd like to know who this guy is and if he's already in Montana."

"I'll put my ear to the ground and see what I can find out. Aren't most of these old buddies still locked up?" his friend asked.

"A couple of them skated, but most of them are still behind bars, why?"

"You're talking cold-blooded murder. They knew some lowlifes on the street, but not hit men. I'd say they met someone while in the pen and contracted him. Let me see who recently got released and call you back."

Rather than hope for service at the cabin, Silas drove on into Zortman to the bar. He braved the storm and climbed out to go inside even though the last thing he wanted was alcohol. The place was packed with the approaching holiday and the weather. He found a small empty table near the door and sat down where he could see anyone who entered. When the waitress came over he ordered a beer and a burger, realizing he hadn't eaten all day.

He'd finished the burger and half of the beer when Cal called back. A boot-stompin' song was playing on the jukebox so he tossed down some money for the waitress and took the call down the hallway toward the men's restroom.

"I'm good friends with the warden at the local penitentiary," Cal said without preamble. "He says the dirty cops are in a wing by themselves fearing for their lives so they didn't have much contact with inmates. However, there was one they were seen talking to in the yard a few times. He recently got out. He's called Little Huey, a mean son of a bee who's done a lot of time for everything *but* murder. Real name's Herbert Jones. Caucasian, five foot nine, doesn't weigh a hundred and fifty pounds soaking wet, but rotten to the core."

"Might explain why he's so mean. Probably had to be at that size on the streets," Silas said. "If it's him he'll try to shoot me in the back, blindsiding me rather than come right at me."

"That would be my guess. You won't see him coming."

SHERIFF MCCALL CRAWFORD read the letters twice before folding them and putting them back in their envelopes. "You say there have been others?"

TJ nodded. "A dozen or so over the past six months."

"More threatening than these?" the sheriff asked.

"Some. At first True Fan was complimentary, but then that began to change. I didn't listen to the advice the reader was offering."

"Your fan suggested suicide?" McCall asked.

"Highly suggested it so I didn't write any more books that I would be embarrassed by," TJ said.

"And what makes you believe this individual might be in this area other than the postmark on the letter?"

TJ told her about the reams of paper that Melinda Holmes had sold after it had been stored for years in her basement. She told her about Nellie, Dot and Tommy, the people who had bought the paper that Melinda remembered. "It's a rather distinct color that would be hard to match."

The sheriff agreed. "Man or woman?"

"Sometimes I think man. Other times, woman. I have no idea."

"You had a book signing the other day. Anyone come through who made you suspicious?"

TJ laughed. "Everyone makes me suspicious. But I suspect it is someone with a connection to New York City since True Fan sent me a photo taken from the sidewalk outside my apartment. The person wanted me to know how close they were." She thought about mentioning being pushed into traffic but tended to agree with Silas that it might have been accidental.

"There are people in town with connections to New York," McCall said thoughtfully. "Others who have visited. Would be interesting to find out who might have asked one of them to take a photograph of her favorite author's apartment. Or if they did it themselves. Is that information public knowledge?"

"No, but Silas suggested that someone could have followed me from one of my book signings. I've done signings only blocks from my apartment and walked home afterward. I wasn't paying attention. Anyone could have followed me without my knowledge, waited on the street and seen me close my curtain before turning on a light on the third floor."

The sheriff nodded. "I noticed in one of your social media photos there is a pretty good view of the interior of your apartment. The curtains were open and I could see not only their design—but the building across the street. Probably wouldn't take anyone with a knowledge of the area long to find you."

TJ shivered. While she was writing about stalkers and killers and how they found their victims, there was one stalking her—and she'd probably made it easy for True Fan. She could have even given her stalker ideas on how to find her in her books.

"Mind if I take these with me?" McCall asked as she got to her feet, still holding the letters.

"Please take them," TJ said, and watched the sheriff pocket the envelopes. "You agree that it's someone here in Whitehorse?"

"It would certainly appear that way. Let me see what I can find out. If you get any more or you think of anything else, please contact me at once," the sheriff said.

"I will." TJ walked her to the door and stood on the porch hugging herself against the storm as the sheriff drove away.

As she started to turn back inside the house, she looked out at the neighborhood wondering if she was being watched at this moment by True Fan.

SILAS FINISHED HIS call and rather than walk back through the bar, decided to exit through the back. He circled around to his pickup. He'd already checked out the clientele enjoying themselves in the bar and hadn't seen anyone suspicious, let alone Little Huey. He had looked for the man who would be sitting alone. Even if Little Huey tried to blend in, he would stick out like a sore thumb in Montana.

He'd been aware of that very thing when he'd first moved here. It hadn't mattered how he'd dressed; it wasn't as if he could just put on a Stetson, jeans and boots and no one would know he wasn't from here.

That's why he knew his would-be killer would be sitting alone nursing a drink. That's if he'd already gotten this far.

Now as he walked out into the cold snow, Silas tried to think like a killer. If he was after a man like him in a state he didn't know, where would he start?

He'd fly in, rent an SUV or a pickup. A town like Whitehorse had a ten trucks to one car ratio. Then he would drive up the three hours from the airport to the western town.

Then what? If he asked a lot of questions, people would notice and say something about it. So he'd come armed with not just weapons. He'd know as much of his victim's backstory as he could get out of the men who'd hired him.

So he'd know about the cabin outside of Zortman. Silas thought of his mailbox down by the road. He couldn't have made it easier for someone to find him. Look how TJ had found him in a blizzard.

Climbing into his pickup, he started the engine and let it run. Snow had piled up on the windshield and now frozen down. His wipers were covered with ice. He let the defrost run while he thought it out.

His would-be killer would have to come prepared for the weather. That might be tougher. Unless he'd been in a Montana blizzard he would have no idea how hard it was to see—let alone get around—in the deep snow. He would have had to have purchased good boots, snow gear, a hat, goggles. Even that might not save him if he got turned around in the storm or stuck on the road.

Most people, with towns so far apart, carried food, water, blankets and matches. Silas had taken to carrying a sleeping bag behind the seat of his pickup. He never knew when he might need it. Which was also why he carried the shotgun on the rack behind his head—and the pistol under his seat.

But neither would protect him if Little Huey shot him in the back.

He saw that some of the snow had melted on the windshield, but the wipers would have to be cleaned off. He started to climb out when through the small defrosted spot on his windshield, he saw a man exit an SUV and head toward the front of the bar.

Silas felt his heart drop like a stone. His buddies hadn't sent Little Huey.

Chapter Seventeen

Kenny "Mad Dog" Harrington. Silas thought about
ending this right here and now as he watched the man
go into the bar. Kenny hadn't seen him with the windshield still mostly covered with snow and ice.

Silas stayed where he was for a moment and then
hit his wipers. Enough snow and ice came off that he
could see well enough to drive. Eventually the falling
snow would cake on the wipers and he'd have a blurry
mess on his windshield, but right now that was the
least of his worries.

He drove out of town, watching his rearview mirror.
Had Mad Dog already been out to his cabin? He would
know soon enough. On the way, he tried to think. Little Huey would have been waiting in the trees to am-
bush him. Mad Dog was a whole other breed of violent
criminal. He'd come head-on. It would take a cannon
to stop the crazy bastard.

Turning on to the road into his cabin, he saw that
there were two sets of tracks. Someone had gone in—
and come back out. Mad Dog had been to his cabin.
Which meant he would be back. Silas had no idea how
much time he had to get ready for the killer.

His mind raced as he drove, all the time keeping an

eye on the rearview mirror. No Mad Dog yet. Maybe he would have a few drinks, snort some coke or take some uppers. Silas knew how hard it was to stop a junkie. A junkie with Mad Dog's size and determination would be almost impossible to stop even filled with lead shot. But Silas had no choice unless…

He was almost to the cabin when a plan began to crystallize. It would be damned risky. Crazy under other circumstances. But worth a shot, he told himself as he pulled in front of the cabin and cut the engine. He would have to move fast. He had one thing going for him: Mad Dog wasn't smart. Also it was snowing so hard, his tracks would be covered quickly.

TJ's CONCERN FOR Silas had been growing by the hour. The thought of him alone at the cabin was driving her crazy. She kept telling herself that he was an ex-cop; he could handle himself. But she'd seen his reaction to the man.

"Can you sit still for five minutes?" her sister Chloe snapped. "This is about Silas Walker, isn't it? What has you so worked up?"

She wasn't about to tell Chloe. Her sister already thought that he was the wrong man for her. If she knew the danger he was in right now… "We left things a little…up in the air," she said truthfully.

Chloe shook her head.

"He isn't anything like Marc," TJ said in her defense.

"Nothing at all," her sister repeated sarcastically.

"What are you two arguing about?" Annabelle asked as she came into the living room with a plate of cookies. "Who wants milk?"

"Leave it for Santa," Chloe joked as she took a cookie. "We were arguing about men."

"So who's the right one for you?" Annabelle asked Chloe as she curled up in a chair and took a warm cookie.

"Justin," TJ said. "Is he still in town?" she asked Annabelle.

"Sorry, he moved away after he married some rich movie star." Annabelle almost choked on her cookie at her joke, before she said, "No, seriously, after Nici married, he was single for a long time. About five years ago, he married Margie Taylor and they moved to Bismarck, North Dakota, to farm her father's place. The marriage didn't last."

TJ raised a brow. "I'm amazed after being in town for such a short period of time how quickly you got caught up on all the local news."

Chloe groaned. "Excuse me, but we weren't talking about my lack of love life. We were talking about Silas Walker."

Her cell phone rang and she sprang to her feet. "Saved by the bell." She headed for her bedroom as she took the call from her agent.

"How are you doing?" Clara asked.

"Okay. I did the signing."

"I heard. Nice turnout?"

"Not bad."

"You made *The New York Times* Best Seller list," her agent said.

TJ knew she should be more excited about that. "That's wonderful."

"Not as high as last time, but it's early. Let's see if it stays where it is or goes even higher."

She was amazed how little any of this mattered right now.

"Have you heard from your True Fan?"

"A few letters, but I'm fine."

"Okay, but you don't sound fine. Maybe True Fan will give you a break over the holidays. When are you coming back?"

That was the question, wasn't it? "Not sure yet." She hadn't booked round-trip. Getting a flight could be difficult. But that didn't worry her either.

"Okay, I'll let you go. If you need anything..."

"I'll call. Have a wonderful holiday." She disconnected. She hadn't even asked where her book had hit on the *Times* list. Lower than last time. That was enough to know. She wasn't even tempted to check online. Normally, she watched closely the first few weeks of a release.

When she came back downstairs, Annabelle's fiancé Dawson Rogers was sitting in the living room. He got to his feet when he saw her, hugged her, wished her a Merry Christmas, then announced that he'd come to get them all for dinner out at the ranch.

"I decided to drive in for you since the visibility is poor and the roads are a little slick," he said.

She glanced out the window and realized he was downplaying how bad it was. "I hate to be a party pooper, as Grandma Frannie used to say, but I'm going to have to pass. Please give my best to your mother. I'm sure I'll see her over the holidays."

Her sisters started to put up an argument, but gave up quickly when they realized she had dug her feet in and wasn't going to change her mind. She wasn't in the mood for dinner and polite conversation. She had a terrible feeling about Silas that she couldn't shake.

As they all departed, she noticed that Annabelle had left the keys to her SUV on the hook by the door. She told herself that going out in this storm was more than risky. It might prove to be suicidal. Worse might be going to Silas's cabin when from what she could gather, there was a killer after him.

She thought about calling the sheriff. And telling her what? That Silas's former cop friends wanted to kill him? McCall couldn't do anything more than TJ could. That's when she knew that if she really wasn't going to do this, then she had not only to dress for the winter storm, but also to go armed.

"You're acting as if you think you really are Constance Ryan from one of your books," she said to herself as she went around the property getting things she thought she might need.

Silas worked as quickly as he could, given the weather. Another storm had blown in. Snow whirled around him, the cold wind biting at any exposed skin. When he'd first bought the land and begun to build on this spot, he'd thought about booby-trapping the area around it.

That was back when he'd been more worried about his former cops' plotting vengeance. He'd ditched the idea, fearful that he'd catch hikers or hunters in his traps and find himself in a lawsuit—if not worse. Also he hadn't wanted to live like that—fearing for his life every day.

Instead, he'd told himself that if they came for him, he'd deal with it then. As time went on, he'd begun to relax. Montana had that effect on him. He had liked feeling safe here, even knowing that it could change at any point.

Now as he finished loading the last booby trap, he stopped to listen. It was hard to hear anything over the wind whipping the pines and howling off the eaves of the cabin. He stared out into the storm, unable to see more than ten feet through the whirling snow.

Mad Dog would have the same problem.

Silas had worked hard since returning to the cabin. He'd known he didn't have much time. From the tracks around the cabin, he'd been able to surmise that Mad Dog had looked around, probably deciding how to come at him.

Now all he could do was wait. The question was where? Inside the cabin would make it too easy for his would-be killer. He couldn't depend on his booby traps stopping Mad Dog. All he could hope for is that one of them would delay the man long enough to give him the upper hand.

TJ STARTED THE SUV, then remembered something she'd forgotten in the house and, leaving the motor running, had run back inside.

Her heart was pounding. Common sense argued that she was doing a foolish thing. But that ache in her stomach, the feeling that Silas needed her, wouldn't let her turn back.

Inside the house, she found the flashlight she'd forgotten. It would be dark by the time she reached the cabin. She thought about texting Silas to tell him she was coming but he would just try to talk her out of it and right now she feared any reasonable argument would be all she needed to change her mind.

Back at the SUV, she was delighted to see that part of the windshield had cleared off. She used her gloved hand to take care of the rest. The snow was still falling so hard that it would cover it again if she didn't jump inside and use the wipers.

She climbed in, cranked up the heater even higher and turned on the wipers. To the steady clack, clack, clack, she shifted into Reverse and backed out.

It wasn't that far to the cabin. Once she was sure that Silas was all right... *Text him*, the voice in her head said. *Text him. Don't make this drive in this kind of weather. Not to mention the fact that he wants you to stay away while he handles this.*

She thought of Marc. She'd begged him to come home, but he was having too much fun. He loved the danger. He loved telling her about the close calls he'd had. She'd heard it in his voice. He thrived on the near misses.

Silas was different. He didn't want this. She remembered seeing both fear and dread on his face. *He knows he's mortal*, she thought. *He's strong, courageous, but only when it is demanded of him. He doesn't go looking for trouble.*

She was almost to the Zortman turnoff. She began to slow when she heard a sound in the seat behind her. Her gaze shot to the rearview mirror, her pulse taking off like a rocket as a face appeared a second before Tommy dove over the seat and dropped in beside her.

TJ screamed. The SUV swerved.

"Don't do anything stupid," he cried. "Keep driving or you're going to kill us both.

"Don't hit the brakes," he yelled as she hit the brakes.

The SUV went into another skid, but straightened as she jerked her foot from the pedal. Fortunately, there weren't any other vehicles on the road.

"What are you doing?" she demanded of him. "How long have you been back there?"

"I climbed in when you went back inside the house

for your flashlight." He sounded so reasonable. "I couldn't leave things the way we did earlier."

"You were back there all this time and didn't say anything?" she demanded, furious with him.

"I wanted to see where you were going," Tommy said. "I had a pretty good idea. Nice to see that I was right."

"What do you want?"

He looked over at her in that irritatingly calm way he had about him. "Why would you drive up here in this storm? You're worried about him. You think he might have another woman in his cabin?"

"No!" She slammed her palm on the steering wheel. "I think he's in trouble. That's why you shouldn't have gotten into this vehicle. You're messing up everything."

"Wait a minute. You think this ex-cop is in trouble and you've come to save him?" Tommy reached down to look into the bag she'd brought. His gaze shifted to her at the sight of the makeshift weapons. He shook his head. "It's a good thing I came along."

"How do you figure that?" She didn't want him here, nor did she like him knowing the impulsive and no doubt foolish thing she'd done. Because seeing it through his eyes, she knew that's exactly what it had been.

The realization moved her to tears. She wiped angrily at them.

"What are you doing?" Tommy asked.

"Turning around and taking you back to town."

He stopped her with a hand on her arm. "I can help."

She looked over at him. Her skepticism must have showed.

"I have a little training for this sort of thing."

She continued to look at him.

"In the service. You do know that I was in the military, right?"

Did she know that?

"Just tell me one thing. Who wants him dead? The cops he put in prison?"

It surprised her that he knew so much about Silas. It made her wonder if his interest was before she came back to Whitehorse or if it was more about her.

"That's my guess. There's a man in town who wants him dead I'm afraid," she said.

Tommy nodded. "I wish I'd known that before we got here, but not to worry. Turn around and go into Zortman. I have a friend I can borrow a few real weapons from. Do you know how to shoot a gun?"

She shook her head as she turned around. That Tommy was taking this seriously made her feel less foolish about driving here, but just as ill-prepared.

Tommy told her where to turn once they drove into the tiny town. "Stop here." The moment she cut the engine, he grabbed the keys. "No offense," he said, and jumped out.

She waited, wondering what she'd gotten herself into. If Silas wasn't in trouble... Or even if he was, what would he think of her showing up with Tommy?

She didn't have long to consider that before he was back with two handguns and a rifle and who knew what other weapons he had under his coat. He tossed them into the SUV and then slid into the passenger side again.

"Let's go," Tommy said as he handed her the keys. "I know a back road."

She stared at him for a moment, realizing she'd never seen this Tommy, before she started the SUV.

Chapter Eighteen

Mad Dog came out of the trees and rushed the cabin like the wild man he was. He was almost to the door when he hit the first trip wire. The hatchet struck him in the thigh, falling short of the chest where it had originally been aimed.

The hit man let out a shriek of pain. The blade had left a nasty bleeding gash but did little to stop Kenny. He roared and charged the porch. The second booby trap sprung, this time working better than the first. Mad Dog was caught by his ankle and jerked off his feet.

He was hanging upside down from a tree limb five feet off the ground when Silas came around from the back of the cabin. He had only a second, not long enough to raise his rifle and shoot before Mad Dog fired.

The bullet grazed the size of his head. He rocked back, connecting with the corner of the cabin as he got off a shot. It went wild. He pumped another cartridge in and fired. Mad Dog howled with pain, swung around and let loose a barrage of bullets.

As Silas was diving behind the corner of the cabin, he caught another one; this one grazed his shoulder. He fired another three shots, all of them hitting their mark, but Mad Dog showed no sign that any of them had done mortal damage.

Silas's head wound was losing blood fast. He could see that Mad Dog was also bleeding, but not bleeding out fast enough. Mad Dog tossed a handgun away and pulled another. Even hanging upside down, the man didn't stop.

Silas ducked back as bullets pelted the corner of the cabin. He wiped at his temple and felt the darkness wanting to close in. He felt himself getting lightheaded. He had to finish this one way or another.

Firing around the edge of the cabin, he heard his bullets hit their mark but Mad Dog's only reaction was a roar of anger. Another barrage of bullets pelted the ground and the corner of the cabin as Silas ducked back again. Even upside down, Kenny was still a damned good shot.

He heard a loud crash and the splinter of wood and knew that Mad Dog had cut the rope he'd been dangling from and had crashed down on the bottom steps of the porch. He also knew that the man would be coming for him. There was a reason Kenny had been tagged Mad Dog Harrington.

With so many bullets pumped into the man, Kenny should be down for the count. But given the drugs he'd no doubt taken, Silas was wondering if he would be able to kill him before Mad Dog killed him.

Darkness faded in and out at the side of his vision. He blinked, trying to stay on his feet but feeling the effects of his blood loss. If he didn't finish this, and soon…

TOMMY INSTRUCTED TJ to kill the engine. "This is where we get out."

She looked into the storm raging around the vehicle and could see nothing but snow and the blur of the green pines beyond it.

"You might want to stay here," he said. "I'll come back and let you know what's happening."

TJ shook her head. She'd come this far. Now she had Tom involved in this. She had begun thinking of him as Tom—not Tommy anymore. He offered her a gun. She shook her head. "I'd probably shoot myself." Instead she grabbed one of her simple-to-operate weapons, ready to brave the storm and whatever else was waiting for them.

They exited the vehicle and Tom led the way through the woods as they dropped down the mountain. He motioned for her to be as quiet as possible. She could hear nothing but the wind high in the pines and the pounding of her heart as she tried to see through the snowstorm. All her instincts were still telling her that Silas needed help. But what if she was wrong? What if it was too late?

Snow whipped in her face and down her neck. She pulled her hat lower and coat tighter around her. They hadn't gone far when she spotted part of the cabin's roof through the trees. Tom motioned for her to stay back as he moved forward toward the back of the house.

They reached the outhouse. Tom stepped around it, TJ right behind him. She saw Silas first. He lay against the side of the cabin at its corner as if he'd just decided to sit down there. She couldn't tell if he was dead or alive, but the snow was red around him. She started to run to him, but Tom held her back.

A huge man came around the corner of the cabin holding a gun. He stopped to look down at Silas. As the man raised his weapon to finish the job he'd started, Tom lifted his rifle and fired. He kept firing as he charged forward until the big man returned fire.

Tom stumbled and went down. The big man limped over to him. She could see that the man was wounded and bleeding badly, but he was still on his feet—and still about to kill both men.

As the man raised his gun, TJ did something that even her heroine Constance wouldn't have done. She charged the man.

SILAS KNEW HE must have blacked out because when he came to, he was sitting in the snow. Confused for a moment, he saw his rifle in the snow next to him and wasn't sure if it was still loaded or not. Snowflakes drifted around the corner of the cabin to melt on his face. He turned his head, not sure what he was seeing.

Mad Dog stood over someone lying in the snow a few yards from him. As the hit man raised his rifle to shoot the person, a figure came screaming out of the storm. With a jolt, Silas saw that it was TJ. She had a baseball bat in her hands.

Turning slowly as if not so steady on his feet, Mad Dog looked over at her as if he didn't believe what he was seeing. Silas felt the same way. She was so small compared to him. Mad Dog looked almost amused.

Silas tried to sit up, but felt his head swim again so he laid back. Just the act of pulling his handgun from his shoulder holster, almost made him black out again.

He finally managed to get it loose just as TJ, still charging the man, swung the bat. The sound reminded him of a pumpkin left by kids in the street being crushed by a car tire. Blood shot out of Mad

Dog's mouth and flew over the snow, leaving a bright red trail. Silas fired the handgun, emptying it into the crazed man.

For too many seconds, Mad Dog didn't move. Silas could see that TJ was ready to swing the bat again if need be. As Mad Dog started to lift his weapon in her direction, Silas yelled his name and tried to get up. The darkness closed in.

TJ SAW WHAT the big man planned to do. Silas sat bleeding by the corner of the cabin. Tom was down in the snow just feet away. She looked into the big man's eyes and knew she was about to die as he raised the gun in his hand and pulled the trigger.

There was a click, then another one, followed by two more, but no gunshot. The man looked down at the gun in his hand, as confused as TJ for a moment. Her heart pounded so hard her chest ached. Her throat had gone dry. She'd looked death in the face.

She swung the bat. It caught him completely off guard. This time, his head snapped back as the bat connected with his temple. He dropped like a sack of potatoes. She stood there, the bat ready to hit him again if need be, trembling so hard she could hardly hold on to the weapon, terrified that he would get up again.

But he lay in the snow, his eyes open and blank, and after a few moments she dropped the bat and fumbled out her phone. As she did, she heard the sirens. How was that possible? She rushed to Tom. He was still breathing. Then she went to Silas. He too was breathing. He smiled up at her, then closed his eyes and dropped off into unconsciousness.

From behind her, she heard movement and swung around. Tom was on his feet. "I called the sheriff when I went in to get the guns," he said as he approached her. Then he smiled. "You really are Constance."

Chapter Nineteen

TJ had plenty of time to think about Tom's words as she waited at the hospital for word on him and Silas. She still couldn't believe what she'd done. She'd acted on instinct and it had almost gotten her killed. If the crazy big man hadn't run out of ammunition in his gun...

Her sisters spotted her and came running down the hall, only to be reprimanded by the head nurse. They pulled her into the waiting room, both talking at once. She held up her hand and realized it was still covered with blood.

Both of her sisters saw it, their eyes widening. Chloe dropped into a chair. Annabelle just stood there, mouth open for a moment.

"It's kind of a long story," TJ said. She told them what Silas had told her about the police officers sending someone to kill him and how she'd had this bad feeling that he needed her, so she'd decided to drive up to his cabin.

Chloe looked at her as if she'd lost her mind.

"I had just turned onto the road to Zortman when Tom popped up from the back of the SUV. He'd been hiding there waiting to see where I was going."

"Tom?" Chloe repeated, having noticed that she was no longer calling him Tommy.

"He told me he had experience in the military and wasn't letting me go alone after I told him why I was determined to check on Silas." Her breath caught in her throat at the memory of the crazed big man standing over Silas about to kill him when Tom starting firing at him.

"If Tom hadn't been there, Silas would be dead. You can't believe this hit man. The EMTs said when they're high on all these drugs these kind of men are nearly impossible to kill. I don't know how many times the man had been shot…" Her voice broke. "Tom was shot. He's in surgery."

"What about you?" Chloe asked as she reached over and took TJ's trembling hands in hers. "The sheriff mentioned something about a baseball bat?"

TJ nodded. Looking back it was as if it had been Constance Ryan who'd leaped out of her books to swing that bat. "He would have killed us all but he'd run out of ammunition in his gun. He pointed it right at me. The look in his eyes…" She shuddered at the memory. "I watched him pull the trigger again and again, but there was only this loud *click, click, click*."

"What did you do?" Annabelle asked, on the edge of her seat.

"I'd already hit him with the baseball bat once and it barely fazed him. But I swung it again and that time…" She shook her head. "That time he went down and he didn't get up. Tom had called the sheriff when he went into a friend's house in Zortman to get guns. I've never seen him like that."

"And Silas?" Chloe asked.

"He's going to make it. He's lost a lot of blood and has a concussion, but he's going to be fine, the doctor said. Now I'm just worried about Tom. If he hadn't come along with me…"

Her sisters got up to come over and hug her as the doctor appeared at the door to tell them that Tom Harwood had come out of surgery and was doing fine.

SILAS OPENED HIS EYES. The room seemed too white. Was he dead? He blinked and brought everything into focus. A hospital room. For a moment, he couldn't remember what had happened. He touched his head. Bandaged and hurting like hell. Something shifted on his bed. He looked down to see TJ. She'd pushed her chair over so she was right next to his bed. Then she'd apparently fallen asleep with her head on the edge of her mattress.

He stared down at her, enough of last night coming back to him to make him scared for her all over again. She'd been at the cabin carrying a baseball bat? Or had he only dreamt it? He touched his bandage again and this time TJ stirred awake.

She blinked at him and brushed some stray locks from her face. "You're awake. How are you?"

"Alive. I think I have you to thank for that."

"Actually, it was more Tom Harwood. I'm sure you'll hear all about it. Right now, the doctor said you just need to rest."

"There is something about a baseball bat," he said.

"Don't concern yourself with that right now," she said, avoiding his gaze.

He wanted to throttle her. "I should turn you over my knee…"

She shifted her gaze to him and smiled. "There's time for that when you get out of here."

He laughed, even though it hurt his head. "You saved my life. I owe you."

"We can discuss that too," she said, still smiling as she took his hand and brought it to her lips.

TJ COULDN'T REMEMBER the last time she'd decorated a Christmas tree. She'd done little to her apartment during the holidays. From the back of her closet she would pull out a small fake tree that was already decorated and plug it in.

She had found herself dreaming sometimes of Christmas back in Whitehorse. Sledding and snowball fights with the boys in the neighborhood, hot chocolate back in the kitchen with their grandmother before decorating her truly ugly fake tree.

Today though, their grandmother's house smelled of pine and gingersnap cookies. Annabelle couldn't seem to quit baking. Her sisters had dragged in the tree they'd cut up in the Little Rockies and they'd stood it up. Instantly, it was like being in the woods again. Being at Silas's cabin, TJ thought.

"Is this practice for marriage?" Chloe had wanted to know when they'd found Annabelle in the kitchen early that morning baking. The house smelled of ginger and cinnamon, and TJ breathed it in as if it was her last breath. Her apartment never smelled like this, not that she baked. In the city, it was too easy to run down and pick up anything you wanted to eat.

This morning, the three of them had sat around the kitchen table reminiscing about Christmases past. They'd eaten warm cookies and milk for breakfast, laughing about some of their Grandma Frannie memories before deciding it was time to tackle the tree.

TJ had been the first one up, long before Annabelle began baking. Even before the sun was up, she'd gone to the hospital to see how Tom was doing. He was sitting up and had more color than the first time she'd seen him right after surgery.

"How are you feeling?" she'd asked.

"Not bad." He'd smiled. "You were amazing."

She'd laughed. "I could say the same about you. You saved my life and Silas's."

He'd given her an embarrassed shrug.

"Thank you, Tom."

"Tom," he'd said and grinned. "Does this mean that Tommy is behind us?"

She'd nodded.

"I'd ask if you've fallen for this ex-cop, but it's clear you have. Does this mean you'll be staying in Whitehorse? I'd like it if we could be friends. Just friends."

"Truthfully, the future is a bit blurry right now. But we can definitely be friends."

Now, she stood back for a moment to look at the beautiful tree her sisters had found and cut down all on their own in the mountains. It was a fir and smelled wonderful. The branches were thick and already naturally decorated with tiny pinecones.

"I'm so glad you saved Grandmother's ornaments," TJ said as she dug in the last of three boxes that had been full. She held up a paper angel. "Remember this one?"

The whole morning had been like that. Each ornament had a memory for one of them. That's why it was taking so long for the tree to get decorated. All those trips down memory lane had derailed them multiple times.

At the sound of someone at the door, they all turned and then shared a troubled look.

"I'll get it," TJ said and hurried to the door, expecting to see Carol from the post office standing outside. But it wasn't Carol. "Silas? I thought you weren't being released until tomorrow."

"I talked the doctor into letting me out. I had to see you."

TJ ushered him inside. He was limping badly, he had a smaller bandage on his temple, but he was alive and smiling. Her sisters said hello, asked about his health and then discreetly left them alone.

"The sheriff filled me in on everything that happened," Silas said after she'd offered him a seat. He leaned toward her. "TJ, you could have been killed!" He shook his head. "What were you thinking?"

"That you were in trouble. The feeling was so strong I couldn't ignore it."

His gaze softened. "I don't know how to thank you and at the same time, never do anything like that again."

She smiled. "I can't promise that. If I feel like you need me…"

He rose and pulled her to her feet and into his arms. "I do need you. But what am I going to do with you?"

"I bet you'll think of something," she said and he kissed her, pulling her into him as if he needed to feel her body against his as much as she did.

"Go to the Christmas dance with me?"

She laughed. "I haven't danced in years."

"Me either. But I heard there will be mistletoe." He grinned.

"Are you sure you're up to dancing? You just got out of the hospital."

His grin broadened. "Oh, I'm up for a lot more than dancing."

Just then Annabelle came careening down the stairs to race into the kitchen. Smoke billowed up from the oven. "I forgot my last batch of cookies," she cried, making them both laugh.

Silas pulled TJ to him and kissed her, backing her up against the wall. His gaze locked with hers. Then something crashed in the kitchen and they heard footfalls on the stairs and moved apart, laughing as Chloe appeared.

TJ couldn't remember being so happy. She wanted to pinch herself. When Silas looked at her like he was right now, she almost forgot about True Fan.

THE OLD GYM was rocking with the sound of loud music and the roar of voices as the Christmas dance kicked off for the season. It was a huge yearly event. Some listened to the music and watched from the bleachers as others danced. It appeared that the whole town had turned out.

The old gym had been decorated with lots of sparkly lights. It reminded TJ for a moment of the only prom she'd attended, which made her grimace. Then Silas had put his arm around her, bringing her back to the wonderful, amazing present.

Chloe hadn't wanted to come. "You both have dates."

"You're going," Annabelle had told her. "I promise you'll have fun."

Chloe had made a face but had finally agreed to come at least for a little while. TJ had seen her talking to three cowboys they had gone to school with and later dancing.

As Silas pulled her out onto the dance floor, TJ put her head on his shoulder and closed her eyes. She loved the smell of him, fresh from the shower and yet so male. He pulled her closer as they swayed with the music. She felt so safe in his arms. But it was so much more than that. That feeling of being complete, being content, being happy filled her.

She never thought she'd ever experience this. She'd been such a loner all of her life. All she'd ever wanted was to write. That had been her driving force for so long. Silas made her want more. Opening her eyes, she looked around the room and felt such a sense of community. She'd forgotten what it felt like being part of a small town.

As the song ended, she was shoved hard against Silas. She turned to see Joyce stumbling away. It appeared she'd been drinking because she turned to sneer at TJ and kept going.

"You know her?" Silas asked.

"Went to school with her."

He chuckled. "What did you do to her?"

"That's just it. Nothing that I can recall. Sometimes I think I get blamed for things I didn't do."

As they both watched Joyce weave unsteadily through the crowd and disappear out the door, TJ wondered if Joyce could be the one writing her the threatening letters. The woman seemed so angry, she could be True Fan.

"Can I get you a drink?" Silas asked as they stepped

off the dance floor. She could tell his leg was bothering him and said as much. He denied it.

"Fine," she said. "But let's sit out a few dances."

He smiled at her, cupping her cheek, his gaze locking with hers. "After this is over, I was hoping to get you alone."

Her heart hammered in her chest. Heat rushed through her, colliding at her center to make her cheeks flush. Pulse pounding at the thought of being alone with him, all she could do was nod. She watched him walk away and could tell that he was trying not to limp. She headed over to where her sisters had gathered.

"Who was that I saw you dancing with?" she asked Chloe.

"Cooper Lawson."

"Justin's best friend from high school," Annabelle said.

"Don't read anything into it, all right?"

TJ laughed. "So you didn't ask him anything about Justin?" Chloe shot her a warning look, but TJ noticed that her sister looked happier than she'd been for some time.

"Where's Dawson?" she asked Annabelle.

"Drink line."

TJ looked in that direction but she didn't see Silas. "Oh, no, there's Mrs. Brown."

Annabelle looked toward the door where Ester had just come in and now stood brushing snow from her sleeve. "I heard she had a series of ministrokes and it's changed her personality."

"Maybe she isn't as grumpy as she used to be," Chloe said, and laughed.

"Or worse," Annabelle said.

"I just remember how upset she used to get with me in her advanced English class," Chloe said. "She would go to write something on the board and actually break the chalk in her fury. She once threw the chalk at me, missed, but almost hit Kirt, who was behind me. Later I saw her in the teachers' lounge crying. I know I was terrible. But she was always singling me out, especially when she knew I hadn't been paying attention."

"No wonder she is always glaring at *me*," TJ said with a groan. "I swear she's mad at me because she has me confused with the two of you. I was the good sister." She was distracted for a moment as she noticed Joyce standing by the entrance. The woman was looking right at her before she pushed out the door. The look gave her a shiver.

SILAS INSISTED ON a last dance since it was a slow one. "I like holding you," he said as he drew her to him. "The problem is that I don't like letting you go and the holiday will be over before we know it." He drew back to look at her. "I was wondering if you'd like to come up to the cabin for a few days after Christmas. I know you'll want to be with your sisters for the holiday—"

"I would love to."

He smiled and let out a breath as if he'd been holding it. "I might even decorate the cabin."

"There's no need. The cabin is perfect just like it is."

"You really do like it," he said, sounding a little surprised.

She frowned. "Of course. I have such good memories…" Her voice trailed off. "I know it was only one night, but I felt as if I—"

"As if we'd known each other a lot longer." His smile

broadened. "I felt the same way. I've never had that happen before. Dates are always so—"

"Awkward, and you promise never to go through it again," she said with a laugh.

"Exactly." His blue eyes sparkled in the twinkling Christmas lights. "But with you, it was different. With you—"

"It was nice."

He nodded and leaned down to kiss her as the song ended. They stood on the dance floor as people began to leave. He kissed her again, then stepped back as if just then realizing the dance was over. "I'll get our coats," he said, his voice sounding rough with no doubt the same desire she was feeling.

Her legs felt a little wobbly as she made her way toward the bleachers where her sisters had gathered along with Dawson and some other friends. She heard them discussing going down to one of the local bars for a nightcap or two.

She'd almost reached them when someone grabbed her arm.

"Dear, would you mind walking me out to my car," Ester Brown said as she latched on to TJ's arm with shaking bony fingers. "I think I might have overdone it."

TJ looked toward the cloakroom and the huge line. It would be a while before Silas could get their coats. Ester apparently had never taken hers off.

"It's just right outside," Ester said, as if seeing her hesitation. "It won't take you a minute." She tugged on TJ's arm and the two of them headed for the door.

TJ shot a look over her shoulder at her sisters. She

got Annabelle's attention and called, "Tell Silas I'll be right back."

"Silas," Ester said as they reached the side door. "Is he your beau now?"

Was he? She supposed so. At least until the holiday ended. "He's just a friend."

"Sure he is," the woman said under her breath. "My car's right over there." They walked through the freezing night air. Unlike Ester, who was all bundled up and in snow boots, TJ wore only a party dress and high heels.

As they stepped outside, TJ saw Joyce standing in the shadow of the building having a cigarette. She could feel her dark eyes on them as they crossed the parking lot.

"That woman doesn't like you," Ester said, following her gaze. She still had a bony-fingered grip on TJ's arm.

"I can't understand why."

Ester chuckled. "Maybe she's read one of your books."

TJ glanced over at her. Mrs. Brown had a sense of humor? She was still chuckling as they crossed the parking lot.

Fortunately, Ester didn't seem to have the breath for walking—and talking. She'd thought her former teacher might want to bend her ear about her books, but that didn't seem to be the case. While in apparently good shape other than those minor strokes she'd had, Ester appeared to be winded by the time they reached her car.

"You know, I'm not really feeling up to driving," the elderly woman said. "I hate to impose, but would you mind, dear? My house is so close by. You're welcome to bring my car back."

"I can walk. It's no problem." She was already freezing, but she couldn't say no. Ester seemed to be breathing hard. What if she was about to have another stroke? TJ definitely didn't want her driving.

"You are such a dear," Ester said as TJ helped her into the passenger side, then, taking the keys the woman handed her, climbed behind the wheel.

Ester's home was only three blocks from the old gym where the Christmas festivities had been held. Snow crystals hung in the air as she drove, the night clear and cold. All TJ could think about was getting Ester home and then returning to the old gym—and Silas. Right now, in his warm, strong arms was the only place she wanted to be.

She started to park the car in the driveway, but Mrs. Brown had already hit the garage door opener.

"I prefer to keep my car in the garage," she said as the door yawned open.

TJ pulled the car in and had barely stopped before Ester had the garage door closing behind them. She turned off the motor and started to turn to the elderly woman when she saw what Ester was holding. Her heart slammed against the walls of her ribs. "What?" The word came out on a surprised and suddenly scared breath.

"Not very succinct for a woman who makes her living writing," her former English teacher said as she waved the gun at her. Ester was still breathing hard, but she didn't look at all incapable of pulling the trigger.

"In case you're wondering, I know how to use this," the woman said. "I'm an excellent shot. Get out of the car. I don't want to shoot you in my garage, but I will if you don't do exactly as I say. It will be a first for you."

"Why are you doing this?" TJ cried.

"Because I can't let you write another one of those awful books," Ester said. "You had so much promise." She shook her head. "Parents over the years have chastised me for being too blunt." She huffed at that. "Honesty, that's what kids need. Good, old-fashioned honesty. That's what I've tried to give you. But did you listen? Of course not."

TJ stared at her as realization froze her in place. "You're True Fan."

"Not anymore," the elderly woman said. "I said I would be until the end. Well, this is the end. Now get out of the car and don't test me, Tessa Jane. If you had listened to me back when you were in my classes... Well, it's too late, isn't it. You won't be embarrassing me any further."

Ester pressed the barrel end of the gun into her back and shoved her toward the door into the house. They moved through the kitchen and into the living room. TJ's mind raced. What was Ester planning to do? She'd said that she couldn't let her write another book. Was she going to shoot her?

As they moved through the house, she looked for something she could use as a weapon. But she saw nothing that would allow her to spin around and disarm the woman before Ester shot her.

She tried to calm down, telling herself that her sisters would realize she hadn't come back. They would look for her. Silas had gone to get their coats. When he returned and they told him where she'd gone he would eventually come looking for her. If Annabelle remembered to tell him. She had to believe that he would find her—that someone would find her—as Ester jabbed her with the gun and pointed toward a door ahead.

TJ heard the word "basement" and knew that she had to do something. Surreptitiously she slipped off her bracelet. Silas had commented on it earlier. It was silver with tiny silver trees on it. She'd bought it the day before because it had reminded her of his place in the woods.

"Mrs. Brown, you can't do this," she said rather loudly to cover the sound of her dropping the bracelet next to one of the chairs in the living room. If the woman didn't find it before someone came looking for her, they might see it; they might know that she was here.

"I've already done it," Ester snapped and, reaching around her, opened the basement door.

All TJ could see was darkness. Before she could react, Ester shoved her. She fell forward, screaming as she tumbled downward.

Chapter Twenty

When Silas returned with their coats he looked around, but he didn't see TJ. Her sisters, though, were standing over by the bleachers. Most everyone had already cleared out. A few stragglers were standing around.

"We were just going uptown for an after-the-party drink," Annabelle announced when she saw him. "Do you and TJ want to come along?"

The last thing he wanted was a drink, and he was considering how to decline without hurting anyone's feelings when he asked, "Where is TJ?" He thought she might have gone to the women's room and looked in that direction.

"She just took our former English teacher out to her car," Chloe said. "It will give us a chance to talk."

He tried not to laugh as she drew him away from the others. He'd been expecting the third degree from TJ's older sister so he wasn't surprised. "I love TJ."

Chloe waved that off as if it wasn't important.

"I want to marry her. I was thinking of asking her on New Year's Eve," he said. "But I was worried that it's too early. I don't want to scare her off."

"You hardly know each other," Chloe said, sounding shocked.

"I know her. I knew her through her books before I met her."

She huffed at that. "You think she's Constance Ryan?" Chloe shook her head. "She's not. She's a prude. She's a chicken. She's—"

"She's braver than you know," he said, remembering the woman who'd saved his life. "She and Constance have a lot in common."

"She's been hurt by a dangerous man before."

He nodded. "She told me about Marc. I'm not him." He realized he was still holding their coats. He looked toward the door. "Shouldn't TJ be back by now?"

"Mrs. Brown is probably out there chastising her for some improper grammar she found in one of her books," Annabelle said, joining them. "Remember what a stickler the old bat was? All that stuff about participles and gerunds? It's a kick that Ester reads TJ's books. But then again, TJ was one of her best students. She should be proud that TJ has made a career as a writer."

Silas looked at Annabelle, hating the sudden worry that had begun roiling in his stomach. "How long have they been gone?"

"Quite a while," Chloe said, now frowning. "We'd better go save TJ from her."

Silas pulled on his coat and, taking TJ's with him, said over his shoulder, "I'll check on her. You guys go on to the bar." He headed for the door, but stopped before going out. "What kind of car does Ester drive?"

"An older model. As big as a tank," Annabelle said. "Blue, I think."

Silas told himself TJ was fine, but all his instincts told him otherwise. He thought about the boxes of old

discolored paper. Mrs. Taylor had said she'd sold one
of the boxes to someone from the school. A teacher?
A former teacher?

Once outside he looked around. A few people were
coming and going. He didn't see a big blue car. He
didn't see TJ or Ester Brown. Maybe TJ had decided
to drive her home. He ran back inside, asked for directions to the woman's house and then ran to his truck.

He told himself that TJ could hold her own with an
elderly woman. But his fear was that she wouldn't see
it coming.

TJ GASPED AS a glass of cold water was thrown in her
face. She didn't know how long she'd been knocked
out. After the shock of the cold water, she became
aware of the pain. She hurt all over. Worse, she found
herself bound with tape on the floor. In the dim overhead bulb Ester had turned on, she could see that her
ankles were bound, along with her hands. Her arms
and one knee were scraped and bleeding, and her head
ached.

She looked up into Ester's weathered face, still feeling as if this couldn't be happening. Her former teacher
had pushed her down the basement stairs. It was a wonder the fall hadn't killed her, and yet Ester didn't seem
to be in the least bit concerned. *Probably because she
plans to kill me anyway.*

She looked around the basement, still feeling as if
her brain was fuzzy. She spotted a small desk with the
old manual typewriter sitting on it. Next to it was an
open ream of the discolored paper. The rest of the box
sat on the floor next to the desk. She thought as her

mind seemed to be clearing that this was the teacher who'd said she bought it to give to the school.

Ester had been down here secretly writing the letters? But not just those, she saw. The trash can next to the desk was filled with wadded-up paper. Even from where she was tied up TJ could see what appeared to be a stack of typed pages on the other side of the typewriter. A book Ester was working on? Why write down here and not upstairs? Why keep it a secret?

She saw that Ester was fiddling with something over by the stairs. TJ began working at the tape binding her wrists behind her. It felt a little loose. If she could get her finger under the last loop…

Ester, she realized, had been wiping TJ's blood off the basement stairs railing. The thought made her stomach drop. How long did she plan to keep her in this basement? Or was she going to kill her and maybe bury her down here? Ester knew that surely she'd never get away with this.

Unfortunately, as the woman turned toward her, TJ saw something in her eyes that told her Ester wasn't worried about getting away with it.

"Did you know that I used to do some writing myself?" Ester asked conversationally as she pulled up a chair in front of her.

TJ stared at her, wondering if she was hallucinating all of this. "I didn't know," she managed to say, since it appeared Ester was waiting for a response.

"Of course you didn't. I was talented, but I needed to make a living." At the edge of the bitterness was pain and regret. TJ had heard it before from aspiring writers. "I dreamed of writing books and being famous like you." Her voice broke.

TJ didn't know what to say. "Now that you're retired—"

Ester shook her head, the gun in her hand still pointed at TJ's heart even though she was bound to the chair. "It's too late."

She decided now wasn't the time to point out that Ester could have written in her spare time as a teacher. The woman had never married or had more to look after than a cat. Maybe she could have found time to write.

But it was clear Ester wanted to blame someone for the fact that she'd never written the books that she'd dreamed would have brought her fame and fortune.

TJ felt badly for her because there'd been a time when she'd had to work at an eight-to-five job. All she'd wanted to do was write. She remembered the frustration. She had the feeling that if she could just write full-time, she could get published. She could support herself on her writing.

It had been hard back then, but she'd gotten up early in the morning and written as much as she could before she had to go to work. Then she'd written late into the night. It hadn't been easy and what she'd written wasn't that great, but she wasn't the only writer who'd had to make a living as well as write starting out.

"That's why you're so angry with me," TJ said, realizing what this really was about. Tessa Jane had the audacity to become a writer while Ester felt she'd been kept from it by students like TJ and her sisters.

"I had talent," Ester said angrily. "I tried to share that talent as a teacher with students like you. But you never appreciated it. When I wrote you the letters, I knew you wouldn't take them seriously if they were from me. That's why I didn't sign them. I thought I could help you…" Her voice broke.

So instead of writing her own books, Ester had wanted to rewrite TJ's.

She didn't know what to say, but she knew she had to say something. Ester seemed confused, as if now that she'd taken TJ, she didn't seem to know what to do with her. Had she just wanted her to know the truth?

"Ester, I'm so glad you've finally told me that the letters were from you. I didn't realize that you were just trying to help me."

Ester stared at her. "How could you not realize it? I told you—"

"But how could I trust it not knowing who the advice was coming from?"

The older woman stared at her. "As if you would have listened even if you'd known. You were impossible in my class."

"I think that was my sister Chloe, or maybe Annabelle. Mrs. Brown—"

"You're just trying to confuse me. I need to think." Suddenly she seemed agitated. The hand holding the gun was shaking.

"You don't want to hurt me. You need to let me go. This is not the way you want to end your teaching career."

Ester huffed. "I didn't even get a gold watch. A luncheon and a pat on the head before I was replaced with a young teacher who doesn't know grammar and couldn't care less."

"I'm sorry," TJ said, not knowing what more there was to say. Ester felt as if her life hadn't mattered. TJs heart went out to her.

"Actually, I owe you so much. I learned a lot in your class. I wouldn't have been as successful as I've been without you."

Ester cocked her head at her as if trying to judge if she was just saying this.

She rushed on, all the time still working at the tape around her wrists. "I loved the writing assignments you gave us," she said, trying to remember one of them that Ester might also recall. High school had been so long ago and yet for Ester it had been only months ago. It was no wonder the students had all run together in Ester's mind—at least TJ and her sisters.

She thought about what Annabelle had said about Ester having a series of ministrokes. That could account for some of this strange behaviour as well, especially if Ester had had them in the past six months.

"My favorite writing assignment was a character study. Do you remember that?"

"Of course I do," her former teacher snapped. "I used it in all my classes."

"I wrote mine about the hall bully. You liked it so much that you read it to all your classes. It was the first time I realized that I might actually be a writer. That I might actually succeed at it."

Ester got a faraway look in her eyes for a moment. "Rick. That was the boy's name."

TJ nodded and felt a ray of hope even though Ester was still holding the gun steady and pointed at her heart.

"I do remember that," Ester said, and looked confused again. Her gaze met TJ's. "Tessa Jane Clementine. Yes, that was one of my best." She frowned. "Your sister wrote about a character on television." She shook her head and sighed.

"You gave me hope that day. All I ever wanted to do was write."

Ester nodded, tears in her eyes. "That's all I wanted too."

"So you need to let me go. This is just a misunderstanding."

Unfortunately, the woman shook her head again. "I can't do that."

ESTER BROWN'S HOUSE was only a few blocks away. The moment Silas pulled up in front of the small white home, he saw that there were no lights on inside. Also there was no blue car parked outside. But there was a garage to one side.

Is it possible they would have gone somewhere else? He couldn't even be sure that TJ was with the older woman. But both Annabelle and Chloe had seen her leave with Ester. He told himself that TJ was so accommodating that she might have taken her by the gas station to fill up the car for her. Or even the grocery store for milk and bread.

But his gut told him that wasn't the case. Fear gripped him as he climbed out of the truck and ran up to the garage. He peered in. A big blue boat of a car filled the small space. He ran up the front steps, rang the doorbell and then hammered with his fist before trying the door. Locked.

Where the hell were they?

He tried to calm down. But he knew that something was terribly wrong.

He saw a loose brick in the planter that ran the full

length of the house and jumped down to retrieve it. Back up on the porch, he threw the brick through the small window next to the door. The glass shattered. He knocked the lethal-looking shards aside and reached in to unlock the door.

AT THE SOUND of breaking glass upstairs, Ester jumped, and for a moment TJ flinched, fearing that she would accidently pull the trigger. They both froze, listening. Someone was breaking into the house.

TJ opened her mouth to scream only to have a balled-up sock stuffed down her throat. She gagged and tried to spit it out, but Ester held it in place with a strip of tape.

"Stay here," she ordered before taking the gun and starting for the stairs.

Like she was going anywhere bound like this. But she had managed to loosen the tape on her wrists. She waited until Ester's back was turned as she headed up the stairs before she worked frantically at the tape. Whoever had come to rescue her wouldn't be expecting Ester to be armed. That could be a fatal mistake.

SILAS HAD JUST gotten the door open when Ester Brown appeared. She still wore her coat as if she hadn't been home long. Her hands were in the pockets. She didn't look that surprised to see him or that upset that he'd just broken into her house.

"What do you think you're doing?" she demanded in a voice that reminded him of a teacher he'd had in middle school.

"Where's TJ?"

"TJ?" she asked, and frowned as if the name didn't ring a bell.

"Tessa Jane. She helped you out to your car, possibly drove you home?"

Ester frowned. "Well, yes, but the last I saw her was in the parking lot with Joyce Mason."

He thought of the woman who'd seemed to purposely bump into TJ at the dance. He'd seen Joyce's expression. It had been hateful. For a moment, he thought he'd broken into the wrong house. But then he saw something over by one of the chairs and recognized it at once as the bracelet TJ had been wearing at the dance tonight.

Ester had followed his gaze—and seen it as well. She stepped to the side as if to block his view, but then must have realized it was too late. Her face filled with anger.

"Ester, what have you done with TJ? TJ!" he called.

"She can't hear you."

He started to rush past her when she pulled the gun. It looked so incongruous that for a moment he thought it was a joke.

But one look in her eyes and he knew this was no joke. His heart dropped at the thought of what she could have already done.

"As I told Tessa Jane, don't try me," she said. "I know how to use it. I don't want to shoot you, but I will." Her voice was so calm he froze. He wasn't quite close enough to her to disarm her. Nor did he doubt she would shoot him. Something in her eyes.

"Where is TJ?"

"You'll see soon enough," Ester said. "Close the

door. You'll have to pay for that window you broke."
She leveled the gun at him. "Unless you're dead too."

TJ HAD HEARD Silas calling for her. Fear gripped her for
a moment as tears blurred her eyes. Ester had taken her
gun when she'd gone upstairs. The woman didn't look
like someone who would carry one—let alone use it.

And that could be Silas's fatal mistake. TJ had
certainly underestimated the woman. She wouldn't
make that mistake again, but Silas might not get a second chance. I might not either, she thought, her heart
pounding.

She heard nothing from upstairs. No gunshot. Ester
hadn't killed him. Yet. She waited a moment as if expecting to hear a gunshot and praying she wouldn't.

Then she went to work on the ropes on her wrists
again. Now she worked even more frantically, feeling
as if time was running out. As she worked, she listened.
Earlier, she'd heard someone ring the doorbell numerous times and then the loud knock; she should have
known it was Silas. Of course he would come looking
for her. The sound of breaking glass had startled her
as well as Ester.

What terrified her was that Ester seemed to know
that she would never get away with this. She didn't
seem to care. It was as if this was something she'd decided to do before she died. Ester was determined to
see this through even though it made little sense.

But TJ had seen the anger that had been apparent
in the letters. Ester was furious with herself, with the
world. And TJ had become the object of that anger.

The tape gave. She shoved it away, aware of the pain
in her shoulder. Her arms were scraped and bleeding,

her wrists aching from being taped up for so long behind her. But she barely noticed.

Tearing off the gag, she thought about calling to Silas to warn him, but realized that might put him in more jeopardy. But what if he believed Ester when she said that she wasn't here? What if he left?

Instead, she hurriedly untied her ankles and got to her feet, blood rushing into her extremities as she looked around for a weapon before she started up the stairs at a run.

SILAS COULD SEE that Ester seemed out of breath, but she still held the gun in her hand plenty steady enough to kill him. He'd complicated whatever plan she'd had and he knew it. But he could see the wheels in her head turning as she motioned for him to lead the way down the hallway.

"Where are we headed?" he asked, walking slowly. He could feel her behind him, intent on keeping that gun leveled at the middle of him.

"Don't worry about it," she snapped. "Just keep walking a little farther."

Ahead he could see a door on his left and an opening into the kitchen off to his right. The tension in the air was thick as salami. Ester was in planning mode and that was making him very nervous.

He was almost to the door on the left when he heard footfalls. It dawned on him that someone was running upstairs from the basement about the time the door was flung open. TJ came bursting through it.

Silas only had a second to decide what to do. He spun around, bringing up a foot. Ester had been distracted for only a moment, but it was long enough that she hadn't gotten a shot off. He kicked at the gun in her hand, but the woman must have had a death grip on it. All he accomplished was shoving the gun off to the side.

The report of the shot was deafening in the small hallway. Sheetrock exploded on the wall to the right, sending a cloud of chalky dust into the air. Silas rushed Ester, but not before she fired again. She was already swinging the gun back in his and TJ's direction when it went off.

He grabbed the woman's arm, heard her cry out as he wrenched it hard enough to take the gun from her bony fingers. She attacked him with her hands, flying at him. For her age, she was much stronger than he'd expected. With the gun still in his hand it was hard to wrestle her into compliance. He finally shoved her face-first into the wall and held her there as he pocketed the gun.

He realized he hadn't heard a sound out of TJ. Turning to look, at first all he saw was the open basement door. Past it was a bare foot, the high heel shoe she'd been wearing lying next to it.

"TJ?"

No answer.

He fought to move the struggling Ester along the wall so he could see TJ. Reaching the door, he slammed it closed. Sitting in the hallway staring was the woman he'd fallen in love with even before he'd met her. She had a hand over her side, blood leaking from between her fingers.

"TJ!" he cried, giving up on trying to hold Ester. He opened the basement door and put her down on the first step before closing the door and locking it. Then he dropped beside TJ and tried to call 911 at the same time as he worked to stanch the bleeding. "You're going to be all right," he kept saying, praying it would be true. "You're going to be all right."

He held her as the sound of sirens filled the air.

Chapter Twenty-One

TJ remembered little after she was shot other than being in Silas's arms and then holding his hand in the ambulance. It had all seemed like a bad dream. Or an ending to one of her books. The scream of the sirens. The blood. The feeling that it was over and yet not knowing if everyone would get out alive.

She vaguely remembered seeing her sisters as she was being wheeled down to surgery. They were both crying. Chloe telling her not to die. Annabelle saying something about Christmas. And Silas standing at the end of the hall, his face a mask of pain and worry. The rest was a blur of dreams and waking up in the middle of the night to see a nurse bending over her.

"It's all right," one nurse had said when TJ had been startled by her, making one of the machines go off. "You're safe here. It's all right."

She was in and out of consciousness so much that she hadn't known what was real and what wasn't. At one point there was a doctor standing over her. He was talking to someone. Silas. She'd felt his hand take hers and when she woke again it was still dark and she could hear Chloe arguing with the nurse outside her door.

Or maybe she'd dreamed it all. When she finally did

surface in the daylight, TJ thought all of it had been a bad dream. But she was groggy from the drugs, lying in a hospital bed, so she knew that at least getting shot had been real.

Silas sat beside her bed—just as she had sat beside his. He rose when he saw she was awake. "How are you?"

She tried to speak but her mouth was so dry. He poured her some water and helped her with the straw. The doctor came in then and told Silas he needed to check his patient.

"I'll be right outside in the hallway," Silas said, and left.

"You were lucky, young lady," the doctor said after checking her wound. "I was able to get the bullet out. No major organs were involved. It should heal nicely. Any questions?"

She shook her head because she had way too many questions. Some of her ordeal had come back, but the last part had happened so quickly...

The doctor hadn't been gone long when her sisters came in. She heard the nurse warn them that they couldn't stay long. One on each side of the bed, they looked at her with concern.

"I'm fine," she said, the words coming out in a hoarse whisper.

"That crazy old woman," Chloe said. "Who would have thought she was the one?"

"As mean as she was to me in English class?" Annabelle said. "I was scared of her."

"She was sick," TJ managed to say.

"Aren't they all," Chloe said. "She could have killed

you. Almost did. If Silas…" She seemed to catch herself. "But you're safe here and it's all behind you."

"The doctor said you might be out before Christmas," Annabelle said. "But if you aren't, we're going to hold Christmas until you are."

"She doesn't care about Christmas right now," Chloe scolded their youngest sister. "Look at her. She's drugged up and probably in pain. Are you in pain?"

TJ was, but she shook her head anyway.

"If you're in pain, you just push this button," Annabelle said. "They told you that, right?"

Maybe they had. TJ couldn't remember. She struggled to keep her eyes open.

"Okay, that's long enough," a female nurse said from the doorway, and her sisters were shooed out.

TJ closed her eyes. A few moments later she heard the door to her room open and close softly. She knew who it was before he took her hand. She kept her eyes closed, feeling herself drawn back into the darkness. With her hand in his, she slept.

THE DOCTOR FINALLY insisted Silas go home and get some sleep. He knew he needed a shower, a shave and clean clothes. He also needed sleep. He hadn't had much since the dance.

But when he closed his eyes, he kept reliving the scene at Ester Brown's house. The sound of the gunfire, seeing that one bare foot and high heel shoe lying next to it. The scene was the kind nightmares were made of.

Even when he told himself that she was going to be all right, he still couldn't sleep. He'd never been so afraid. Even Mad Dog hadn't terrified him the way

Ester had because he'd looked into her eyes and he'd known that she had nothing to lose. She would have killed them both that night. As it was, she'd almost killed TJ.

"So you don't know when you're coming back to the city?" Cal had said when he'd called him.

"No. Honestly, I'm not sure I am. Things are too up in the air right now."

"Are you worried that the cops you fingered will hire someone else to come after you?" his friend had asked.

"No, Kenny 'Mad Dog' Harrington did me a favor," Silas had said with a chuckle. "He taped their conversations, including when my former NYPD partner paid him for his services. Mad Dog wasn't as stupid as they thought he was. He was worried that he'd take care of me and then they would turn on him to insure that he wouldn't rat them out some day when he got picked up for another crime. Mad Dog would have sold them out for a lesser sentence and they knew it. He was right. They would have had him killed to tie up the loose ends."

"Why haven't I heard about these tapes?" Cal asked.

"Could be because he made copies and made sure I had one. He left it for me in my cabin. I didn't see it until after he was dead. Apparently he wanted me to know who'd hired him before he killed me. So now, if they ever make a move on me, the tapes will surface."

"Tapes?"

"He made copies. Now the copies are being held in several safe places as…insurance. There's one on its way to you," Silas said. "My former…associates have been notified. They don't want any more years behind bars, or, in my ex-partner's case, he doesn't want to go straight to prison."

"So," Cal said. "This has to be about a woman."

Silas laughed. "Isn't it always? Only this woman, well, she's a keeper. That is if she'll have me."

THE NEXT TIME TJ WOKE, she found Sheriff McCall Crawford next to her bed. "The doctor said I could ask you some questions if you're up to it."

She nodded. "Ester?" The moment she saw McCall's expression she knew.

"Ester had another stroke," the sheriff said. "She didn't make it."

TJ felt a well of sadness. Yes, the woman had terrorized her and almost killed her, but she felt sorry for her too. "She felt she was never appreciated. She gave up her dream to be a teacher—at least that's the way she saw it."

The sheriff pulled out her notebook and recorder. "Why don't you tell me what happened."

She did, finishing with, "I don't remember all that much after I was shot."

McCall closed her notebook and shut off the recorder. "We found the typewriter and paper downstairs. She was definitely the person who'd been sending you the threatening letters."

TJ nodded. "There were other typewritten papers down there. Is there any chance I could have them?"

The sheriff hesitated. "It would be up to her relatives. I've been trying to find out if there are any. So far I've had no luck."

"What Ester wanted more than anything was to publish," TJ said. "I don't know if she even finished the book she was working on, but if there is any way it is publishable… I'd like to do that for her."

McCall smiled. "I'll make sure you get whatever there is."

Chapter Twenty-Two

TJ made it home for Christmas. She was still sore and had been forced to assure the doctor that she would take it easy. But Christmas Eve she was with family. Annabelle had always been like a kid in a candy store at Christmas. She'd baked and her future mother-in-law had brought over more food than they could eat in a month.

"Willie's teaching me to cook," Annabelle had said. "But we both think I have a way to go before I serve it to humans. The pigs out at the ranch love my cooking though," she added, making them laugh.

"Wait," TJ said as she remembered. "Belle, you were going to get married on Christmas!"

Her sister shook her head. "It just didn't work out. I couldn't get married without you there."

"I don't want to be the reason you didn't get married," she said. "I know how anxious you and Dawson are to tie the knot."

"It's not that big of a deal. We're thinking New Year's Day. It's just going to be a few people, nothing extravagant. Willie is insistent that it be held at the ranch and we let her take care of everything. I have the coolest mother-in-law-to-be ever." They agreed she did.

They ate, opened presents and sat around talking. TJ hated the months they'd been estranged and swore she was never going to let it happen again. "I wish Grandmother was here."

"Me too. I would love to ask her some questions," Annabelle said.

Chloe got up to adjust one of the ornaments on the tree. "It just goes to show that you never really know a person. Grandmother. Ester. Who knows what secrets everyone in this town has?"

"You're talking about how I make a living," TJ said. "If you assume everyone has a secret, well, it makes a good story."

"Have you read Ester's novel?" Chloe asked.

She nodded. "The sheriff said that no relatives have come forward. Once Ester's estate is settled, I'm going to self-publish it under her name."

"Is it any good?" Annabelle asked.

TJ hesitated, making Chloe laugh.

"You can tell us if it's awful," her sister said.

"After all, she tried to kill you," Annabelle added, and was quickly chastised by Chloe for bringing that up on Christmas Eve. "Come on, it's like the elephant in the room. If it hadn't been for Silas, TJ would be—"

"The book isn't very good, but it was Ester's first," TJ interrupted.

"And last," Chloe said.

She nodded. "I know it probably seems silly to publish it."

"No," Annabelle said. "It's sweet and more than the old bat deserves." She mugged a face at Chloe.

"So does this mean you're ready to go back to writing soon?" Chloe asked her.

"In a while."

Annabelle grinned. "She has other things on her mind."

"Speaking of Silas," Chloe said. "I hope the two of you are going to give it some time before you do anything rash."

TJ laughed. "Anything rash?"

"Leave her alone," Annabelle said. "Let her do whatever she wants to. It's her life and Silas is…"

"At the door," TJ said after there was a knock and he put his head in.

"I don't want to interrupt."

"You're not," Annabelle said, getting to her feet and motioning for Chloe to do the same. "We were just leaving." She ushered Chloe up the stairs, the two arguing all the way.

"I didn't mean to run them off," Silas said.

"It's fine. We just finished opening our presents. The two of them were starting to argue over me."

"Good thing I showed up, then," he said with a grin. "How are you?"

"Still sore, but the doctor said I am healing well."

"What about mentally? You've been through some traumatic holidays," he reminded her.

As if she needed to be reminded. "It hasn't been dull, that's for sure. But there won't be any more True Fan letters. There's no reason I can't get back to work. I have a deadline looming… What about you?"

Silas sat down across from her and took both of her hands in his. "Are you well enough that you still want to come up to the cabin with me?"

She smiled. "It's just what I need. *You're* just what I need. That and your homemade bread."

"You've got it. I'll pick you up tomorrow. Say, nine? Will your sisters be all right with it?"

"I don't need their permission."

"How about their blessing?" he asked. "I want them to like me because if I have my way…" He shrugged.

"I'll see you in the morning."

She went to the window and waved as he drove away, wondering if she would be able to sleep tonight. She was excited about returning to the cabin, but even more about spending the next few days with him up in the mountains away from everyone.

"You can come back down now," she called up the stairs to her sisters. She knew they hadn't gone far and had been listening to everything she and Silas had said. Annabelle because she was nosy. Chloe because she was worried.

They both came down the stairs, Annabelle all starry-eyed. "He wants us to like him because he's going to ask you to marry him," she said in a sing-song fashion.

"And live in that one-room cabin?" Chloe demanded.

TJ shook her head. "You're both way ahead of yourselves. Slow the roll," she said, something she hadn't said since high school. Both sisters laughed.

"Then why are your cheeks flushed?" Annabelle asked. "You're in love with him and he's crazy about you. Just make sure that you're back for my wedding on New Year's Day."

"I wouldn't miss it for anything," TJ said.

Chapter Twenty-Three

TJ almost didn't recognize Silas. He'd shaved off his beard and trimmed his hair. He no longer looked like a mountain man when he came to pick her up.

"Are you leaving?" she asked, thinking he'd done this because he had been called back to his job in New York City.

He shook his head. "I thought you might want to see what I really looked like."

She laughed, amazed that the man could be even more handsome without the full beard. She reached out and cupped his cheek, his strong jaw covered in designer stubble. "I'd take you either way."

He grinned as he stepped closer. "That's what I wanted to hear." He pulled her to him. "Ready to spend a few days at the cabin?"

TJ had never been more ready for anything. Silas drove through the snowy landscape toward the Little Rockies. It was one of those incredible winter days in Montana, not a cloud in a robin-egg blue sky, the sun making the new snow shine like fields of diamonds.

She felt herself relax. She'd come home to hide out from True Fan and make up with her sisters. Instead True Fan had been here waiting for her. The sheriff had told her that Ester used former students who'd moved away to mail the letters for her, including one now living in New York City.

"I suspect she was the one who took the photograph of your apartment," McCall had told her. "They just thought Ester was a fan."

She felt only sadness when she thought of Mrs. Brown. All those years when Ester was teaching, she had yearned to write, not realizing the only thing that had held her back was her own fear, her own misgivings about her talent.

"It is so heartbreaking," she'd said. "And yet what I told her was true. She helped me become a writer. She felt she'd wasted her life and it just wasn't true. I'm just sorry that I never thanked her for what she did do for me. Not until it was too late."

"But you got to tell her," McCall had said. "I'm thankful it ended without either of you being killed. The doctor said a lot of her behavior was due to the strokes she'd been having for some time. I don't think she realized what she was doing."

TJ looked out at the passing snowy foothills and reminded herself that it was over. She'd had a wonderful Christmas and felt closer to her sisters than she had in years. Glancing at Silas, she had to smile to herself. Annabelle was right. She was in love.

"I don't think I'm going back to New York," he said, and glanced over at her. "I don't need the job financially or emotionally or mentally. To tell you the truth I don't want to leave Montana."

She chuckled, as she'd been thinking the same thing since her return. "I love being here. And as you said, I can write anywhere. I was thinking earlier that I would let my New York apartment go. Chloe will be going back home to work and Annabelle will be getting married New Year's Day and moving in with Dawson, so the house will be empty. There's no reason I can't stay."

He grinned over at her. "I can't tell you how much I was hoping you would say that." He sounded relieved. "I want to spend as much time as I can at the cabin, but eventually either build a larger place or buy one."

"You wouldn't sell the cabin though, right?" she asked.

"No. Never. It's even more special to me since I got to share it with you."

As Silas pulled up in front of the cabin, she saw that the woodstove was going. Smoke curled up into the snow-filled pines. She couldn't wait to get inside, but he had other plans. As she started to open her pickup door, he stopped her.

"There's something I want to do first," he said, and reached into the pocket of his sheepskin coat to pull out a small jewelry box.

TJ felt her heart leap as she looked from it to his blue-eyed gaze.

"I know this is silly, but once we get into that cabin with that bed right at the center of the room, I'm going to want to make love to you. And maybe it's old-fashioned, but I want to do this right." He shifted in the seat and found a way even in the cab of the pickup to get down on one knee.

Sunlight poured through the window. Outside the fresh snow gleamed. In the warm cab of the pickup, Silas said, "Tessa Jane Clementine, will you marry me?"

She broke into a wide smile as tears filled her eyes. "Yes. Oh yes."

Silas slipped the ring on her finger. The pear-shaped diamond shone like the snow outside the windows. The ring fit perfectly.

TJ threw herself into his arms. The kiss was a promise of what was to come. Years cuddled up in that cabin. Late-night card games. Homemade baked bread. Best friends forever.

But for tonight, all TJ wanted was to spend it in this man's arms listening to the wind in the tall pines and the crackle of the fire in the woodstove. She was home.

SILAS FELT LIKE a man who'd won the lottery. He turned off the pickup engine, ran around and pulled TJ out and into his arms.

"I believe you're supposed to do this *after* we're married," she said, laughing as he carried her up the porch steps and over the threshold into the cabin.

"I feel as if our lives are starting now," he said as he put her down. He looked into her blue eyes. "Beautiful and smart and talented. How did I get so lucky?"

"You liked my books."

He laughed. "But nothing like I like their author." He kissed her, pulling her close. Outside, snow crystals danced in the air against the big sky. Inside, the woodstove crackled and popped invitingly. "How soon can we get married?"

She looked up at him in surprise. "As soon as we can find a preacher."

"I love you," he said, his gaze locked with hers. "I think I left that out earlier. Also I forgot to ask you how you feel about kids."

"I'm for them," she said. "Two, three…"

"Four, five…" He laughed, still feeling as if he needed to pinch himself. "Tell me this isn't a dream."

"If it is, I don't want to wake up," she said. "I love you, Silas Walker. I know this happened fast. But I know it's right."

"I've never been this sure of anything." He kissed her, determined to find a preacher soon and make her his wife.

* * * * *

SPECIAL EXCERPT FROM

HQN™

*When wealthy cattleman Callen Laramie is called
back home to Coldwater, Texas, for a
Christmas wedding, he has no idea just how much
his attendance will matter to his family...
and to the woman who's never been far from
his thoughts—or his heart.*

Read on for a sneak preview of
Lone Star Christmas
by USA TODAY *bestselling author*
Delores Fossen.

CHAPTER ONE

DEAD STUFFED THINGS just didn't scream Christmas wedding invitation for Callen Laramie. Even when the dead stuffed thing—an armadillo named Billy—was draped with gold tinsel, a bridal veil and was holding a bouquet of what appeared to be tiny poinsettias in his little armadillo hands.

Then again, when the bride-to-be, Rosy Muldoon, was a taxidermist, Callen supposed a photo like that hit the more normal range of possibilities for invitation choices.

Well, normal-ish anyway.

No one had ever accused Rosy of being conventional, and even though he hadn't seen her in close to fourteen years, Billy's bridal picture was proof that her nonnormalcy hadn't changed during that time.

Dragging in a long breath that Callen figured he might need, he opened the invitation. What was printed inside wasn't completely unexpected, not really, but he was glad he'd taken that breath. Like most invitations, it meant he'd have to do something, and doing something like this often meant trudging through the past.

Y'all are invited to the wedding of Buck McCall and Rosy Muldoon. Christmas Eve at Noon in the Lightning Bug Inn on Main Street, Coldwater, Texas. Reception to follow.

So, Buck had finally popped the question, and Rosy had accepted. Again, no surprise. Not on the surface anyway, since Buck had started "courting" Rosy several years after both of them had lost their spouses about a decade and a half ago.

But Callen still got a bad feeling about this.

The bad feeling went up a notch when he saw that the printed RSVP at the bottom had been lined through and the words handwritten there. "Please come. Buck needs to see you. Rosy."

Yes, this would require him to do something.

She'd underlined the *please* and the *needs*, and it was just as effective as a heavyweight's punch to Callen's gut. One that knocked him into a time machine and took him back eighteen years. To that time when he'd first laid eyes on Buck and then on Rosy shortly thereafter.

Oh man.

Callen had just turned fourteen, and the raw anger and bad memories had been eating holes in him. Sometimes, they still did. Buck had helped with that. Heck, maybe Rosy had, too, but the four mostly good years he'd spent with Buck couldn't erase the fourteen awful ones that came before them.

He dropped the invitation back on his desk and steeled himself up when he heard the woodpecker taps of high heels coming toward his office. Several taps later, his assistant, Havana Mayfield, stuck her head in the open doorway.

Today, her hair was pumpkin orange with streaks

of golden brown, the color of a roasted turkey. Probably to coordinate with Thanksgiving, since it'd been just the day before.

Callen wasn't sure what coordination goal Havana had been going for with the lime-green pants and top or the lipstick-red stilettos, but as he had done with Rosy and just about everyone else from his past, he'd long since given up trying to figure out his assistant's life choices. Havana was an efficient workaholic, like him, which meant he overlooked her wardrobe, her biting sarcasm and the occasional judgmental observations about him—even if they weren't any of her business.

"Your two o'clock is here," Havana said, setting some contracts and more mail in his inbox. Then she promptly took the stack from his outbox. "George Niedermeyer," she added, and bobbled her eyebrows. "He brought his mother with him. She wants to tell you about her granddaughter, the lawyer."

Great.

Callen silently groaned. George was in his sixties and was looking for a good deal on some Angus. Which Callen could and would give him. George's mother, Myrtle, was nearing ninety, and despite her advanced age, she was someone Callen would classify as a woman with too much time on her hands. Myrtle would try to do some matchmaking with her lawyer granddaughter, gossip about things that Callen didn't want to hear and prolong what should be a half-hour meeting into an hour or more.

"Myrtle said you're better looking than a litter of fat spotted pups," Havana added, clearly enjoying this. "That's what you get for being a hotshot cattle broker with a pretty face." She poked her tongue against her cheek. "Women just can't resist you and want to spend time with you. The older ones want to fix you up with their offspring."

"You've had no trouble resisting," he pointed out—though he'd never made a play for her. And wouldn't. Havana and anyone else who worked for him was genderless as far as Callen was concerned.

"Because I know the depths of your cold, cold heart. Plus, you pay me too much to screw this up for sex with a hotshot cattle broker with a pretty face."

Callen didn't even waste a glare on that. The *pretty face* was questionable, but he was indeed a hotshot cattle broker. That wasn't ego. He had the bank account, the inventory and the willing buyers to prove it.

Head 'em up, move 'em out.

Callen had built Laramie Cattle on that motto. That and plenty of ninety-hour workweeks. And since his business wasn't broke, it didn't require fixing. Even if it would mean having to listen to Myrtle for the next hour.

"What the heck is that?" Havana asked, tipping her head to his desk.

Callen followed her gaze to the invitation. "Billy, the Armadillo. Years ago, he was roadkill."

Every part of Havana's face went aghast. "Ewww."

He agreed, even though he would have gone for something more manly sounding, like maybe a grunt. "The bride's a taxidermist," he added. Along with being Buck's housekeeper and cook.

Still in the aghast mode, Havana shifted the files to her left arm so she could pick up the invitation and open it. He pushed away another greasy smear of those old memories while she read it.

"Buck McCall," Havana muttered when she'd finished.

She didn't ask who he was. No need. Havana had sent Buck Christmas gifts during the six years that she'd worked for Callen. Considering those were the only personal gifts he'd ever asked her to buy and send to anyone, she knew who Buck was. Or rather she knew that he was important to Callen.

Of course, that "important" label needed to be judged on a curve because Callen hadn't actually visited Buck or gone back to Coldwater since he'd hightailed it out of there on his eighteenth birthday. Now he was here in Dallas, nearly three hundred miles away, and sometimes it still didn't feel nearly far enough. There were times when the moon would have been too close.

Havana just kept on staring at him, maybe waiting for him to bare his soul or something. He wouldn't. No reason for it, either. Because she was smart and efficient, she had almost certainly done internet searches on Buck. There were plenty of articles about him being a foster father.

Correction: the hotshot of foster fathers.

It wouldn't have taken much for Havana to piece together that Buck had fostered not only Callen but his three brothers, as well. Hell, for that matter Havana could have pieced together the rest, too. The bad stuff that'd happened before Callen and his brothers had gotten to Buck's. Too much for him to stay, though his brothers had had no trouble putting down those proverbial roots in Coldwater.

"Christmas Eve, huh?" Havana questioned. "You've already got plans to go to that ski lodge in Aspen with a couple of your clients. Heck, you scheduled a business meeting for Christmas morning, one that you insisted I attend. Say, is Bah Humbug your middle name?"

"The meeting will finish in plenty of time for you to get in some skiing and spend your Christmas bonus," he grumbled. Then he rethought that. "Do you ski?"

She lifted her shoulder. "No, but there are worse things than sitting around a lodge during the holidays while the interest on my bonus accumulates in my investment account."

Yes, there were worse things. And Callen had some firsthand experience with that.

"Are you actually thinking about going back to Coldwater for this wedding?" Havana pressed.

"No." But he was sure thinking about the wedding itself and that note Rosy had added to the invitation.

Please.

That wasn't a good word to have repeating in his head.

Havana shrugged and dropped the invitation back on his desk. "Want me to send them a wedding gift? Maybe they've registered on the Taxidermists-R-Us site." Her tongue went in her cheek again.

Callen wasted another glare on her and shook his head. "I'll take care of it. I'll send them something."

She staggered back, pressed her folder-filled hand to her chest. "I think the earth just tilted on its axis. Or maybe that was hell freezing over." Havana paused, looked at him. "Is something wrong?" she came out and asked, her tone no longer drenched with sarcasm.

Callen dismissed it by motioning toward the door. "Tell the Niedermeyers that I need a few minutes. I have to do something first."

As expected, that caused Havana to raise an eyebrow again, and before she left, Callen didn't bother to tell her that her concern wasn't warranted. He could clear this up with a phone call and get back to work.

But who should he call?

Buck was out because if there was actually something wrong, then his former foster father would be at the center of it. That *Please come. Buck needs to see you* clued him into that.

He scrolled through his contacts, one by one. He no longer had close friends in Coldwater, but every now and then he ran into someone in his business circles who passed along some of that gossip he didn't want to hear. So the most obvious contacts were his brothers.

Kace, the oldest, was the town's sheriff. Callen dismissed talking to him because the last time they'd spoken—four or five years ago—Kace had tried to lecture Callen about cutting himself off from the family. Damn right, he'd cut himself off, and since he would continue to do that and hated lectures from big brothers, he went to the next one.

Judd. Another big brother who was only a year older than Callen. Judd had been a cop in Austin. Or maybe San Antonio. He was a deputy now in Coldwater, but not once had he ever bitched about Callen leaving the "fold." He kept Judd as a possibility for the call he needed to make and continued down the very short list to consider the rest of his choices.

Nico. The youngest brother, who Callen almost immediately discounted. He was on the rodeo circuit—a bull rider of all things—and was gone a lot. He might not have a clue if something was wrong.

Callen got to Rosy's name next. The only reason she was in his contacts was because Buck had wanted him to have her number in case there was an emergency. A *please* on a wedding invitation probably didn't qualify as one, but since he hated eating up time by waffling,

Callen pressed her number. After a couple of rings, he got her voice mail.

"Knock knock," Rosy's perky voice greeted, and she giggled like a loon. "Who's there? Well, obviously not me, and since Billy can't answer the phone, ha ha, you gotta leave me a message. Talk sweet to me, and I'll talk sweet back." More giggling as if it were a fine joke.

Callen didn't leave a message because a) he wanted an answer now and b) he didn't want anyone interrupting his day by calling him back.

He scrolled back through the contacts and pressed Judd's number. Last he'd heard, Judd had moved into the cabin right next to Buck's house, so he would know what was going on.

"Yes, it came from a chicken's butt," Judd growled the moment he answered. "Now, get over it and pick it up."

In the background Callen thought he heard someone make an *ewww* sound eerily similar to the one Havana had made earlier. Since a chicken's butt didn't have anything to do with a phone call or wedding invitation, it made Callen think his brother wasn't talking to him.

"What the heck do you want?" Judd growled that, too, and this time Callen did believe he was on the receiving end of the question.

The bad grouchy attitude didn't bother Callen because he thought it might speed along the conversation. Maybe. Judd didn't like long personal chats, which explained why they rarely talked.

"Can somebody else gather the eggs?" a girl asked. Callen suspected it might be the same one who'd ewww'ed. Her voice was high-pitched and whiny. "These have poop on them."

"This is a working ranch," Judd barked. "There's

poop everywhere. If you've got a gripe with your chores, talk to Buck or Rosy."

"They're not here," the whiner whined.

"There's Shelby," Judd countered. "Tell her all about it and quit bellyaching to me."

Just like that, Callen got another ass-first knock back into the time machine. Shelby McCall. Buck's daughter. And the cause of nearly every lustful thought that Callen had had from age fifteen all the way through to age eighteen.

Plenty of ones afterward, too.

Forbidden fruit could do that to a teenager, and as Buck's daughter, Shelby had been as forbidden as it got. Callen remembered that Buck had had plenty of rules, but at the top of the list was one he gave to the boys he fostered. *Touch Shelby, and I'll castrate you.* It had been simple and extremely effective.

"Buck got a new batch of foster kids," Judd went on, and again, Callen thought that part of the conversation was meant for him. "I just finished a double shift, and I'm trying to get inside my house so I can sleep, but I keep getting bothered. What do you want?" he tacked onto that mini-rant.

"I got Buck and Rosy's wedding invitation," Callen threw out there.

"Yeah. Buck popped the question a couple of weeks ago, and they're throwing together this big wedding deal for Christmas Eve. They're inviting all the kids Buck has ever fostered. All of them," Judd emphasized. "So, no, you're not special and didn't get singled out because you're a stinkin' rich prodigal son. *All of them,*" he repeated.

Judd sounded as pleased about that as Callen would

have been had he still been living there. He had no idea why someone would want to take that kind of step back into the past. It didn't matter that Buck had been good to them. The only one who had been. It was that being there brought back all the stuff that'd happened before they'd made it to Buck.

"Is Buck okay?" Callen asked.

"Of course he is," Judd snapped. Then he paused. "Why wouldn't he be? Just gather the blasted eggs!" he added onto that after another whiny *ewww.* "Why wouldn't Buck be okay?"

Callen didn't want to explain the punch-in-the-gut feeling he'd gotten with Rosy's *Please come. Buck needs to see you,* and it turned out that he didn't have to explain it.

"Here's Shelby, thank God," Judd grumbled before Callen had to come up with anything. "She'll answer any questions you have about the wedding. It's Callen," he said to Shelby. "Just leave my phone on the porch when you're done."

"No!" Callen couldn't say it fast enough. "That's all right. I was just—"

"Callen," Shelby greeted.

Apparently, his lustful thoughts weren't a thing of the past after all. Even though Shelby was definitely a woman now, she could still purr his name.

He got a flash image of her face. Okay, of her body, too. All willowy and soft with that tumble of blond hair and clear green eyes. And her mouth. Oh man. That mouth had always had his number.

"I didn't expect you to be at Judd's," he said, not actually fishing for information. But he was. He was also trying to fight back what appeared to be jealousy. It was something he didn't feel very often.

"Oh, I'm not. I was over here at Dad's, taking care of a few things while he's at an appointment. He got some new foster kids in, and when I heard the discussion about eggs, I came outside. That's when Judd handed me his phone and said I had to talk to you. You got the wedding invitation?" she asked.

"I did." He left it at that, hoping she'd fill in the blanks of the questions he wasn't sure how to ask.

"We couldn't change Rosy's mind about using that picture of Billy in the veil. Trust me, we tried."

Callen found himself smiling. A bad combination when mixed with arousal. Still, he could push it aside, and he did that by glancing around his office. He had every nonsexual thing he wanted here, and if he wanted sex, there were far less complicated ways than going after Shelby. Buck probably still owned at least one good castrating knife.

"I called Rosy, but she didn't answer," Callen explained.

"She's in town but should be back soon. She doesn't answer her phone if she's driving."

Callen couldn't decide if that was a good or bad thing on a personal level for him. If Rosy had answered, then he wouldn't be talking to Shelby right now. He wouldn't feel the need for a cold shower or an explanation.

"Rosy should be back any minute now. You want me to have her call you?" Shelby asked.

"No. I just wanted to tell them best wishes for the wedding. I'll send a gift and a card." And he'd write a personal note to Buck.

"You're not coming?" Shelby said.

Best to do this fast and efficient. "No. I have plans. Business plans. A trip. I'll be out of the state." And he cursed himself for having to justify himself to a woman who could lead to castration.

"Oh."

That was it. Two letters of the alphabet. One word. But it was practically drowning in emotion. Exactly what specific emotion, Callen didn't know, but that gut-punch feeling went at him again hard and fast.

"Shelby?" someone called out. It sounded like the whiny girl. "Never mind. Here comes Miss Rosy."

"I guess it's an important business trip?" Shelby continued, her voice a whisper now.

"Yes, longtime clients. I do this trip with them every year—"

"Callen, you need to come," Shelby interrupted. "Soon," she added. "It's bad news."

Don't miss
Lone Star Christmas *by Delores Fossen,*
available now wherever
HQN Books and ebooks are sold.

www.HQNBooks.com

HUNTING DOWN THE HORSEMAN

I always wanted a sister,
but my mother didn't cooperate. So I'm not sure
how it was that I came to write a book about sisters.
But I did. Fortunately, I have two women in my life
who have been like sisters—sisters-in-law who
also became good friends. That's why this book is
dedicated to Frances Demarais and Annie Rissman
for being the sisters I never had.

Chapter One

According to the legend, the town of Lost Creek is cursed. Only a few buildings remain along the shore of the Missouri River in an isolated part of Montana.

The story told over the years is that a band of outlaws rode into the fledgling town and killed a mother and child, while the rest of the residents watched from a safe distance.

When the husband returned, he found his wife lying dead in the dirt street, his child and her doll lying next to her, and the townspeople still hiding from the outlaws.

He picked up his daughter's doll from the dirt and swore revenge on the townspeople.

One by one, residents began to find a small cloth doll on their doorsteps—and then they'd die. According to one story, the rest of the townspeople fled for their lives.

But another story tells of a pile of bones found at the bottom of a cave years later. Men, women and children's bones—the residents of Lost Creek and evidence of a story of true retribution.

THE SUN SINKING into the Little Rockies, Jud Corbett spurred his horse as he raced through the narrow canyon. Behind him he could hear the thunder of horses growing louder. The marshal star he wore on his leather vest caught the light as the canyon heat rose in waves, making the towering rock walls shimmer. Sweat trickled down his back. His mouth went dry.

Just a little farther.

His horse stumbled as he rounded the last bend and almost went down. He'd lost precious seconds. The riders were close behind him. If his horse had fallen...

His gray Stetson pulled down low over his dark hair, he burst from the canyon. On the horizon, the ghost town of Lost Creek wavered like a mirage under the cloudless blue of Montana's big sky.

Jud felt his heart leap as he spurred his horse to even more speed, adrenaline coursing through his veins.

Almost there.

The loud report of a rifle shot punctuated the air. Jud grabbed his side, doubling over and grimacing with pain. The second shot caught him in the back.

Tumbling headlong from his horse, he hit the ground in a cloud of dust.

"Cut! That's a wrap."

FROM THE SIDELINES, assistant director Nancy Davis watched Jud Corbett get up grinning to retrieve his Stetson from the dirt.

"He's such a showoff," stuntwoman Brooke Keith said beside her, her tone a mixture of envy and awe.

"The man just loves his work," Nancy said, cutting her gaze to the stuntwoman and body double.

That got a chuckle from Brooke. "Kind of like the way the leading lady just likes to be *friendly.*"

Nancy watched as Chantal Lee sauntered over to Jud and, standing on tiptoes, whispered something in his ear. Jud let loose that famous grin of his as Chantal brushed her lips against the stuntman's suntanned cheek before she sauntered away, her hips swaying provocatively.

"Easy," Nancy warned.

"Easy is exactly what she is," Brooke said with obvious disgust as she walked off toward Jud.

Jud Corbett was shaking his head in obvious amusement at Chantal. Whatever she'd offered him, he wasn't taking the bait.

As Brooke joined Jud, Nancy couldn't help the sliver of worry that wedged itself just under her skin. All she needed was Chantal and Brooke at each other's throats. There was enough animosity between them as it was. She'd have to talk to Chantal and tell her to tone it down.

As for Brooke… Nancy watched the stuntwoman sidle up to Jud and knew the signs only too well. A catfight was brewing, and Jud was about to be caught right in the middle. Nancy wondered if he realized yet what a dangerous position he was in.

"NICE STUNT," BROOKE said with an edge to her voice as she handed Jud a bottle of water.

"Thanks," he said and took a long drink. "But you could have done that stunt blindfolded."

She smiled at that, but the smile never reached her eyes. "I was referring to Chantal's stunt."

"I hadn't noticed." He'd noticed, though he certainly hadn't taken it seriously. Chantal liked to stir things up.

Brooke chuckled. "You noticed."

"Good thing I never date women I work with while on a film."

Brooke eyed him. "That's your rule?"

"The Corbett Code," Jud said, lifting his right hand as if swearing in.

She laughed. He liked Brooke. He'd worked on a couple of films with her. She was a grown-up tomboy.

Chantal Lee, on the other hand, was a blue-eyed blond beauty, all legs, bulging bosom and flowing golden hair. While Brooke was the perfect stunt double for the star, she dressed in a way that played down her curves. The two could have passed for sisters, but they were as different as sugar and salt.

Brooke was scowling in the direction of Chantal's trailer. "Did you know Chantal demanded another stuntwoman and body double? Zander refused, even though Chantal threatened to break her contract."

That surprised Jud. Not about Chantal, but about director Erik Zander, who had never seemed like a man with much backbone. But if the rumors were true, Zander was betting everything on this film, a Western thriller. Apparently, it was do or die at this point in his career.

According to the rumor mill, the director was in debt up to his eyeballs from legal fees after a young starlet had drowned in his pool and the autopsy showed that the woman was chockfull of drugs—and pregnant with Zander's baby.

He'd managed to keep from getting arrested, but it had cost him not just his small fortune but his fiancée, the daughter of a wealthy film producer. She broke their engagement, and that was the end of her wealthy father backing Zander's films.

Jud paid little attention to rumors but he did have to wonder why Erik Zander had decided to produce and direct *Death at Lost Creek*, given the publicity after the death at his beach house. On top of that, Zander had cast Chantal Lee and Nevada Wells, former lovers who'd just gone through a very nasty public breakup. Jud feared that would be the kiss of the death for this film.

Jud had gotten roped into the job because Zander had made him an offer he couldn't refuse—complete control over all the stunts in the movie as stunt coordinator.

Suddenly Chantal's trailer door slammed open. The star burst from it, clutching something in her hand as she made a beeline for them.

As she drew closer, Jud saw that the star had one of the small rag dolls from the film gripped in her fist. She stalked up to the two of them and thrust the doll into Brooke's face.

"I know you left this on my bed, you bitch!" Chantal screamed. "If I catch you in my trailer again…" She threw the doll at Brooke.

Jud watched Chantal storm away. Everyone in the common area had witnessed the scene but now pretended to go back to what they were doing.

Beside him, Brooke stooped to pick up the doll that had landed at her feet.

Jud saw at once that the doll wasn't one from the prop department. He took the tiny rag doll from her. It was so crudely made that there was something obscene about it.

Brooke wiped her hands down the sides of her jeans as if regretting touching the ugly thing. "I didn't put that on her bed." She sounded confused and maybe a little scared.

"You're not buying into that local legend," he said with a chuckle. "Not you."

She smiled at that but still appeared upset. According to the script for *Death at Lost Creek* and local legend, the recipient of one of these dolls was either about to have some really bad luck, or die.

"I'll take that," Nancy snapped as she came up to them and held out her hand.

Jud dropped the tiny rag doll into it. From the look on the assistant director's face she was not amused. But then Jud didn't think he'd seen her smile since he'd gotten to the set.

"I can't wait until this is over," Brooke said, her voice breaking after Nancy walked away. "I hate this place."

He'd heard the crew complaining about the isolation since the closest town was Whitehorse, Montana, which rolled up its sidewalks by eight o'clock every night.

But Jud suspected it was the script—not the location—that was really getting to them. Their trailers were circled like wagon trains, one circle for the crew, another for the upper echelon in what was called the base camp.

Not far from the circled RVs was the catering tent and beyond it was the false fronts and main street depicting the infamous town of Lost Creek.

But it was the real town of Lost Creek farther down the canyon that had everyone spooked. Now a ghost town deep in the badlands of the Missouri Breaks, with its history it was a real-life horror story.

All that was left of the town were a few rotting wooden buildings along the creek and the Missouri

River. The town, like so many others, had been started by settlers coming by riverboats up the wide Missouri to settle Montana.

The wild, isolated country itself was difficult enough for the settlers. The river had cut thousands of deep ravines into the expanse, leaving behind outcroppings of rocks and scrub pine and hidden canyons where a person could get lost forever. Some had.

But even more dangerous were the outlaws who hid in the badlands of the Breaks and attacked the riverboats—and the towns. Lost Creek had been one of those towns.

"I have to get away from here for a while," Brooke said suddenly. "Are you going into town tonight?"

"Sorry, I've been summoned to a family dinner at the ranch. Which means something is up, or I'd ask you to come along."

"That's right, your family lives near here now. Trails West Ranch, right?"

He nodded, wondering how she knew that. But it wasn't exactly a secret given who his father was. Grayson Corbett had graced the cover of several national magazines for his work with conservation easements both in Texas and Montana.

"I'm dreading dinner tonight," Jud admitted. He had been ever since he'd gotten the call from his father's new wife, Kate. That in itself didn't bode well. Normally Grayson would have called his son himself. Clearly Kate had extended the invitation to make it harder for Jud to decline.

"Family," Brooke said. "That's all there is, huh."

"Are you sure you're all right?"

She smiled. "I'm fine. You're a nice man, Jud Corbett, but don't worry, I won't let it get around."

He watched her walk away, strangely uneasy. He'd worked with Brooke before. She was a beautiful, talented woman with a core of steel—much like Chantal. She didn't scare easily. He suspected whatever was bothering her had nothing to do with a silly rag doll or the horror stories that went with it.

BABY SHOWERS WERE enough to make any twentysomething female nervous. For Faith Bailey it was pure torture. But she had no choice.

This was a joint shower for the very pregnant Cavanaugh sisters, who Faith had grown up with.

Laci Cavanaugh had married Bridger Duvall, and the two owned the Northern Lights Restaurant in downtown Whitehorse. Laney Cavanaugh had married Deputy Sheriff Nick Giovanni, and they had built a home near Old Town Whitehorse, where the girls' grandparents lived. Both sisters were due any day now—and looked it.

The shower was being held at the Bailey Ranch in Old Town Whitehorse, the only place Faith had ever considered home in her twenty-six years. Another reason Faith had to be here.

But as she sat in her own ranch house living room, she couldn't help feeling out of place. Almost all of her close friends were married now, except for Georgia Michaels, who owned the knitting shop in town, In Stitches. And everyone knew what followed marriage: a baby carriage.

"Can you believe this population explosion?" her friend Georgia whispered. On the other side of Georgia, their good friend Rory Buchanan Barrow was fighting morning sickness even though it was afternoon.

When they were all kids, growing up in this isolated part of Montana, they'd all vowed not to get married until they were at least thirty-five, and none of them was going to stick around Whitehorse. Instead, they'd sworn they would see the world, have exciting adventures and date men they hadn't grown up with all their lives and dated since junior high.

While some hadn't married the boy next door, they'd all fallen hard for their men and totally changed their big plans for the future.

Faith couldn't help but feel annoyed with them as she looked around the crowded living room and saw so many protruding bellies and wedding bands. To make matters worse, they all looked ecstatically happy.

A man and marriage just wasn't Faith Bailey's secret desire, she thought as she looked wistfully out the window at the rolling grassland and the rugged edge of the Missouri Breaks in the distance.

"I had to add a baby bootie knitting class at the shop," Georgia whispered to her. "Something about getting pregnant makes a woman want to knit. It's *really* spooky."

Faith laughed, imagining her sister McKenna knitting booties in the near future. McKenna had started her Paint horse farm, and her husband, Nate, was busy building them a home on a hill overlooking the place, but neither had made a secret of their plans to start a family right away.

It was her older sister, Eve, who Faith thought would be hesitant. While all three Bailey sisters were adopted and not related by blood, Eve was the one who was driven to find her birth mother. Before bringing a child into the world, Eve would be more determined than ever to know about her genes and the blood that ran through her veins.

Faith watched Laci and Laney open one beautifully wrapped box after another of darling baby clothing and the latest in high-tech baby supplies, all the time wishing she was out riding her horse. After all, she was only home for the summer, and she'd promised herself she was going to spend every waking moment in the saddle.

"If I see one more breast pump, I'm going to be sick," she whispered to Georgia who laughed and whispered back, "Do you have any idea what some of that stuff is for?"

Before Faith could tell her she didn't have a clue, Laci's water broke, and not two seconds later, so did Laney's.

Faith smiled to herself. She was going to get in that ride today after all.

SHOWERED AND CHANGED, Jud came out of his trailer to find Chantal Lee waiting for him beside his pickup. He groaned under his breath as he noticed Nevada Wells sitting in the shade of his trailer with a half-empty bottle of bourbon on the table next to him. Nevada was watching Chantal with a look of unadulterated hatred on his face.

The two stars had made front-page tabloid news for months beginning with their scorching affair, their torrid public shows of affection and their scandalous breakup—all in public.

Jud wondered what director Erik Zander had been thinking, throwing the two together in this Western thriller, given their recent past. How were they going to get an audience to believe they were crazy about each other in this film and not just plain crazy?

As Jud neared his pickup, Chantal sidled up to him in a cloud of expensive perfume and a revealing dress that accented her every asset. She looped her arms around his neck and smiled up at him.

Across the compound, Nevada grabbed up his bourbon bottle and stormed into his trailer.

"If you're trying to make Nevada jealous," Jud said to Chantal, "you can stop now. He's gone back into his trailer."

"Don't you read the tabloids?" she asked as he disengaged her from around his neck. "I've moved on. So," she said, "how about showing me the town tonight?"

"Whitehorse? As flattering as the offer is, I'm afraid I have other plans."

"Brooke." Chantal made a face as she said the stuntwoman's name.

He shook his head, knowing whatever fueled this battle between the two women had started long before now. "I don't date anyone I work with during filming. I'm having dinner with my family."

Chantal brightened. "Take *me*," she pleaded. "I am bored beyond belief out here in the middle of nowhere. You'll be saving my life."

"Sorry," he said, thinking about what would happen if he took her home with him. He'd dodged a bullet by sacrificing his brother Shane to the marriage pact he and his four brothers had made. But he was still in the line of fire.

It would be fun, though, to see his family's expressions if he pretended interest in Chantal for a wife. But even he couldn't do that to them.

No, the last thing he wanted was to call attention to himself right now. He'd hoped that karma would be on his side when he and his brothers had drawn straws to see who would have to find a wife first. Then he'd drawn the shortest straw and known he had to do something fast, so he had. He'd found the perfect woman— for his brother Shane.

That little maneuver had really only delayed the problem, though. Jud knew in his heart that what his father wanted wasn't so much for each of his sons to marry but for them to settle in Montana closer to Trails West Ranch, the ranch Grayson Corbett had bought for his new bride, Kate.

Grayson was no fool. He had to know that getting all his sons to settle down in Montana probably wasn't going to happen, no matter what kind of carrot he dangled in front of them. But it *was* some carrot.

Grayson's first wife, the boys' mother, had written five letters, one to each son, before she died. The letters, only recently found, were to be read on each son's wedding day. Her dying wish in a letter to Grayson was that the boys would marry by the age of thirty-five— and all marry a Montana cowgirl.

It was hard to go against the dying wishes of his mother, even a mother Jud, the youngest, couldn't remember, since she'd died not long after he and his twin brother, Dalton, were born. Being a Corbett demanded that he go along with the marriage pact the five brothers had made—and eventually live up to the deal.

The problem was that he'd never met anyone he wanted to date more than a few times, let alone marry.

But then most of the women he knew were like Chantal, he thought, as beside him she pretended to pout.

"You're going to hate yourself in the morning for leaving me behind," she cooed.

Jud nodded ruefully. "Ain't that the truth."

"Your loss," she said, and turned in a huff to storm off, again putting a whole lot of movement into those hips of hers.

Jud smiled as he headed for his pickup. He had a weakness for beautiful women and a whole lot of oats left to sow, but his real-life exploits could never live up to those that showed up in the movie magazines about him.

When he thought about it, what woman in her right mind would want to marry a man who did dangerous stunts for living? And he had no intention of quitting until he was too old to climb into the saddle, he thought, as he headed for the ranch.

FAITH BAILEY RODE her horse to the spot where she always went when she wanted to make sure no one saw what she was up to. She'd been coming here since she was a girl. It was far enough from the ranch house and yet not too far away should she need help.

As she got ready, she recalled too vividly the time she'd taken a tumble and broken her arm.

"Were you thrown from your horse?" her mother had demanded when she returned to the house holding her arm after one of her "rides."

Not exactly. "All of a sudden I was on the ground," Faith had said, determined not to lie—but at the same time, not about to tell the whole truth, which she'd feared would get her banned from horseback riding altogether.

She'd kept the truth from even her two older sisters, Eve and McKenna. They couldn't have kept her secret, afraid she'd break her fool neck and they'd get blamed for it.

Now with her mother remarried and living in Florida, Faith still didn't like to upset her family. They'd all been through enough without that. So she kept her trick riding to herself. It was her little secret—just like her heart's desire.

Faith had taken more precautions after the broken arm incident, and while she'd gotten hurt occasionally as she'd grown older, she'd also kept that to herself.

She made a few runs along a flat spot at the far end of a pasture before she got her horse up to a gallop and slipped her boots from the stirrups to climb up onto the back of the horse behind the saddle.

It was a balancing act. Standing, she galloped across the flat area of pasture, feeling the wind in her face and the exhilaration. She always started with this trick, then moved on to the harder ones.

Her mind was on the task at hand. Over the galloping of her horse, the pounding of her heart and the rush of adrenaline racing through her veins, Faith didn't hear the sound of the vehicle come up the dirt road and stop.

JUD CORBETT BLINKED, telling himself he wasn't seeing a woman standing on the back of a horse galloping across the landscape.

He'd stopped his pickup and now watched with growing fascination. The young woman seemed oblivious to everything but the stunt, her head high, long blond hair blowing back, the sun firing it to spun gold.

She still hadn't seen him and didn't seem to notice as he climbed out of his truck and walked over to lean against the jackleg fence to watch her go from one trick to another with both proficiency and confidence.

He'd seen his share of stuntmen and women do the same tricks. But this young woman had a style and grace and determination that mesmerized him.

She reminded him of himself. He'd started on the road to his career as a kid doing every horseback trick he could think of on his family's ranch in Texas. He'd hit the dirt more times than he wanted to remember and had the healed broken bones to prove it.

The young woman pulled off a difficult trick with effortless efficiency, but as she slowed her horse, he could see that she still wasn't quite happy with it and intended to try the stunt again.

"Hey," he called to her as he leaned on the fence.

Her head came up, and, although he couldn't see her face in the shadow of her Western hat brim, he saw that he'd startled her. She'd thought she was all alone.

"Didn't mean to scare you," he said, shoving back his hat and smiling over at her. "On that last trick, try staying a little farther forward next time. It will help with your balance. I'm Jud Corbett, by the way." No reaction. "The stuntman?"

She cocked her head at him and he thought as she spurred her horse that she intended to ride over to the fence to talk to him.

Instead, she turned her horse and took off at a gallop down the fence line. He knew what she planned to do the moment she reined in. She shoved down her Western straw hat and came racing back toward him.

This time the trick was flawless—right up until the end. He saw her shoot him a satisfied look an instant before she lost her balance. She tumbled from the horse, hitting the dirt in a cloud of dust.

Chapter Two

Jud scrambled over the fence and ran to the young woman lying on the ground, wishing he'd just kept his big mouth shut and left her alone.

She lay flat on her back in the dirt, her long, blond hair over her face.

"Are you all right?" he cried as he dropped to his knees next to her. She didn't answer, but he could see the rise and fall of her chest and knew she was still breathing.

Quickly, he brushed her hair back from her face to reveal a pair of beautiful blue eyes—and drew back in surprise as one of those eyes winked at him and a smile curled the bow-shaped lips.

From a distance, he'd taken her for a teenager. Even up close she had that look: blond, blue-eyed, freckled. Now, though, he saw that she was closer to his own age.

His heart kicked up a beat, but no longer from fear for her safety. "You did that on purpose!"

She chuckled and shoved herself up on her elbows to grin at him. "You think?"

He wanted to throttle her, but her grin was contagious. "Okay, maybe I deserved it."

"You did," she said without hesitation.

"I was just trying to help." He'd seen so much potential in her and had wanted to— What had he wanted to do? Take her under his wing?

That was when he thought she was a teenager. Now he would have preferred taking her in his arms.

Rising, he offered her a hand up from the ground. She stared at his open palm for a moment, then reached up to clasp his hand. Hers was small, lightly callused and warm. He drew her up, feeling strangely awkward around her. The woman was a spitfire.

She drew her hand back from his, scooped up her Western hat from the dirt and began to slap it against her jean-clad long legs, dust rising as she studied him as if she didn't quite trust him. She didn't trust *him*?

"Look, I feel like we got off on the wrong foot," Jud said as she shoved the cowboy hat down on her blond head again. "How can I make it up to you?"

She grinned. "Oh, you've more than made it up to me, Mr. Corbett." She whistled for her horse and the mare came trotting over. As she swung up into the saddle, she said, "Thanks for the *tip*."

He couldn't help smiling at the sarcasm lacing her tone and wished he wasn't so damned intrigued by her. She was cocky and self-assured and wasn't in the least impressed with him. It left him feeling a little off balance since he'd always thought he had a way with women.

She reined her horse around to leave.

"Wait. Would you like to have breakfast?"

She drew her horse up and glanced back at him. *"Breakfast?"*

He realized belatedly how she'd taken the invitation. Since he was tied up for dinner tonight, his first thought had been breakfast.

"I already have plans for dinner tonight, but I was thinking—"

"I can well imagine what you were thinking." She spurred her horse and left him standing in the dust.

He watched her ride away, trying to remember the last time he'd been turned down so completely. It wasn't until she'd dropped over the horizon that he realized he didn't even know her name.

FAITH FELT LIGHT-HEADED. She couldn't wipe the grin off her face or banish the excitement that rippled through her as she rode her horse back to her family ranch house.

Jud Corbett. The most notorious stuntman in Hollywood. There wasn't a stunt he couldn't do on a horse. And he had seen her ride!

She chuckled to herself at the memory of his expression when she'd winked at him. She hadn't been able to help herself. She'd wanted to show off. She was lucky she hadn't broken her fool neck doing it, though.

Her heart had been pounding in her chest when she opened her eyes fully and had seen him in the flesh. The Hollywood movie and stuntman magazines hadn't done Jud Corbett justice. The man, who'd made a name for himself not only for his stunts, but also as a ladies' man, was *gorgeous*.

He'd taken her breath away more than her pratfall. She knew about the film being shot down in the Breaks since her sister McKenna was providing some of the horses.

But Faith had never dreamt she'd get the chance to

meet Jud Corbett—let alone be asked to breakfast, even
though she knew what *that* meant, given his reputation.

What had he been doing on that old road, anyway?
No one used it. Or at least she'd thought that was true.
Wait a minute. That road led to the Trails West Ranch
property, and hadn't she heard that someone named
Grayson Corbett had bought it?

Corbett. Of course. She'd just never put two and two
together. Jud must be one of Grayson Corbett's five
sons she'd been hearing about. Which meant Jud was
on his way to the ranch when he'd seen her.

Her grin spread wider. She still couldn't believe it.
She'd fooled the legendary Jud Corbett with one of
her tricks.

As she neared the house, she tried to compose herself. Her older sister Eve's pickup was parked out front.
Faith would have loved to burst into the house and
tell Eve all about her afternoon. But this didn't seem
the time to reveal her trick-riding secret. Eve worried
about her enough as it was, and Eve had her own concerns right now.

Faith knew not wanting to worry her family wasn't
the only reason she'd kept her secret. It was *hers*, all
hers. Growing up, she was always lumped with her sisters as one of the wild Bailey girls. Eve and McKenna
had been stubborn, independent and outspoken.

Faith herself had been all of those and then some,
but she'd thought her trick riding as a girl had made
her the true daring one.

And now Jud Corbett, of all people, knew.

She tried to assure herself that he wouldn't tell anyone. Who *could* he tell? He probably didn't even know
who she was—or care. Faith tried to relax as she took

care of her horse, then walked up to the house, only a little sore from her stunts.

"Everything all right?" Eve asked from the front porch.

Faith hadn't seen her sister sitting on the swing in the shade. Eve lived with her husband, Sheriff Carter Jackson, down the road, but she spent a lot of time in the family ranch house when Faith was home, acting as surrogate mother since their mother had remarried and moved to Florida.

"I didn't see you there," Faith said as she mounted the steps.

Eve was studying her. "You look flushed. Are you feeling all right?"

"Great." It was true. "I wish you wouldn't worry about me, though." Also true, but she hadn't meant the words to come out so sharply. At twenty-six, she was too old to be mothered by her thirty-three-year-old big sister. But mostly, she didn't like worrying Eve.

Eve's silence surprised her—as well as what she saw her sister holding on her lap.

"Is that your baby quilt?" Faith asked, frowning. "Does this mean…?"

Eve shook her head. "I'm not ready to have a baby yet."

"Well, you're the only one in the county," Faith said, dropping onto the swing beside her. "Have you heard if Laci and Laney had their babies yet?"

Eve shook her head, fingering the quilt on her lap. "I was just thinking about *my* biological mother and the night she gave birth to me and Bridger."

Faith had hoped that once Eve was married to the only man she'd ever loved, she might not need to keep up her search. Eve and her twin brother, Bridger, had only been reunited a year ago, brought together by the mutual need to find the woman who'd given them up.

"We know her name," Eve said, surprising Faith. "It's Constance Small."

"You found her?" Faith asked, shocked.

"Not yet. All we have so far is a name and a little information. She was seventeen, possibly a runaway. She disappeared right after she gave birth to us."

"I'm sorry." Faith, like her sisters, was also adopted, but she had no desire to know her birth mother or the circumstances. She couldn't understand Eve's need. Clearly, it could lead to disappointment—if not worse.

Eve put the quilt aside. "Are you sure you're all right? Stay here in the shade. I'll get you some lemonade."

Faith laughed, glad that her sister had something to keep her mind off finding Constance Small. "Thanks, but I just need a shower."

"You haven't forgotten the fund-raiser tonight at the community center, have you?"

Faith had. She frantically searched around for a way to get out of it.

"Don't even think about backing out," Eve said. "McKenna called a little while ago to make sure we were both going."

Faith groaned at the thought of going to the dance.

"Faith?" her sister said in a voice that reminded Faith of her mother's.

"Of course I'm going." She couldn't let her sisters down. Even though they weren't blood related, there was a bond between them that nothing could break.

"Wear your red dress."

Not even the thought of a county dance could dampen Faith's mood for long. As she went into the house she hugged her latest secret to her, treasuring what had happened this afternoon.

But minutes later as she stepped into the shower, Faith realized that Jud Corbett had awakened something inside her. A secret impossible desire that she'd put away the same way she'd put away her dolls and her childhood daydreams.

Like a genie freed from its bottle, her secret yearning had emerged now and, even if Faith had wanted to, she knew no matter how dangerous, it wasn't going back into that bottle.

JUD OPENED THE front door of the Trails West Ranch house and breathed in the mouthwatering scents of chile rellenos, homemade refried beans and freshly fried corn tortillas with Juanita's special spices. He'd bet she'd made flan for dessert.

His favorite meal. He closed his eyes, pausing to hang up his jacket and brace himself for whatever was awaiting him. The only good news about his father's move to Montana was that he'd somehow talked Juanita into making the move with him and Kate.

The menu alone was a tip-off, even if Jud hadn't seen his brothers' vehicles parked out front. It was just as he'd suspected: a family meeting.

Hearing the tinkle of ice in crystal glasses and the hum of voices in the bar area, Jud headed toward it, pocketing the pleasurable thoughts of the young woman horseback rider he'd seen.

"Jud," his father said as he spotted him. Grayson

looked at his watch and frowned. He was a big, handsome, congenial man, as open as the land he lived on.

"Sorry I'm late." Jud thought about mentioning the woman he'd seen but changed his mind. He got razzed enough about women, his own undoing since he'd made the mistake of sharing some of his exploits, embellishing, of course, to make the stories better—just as the movie magazines did.

"Dinner smells amazing," he said, hoping to cut short whatever this summit meeting might be about.

Everyone was gathered in the large family room, a bad sign. His oldest brother Russell stood behind the bar nursing a beer; Lantry was propped on a stool talking to their father's wife, Kate; Shane was sprawled in a chair by the window—no sign of Maddie, his fiancée, another bad sign; and fraternal twin Dalton was whispering with Juanita and stealing tortilla chips from the large bowl in her hands.

"So what's up?" Jud asked as he helped himself to a beer from the bar fridge, just wanting to get this over with.

He saw a look pass between his father and Kate. Uh-oh. He felt his heart dip. For years after their mother, Rebecca, had died, Grayson had been alone. They'd thought he would never remarry.

Then along came Kate. Kate had shown up at their Texas ranch with a box of photographs of their mother. Rebecca had been the ranch manager's daughter. Kate the daughter of the ranch owner. The two had grown up together on Trails West Ranch outside of Whitehorse, Montana.

Kate had lost touch with Rebecca over the years. When she'd found the photographs, she'd said she'd thought enough time had passed since Rebecca's death that Grayson might want them.

He had. And it wasn't long before he'd wanted Kate, as well. All these years Grayson hadn't been able to go through his deceased wife's belongings. With Kate's love and support, he finally had—and found the letters from their mother, triggering this marriage pact among the sons.

Grayson had fallen hard for Kate. So hard that he'd sold his holdings in Texas and bought Kate's long-lost family ranch in Montana as a present for her, then moved them to Montana.

His father had been so happy with Kate. Jud couldn't bear it if that was no longer the case.

"Kate and I have something to tell you," Grayson said now, his expression way too serious for Jud's tastes.

Jud took a swig of his beer and braced himself for the worst. All five brothers had thought their father's marriage and the move to Montana was impulsive and worried, since even Jud had noticed that Kate had seemed different here at the ranch.

She should have been happy to have her family ranch back after it had been lost when her father died. But she hadn't been.

"Kate?" Grayson said, giving his wife's shoulder a squeeze.

She raised her head, glancing around as if looking for someone. Her gaze settled on Shane sitting by the window, his back to them.

What the hell, Jud thought, feeling the tension in the room crank up several notches.

"I have a daughter."

They all stared at Kate, knowing she'd never been married and as far as they'd known had never had a child.

"I gave birth to her when I was in my early twenties, right after my father died, right before I left Montana," Kate said, her voice strong. "I gave her up for adoption when she was only hours old." She swallowed. "I've regretted it ever since."

What was this? True confessions?

"You weren't in any shape to raise a child alone," Grayson said. "You had little choice given your situation."

She cut her eyes to him and he fell silent again. "The father of my child was married." Her back stiffened visibly. "He wasn't going to leave his wife. I was hurt. I told him the baby had died. It wasn't until recently that I told him the truth."

You could have heard a pin drop in the room. Everyone was staring at Kate. Except Shane. His back still to them, he appeared to be gazing out the front window as if uninterested. Or had he already heard this?

Jud felt his chest tighten. "What happened to your baby?"

Kate turned toward him. "Adopted by a local family, she grew up in Old Town Whitehorse."

Jud did the math. "So she would be in her mid-twenties."

"Twenty-six," Kate said.

He could see what was coming. "Does she know who you are?"

Kate nodded.

"Of course, she was surprised," Grayson said. "So

it is going to take some time to get to know her and her to know us."

"So when do we get to meet her?" Dalton asked.

The silence said it all.

"You've already met her," Kate said. "Her name is Maddie Cavanaugh."

Jud shot a look at Shane.

"Shane's fiancée?" Lantry demanded, glancing at his older brother, as well. Shane still didn't say anything or look in their direction.

"I take it Maddie is upset," Jud said, stating what he knew was the obvious.

"She'll come around," Grayson said, always the optimist.

"I wanted you all to know so you understood that it might be tense when Maddie is around. She's having trouble forgiving me. I'm having trouble forgiving myself."

For the first time, tears shone in her eyes, but she seemed to hold them back with sheer determination.

"Are you worried about the legal ramifications, Kate?" Lantry asked, always the lawyer.

"No," Grayson said. "She is Kate's daughter and will be treated like any other member of this family."

"But the wedding is still on, right?" Jud asked.

Russell shot him a warning look.

Juanita announced dinner was ready as if on cue, but no one moved.

"This calls for margaritas," Grayson announced.

Kate touched his arm. "Maybe after dinner," she suggested.

Everyone except Shane headed in for dinner. Jud

hung back. "I wasn't only thinking of myself just now," he said to Shane.

"I know." Shane got to his feet. "We should join the rest of the family." He looked like hell. Clearly this was taking a toll on him.

"Maddie will come around. You know she will," Jud said. "She loves you. It would be a damned shame if you let this come between you. You're made for each other."

Shane smiled. "Not to mention the pressure it would put on you to tie the knot."

"Yeah," Jud said smiling ruefully. "Not to mention that."

EVE WISHED SHE didn't know her two younger sisters so well. The moment she'd seen Faith's face on her return from her ride, she'd known something had happened.

Whatever it had been, Faith was keeping it to herself. Eve had noticed right away that Faith had been thrown from her horse. There was dirt ground into the seat of her jeans and into the elbows of her Western shirt.

This wasn't anything new. Over the years Faith had returned many times from rides fighting to hide the fact that she'd been thrown. Often also trying to hide her hurt pride.

This time, however, Faith seemed jubilant, and that had Eve as perplexed as anything. She would have thought a man was involved, but at this point in Faith's life, she seemed to prefer the company of her horse.

Eve looked up at the knock at her screen door to find her twin brother, Bridger, standing just outside.

She couldn't help thinking about the first time she'd seen him.

Unlike her, he'd known he was adopted. He'd even known he'd had a twin sister. Their shared blood had thrown them together as they'd tried to find out the truth about their illegal adoptions.

"Hey," he said as he met her gaze through the screen. He was dark haired like her. Eve had always known she was different from her mother, father and two sisters, who all had blond hair and blue eyes. Now she knew why.

"Just the person I wanted to see," she said as he came into the house, and she gave him a hug.

"Faith must be home," he said, glancing at the supper she had started. Eve had remodeled her grandma Nina Mae's home down the road when Nina Mae had to go into the rest home with Alzheimer's.

The Bailey ranch house sat empty except when Faith was home. Eve didn't want her sister, who insisted on staying at the ranch house, to come home to an empty house, so she spent time here trying to make it a home for Faith.

Faith had taken their parents divorce the hardest. Now their father lived in town with his girlfriend and their mother in Florida.

"You're an awfully nice sister," Bridger said as he sat down at the kitchen table where everyone always congregated.

Eve would have argued how nice she was. She felt she'd let down her family because from the time she was very young, she knew she was different and resented it, always searching for her real self. Her real family, as she thought of them. She'd just wanted someone who looked like her. Now she had Bridger, at least.

"Any luck?" Bridger asked picking up one of the papers spread out on the kitchen table.

"I called all of the Constance Smalls I've found so far," Eve said pouring him a cup of coffee before sitting down at the table with him. Later she would try the C. Small listings.

"You realize she probably married and changed her name. Her name might not even have been Constance Small. She could have lied about that, given she was a runaway."

"I know." Eve could hear Bridger's reservations. Once they'd found out that Constance Small was probably a runaway, he seemed to back off in the search.

She couldn't blame him. It did feel hopeless. Even if Eve lucked out and found the woman, she'd probably wish she hadn't.

"So? Did Laci have her baby?" she asked, changing the subject.

Bridger's expression quickly shifted from a frown to a broad smile. "She sure did. Jack Bridger Duvall."

"Laci beat her sister and got the name Jack?" Eve laughed. The two sisters had both wanted the name Jack from the time they'd found out they were both carrying boys. They'd agreed that whoever gave birth first got the name.

"Laney went with Jake," Bridger said with a shake of his head. *"Sisters."*

Eve smiled. "I know you brought photographs. Come on, let's see 'em."

"I thought you'd never ask," he said pulling his chair closer to her as he dug out his digital camera.

Eve pushed away the papers with the names of the women who could possibly have given birth to her and her brother, wishing she was more like Bridger. He'd moved on. Why couldn't she?

Chapter Three

"Excuse me, can you tell me who that woman is?" Jud Corbett asked the elderly woman standing next to him. "The one in red."

The Old Town Whitehorse Community Center was packed tonight, the country-western band made up of oldtimers who cranked out songs that took Jud back to his youth in Texas.

A smile curled the elderly woman's lips as she glanced across the dance floor, then up at him. "They're the Bailey girls—Eve, Faith and McKenna. Faith is the one in red. Pretty, isn't she?"

"Very," Jud said. "Faith Bailey, huh?" He liked the sound of her name.

The woman beside him cut her eyes to him, her smile knowing. "So why don't you ask her to dance?"

He chuckled. Dancing with him would be the last thing Faith Bailey wanted to do. "That's a good idea."

"Yes, it was in my day, too," the elderly woman said sagely.

Jud moved across the worn wooden dance floor toward Faith, who was flanked on each side by her sisters. After dinner tonight, he'd opted not to stay at the ranch but drive back to his trailer on location to be ready for an early shoot in the morning. At least that had been his excuse to escape the tension at the ranch.

As he was driving through Old Town Whitehorse, he'd seen all the rigs parked around the community center. Slowing, he'd heard the old-time country band. He'd bet himself that the band members wouldn't be a day under seventy—and that his trick-riding cowgirl would be there.

He'd parked and walked back to the community center to find he'd been right on both counts.

As he crossed the dance floor toward Faith Bailey now, he realized she'd already seen him and was trying to look anywhere but at him. Clearly, if she'd had somewhere to run in the crowd of people, she would have.

"Hello again," he said, tipping his Stetson as he stopped directly in front of her.

Seeing that she was trapped, her blue eyes flashed like hot flames. "I'm sorry. Do I know you?"

"I would have sworn we'd crossed paths before," he said and grinned. It had bothered him why she'd been practicing her stunts so far away from her ranch house.

But from the imploring look she was giving him now, he'd wager that she hadn't wanted anyone to see her doing the stunts. Was it possible that not even her sisters knew?

"I guess I could be wrong," he said in a slow Southern drawl. "Why don't we dance and see if we can sort it out? Unless you'd like to discuss it here," he added quickly when he saw she was about to decline.

Her cheeks flushed with heat, those big blue eyes hurling daggers at him. "If you insist."

"I do." He took her hand and drew her to him.

The band had broken into a cowboy jitterbug. He swung her away from her sisters and deeper into the other dancers on the floor.

She was a good dancer, staying with him, matching any move he made even though anger still blazed in her eyes. She apparently didn't like being blackmailed into dancing with him. Talking over the band was out of the question, which was fine since he was enjoying dancing with her and had a bad feeling where their conversation would go.

He swung her around, catching her around her slim waist, their gazes meeting, hers challenging. He liked everything about her, from the fire in her eyes to the arrogant tilt of her chin and the easy, confident way she moved. Faith Bailey was apparently just as at home on a dance floor as she was on a horse.

And she wasn't about to let him get the better of her.

He smiled, thoroughly enjoying himself. He was sorry when the song ended and she started to pull away. He drew her back as the band went right into a slow dance.

"So, Faith Bailey," Jud said as he pulled her close, breathing the words at her ear. "Why is it you don't want anyone to know about your trick riding?"

She tensed in his arms. Drawing back slowly, her gaze a furious slit, she said, "Blackmail will only get you so far, Mr. Corbett."

He chuckled. "Come on, why the secrecy? You're good. Damned good. Why hide your talent?"

"We're not all like you, Mr. Corbett," she said. "Some of us have no need to be in the spotlight."

"Jud. Mr. Corbett is my father." His grin broadened. "And you and I are more alike than you think. I recognized myself in you the moment I saw you riding across the prairie. You *love* trick riding, and don't tell me you don't like an audience after that stunt you pulled earlier today. So what are you afraid of?"

"Nothing," she said too quickly, and he knew he'd hit a nerve. The song ended. "Thank you for the dance." She tried to pull free, but he held her a moment longer.

"Don't worry," he whispered, his gaze locked with hers. "I'll keep your secret."

He'd expected relief in her expression. But instead her eyes narrowed, making it clear she didn't like the fact that it was something else they shared.

As he released her and she disappeared into the crowd on the dance floor, all Jud could think about was seeing her again.

FAITH TRIED TO still the trembling in her limbs. She went straight to the punch table and downed a glass. Dancing with Jud Corbett had shaken her badly. She feared there was some truth in what he'd said about them being alike.

A man like that could confuse a woman. Not Faith Bailey, who wasn't susceptible to him. But she pitied other women, who she realized could be easily mesmerized by his good looks and easygoing charm.

She shook off those thoughts, reminding herself that she was furious with him for blackmailing her into dancing with him. A man like that, well, he wasn't one she wanted knowing her secret. Not just about the trick riding.

But another secret, one she'd kept hidden from even herself until she'd opened her eyes and seen Jud Corbett leaning over her earlier today.

Faith now feared Jud Corbett knew her most secret desire.

She shivered, feeling exposed and more vulnerable than she'd ever felt. How was it possible that a man she'd only danced with could know her so well?

"I wondered where you had gone off to," McKenna said, joining her. "That was one of the Corbett brothers you just danced with, wasn't it?"

Faith thought about feigning ignorance. "Uh-huh." She took another glass of punch and sipped it this time, needing something to do with her hands.

"He is certainly good-looking," McKenna commented.

"I hadn't noticed."

McKenna laughed. "You *have* to be kidding. Are you going to pretend you also didn't notice the way he was looking at you?"

Faith remembered only too well how his gaze had locked with hers as he'd tipped his hat. Time had stretched out interminably as she'd stood at the edge of the dance floor praying he would just go away.

Her heart had been beating so hard it seemed the only sound in the room as he'd pulled her to him and out onto the dance floor. She'd feared everyone was watching and getting the wrong idea. Especially her sisters.

And they had.

"You're mistaken," Faith said, knowing her cheeks were still flushed. "He looks at every woman that way."

"Are you talking about Jud Corbett, the stuntman?"

Eve asked, joining them. She helped herself to a glass of punch.

Faith shrugged and glanced across the room to where Jud Corbett was standing, his gaze on her. She quickly averted her eyes, feeling her cheeks warm even further.

"I heard Jud Corbett is fearless when it comes to stunts," McKenna said.

"He sounds dangerous," Eve said, and Faith could feel her sister's gaze on her.

"Dangerous" described Jud Corbett perfectly, Faith thought, as she saw the look Jud Corbett gave her as he left the dance.

AFTER THE DANCE, Eve Bailey Jackson got on the phone again. Carter was working late tonight at the sheriff's department—some annual report or something or other.

"I don't like you staying home alone so much," Carter had said earlier. His gaze said he knew about the list of phone numbers, knew the long hours she'd spent gathering them—and calling trying to find her birth mother.

He'd seemed about to say something else but changed his mind. Eve knew he worried that she'd never quit looking for her birth mother and that her unfulfilling quest would sour her and their life together. Or worse, that she'd find her mother and be even more disappointed.

Eve had gone through the long list of C. Small numbers, each time telling herself that this would be the call that would end it.

Now as she started to dial yet another, she felt her heart pound with anticipation and fear. This was the last number on the list.

If this number was another dead end, then it was a sign, she told herself. Her fingers shook as she tapped in each number, a silent prayer on her lips and tears in her eyes as she promised herself this would be the last of it. Her search would end here.

Like her brother, she would move on. Carter wanted to have children. He wanted the two of them to get on with their lives.

She made a solemn promise to herself as the phone at the other end of the line began to ring. She'd run out of options and couldn't bear any more dead ends. She would give up her search for the mother who'd given her and Bridger away. This had to stop.

"No more," she said under her breath as the phone rang once, twice, three times and then, just when Eve was about to hang up, give up for good, a female voice answered.

"Hello?"

Eve had to clear her throat. "Is this Mrs. Small?"

"Yes?"

"My name is Eve Bailey Jackson. I'm trying to locate a Constance Small who lived near Whitehorse, Montana, thirty-four years ago."

"Constance?" the woman repeated. The line went dead.

As hard as she tried to hold them back, Eve felt the tears flow down her cheeks. Another dead end. Her last.

THE CALL CAME out of the blue. Mary Ellen was in the middle of baking cookies for the church fund-raiser.

Quickly dusting the flour from her hands, she answered the phone with a cheerful, "Hello."

"Mary Ellen?"

"What's wrong, Mother?"

"I got another one of those calls about Constance." Her mother was crying. "After all these years…I just can't bear it. I know it's just another prank call, someone wanting money, like the others professing to have information about Constance."

"It's all right, Mother." But Mary Ellen feared it wasn't. As she'd said, it had been years. Why would someone be calling now?

"I took down the woman's number from caller ID. She said her name was Eve Bailey Jackson. She was calling from Montana."

Mary Ellen drew up a chair and sat down hard.

"She sounded nice." Her mother thought everyone was nice. "But I just can't do it. Would you call her?" Her mother began to cry, and Mary Ellen hated this Eve Bailey Jackson.

"I'll take care of it. I'm sure it's just as you say— nothing. So don't worry yourself over it."

For years Mary Ellen had feared this day would come. But as time had gone by, she'd started to think that the truth would never come out.

"Bless you, dear. Here's her phone number."

Mary Ellen listened as her mother rattled off the Whitehorse, Montana, telephone number, but she didn't write it down. She had no intention of returning the call. She told herself she was doing them all a favor as she hung up the phone.

Turning back toward the kitchen, she saw black

smoke billowing from the oven. She'd burned the cookies for the church fund-raiser. Only then did she let herself break down.

Chapter Four

The prairie glistened in the morning sun, tall green grasses undulating in the slight breeze, the smell of summer sharp and sweet. Overhead, puffy white clouds floated in a crystalline blue sky.

Faith saw the plume of dust curling up off the dirt road that ran through Old Town Whitehorse past the Bailey Ranch.

She watched as the vehicle slowed, squinting into the morning sun as a vaguely familiar pickup pulled to a stop in front of the house.

"Is that Jud Corbett?" Eve asked from behind her as the cowboy climbed out of the truck. Tilting his Stetson back, he walked toward the front door.

Faith cursed under her breath. Jud Corbett hadn't taken her warning to stay away. The man was impossible. What could he want? Not to help protect her secrets, she'd bet money on that.

Faith hurried out on the porch and down the steps to cut him off. He was tall and muscled, but there was grace and fluidity to his movements. She easily recognized him in the movies where he did the stunts. There was just something about him. A confidence.

Arrogance, she thought now.

He saw her and slowed as if only now thinking twice about coming here. His mistake.

"I thought we had an understanding?" she demanded through gritted teeth as she faced him.

He grinned then, his eyes sparkling with humor. "Did we?" He took a step toward her. She took two back. "Do I scare you?"

"Of course not," she snapped, a clear lie. What was it about him that made her feel she always had to be on guard around him? She knew the answer to that one, actually.

"Fearless, are you? Then you're just the woman I'm looking for."

She irritably brushed away his words like a cobweb in her path. "Do not even try to charm me. I can assure you it won't work." Another lie.

"That wasn't charm. That was honesty." He said the words simply, and if she hadn't known better, she might have believed him. "I need to talk to you about something that will make you very happy."

She eyed him suspiciously. "If this is about *break-fast—*"

He laughed. "While I would hope *breakfast* with me would make you more than *very* happy, that's not it." The grin faded. "Could we talk somewhere?"

Eve was just inside, probably watching them from the window.

"Down by the creek," Faith said, and turned toward the copse of cottonwoods that stood along the banks. She planned to set the man straight once and for all. The last thing she needed was him showing up on her doorstep again.

While he'd promised to keep her secret, she knew

given the way he'd blackmailed her into dancing with him last night that he couldn't be trusted. What was he doing here? And what could he possibly have to talk to her about? Whatever it was, she was on her guard. She wouldn't put anything past him.

When they reached the creek and were out of sight of the house, she turned to face him, hands on hips, her expression as impatient as she could make it.

"This had better be good," she warned him.

"Our stunt double was bitten by a rattlesnake this morning. She isn't going to be able to finish the shoot."

"Brooke Keith?" Faith said on a surprised breath. She'd heard that the stuntwoman was working on the film. An old flame of Jud's, according to the tabloid movie magazines.

He raised a brow. "You *know* her?"

"Know *of* her. I've read about her." The moment those words were out, Faith wanted to snatch them back.

Jud's brows shot up. "So that's it. You don't really believe that stuff Hollywood gossip rags print, do you?" He shook his head as if disappointed in her.

"Where there's smoke, there is usually fire," she said, grimacing at how much she sounded like her sister Eve.

"Look, I'd like to try to convince you that you're all wrong about me, but I don't have the time," Jud said. "We need someone to fill in for Brooke and finish the film. There are only a few more days of stunts to be shot. I suggested you to our director."

He rushed on. "The director checked and found out that you already have a SAG card." His gaze narrowed. "Apparently you've done some ride-on parts in movies, not stunts, just horse-related shots—this woman who shuns the spotlight."

He held up his hand to stop her from commenting. It was a wasted effort on his part. She'd opened her mouth, but nothing had come out. A small gust of wind could have knocked her over.

Jud Corbett hadn't just known her secret heart's desire—he'd just offered it to her.

"If you pass this up," he said. "You'll regret it the rest of your life."

"I…"

"Just think about it." He thrust a business card into her hand. "My cell phone number's on it. I'll just need to know by noon." With that he turned and walked away, leaving her too stunned to move.

DIRECTOR ERIK ZANDER couldn't believe his bad luck. Just the thought made him curse as he poured Scotch into his fourth cup of coffee of the morning. Probably wasn't the best way to start the day, but what the hell, given the way his life was going.

Last night Keyes Hasting had called.

"I heard about the film you're making and am intrigued," Hasting said. "You don't mind if I come up."

Like hell he didn't mind, but he'd been too shocked to say so, especially when Hasting had added, "The theme of this film is close to my heart. Retribution, isn't it?"

Those last words registered like a gun to his head.

"I heard your stuntwoman was bitten by a rattlesnake," Hasting had said. "I hope you can find someone else so you can finish the film."

"My stunt coordinator has someone in mind," he'd

said, all the time thinking, *That son of a bitch Hasting has a spy on the set.*

Hasting was an old reprobate with too much money and alleged mob connections. Zander had hung up the phone and gotten skunk drunk. And this morning, hungover, he was dreading Hasting's visit like a root canal.

Snapping open his cell phone, Zander checked to see if Jud had called. No voice mail. Jud had promised to let him know the moment he had a verbal agreement from the new stuntwoman. Why hadn't he heard something yet?

Fortunately, he would be able to shoot around the problem today, but by tomorrow when Hasting arrived…

"Anyone seen Jud Corbett?" Zander bellowed as he stepped out of his trailer, wishing he'd never laid eyes on the script for this film. It had arrived on his doorstep. Along with a blackmail threat.

FAITH WAS STILL standing by the creek when Jud Corbett drove away in his pickup. He had her stirred up good, and no matter how hard she tried to put him—and his offer—out of her mind, she couldn't.

She'd always dreamed of being a stuntwoman, specializing like many did with horse trick riding.

But it had only been a dream. She'd told herself her riding gave her so much pleasure, she didn't need to take it any further. Only men like Jud Corbett needed the applause and exaltation.

But he'd called her on it and now the truth was out. She wanted this more than she'd ever wanted anything, she thought, as she walked back toward the house. She'd just never admitted it. Until now.

Faith looked up to see her sister waiting on the porch for her, a worried look on her face. Faith swallowed and said, "There's something I need to tell you."

As she took a seat beside Eve, she spilled it all, the years of practice and Jud Corbett's offer—her most secret of all desires.

"I wondered how long it would take you to tell me," Eve said when Faith had finished.

"You *knew*?"

"Oh, Faith, I've known since that time when you were a girl and you broke your arm. I'd hoped you would outgrow it. I was afraid for you. But when you didn't… It's what you've always wanted, isn't it?"

She nodded, tears in her eyes. "When we were kids, I thought you'd tell Mother, then after I went away to college, I just didn't want to worry you."

"You've been headed in this direction for a long time."

Just as Jud had said, in college Faith had done some ride-on parts in movies being filmed around Bozeman. None involved stunts, though.

"Don't think it doesn't worry me," her sister continued. "Stunt work is dangerous."

"It can be," Faith allowed. "You have to use your head, expect things to go wrong. It's all part of it."

Eve shook her head. "McKenna will probably have a fit, not to mention what Mother will have to say about it. But Dad, well, he'll just be proud of you."

Faith smiled. If she had expected anyone to have a fit, it was Eve. Life was just full of surprises. She hugged her older sister. "Thank you. I have to call Jud and tell him I'll do it."

"You hadn't already agreed?" Eve asked in surprise.

"I wanted to talk to you first."

Tears welled in her sister's eyes. "I would never stand in your way. But just so you know, I intend to be on that set every day you're doing a stunt."

Faith laughed and went to make the call. Jud answered on the first ring as if he'd been waiting for her call.

"So you're going to do it," he said before she could say a word. He sounded pleased, an underlying excitement in his voice that tripped something inside her.

"You're that sure I can do this?" she had to ask.

He chuckled. "You know you can or you wouldn't have called me back."

"Don't be so sure about that."

"We resume shooting in the morning, but come over this afternoon. I've made sure there will be a trailer here for you to stay in so you'll be ready for early shoots. Bring your horse. There will be time to get in some riding."

He had everything arranged already? "What if I hadn't called?"

"I saw you ride, remember? You and I are cut from the same cloth."

"Except I will never be as cocky as you are."

He laughed. "Trust me, you already are." She could tell he was smiling. "This is a great break for you. I'm as excited about it as I was when I did my first film."

Faith swallowed, thinking that her break had come at the expense of the stuntwoman who'd been bitten by a rattlesnake and said as much.

"Brooke's going to be fine. The doctor said she's one of those rare cases. She had an adverse reaction to the snakebite antidote. Fortunately, we have a helicopter on the set and rushed her to the hospital."

"Once she gets better, she'll want her job back," Faith said, worried that was true.

"Nope. You'll be doing what's left of her stunt work for the remainder of the shoot. She talked the director into hiring her as assistant stunt coordinator. She can't do stunts, but she can help set them up."

Faith swallowed back her guilt at that news. She couldn't help but be anxious and thrilled at the same time. Jud had seen to everything. "Are you always so accommodating?" she asked only half-joking.

"I made an exception just for you. I should warn you," he added, "this film is pretty low budget. As well as doing stunts, I'm also the stunt director. But don't worry. I think you'll be pleased with what I got you for pay."

As if she wouldn't have done it for free, Faith thought.

"Celebrate," Jud said.

Again she felt that small insistent thrill that seemed to warm her blood. "Jud?"

"Yes?"

"Thank you."

He laughed. "Thank me after this film is over. This will either cure you of your need to trick ride or—"

"Or kill me?" she asked with a nervous laugh.

"Or hook you so badly you won't want to ever quit," he said. "Either way, you may not thank me when it's over."

She wondered about that as she hung up and felt like pinching herself. Her secret desire was about to be realized. She just had to be careful that Jud Corbett didn't ignite any other secret desires in her.

As she started to leave, she noticed some wadded-up papers in the wastebasket near the phone. She pulled one out and saw that it was the list of numbers for Constance Small and C. Small. Every name had been scratched out.

Dropping the paper back into the trash, she glanced toward the porch where Eve was still sitting and felt an overwhelming sadness for her sister. If only her dreams could come true.

MARY ELLEN HATED FLYING. She'd brought along some needlepoint for the flight, but she hadn't touched it. Her mind was reeling. What did she hope to accomplish by flying to Montana? Just the thought of returning to Whitehorse made her blood run cold.

Had she been able, she would have gotten off the plane and gone home where she belonged. But as she felt the plane begin its descent into Billings, Mary Ellen knew she'd come too far to turn back now. She had to see why after all these years someone would call about Constance.

There would be a rental car waiting for her at the airport on the rock rims above Montana's largest city, but she was arriving so late that she planned to spend the night and drive the three hours to Whitehorse in the morning.

From Billings she could drive north through Roundup and Grass Range, the only two towns for hundreds of miles between Billings and Whitehorse. Roundup was small, and Grass Range was even smaller.

Mary Ellen tightened her seat belt and closed her eyes. She hated cold even more than flying. At least it was July in Montana. Had it been winter like the last time she was in Whitehorse, Mary Ellen knew she wouldn't have come.

It would be hard enough returning to the past.

As the plane began its descent into Billings, Mary Ellen wished she were on speaking terms with God. But she suspected any prayers from her would be futile given all her sins—her greatest sin committed in Whitehorse, Montana, thirty-four years ago.

As FAITH TOPPED the hill in her pickup, her horse trailer towed behind, she saw the movie encampment below: the two circles of trailers and past it the small town that had been erected. All of it had a surreal feel to it— not unlike this opportunity that had landed in her lap.

Captured in the dramatic light of the afternoon sun, the small Western town in the middle of the Montana prairie looked almost real with its false storefronts, wooden sidewalks, hitching posts with horses tied to them and people dressed as they would have been a hundred years ago.

She'd barely gotten out of her pickup when Jud Corbett walked up.

"Feel like saddling up and going for a ride?" he asked.

"Sure." She hadn't been on her horse all day, and the offer definitely had its appeal. Even more so because it would be with Jud, although she wasn't about to admit that, even to herself.

They saddled their horses and rode along the edge of the ravine overlooking the movie camp. She and Jud compared childhoods, both finding that they'd grown up on ranches some distance from town, both loved horses and both had begun riding at an early age.

"I can't believe how much we have in common," Jud said, his gaze warming her more than the afternoon summer sun. "Do you believe in fate?"

She chuckled. "Let me guess. It's *fate* that you and I met?"

"Don't you think so?" he asked. He was grinning, but she saw that he was also serious.

"I suppose I do." If he hadn't taken the back road to his family ranch that evening, and if Laney and Laci hadn't gone into labor when they had so Faith could go riding, then what was the chance that she and Jud would be here right now?

"Fate, whatever, I'm just glad you and I crossed paths," he said, then drew up his horse, as below them the ghost town came into view.

Jud leaned on his saddle horn to stare down at it. "Spooky looking, even from here."

She felt a chill as she followed his gaze. A tumbleweed cartwheeled slowly down the main street of the ghost town to come to rest with a pile of others against the side of one of the buildings. Remarkable there were any buildings still standing.

"So are the stories true?" Jud asked.

"At least some of them," she said. "The descendants of the Brannigan family still live on down the river." She saw his surprise. "Some of the descendants of Kid Curry and his brothers also still live around here."

He shook his head. "But what about the town and this thing with the rag dolls?"

She looked down at what was left of Lost Creek. "I'm sure you've heard the story, since apparently it's what the script of this film is based on."

"Some outlaws rode into town and killed a woman

and her little girl while the townspeople stood by and did nothing. The husband and eldest son returned, saw his dead wife and child in the middle of the street and picking up the little girl's rag doll from the street, swore vengeance on everyone who'd stood back and let it happen. Does that about size it up?"

She smiled. "Just about."

"Then the townspeople started finding rag dolls on their doorsteps and terrible things began to happen to them until one night everyone in town disappeared."

"That's the way the story goes," Faith admitted.

"Don't you think its more than likely the townspeople left knowing that the outlaws would be back and more of them would die?" Jud asked.

She said nothing.

"What happened to the father?"

"Orville Brannigan and the rest of his children moved downriver to live like hermits. Their descendants still do. The little girl's gravestone is about all that's left up at the cemetery on the hill. Emily Brannigan. The historical society comes out a couple of times a year and puts flowers on her grave."

"The poor family," Jud said.

"It always amazes me how many families struggled to tame this land and still do."

"Like *your* family."

She nodded, remembering the school field trip she'd taken to the Lost Creek ghost town and the frightening sensation that had come over as she'd stood among the old buildings on the dirt street where Emily Brannigan and her mother had lost their lives.

That sensation had been the presence of evil. Evil fueled by vengeance. She'd known then that the settlers had never left town. Some years back, a local named Bud Lynch had sworn he found a pile of human bones in a cave west of the ghost town.

The bones, as well as any evidence of the more than hundred-year-old crime, had mysteriously disappeared before his story could be confirmed by the sheriff.

The Brannigans and their relatives called Bud Lynch a liar, but Faith had seen the man's face when he told of what had to have been the skeletons of dozens of men, women and children, piled like kindling in the bottom of the cave.

There was no doubt that Bud Lynch had seen evil.

DIRECTOR ERIK ZANDER woke on the couch, confused for a moment where he was and how he'd gotten there. On the floor next to him lay an overturned empty Scotch bottle. He groaned when he saw it.

He had to quit drinking like this. He sat up, his head aching, the room spinning for a moment. The trailer rocked to the howl of the wind outside, the motion making him ill.

He glanced at his watch. Past two in the morning. With an early call, he really needed to get some sleep. Hasting would be arriving today, and who knew what the hell he really wanted.

Pushing himself to his feet, Zander stumbled toward the bedroom, slowing as he passed the kitchen and the fresh bottle of Scotch he knew was in the cabinet within reach.

"Don't even think about it," he mumbled to himself. He was already so drunk he had trouble navigating the narrow hallway, bumping from wall to wall like a pinball. Something about that made him laugh.

He was still chuckling when he reached the small bedroom. The trailer room was just large enough for a bed and a built-in dresser.

As he aimed himself for the bed, he spotted the doll propped against the pillow and lurched back, stumbling into the wall and sitting down hard. Now eye to eye with the damned doll, he saw that it had to be the ugliest thing he'd ever seen.

Worse, it appeared to be looking right at him, reminding him how much he hated this script. A Western *thriller*? As if his life couldn't get any worse.

He reached for the doll, squeezing it in his big hand as he stared into its grotesque face. It wasn't until then that it registered in his alcohol-saturated brain that it wasn't one of the dolls from props.

He stumbled to his feet, still clutching the doll. "What the hell is this?" If it wasn't from props, then where had it come from? And why had someone left it on his bed?

At least that answer was easier to come up with. Anyone who'd read the script knew that the rag dolls were the harbinger of bad luck and had made it thinking to scare him.

Erik Zander began to laugh, a big belly laugh that sent him sprawling backward on the bed. As if some ugly doll could make his life any worse.

Chapter Five

"It's a *ruse*," Nancy told Zander the next morning. She'd come straight to his trailer before the others were even up.

The director had stumbled to the door, still half-asleep, wearing blue cotton pajama bottoms. His graying blond hair stuck out at all angles, and there was a red crease line on his unshaven jaw where he'd slept on something that had left a mark.

Although in his early fifties, he still looked like the boy next door—the drop-dead good-looking boy who never gave a second glance to nondescript girls like Nancy Davis.

She couldn't help but stare at his muscular bare chest. It was covered with blond-gray fuzz that fell in a V to the tied pj bottoms. Even at this age, he was still a damned good-looking man. She felt her face heat and hurriedly averted her eyes.

"I have to talk to you," she stammered.

"What the hell time is it?"

"I came by before anyone else was up so we wouldn't be interrupted."

He grunted. "Well, come in then." After a hasty retreat to the back of the trailer, he returned wearing a faded and worn publicity T-shirt from his last movie over the pajama bottoms.

"I'm sorry to wake you so early, but I knew you'd want to know," Nancy said. "It's about Chantal and Nevada."

He held up a hand as he got the coffee going. "It's too damned early to even talk about them, okay?"

"They're only pretending to hate each other," she blurted. "I saw them together last night."

"The moment will pass, believe me. Like the quiet before the storm." He hovered over the coffeemaker as if intimidation could force it to brew faster. "Don't you know? They do this all the time."

"I've seen their fights on YouTube. I didn't buy it then and I certainly don't now. They're deceiving everyone."

He turned to frown in her direction. "*Okay.* Who cares?"

Nancy was surprised by his lack of interest. Was the man daft?

"Believe me, by this morning they'll be at each other's throats again and trying to destroy this film," he said with a sigh as he lifted the coffeepot and motioned in her direction.

"No, thanks," she said and watched him pour himself a cup. He turned his back to her to add a shot of Scotch to the coffee, as if everyone didn't know about his drinking.

"It just seems strange that they'd want everyone on the set to think they hate each other. I mean, they've hung their dirty laundry out for everyone to see for months now. Why the secrecy? It has to be a publicity stunt to keep their photos on the front of every tabloid out there."

Zander scowled as he took a gulp of his coffee and leaned back into the kitchen counter as if he needed the support. "When I think of the heated battles they've put us all through on the set…" He shook his head and took another gulp of coffee. "But quite frankly, I could give a damn what they do as long as they don't destroy this film, and this morning I'm not even sure I care about that."

She gave him a disapproving look. "Well, I just thought you should know since I'm aware how much this film means to your career."

"Yeah," he said and took another gulp of coffee and Scotch.

She rose and walked to the door, turning to look back at him.

He was squinting down into this coffee cup. He'd completely forgotten she was there.

Nancy wondered what would happen if he ever really took a good look at her. One thing was certain. It wasn't going to happen today.

THE SET WAS a beehive of activity the next morning when Faith came out of her trailer. She'd been on other location shoots and knew that filmmaking was a lot of standing around and waiting. It was never as exciting as she'd originally thought it would be.

But today was completely different. She couldn't have been more excited. Jud was waiting for her at catering, a bunch of tables and chairs under a tent with a trailer next to it. The set was too far away from anything to be catered, so cooks had been hired to feed everyone.

He handed her a cup of coffee, smiling broadly.

"How's the nerves?" he asked.

"Steady as a rock."

He laughed. "I'll bet. Have some coffee and then I'll fill you in on what's planned for today. Once we get your paperwork taken care of, next stop is makeup and wardrobe."

Since she would be standing in for the leading lady, Faith was going to be dressed identically to what Chantal would be wearing today. Her blond hair was close enough in color to the star's that at least she wouldn't have to wear a wig—just a large bonnet, which would hide most of her hair anyway.

"I feel as if I've stepped back a hundred years," Faith said later as she came out of the costume trailer to find Jud waiting for her. She was wearing a prairie dress, lace-up high-heeled boots, her hair drawn up under the bonnet.

His gaze was hotter than the sun peeking over the horizon. "Wow. You look…"

She couldn't imagine him being at a loss for words.

"Perfect," he said finally and laughed.

They walked to a waiting SUV that drove them to the temporary set. A facade of a town had been erected to resemble what Lost Creek would have looked like over a hundred years ago.

The storefronts appeared real enough, but behind each was nothing but supports or, in the case of the hotel, a building that housed a saloon with a staircase up to the second floor where there was a hallway and one room that looked out over the main street.

Horses were already tied to the hitching posts and several wagons were parked along the street. Crew worked to move props and camera equipment into place. The cast and crew were smaller than some of the films she'd worked on, which made it feel more intimate. Or maybe it was just being this close to Jud Corbett.

"That's our leading lady," Jud said, as Chantal Lee came out of the saloon and stopped on the wooden sidewalk. She appeared irritated as she dusted at something on her sleeve. From a distance, she could have been Faith's twin.

"And our leading man, Nevada Wells." Nevada stood in the swinging doors at the front of the saloon as if posing for his picture. But no one was paying any attention to him. He, however, had his gaze on Chantal.

Faith recognized them both from films and the tabloids and movie magazines.

Jud walked Faith through the stunts they would be performing. He would be doing Nevada's stunts and stand-ins, she Chantal's.

He pointed to a wagon pulled by a team of horses. "Have you ever driven a team before? It's not that hard since the object is to let them run so the hero, that would be me, can chase you down and save you. Of course they don't run as fast and as out of control as they will appear on film."

Faith smiled at him, thinking this was a lot like her fantasies as a girl on the ranch. Only in those, she did the saving.

"I'm a quick study," she said as they walked over to the wagon and she climbed up on the seat.

"We're going to do a few slow-motion run-throughs, then the main event later. You ready?"

Faith grinned. She couldn't wait.

THE RUNAWAY WAGON was a stunt straight out of old Westerns. On a higher budget film, most of the action would have been computer generated.

"I want this film as authentic as we can make it," Zander had said to Jud. "None of that computer-generated stuff."

Jud had only nodded, although he knew the director was just being cheap. Computer-generated material was costly. And even though Zander would have to pay Jud more for the dangerous stunts, he would still save money. Stunt money hadn't been as good the last few years because a lot of films had gone with computer-generated action scenes.

Not that Jud worried about making more money. He didn't do this for the money. He liked to do the stunts. The runaway wagon stunt could be dangerous. Driving a team of horses wasn't as easy as it looked. Not that he was worried that Faith couldn't handle it.

But there had already been a few minor accidents on the film. Not unusual in the filmmaking industry, but he just wanted to be sure that Faith was as safe as possible since he'd gotten her into this.

He climbed up onto the wagon seat next to her and unhooked the reins. "Let's take a little ride first to let you get the feel of it."

They took off down the dirt track. They hadn't gone far when she took the reins. At the foothills, she turned the team around.

"Let's try it with some speed," she said with a grin and snapped the reins down. The team took off, gaining speed as they raced back toward the fabricated town.

Faith slowed the wagon on the outskirts of the set and brought the team to a halt. "Well?"

Jud grinned over at her. This woman could handle anything she set her mind to. "The idea is to let them run, but not too fast."

She nodded. "I know. It's all illusion." The team wouldn't actually be out of control. The wagon seat was rigged so it rocked. All Faith had to do was play along.

"You got it." Jud jumped down and lifted her from the wagon. Her waist was slim, her body warm beneath the dress. He set her down and for a moment he had this wild desire to kiss her.

She must have sensed it because she stepped away from him.

At the sound of raised voices he turned to see Chantal arguing with the director.

"You don't need me at all today," Chantal was saying, even though she was down on the call sheet for the first scene, where she has a discussion with the leading man while sitting on the seat of the wagon.

The runaway wagon scene would follow. Although most scenes were shot out of sequence, the cinematographer had wanted these in order to make sure the light was the same and save filming yet another day since, according to the weatherman, a storm was moving in.

Jud walked over to see what was going on.

"Shoot my double," Chantal said. "I told you, I'm ill. I'm going to my trailer." Without another word she stormed over to one of the trucks used to ferry crew and actors from the encampment to the set and took off.

Zander swore and turned to Jud. "We'll shoot around her." It was becoming the film's mantra.

Jud glanced toward Faith, who must have overheard. She gave him a thumbs-up and climbed back onto the wagon bench.

Jud headed for his horse, motioning to the cinematographer and director that they were ready.

The scene would be shot from several angles. This

scene required that Faith as Chantal's body double race across the prairie on the runaway wagon after a fictional gunshot from the saloon spooked her team.

As he started to swing into the saddle, Jud caught movement out of the corner of his eye. Something flew past. The rest happened so quickly, all he could do was react.

One of the horses in the team started for no apparent reason, rearing up, then taking off. Jud saw Faith grab for the reins from where she was sitting on the wagon's seat as the horses panicked and bolted.

Jud leaped on his horse and went racing after her. He could see the film crew scrambling to get out of the way as the wagon careened toward them.

Faith's bonnet blew off, her long blond hair coming loose and blowing back in a wave. She was struggling to get control of the team—and to still stay on the wagon as it rattled across the rough terrain.

Jud rode hard after her. The wagon hit a bump and Faith went airborne for a moment before coming down again half on the seat. She regained her balance but lost one of the reins. The team ran flat out, even more spooked with one of the reins dragging now.

Gaining on the wagon, Jud rode up along the right side. He'd performed this stunt a dozen times—just not at this speed. Nor out in the middle of the prairie without a fail-safe.

"Faith!"

She nodded and slid across the wagon seat toward him. Her blue eyes were wide with fear, but she did as she would have in the actual scene—only at a much faster speed and through the bumpy prairie.

Ahead he could see an outcropping of rocks. The

team of horses was headed right for it. Jud knew he'd get only one chance to do this before the team and wagon reached the rocks.

He reached for Faith.

CHANTAL LEE WATCHED the whole thing from in front of her trailer. She would have assumed that Zander had moved up the stunt. Except there were no cameras rolling.

With horror, she realized that the team of horses had run away for real. This was no movie stunt. And if she hadn't refused to shoot that part today, she would have been on that wagon.

She covered her mouth with her hand as she watched the scene unfold. Just like in the movies—Jud riding to save the cowgirl.

Only this was real.

Chantal heard others join her, a crowd forming around her and cries of horror as Jud reached for the new stuntwoman—an amateur who was about to get killed.

"He's got her!" someone cried.

Chantal blinked, not believing what she'd just seen. The new stuntwoman—what was her name? She'd been told her name this morning, but she hadn't been paying attention. Anyway, she'd made the jump to the back of Jud's horse just before the team veered away from the pile of rocks.

The wagon didn't make the ninety-degree turn, and flipped over, crashing into the rocks, boards splintering and wheels flying as the fail-safe mechanism released the team from the wagon. The team slowed and finally stopped.

Chantal stared at the carnage. "I could have been on that wagon. I was *supposed* to be on that wagon." She glanced across the camp and saw Brooke Keith give her a short nod, a smile on the stuntwoman's face.

Chantal shuddered as she remembered the rag doll she'd found on her bed. Brooke had sworn she hadn't done it. But what if she had? What if it hadn't been a prank, but a warning?

"If you'd been on that wagon, you'd be dead right now," one of the crew said.

"He's right," another said. "If that stuntwoman hadn't known what to do, she'd be in those rocks with her head split open."

"Good thing you were too sick to work," Nancy Davis said.

Chantal hadn't seen the assistant director join them. She heard Nancy's snide tone, but ignored it as Brooke joined them.

"Jud's the one who saved the day, again," Chantal said for Brooke's benefit. "He's the one who killed the rattlesnake that bit you. What would we do without him?"

"Come on, everyone. Let's get back to work," Nancy ordered, shooting a look at Chantal, which she ignored.

The moment everyone else left, Brooke grabbed her arm. "Leave Jud alone, Chantal. I'm warning you."

Chantal jerked her arm free. "You left me that doll."

"It was just a joke."

"Just like that runaway team of horses?"

Brooke shook her head. "I had nothing to do with that. It was just an *accident*."

"Like your snakebite," Chantal said.

As FAITH SLIPPED off the back of the horse, Jud swung down and pulled her to him. She wasn't sure her legs would have held her without his strong arms around her. She looked up into his handsome face, never so glad to see anyone in her whole life.

He held her longer than necessary, but she was glad of it. He seemed to be as relieved as she was.

When he finally let her go, she could see the fear still in his eyes. "You're sure you're all right?"

She nodded. "I thought I was a goner." She was safe, standing on solid ground. So why did being this close to Jud make her feel as if the earth might crumble under her at any moment?

"Did you see what spooked the horses?" he asked.

She shook her head. "There was a thunk, as if a rock hit the side of the wagon," she said, frowning as she tried to remember. "It happened so fast, I can't be sure."

"A rock. Did you see where it came from?"

She thought it an odd question. "No." Was he saying he thought someone might have thrown the rock? And why was he acting as if this wasn't the first accident on the set?

Whatever it had been, the scene was straight out of the movies, with Jud saving her. The realization of just how close a call it had been was starting to settle in. She hugged herself to still the trembling. "You saved my life. Thank you."

He looked ill at ease. "I was just doing my job."

"Too bad they didn't get it on film," she said, making him smile. She could see that he was upset.

"You did great."

"I just did what you showed me to do." That, and she'd studied enough of the stunts on old movies.

He glanced toward the set. One of the SUVs was headed in their direction. He walked over to pick up his horse's reins.

His gaze met hers and held it before they were descended on by the others from the set. "I hope I haven't gotten you into something dangerous," he said quietly.

She frowned as he swung up onto his horse. What did he mean? Of course stunt work was dangerous sometimes.

But she had the feeling he was talking about something else, as if he thought the runaway team hadn't been an accident.

Chapter Six

Jud heard someone come up behind him as he headed for his trailer, but he paid no attention. He was still shaken by what had happened. Faith Bailey was lucky to be alive.

"Saved another one, huh?" said an angry-sounding male voice behind him.

Jud turned to find Nevada Wells, face flushed, eyes bulging, his breathing coming hard and fast. Nevada was Hollywood handsome complete with a cleft in his chin, but apparently just the altitude left the man winded.

"I've got your number," the leading man said, poking a finger into Jud's chest. "If you think I don't know what you're up to, I do. The rest of these people, they're too stupid to see, but not me." His breath smelled of alcohol and he looked as if he hadn't gotten much sleep lately.

"What the hell are you talking about?" Jud asked impatiently. There was nothing about Nevada Wells he liked. The man had gotten this far on looks, not talent, and was known for being a wuss as well as a whiner.

"The snake, now the runaway wagon. Lucky you just happened to be there both times."

"*You* were there, as well," Jud said pointedly, but Nevada clearly wasn't listening.

"You like playing hero."

Jud laughed. "You're the one who *plays* hero."

Nevada narrowed his eyes. "What do you think Erik Zander would say if I told him I know who's behind the accidents on the set?"

"He'd say you were crazy as well as drunk. Don't be ludicrous. What would I have to gain by doing something so malicious?"

"I've been asking myself that."

"Let me know when you come up with an answer," Jud said and walked off.

AFTER A HOT shower and a change into jeans, shirt and boots, Faith left her trailer to find her sister. She had tried Eve's cell phone but had gotten voice mail. Eve hadn't planned to come out to the shoot until afternoon, when Faith had told her she'd be doing her first stunt. A small fib.

Faith suspected her sister had heard about the accident, given the way news traveled in the county. So she wasn't surprised to see Eve among the locals who came out to watch moviemaking from the sidelines.

A rope barrier had been erected to keep back what had been until now only a small crowd. Several crew members were now positioned nearby in case someone tried to get on the set during shooting.

Eve Bailey was standing with some other local residents Faith recognized. From her sister's expression, Faith could see that Eve was upset. No doubt she'd been told that Faith was all right, but Eve would have to see for herself, and the crew wasn't about to let her through to find her sister.

As she drew near, Faith noticed a woman standing off to the side away from the locals. What caught Faith's attention was the way the woman was dressed. She wore a pale green dress and low heels, her hair pulled up in a chignon.

That alone made her stand out since everyone else was dressed in jeans and boots. While Faith would swear she'd never seen the woman before, something about her seemed familiar. She had wide-set dark eyes and dark hair streaked with gray. She wore a scarf around her neck, tied loosely, that picked up the green in the dress.

Something else odd: she didn't seem that interested in what was happening on the set. Instead, she was looking down the rope line, her gaze on the locals.

Faith worked her way around the back of the small crowd, not wanting to block anyone's view of the scene being shot. When she touched her sister's shoulder, Eve turned and, seeing her, dragged her into a tight hug without a word.

"I'm fine," Faith said as others she knew crowded around her, wanting to hear the gory details. "It was just like the real stunt and worked exactly the same," she said, stretching the truth.

When she looked up, she saw the woman in green watching them. Caught, the woman hurriedly glanced away. When Faith looked again, the woman was headed for an SUV with Billings plates.

"Are you sure you're all right?" Eve asked, drawing Faith's attention back.

Faith nodded, looking into her sister's heart-shaped

face framed by her long black hair, the eyes so dark they were almost black, and felt a jolt as she saw the resemblance between the older woman who'd just left in the SUV—and her sister.

MARY ELLEN DROVE to the top of the hill and had to pull over and get herself under control before continuing back to Whitehorse.

At breakfast this morning at the Great Northern, she'd heard the locals talking about the film and Faith Bailey.

The name Bailey had caught her attention. She'd listened as the group of women, who were apparently from some group called the Whitehorse Sewing Circle, discussed an accident on the set this morning. Apparently Eve Bailey was on her way out there, even though early reports were that her younger sister Faith was fine.

"What's that girl doing out there performing stunts anyway?" one of the older women demanded.

"She's a *Bailey.* You know how wild those girls always were," another one said.

"Lila raised them like boys. That was the problem."

"Raised 'em more like wolves, if you ask me." Everyone laughed. "It's no surprise the way that youngest one is turning out."

The women finished their breakfasts and decided to drive out to the set to see just what that youngest Bailey girl was up to before going back to Old Town Whitehorse to finish a couple of baby quilts they were all working on for the Cavanaugh girls.

Mary Ellen had pushed her half-finished breakfast away and followed, hoping they were right about Eve

Bailey being on this movie set. What would it hurt to see the woman? she'd thought. She'd come this far.

And she had seen her. Mary Ellen would have recognized Eve anywhere. The dark hair, those coal-black eyes so much like her own and that face. It was like looking into a photograph taken thirty-some years before.

Her heart was still pounding. She felt sick to her stomach. She wished she'd never come here. Never laid eyes on Eve Bailey Jackson. Never seen the way the sisters had hugged so tightly and realized how much she'd missed the past thirty-four years.

Mary Ellen wiped at her tears and checked her watch. If she hurried back to the motel and packed up she might be able to catch an early flight out.

If she stayed in Whitehorse any longer, she feared what she might do. As she drove away from the movie set, she barely noticed the bank of dark clouds over the Little Rockies.

THE SKY DARKENED to the west, the wind kicking up dust devils as it swept down the river and through the badlands of the Missouri Breaks. A lightning bolt tore through the clouds in the distance, and the rumble of thunder echoed over the set.

Zander cursed. Not even the weather would cooperate. He ran a hand through his hair and scowled at the sky. The whole day had gone this way, beginning with the team of horses taking off the way they had and destroying the wagon.

It was a wonder Faith Bailey hadn't gotten killed. She would have if it hadn't been for Jud Corbett. Hiring him was the best thing Zander had done. Not that it had been his choice. He'd had no choice. And that's what worried him now.

Along with the script and the blackmail note, he'd found instructions on who to cast, what stunt people to use, what crew members. Thinking it was some crackpot, he'd tossed the script and the blackmail note into the garbage.

A day later, when the second blackmail note had arrived with a copy of a very incriminating photograph taken the night of the party at his Malibu beach house—a night that had ended with crime-scene tape and a coroner's van—he'd dug the script out of the garbage and read it.

He'd quickly been convinced that making a Western thriller near Whitehorse, Montana was in his best interests.

Now as he watched the clouds moving fast up the river, he wondered if he'd not only been set up—but also set up to fail. Zander laughed at his own foolishness. Even blackmailed, a part of him believed the person doing this was just someone who was desperate to get his film made.

He'd been able to fool himself—until Keyes Hasting had showed up this morning at his trailer and had mentioned, almost as an offhand remark, that he was in mourning. His godchild, he said, had recently died.

"I'm sorry," Zander had said automatically, since what else was there to say?

"She was a beautiful woman—talented, headstrong and determined, probably too determined, but now we will never know what she might have accomplished in her life," Hasting said.

There was an edge to his voice that should have put

Zander on alert. But he was too busy wondering why Hasting had come to pick up on it.

"You knew her."

Zander had been fiddling with the coffeemaker, but at those words, he stopped and turned, frowning slightly. "Your godchild?"

"That was who we were talking about, wasn't it?" the old man snapped irritably.

Zander had finally picked up on that scalpel-edge tone of Hasting's. "*I* knew her?" His heart boomed in his chest. Had it been some young, starry-eyed actress he'd rejected for a film? Or fired? Or far worse, slept with? He had barely heard Hasting's next words because he'd been breathing so hard, his pulse like a barreling freight train.

"You knew her *well. Very* well. Her name was Camille Rush."

Looking back, Zander could now marvel at how well he'd taken the news that this old mob-connected gangster's godchild was the young starlet Zander had impregnated and refused to marry. The same starlet who'd been found in his hot tub dead and full of drugs.

"Keyes," he'd said, actually using the old man's first name. "I'm so sorry. I had no idea Camille was your godchild. I regret that I didn't realize she was in trouble," he'd said in his defense, his voice filled with true emotion—fear, though, more than true remorse. "But how could I know that she would take her own life?"

Hasting had scowled at him, then laughed. "We both know Camille was too self-centered to ever take her own life."

Zander thought of the way the man had then walked

away, the threat hanging in the air like the dark clouds now gathering.

That's when he knew for certain. This film. Keyes Hasting was the one behind it and the blackmail. The question that had tormented Zander then and now, though, was still *why?* Some kind of warped revenge? Hasting could have had him killed and been done with it. Why go to all this trouble?

True, the way the film was going, this would be a much slower, more painful death, Zander thought. This film wasn't a lifesaving limb for a drowning man. *Death at Lost Creek* was no doubt the nail in his coffin.

Keyes Hasting planned to destroy his career somehow with this film. Or was there more to it?

One thing was clear. Hasting was his mortal enemy. But what could Zander do? Nothing. Hasting had him right where he wanted him.

Zander shivered, less from the dropping temperature than from his own dark thoughts. Whatever—this day was a wash, literally.

"Strike the set!" he called in disgust and headed toward his trailer. "Reschedule for tomorrow morning, weather permitting," he told his mousy assistant director without giving Nancy a backward glance.

"Erik."

He didn't turn around. In fact, just the sound of Chantal's voice made him want to run as far and fast as he could. He'd already had a run-in with Nevada before breakfast.

His trailer had been like Grand Central Station this morning, starting with Nancy carrying gossip about the stars of the movie, then Nevada with complaints about everything from his accommodations to his role, then

Brooke demanding more money since she was now an assistant stunt coordinator.

He felt as if he were on a sinking ship, no life raft and no way to call for help.

After the morning he'd had, he was in no mood to hear Chantal's complaints and demands. He feared he might wring her pretty little neck. If she valued her life, she'd take the hint and leave him alone.

He quickened his step. With luck he would reach his trailer before the rain started and without Chantal. He needed a drink to steady him. He feared the people around him had begun to smell fear coming off him in waves.

"Erik." Chantal's sharp tone cut through his thoughts as the first drops of icy rain splattered down.

He opened his trailer door and stopped under the awning, thinking maybe he could make this quick and painless. One thing he was determined not to do was invite her in.

"You and I need to talk." Her gaze bored into him, harder than the drops of rain pelting down on the awning overhead.

"Later, I have to—"

"Now, unless you want to talk about your personal problems out here where everyone can hear," she said, then lowered her voice. "Problems like Keyes Hasting?"

He met her gaze, his blood turning to slush. "Why don't we step inside?"

THE WIND WHIPPED Faith's hair into her face as the storm moved in. The crowd scattered, everyone rushing to their cars or trailers as the rain fell hard as hailstones.

"Are you staying here again tonight?" her older sister asked as they ducked under Faith's trailer awning.

"We'll be shooting early in the morning if the weather clears up."

Eve hugged her again, running a hand over her blond hair just as she had done when they were children. "Be careful."

She started to say she was always careful. But look what had happened this morning. "I will."

"I'll be back tomorrow morning," Eve promised.

"That isn't necessary."

"Yes, it is." With that, her sister turned and hurried through the rain to her pickup.

Faith wondered where Jud was and swatted that thought away like a pesky fly. She wanted to talk to him about the accident earlier and the nagging feeling she had that it hadn't been the first on the set.

"Faith?"

She turned to see Nancy Davis coming toward her with the next day's call sheets.

"There are a few changes that affect you," Nancy said.

Faith took the sheet. "Nancy, I heard you were the one who found Brooke after she was bitten by the rattlesnake. They say she would have died, if you and Jud hadn't acted quickly to get her to the hospital."

"Everyone should work more and talk less," Nancy snapped.

"I only mentioned it because it seemed so odd that she was bitten by a rattlesnake in her trailer. How in the world did the snake get in there?"

"I have no idea," Nancy said. "I have more important things to worry about." With that she turned on her heel and left.

Odd, Faith thought. No odder than Nancy herself, though.

"You okay?" asked a very male voice coming toward her.

She turned to find Jud Corbett grinning at her.

"I heard you muttering to yourself. Is there a problem with the call sheet?"

She shook her head. "How well do you know Nancy Davis?"

"I *don't* know her. Why? Did one of your movie magazines say I dated her?" His grin broadened.

"You disappoint me. I thought you've dated everyone in Hollywood. Seriously, I'm curious about her." Faith told him what Nancy had just said.

Jud shrugged. "Appears she doesn't like being a hero. Why all these questions?"

"I saw your expression earlier when you asked me if I saw where the rock came from that spooked the wagon team. You think someone did it on purpose."

He held up his hands. "I never said that."

"Not in so many words. But you have to admit, Brooke getting bit by a rattlesnake in her trailer couldn't have been an accident. Snakes can't climb steps or open doors."

Jud hesitated. "Okay, that was suspicious. I think someone did it as a prank."

"A sick, dangerous prank."

"Few people die from snakebites. Brooke just happened to experience complications from the antidote."

"You're not fooling me for a minute, you know,"

she said. "You're scared someone is behind these accidents."

"Or maybe I wanted you to believe the accidents were deliberate so I'd have an excuse to protect you and spend every waking moment with you."

"Nice try."

"I'm serious, at least about wanting to protect you, and I can see now that spending time with you is the only way to keep you out of trouble. I have to go to the ranch tonight. Come with me." He held up his hands in surrender. "It's just dinner with my family. No ulterior motives." He grinned. "*Breakfast* isn't in the package."

She couldn't help but smile. The man was incredibly charming, and she hadn't been looking forward to being cooped up in her trailer.

"I have a stop to make in town first. I could meet you after that, say at Packy's?"

"Great," Jud said and grinned. "I hope you like Mexican food."

Chantal was all business as she stepped past the director into his trailer.

Zander glanced back through the pouring rain toward catering. A few people had taken cover under the huge canopy that sheltered the outdoor eating area. Some were looking in his direction. Even if they didn't hear what Chantal had said to him, he knew they were speculating on what was going. It wasn't like they didn't know about most of his *personal* problems.

He swore under his breath as he stepped into the trailer after his leading lady and slammed the door. Chantal had removed the lightweight jean jacket she'd been wearing. Rain droplets darkened the jacket where she'd hung it over the back of one of his chairs.

The woman herself was at his bar in the small kitchen making herself a drink.

"Scotch, straight up," he ordered. "Since you're pouring," he added when she turned, cocking a brow at his tone.

Zander slouched into the recliner, wondering what Chantal wanted and what she planned to offer in return. He'd been waiting for her to throw herself at him. Chantal Lee had warmed the couches of every director she'd worked with, her exploits as legendary as the remunerations she'd wriggled out of them.

Sex was the last thing on his mind as she handed him his drink and curled up on his couch. She ran a finger around the rim of her crystal tumbler and studied him openly.

"Why don't you cut to the chase," Zander said irritably. He'd never taken Chantal for a woman with brains as well as beauty, but as he met her gaze he wondered if he'd been wrong about that.

"I heard something that has me concerned," she said, still watching him with her laser-intense gaze.

Nothing he loved more than being forced to squash some stupid rumor on the set. "Whatever it is, it isn't true."

"Really?" One perfect brow arched upward. Chantal was like a giant cat curled up on his couch. She looked friendly enough, but he knew she could be purring one moment and scratching out his eyes the next.

"Then you didn't give me the leading role in this film because someone is blackmailing you?"

Zander choked on his Scotch.

"FAITH." SHERIFF CARTER JACKSON rose from behind his desk as his sister-in-law stepped into his office. Outside, lightning splintered the dark sky followed by booms of thunder that rattled the windows as rain fell in a torrent. "I heard about the excitement out on the set. You all right?"

She nodded, shook the rain from her and took the chair he offered across from him. She wasn't surprised he'd heard about the wagon incident. Probably from Eve.

"The accident is one of the reasons I'm here," Faith said. Now, though, she was having second thoughts. Spying on the people she was working with didn't seem like a good idea. Especially if there was even a chance her accident had been anything but.

Carter was waiting.

"I was wondering if you could do some checking for me? Unofficially?"

"What kind of checking?"

"I'm curious about the people I'm working with." She knew the scuttlebutt from movie magazines. What she needed was the behind-the-scenes kind of information that only a law enforcement person could provide.

Reaching in her pocket, she drew out the list of names she'd jotted down before coming in. Erik Zander, Chantal Lee, Nevada Wells, Brooke Keith, Jud Corbett.

She handed him the list.

His eyebrows shot up on the first name. "Erik Zander? He was involved in the death of a woman who drowned in a hot tub during a party at his Malibu residence."

"He was never arrested, right?" Faith asked.

"Not enough evidence," Carter said. "Not the same as being innocent, though."

Every tabloid in the country had picked up the story. What she found interesting was that the others on her list had been at that party, including Jud Corbett.

Carter scanned down the sheet and lifted his gaze back to her again. *"Jud Corbett?"*

Faith wished now she hadn't added his name to the list. "Those are the main people I work with. There is one more I forgot to add, Nancy Davis. From what I can gather, this is her first assistant director job."

"What is it exactly that you're looking for?" the sheriff asked, leaning back in his chair to study her.

"Accidents happen on movie sets all the time," she said quickly. "I think that's all this is. But it doesn't hurt to check out the primary people involved in the film, right?"

Carter sighed. "You sound like a cop. Okay. You'll let me know if there are any more accidents out there, right?"

"Of course," she said, feeling only a little guilty for coming here. She didn't want to betray Jud. Nor did she want anything to keep her from the stunt work on this film.

But she was no fool. Jud was holding something back. If there was a problem on the set, she wanted to know about the people she was working with.

Silently she prayed that the wagon incident would be the last. But a nagging feeling told her she wouldn't have come to the sheriff if she believed that.

ERIK ZANDER WIPED his mouth and said, "Blackmail? That's absurd." He downed the rest of his drink, his heart hammering wildly in his chest.

"So you weren't blackmailed into making this movie?"

"Hell, no. Where would you get such an outrageous idea?" he demanded.

She glanced down at the glass in her hand. He noticed she hadn't touched her drink while his was empty and he already needed another one.

He thought about asking her to get it for him, but his stomach was churning and he didn't trust himself to speak. Not that he expected she'd do it anyway.

When was he going to learn that there were no secrets in Hollywood? What a laughingstock he would be if this got out. The thought was so absurd, he snorted, making Chantal's head jerk up.

"What's so funny?" She looked irritated, as if he'd been making fun at her expense.

He shook his head. "Nothing." Here, just seconds ago, he'd been worried about being the laughingstock of Hollywood when Hasting had evidence that would make a jury send him to the electric chair. Did California have an electric chair, or would it be lethal injection? Hell, Hasting was probably going to kill him when this film was over and save the state the expense.

Was it any wonder Zander had totally lost his perspective?

"You know, if you really had been blackmailed into doing this picture, into giving me this role, then I have to wonder who else you were forced to hire." Chantal's gaze locked with his and he felt his stomach roil.

His head whirled. He held out his empty glass, hoping she'd take the hint.

She didn't. "That's the reason you gave Nevada the role, isn't it? Why else would you throw the two of us together in a film so soon after our breakup?"

Zander opened his mouth to tell her that he knew

they weren't really broken up, but nothing came out. He drew back his glass, which suddenly felt too heavy to hold.

"Which brings up the big question, doesn't it?" Chantal continued. "What could a blackmailer have on you that you'd let yourself be put in such a tenuous, not to mention dangerous, position?"

Zander leaned over to set his glass down on the coffee table. It slipped from his fingers and thudded onto the surface. Suddenly he didn't feel so good.

"Zander?" Chantal sounded far away.

He was having trouble catching his breath. His gaze shot to the table where he'd dropped his empty glass. It was gone. Chantal was standing over him, holding his empty glass and her own full one. No lipstick on the rim. She still hadn't taken a drink.

He opened his mouth, but only a rasping sound came out, each breath a struggle. He tried to get to his feet as he watched Chantal walk over to the sink, pour her drink down the drain and turn on the faucet to rinse her glass.

No! his mind screamed as she put her glass aside and rinsed out his, refilling it with water.

"Here, drink this," she said frowning as she came back over to him. Was that genuine concern in her voice? If so, then she was a better actor than he thought.

She'd poisoned him and he'd just sat here and watched her get rid of the evidence. Or had it been Hasting who'd put the poison in the Scotch this morning and Chantal had just stupidly destroyed the evidence, not realizing what she was doing?

He shoved the glass of water away and tried again

to stand. He had to keep her from getting rid of the bottle of Scotch, the only proof left.

The room swam. He struggled to his feet, doubling over as he fought to catch his breath.

"Erik? You bastard, don't you dare have a heart attack and die before I get what I want."

He pitched forward, sprawling face-first on the floor. From far away he heard Chantal screaming. Down the hall, he caught sight of the doll he'd found on his bed last night. It was lying on the floor where he'd tossed it, those dark sightless eyes staring at him.

The doll appeared to be smiling.

Chapter Seven

"A panic attack?" Chantal stormed around her trailer, too angry to sit. "That's all Erik had? He scared me half to death. I thought he was having a heart attack."

"Apparently you scared him, as well," Nevada said from the couch. He'd come from the hospital emergency room where Zander had been rushed by helicopter earlier. "He thought you'd *poisoned* him."

She swung around. *"What?"*

Nevada nodded, smiling. "The moment Erik regained consciousness he had his girl Friday Nancy rush back out here to his trailer to retrieve the glass and bottle of Scotch that you used to pour his drink."

"And?"

"The Scotch bottle had mysteriously disappeared, along with both glasses the two of you had drunk from."

She stared at him. "I thought you said it was a panic attack?"

"It was. The hospital ran a blood test on him, and there was no poison in his bloodstream." Nevada shook his head.

"Then why would anyone get rid of the Scotch and glasses?"

He shrugged. "It's crazy since obviously the Scotch didn't affect *you*."

"I never got a chance to drink mine," she said.

"How *fortunate*," Nevada said.

"You think I put something in his Scotch?" she demanded incredulous. "That's why you declined a drink when I offered you one a minute ago."

"A man can't be too careful around a woman like you."

She grabbed a nearby couch pillow and threw it at him. He ducked and grinned. She reminded herself that she needed him to believe she gave a crap about him. "If you weren't so handsome…"

He ate that up. Usually. But not now. "Maybe there was something in the Scotch that normal blood test screening wouldn't find," he suggested, eyeing her. "Without evidence there is no way to prove his Scotch was doctored."

"You seem to know a lot about blood screening," she commented. "If his Scotch was 'doctored' then it happened before I got to his trailer. His door wasn't locked."

"Doesn't matter. The doctors say it was a panic attack and Zander overreacted. So you're off the hook."

"I was never *on* the hook." He was starting to irritate her.

"Erik might disagree with that, my love," Nevada said. "Unless you can produce the Scotch and glasses, I'm afraid you'll always appear guilty of something."

"You find that amusing?"

"No, I find that frightening," he said. "And exciting. I always knew you were a dangerous woman. Now I know just how dangerous."

"Someone took the bottle and glasses to incriminate me," she said.

"Or save you," he added. "Calm down. You're in the clear. Erik had a panic attack. And come on, he has reason to panic, the way this movie is going. I just saw Keyes Hasting talking to Nancy. What is he doing here?"

"Isn't it obvious? He's got money in this film," she said, not happy to hear that Nancy had been talking to Hasting. She hated not knowing what was going on.

"Erik wouldn't take money from Hasting," Nevada said. "Not unless—"

"He was desperate? Zander's career is riding on this film."

"And so is ours," he reminded her, as if she needed reminding. A few films that did poorly at the box office and the phones quit ringing. The only thing that had kept her name in the news was her breakup with Nevada.

He stood now and walked to the door as if leaving. She felt a moment's relief. Instead, he locked the door and turned back to her.

"What do you think you're doing?" she demanded as he strode to her, pulled her out of her chair and began to unbutton her blouse.

She tried to shove his hands away. "Everyone knows you're in here with me."

Nevada grabbed the front of her shirt and jerked. Buttons went flying, fabric tore. Roughly he cupped her right breast and squeezed as he gave her a punishing kiss.

She fought to push him away, both of them falling

backward. The chair crashed to the floor, them right behind it.

"Stop it, you bastard!" she bellowed.

Above her, Nevada Wells smiled. "What did I ever see in a bitch like you?" he yelled as he bared her breasts.

Chantal grabbed the lamp cord and jerked it. The lamp crashed to the floor. She let out an obscenity as her hands went to the zipper of his jeans. Only a few more days and *Death at Lost Creek* would be over and she wouldn't need Nevada Wells anymore. But in the meantime...

MARY ELLEN HAD barely made it back to the motel in her rental SUV on the narrow muddy road. Now, as she looked out the window she saw that the rain still fell in a curtain of cold and poured from the rusted motel-room gutters like Niagara Falls. Through the darkness of the stormy afternoon she could see the huge droplets dimpling the ever-expanding puddles.

She'd planned to leave Whitehorse, to return to Billings, to catch any flight out of Montana that she could get on a moment's notice.

But those plans had changed as she drove back from the movie set. A thunderstorm like nothing she'd ever seen had swept in. *A gully washer.*

She blinked and could almost hear those words come out of her father's mouth. She let the curtain fall back over the window and turned to face the desolate motel room.

Rain or no rain, she couldn't stand to spend another moment in this room with nothing but her memories—

and regrets. Everything about this town brought back the last time she'd been here.

Grabbing her suitcase and car keys, she pulled on her coat and, opening the motel room door, ran through the rain to the SUV. Once behind the wheel, she started the engine and turned on the heat to clear the windshield. Her coat was soaked and steaming up the windows faster than the heater could warm to clear them.

As if that wasn't bad enough, Mary Ellen noticed her gas gauge. She couldn't leave here without getting fuel—not with a three-hour drive ahead of her and only two small towns between here and Billings.

She drove beneath the railroad underpass, coming up on Central Avenue, headed south of town on Hwy 191. Her wipers clacked loudly, unable to keep up with the driving rain.

At the last gas station on the edge of town, Packy's, she pulled into the pumps and sat in her car, waiting for the rain to let up a little before she got out to fill her tank.

As she was sitting there, a pickup pulled in on the other side of the pumps. To her shock, Eve Bailey Jackson got out and began filling the truck's gas tank. She wore a cowboy hat, jeans and boots and a slicker and seemed oblivious of the rain.

Mary Ellen wondered what Eve was thinking about as she finished getting gas and went inside to pay.

In the glow of warm light inside the small old-fashioned convenience store, Eve visited for a few minutes with the young woman behind the counter. Mary Ellen couldn't tell what Eve was saying. It didn't matter. She watched her, mesmerized.

"God help me," she whispered, tears welling in her eyes, as Eve Bailey Jackson came out.

Their gazes met for a moment through the rain. Eve slowed her step, frowned, and for a moment Mary Ellen feared she would come over to the car.

Hurriedly, Mary Ellen started her engine and pulled away as Eve walked to her truck and, still standing in the rain, watched as Mary Ellen drove away.

FAITH'S CELL PHONE RANG. She smiled as she saw who it was. "Hello?"

"How're your chores going?" Jud asked. "I was hoping we could meet in an hour."

The last thing she should be doing was having dinner with Jud and his family. But she was curious about him. Curious about his family. "See you then."

She'd barely hung up when she got a call from her brother-in-law.

"I did that checking you asked for," the sheriff said.

"That was fast."

"Stop by my office if you want to see what I came up with. Nothing raises a red flag other than that trouble with the director. It apparently wasn't his first encounter with the law."

When Faith stopped by the sheriff's office, Carter wasn't in, but he'd left an envelope for her. She didn't open it until she reached her pickup.

Inside was a page of information on each of the people she'd asked him about. She scanned it, disappointed. Most of the information was the same as what she'd read in the movie magazines.

In the old days, movie stars often changed their names for Hollywood. That was less likely now. Nevada's parents had been involved in show business and had given each of their children "star" names.

Chantal Lee was actually Chantal Leigh Olsen. Brooke Keith had changed her name from Samantha Brooke Keifer. Nancy Davis was just Nancy Davis.

Nothing new about Jud. He was one of five brothers, raised on a ranch in Texas, started riding horses at the age of two.

Faith started to put the pages away when something caught her eye. Nancy Davis and Brooke Keith were both from the same small town in Idaho.

Looking up through the rain, Faith blinked. Nancy Davis had just pulled up in front of the *Milk River Examiner* and was now getting out of the SUV. The timing was too perfect.

As the assistant director ducked into the local newspaper office, Faith climbed out of her pickup and ran through the rain after her.

Like a lot of businesses in the small Western town, the newspaper didn't just offer news. It sold office supplies, offered photo processing and displayed the latest fundraiser auction items in its front window.

Nancy turned as she heard the door open behind her and quickly checked her expression, but not before Faith had seen dread in the woman's face. Nancy wasn't happy to see her.

Since Faith had come on the film, Nancy had been cordial and businesslike. But definitely not friendly. Faith had wondered if it was because she'd taken Brooke's job. Or if Nancy was just that way, since she seemed to keep her distance from everyone on the set.

"Hi," Faith said to her and pretended interest in a loose-leaf notebook.

Andi Blake came out of the back of the newspaper office to wait on Nancy. Andi was dating Cade Jackson, the sheriff's older brother.

"Hi, Andi. I didn't know you were working here again," Faith said to the pretty Southerner.

"I'm a reporter again." Andi had been a big-city TV anchor before coming to Whitehorse as a reporter and falling in love with Cade.

Faith noticed the diamond engagement ring on Andi's finger. "Congratulations! When did that happen?"

"Just last night," Andi said, blushing. "We haven't had a chance to tell anyone yet."

"Don't worry, it's Whitehorse. By now, word is already circulating."

Andi laughed. "You're probably right. Several of the members of the Whitehorse Sewing Circle were in this morning, so I guess the announcements have been sent. Heard about you working as a stuntwoman on the film and your accident this morning."

"Excuse me?" Nancy said impatiently. "Erik Zander asked me to pick up some old newspapers for the film set?"

"Sorry, I thought you two were together. Just give me a moment. I'll get them." Andi disappeared into the back again.

Faith didn't like Nancy being rude to Andi, who would soon be family, but she hid her feelings as she asked, "Do you have to get right back to the set? I was hoping we could have a cup of coffee."

Nancy looked surprised, then suspicious. "Erik is waiting for—"

"Just a quick cup. I wanted to ask your advice on something."

Nancy raised a brow, but said nothing as Andi returned with a large manila envelope.

"These are replicas of newspapers from the years he asked for," Andi said. "Should I put that on the movie account?"

"Yes, thank you." Nancy shoved the envelope into her large satchel as she turned to Faith. "I suppose I have time for a quick cup of coffee."

Faith told Andi goodbye and she and Nancy walked down the street to the small coffee shop. This time of the day the place was empty. They sat by the window. Nancy gave her a wry smile as she picked up the latte the waitress had put in front of her. "So it's advice you want?"

Faith had thought about breaking the ice by asking Nancy's advice about a career in movies, a ruse she realized the woman would have seen right through.

"I hope this isn't going to be more nonsense about Brooke's snakebite," Nancy said.

"No," Faith said. "But it is about Brooke."

Nancy frowned.

"She mentioned that the two of you went to school together in your hometown. Ashton, Idaho, right?"

All the color left Nancy's face. "Brooke told you that?"

"I'm pretty sure she's the one who mentioned it. Why? Is it a secret?" Faith chuckled as if she'd made a joke.

"Of course not. It's just not true."

"Really?"

Nancy seemed flustered. "Well, I mean, I guess she is from Ashton originally, too, but we didn't know each other."

"Oh, I just assumed you were friends, since it's a small town and you're both about the same age…"

"We went to the same school, but Brooke moved to California our junior year," Nancy said. "I never really knew her."

"So the two of you have never discussed being from the same town?"

"No, this is the first movie we've worked on together, and we have no reason to reminisce about Idaho. I'm sure she's as glad to be out of there as I am."

Nancy seemed to realize what she'd said. "Not that there is anything wrong with Idaho or Montana, it's just…I really have to go." She rose from the table, then hesitated.

"My treat," Faith said, even though Nancy had made no move to pay for their coffees.

"I know it wasn't advice you were after when you invited me for coffee, but I'm going to give you some anyway. Stop being so nosy. None of this has anything to do with you."

Without another word, Nancy turned and walked out. Faith stared after her. None of what had nothing to do with her?

She remembered what the sheriff had said about Zander having an earlier brush with the law and pulled out the papers he'd given her. Apparently there'd been another unfortunate accident that resulted in a death years ago. This one a car accident. Erik Zander had been driving.

A young woman had been killed. That time, too, he escaped being brought up on charges, although it was rumored that he'd been drinking and that the young woman was pregnant.

Sounded like history repeating itself if Erik Zander had been the father of that baby, as well.

That death had happened more than twenty years ago.

Faith paid for the coffee and went out to her pickup before she dialed the sheriff's office. When Carter came on the line she said, "Thanks for the information you left me."

"I warned you there wasn't much to find."

"I'm curious about something else, though. That incident involving the car wreck and Erik Zander twenty-some years ago, can you get me more information on it?"

"What are you doing?" Carter asked with a sigh.

"Satisfying my curiosity."

Carter said something under his breath she didn't catch. It had sounded like, "You damned Bailey girls."

"I'll see what I can find out. There won't be much since Zander was never charged."

Just like in the hot tub death twenty years later.

"Faith, I'm a little concerned about what you might be getting yourself into with this," her brother-in-law continued.

"Oh, come on, Carter, what could be more dangerous than being a stuntwoman?" she joked.

"You have a point there," he said. "Just be careful."

"Not to worry. I am always careful."

"Sure. Just like your sisters. And just as stubborn as them, too."

Driving down to Packy's to meet Jud Corbett she reminded herself that she and her sisters had that in common—curiosity. It had gotten them in trouble more times than she could remember. It had almost gotten both her sisters killed.

THE SCOTCH BOTTLE and the two glasses weren't the only things missing, Erik Zander had found out when he returned to his trailer.

That damned doll was gone. It had been the last thing he'd seen before he'd passed out, and now it was nowhere to be found.

He glanced out his window and saw Nancy returning. He tried to remember what he'd sent her to town to get for him. Whatever it had been, she didn't seem all that anxious to bring it to him.

"Erik?" Nancy looked surprised to see him standing at her trailer door. "I was going to bring you the old newspapers you had me get." She picked up a manila envelope and held it out to him.

He didn't take it.

"Erik? Is something wrong?"

He glanced over his shoulder and saw some of the crew standing a few yards away. "Can I come in?"

"Of course." She moved aside to let him enter. He closed the door behind him, then stood for a moment wishing he hadn't been so impulsive. *Just take the damned envelope and leave well enough alone.*

If he asked her about the doll, she was bound to wonder why he was making such a big deal out of a damned rag doll. It would be all over the set that he believed the evil of Lost Creek was real. Everyone was probably already talking about him after his so-called panic attack.

"Is there something else?" Nancy asked. She looked flushed, even upset. Since she never got rattled, he wondered if something had happened in town.

Not that he cared what had her stirred up. He had

too many problems of his own. His throat felt dry. He would have killed for a drink—if he hadn't been afraid to take one.

"I wanted to ask you if you took anything from my trailer," he blurted out.

Her eyes narrowed. "You asked me to take the Scotch bottle and the two used glasses, but like I told you, they weren't there when I looked for them."

"Not that." He glanced around her trailer, surprised how neat it was. He realized he didn't know this woman, certainly hadn't recognized her name when he'd been blackmailed into making her assistant director on this film. Was she Hasting's spy on the set? She seemed a bit...weak for the part.

"I thought I saw something on the floor of the bedroom right before I passed out," he said regretting this. "You didn't find anything?"

"What did you think you saw?"

He waved a hand through the air. "It's not important."

"Erik," she said as he turned to leave. "I didn't find anything out of place when I searched your trailer for the Scotch and glasses you and Chantal used."

He nodded and pushed open the door. Whoever had gotten rid of the glasses and Scotch had also taken the doll. But why? Someone had entered the trailer after he was flown to the hospital.

Not Nancy, since she'd flown with him in the chopper to the hospital. That left Hasting, Nevada, Chantal and Brooke. All of them had been in his trailer just that morning before his soon-to-be-legendary panic attack.

"Who has keys to the trailers?" he asked as a thought struck him.

"The occupants."

"The company that rents them must keep an extra. They didn't give you a master key?"

She frowned. "No. No one has a key to your trailer but you and the rental company. Why? Have you lost your key? I didn't think you ever locked the door."

He didn't.

"I tried it this morning when I came over. It was open," she explained, looking embarrassed. "It was open when I came back. Anyone could have gone in. I'm sorry I didn't think to lock it."

He stared at her. She was so damned competent. He didn't know what he would have done without her. Hell, she was the one that got both him and Brooke to the hospital before they'd died. He stared at her, seeing her maybe for the first time.

Something about the way she was looking at him nudged a memory. Maybe he had worked with her before and just forgotten. Or maybe they'd met somewhere else...

"Erik? Are you sure you're all right?"

He shook his head as his skin went cold and clammy, the contents of his stomach recoiling. He suddenly felt sick. Stumbling down her trailer steps, he aimed himself at his own trailer, hoping he could reach it in time.

MARY ELLEN DROVE around aimlessly until she realized she hadn't had anything to eat all day and was weak and sick with hunger.

The only place open at this hour was a convenience store on the west end of town. She went in and got herself a cup of coffee and a sweet roll. It was too late to head for Billings, even if she could leave.

She knew she should go back to the motel and get some sleep, but she couldn't rid herself of the image of Eve's face peering at her through the pouring rain. That startled look haunted her.

What had *Eve* seen? A resemblance to her own face? How long had Eve looked for that in every older woman's face, hoping to see her mother looking back?

Mary Ellen paid for the sweet roll and coffee and went back to her car. She forced herself to choke down the roll, knowing she needed sustenance, but unable to taste a bite. Washing down the last of it, she told herself she had to end this.

For years she'd lived with the lies and deceit. She couldn't do it any longer. But telling the truth would mean not only confessing to what she'd done, but also reliving her sins. She'd never been able to face those horrible memories, and yet she'd never been able to escape them, either.

Mary Ellen stared out through the rain, chilled at the sound of it drumming on the car roof. It was too late to do anything tonight. But if she waited she might lose what little courage she had.

She pulled out her cell phone and called Eve Bailey Jackson's number.

The phone rang once. Mary Ellen's hand shook and she almost snapped the cell shut as the phone at the other end rang a second time.

"Hello?" A woman's voice. Eve's?

Mary Ellen swallowed, her throat almost too dry to make a sound. "Eve Bailey Jackson?"

"Yes?"

"My name is Mary Ellen." She swallowed. "Mary Ellen *Small*. Your mother was my sister."

Chapter Eight

Jud had thought about calling ahead to let his family know he was bringing Faith to dinner.

But he didn't want anyone making a big deal of out it. If he made it sound like a spur-of-the-moment invitation, maybe his family wouldn't try to read anything more into it.

He'd told Faith the truth: he didn't like leaving her alone on the set. What he hadn't told her was that he thought he'd seen something right before the team of horses had been spooked. Movement on the fringe and something flying through the air. A rock? He couldn't be sure. And that's what worried him.

But his gut instinct told him that someone had intentionally caused the horses to spook. Had they known, though, that the team would take off and nearly kill Faith? Or had they thought it was Chantal sitting on the wagon, since that's who was supposed to be there at that moment according to the call sheet?

He didn't want to believe the accident had anything to do with Faith. Whoever was deliberately causing the accidents on the set had to be trying to sabotage the film. Why anyone involved in the movie would want to sabotage it was anyone's guess.

Or maybe it had been just a few unlucky accidents and he was making too much of it because he'd gotten Faith into this and now felt he had to keep her safe.

As he and Faith drove through the rain toward Trails West Ranch, Jud was glad to lose himself in the landscape. It was July, the wet grass was still a vibrant green that ran from horizon to horizon.

It surprised him how the land up here had gotten into his blood. When he'd thought of Montana, he'd always thought of snowcapped mountain peaks and towering pine trees—not the prairie with the only mountains in the distance and few if any pines.

But he liked that thousands of buffalo used to race across this expanse of earth and that outlaws holed up in the Missouri Breaks badlands. One of Butch Cassidy's and the Sundance Kid's alleged last robberies took place just outside of Whitehorse. Sometimes he thought he could feel the history as if it was entrenched in the landscape.

He noticed that Faith seemed content to stare out at the country, as well. Probably had a lot on her mind. He didn't mind not talking. He liked the sound of the rain on the roof of the pickup, the steady slap of the wipers, the sound the tires made as they churned up rainwater from the puddles.

"Where will you go after this?" Faith asked after a while. She'd been gazing out the window, looking at the land with a longing he recognized only too well.

"Wherever the next film takes me." Her gaze had shifted to him. He didn't tell her that he had a few months to kill. The downtime was the hardest. He tended to get into trouble, and that trouble usually involved a woman because, ultimately, he always left them to pursue his stunt work.

"What about you?" he asked, glancing over at her.

She shrugged, a secret smile turning up her lips. "I never thought I'd be doing what I am now, so who knows?"

She wore jeans, boots and a Western blouse that made him too aware of her curves. Her blond hair was pulled up into a ponytail and there was just the faintest touch of makeup, a brush of mascara to her lashes, a little gloss to her lips. The high color of her cheeks was all her own, he thought with a smile.

While Faith had earlier resembled Chantal enough to play her body double, right now she looked nothing like the leading lady.

There was an innocence about Faith that Chantal couldn't even act—and a peace, a self-assurance that he'd seen that first day when he'd caught her doing horse tricks on the back forty.

Now he realized too late that this was exactly the kind of woman his father would like to see him marry. Taking her home could be a huge mistake.

"There's something I need to tell you," he said, and cleared his throat. "I...the thing is, about my family..."

"I'm sure they're no worse than mine," she said, humor in her voice.

"Yeah." He smiled at that. "I just need to fill you in before we get there."

"Will I need a scorecard to keep track?" she asked, turning in the seat to face him.

He gave her a quick rundown of the family, from Juanita, the family cook who his father had convinced to come to Montana with them, to his four brothers, Russell, Dalton, Lantry and Shane.

"Shane's engaged to Maddie Cavanaugh, right?" Faith said.

"Yeah. But I'm not sure Maddie will be there tonight," he said, wondering how much he should tell her. "I believe this will become common knowledge soon enough… Kate, my dad's wife, is Maddie's birth mother."

"She's adopted? I had no idea."

"Not even Maddie knew. So things have been a little tense between Maddie and Kate."

"And Shane?"

"They'll work it out. They're perfect for each other, and since I'm the one who got them together…"

"I can't see you playing Cupid," Faith said, grinning.

"Well, that's another thing I need to tell you."

She laughed. "I need to know all this before having dinner at the ranch with your family?"

He was glad she found humor in it. He wished he did.

"Yeah, actually, you do. You see there's a chance my family might get the wrong idea about you and me."

She cut her eyes to him.

He held up a hand. "Not because of me. It's because of these letters my mother left before she died." He explained about his mother's dying wish that her sons marry before the age of thirty-five and marry a Montana cowgirl.

"You drew straws?" She sounded as incredulous as he'd been at the suggestion at the time.

"You had to have been there. The letters, Dad's recent marriage, the move to Montana, this family code we have, it put a lot of pressure on us. I know Dad just wants us all to settle here so we can be closer as a family."

"Realistically, do you see that happening?"

"Hell, no. Nor do I have any plans to get married anytime soon."

"But you drew the shortest straw and there's that family code of yours." She smiled, clearly having fun with him.

"Laugh if you will, but I just wanted to warn you so you know what you might be walking into."

"You're afraid they'll think I'm your date—or worse, your *girlfriend*."

"I'm glad you're enjoying yourself at my expense."

"I had no idea dinner with you and your family could be this…interesting," she said, smiling at him as the ranch came into view.

Trails West Ranch was nestled in a valley of green, the badlands of the Missouri Breaks in the distance. At the center sat the ranch house.

Jud slowed, glanced over at Faith and wondered if it would be so bad if the family thought Faith was his date.

EVE BAILEY CLUTCHED the phone in her hand. "Mary Ellen *Small*? If this is some kind of joke…"

"You called my mother, Mary, looking for a woman named Constance Small. She called me after she hung up with you."

Eve was at a loss for words. "I don't understand." Her voice broke.

"My younger sister was your mother."

"How do I know that's true?" she asked, even as she

remembered the woman she'd seen at Packy's earlier, that feeling of seeing someone she knew, a stranger with a face that had seemed so familiar...

"I brought all the proof you'll need with me, but are you sure you want to know? You may not like what I have to tell you."

Eve felt as if her heart might burst. After all this time, could it be true? "Yes, I've waited for thirty-four years. I'm *sure*."

"It's late. Perhaps we could meet in the morning."

"No, I need to see you now. This can't wait any longer, *please*."

"All right. I doubt either of us will get any sleep tonight anyway. Do you want me to come there?"

"I'll come to you."

"I'm staying at the Riverview Motel. Number six."

"I'll be there in ten minutes." Eve hung up, her heart pounding. Was it possible she was finally going to find out the truth?

But if so, then why hadn't Constance Small come herself? Why send her sister? *Your mother* was *my sister.* That's what the woman had said. Did that mean her mother was dead?

There was only one way to find out. She had so many questions. Eve grabbed the keys to her pickup and headed for the door. Ten minutes. In ten minutes she knew she would be facing the woman she'd seen at Packy's earlier.

Her aunt Mary Ellen Small? Finally someone from her birth family. Someone who resembled her.

Eve knew better than to get her hopes up. She'd been disappointed too many times before. As she drove the five miles into town to the Riverview, she wondered if she should let Carter know where she'd gone.

No. He'd be suspicious and want to come along, and this was something she had to do alone. She didn't even want her brother there, didn't want to get his hopes up until she knew for sure. In truth, she just needed this desperately for herself and had for as long as she could remember.

The rental SUV she'd seen earlier at Packy's was parked in front of room six, just as she knew it would be. Eve braced herself as she pulled in beside it and, cutting the engine, she got out and ran through the rain.

She was trembling with excitement and anxiety and cold dread. For so long she'd feared she would never know what happened the night she was born. Nor would she ever see another person who looked like her, who shared her blood, her coloring, her DNA.

Then her twin brother, Bridger, had come into her life. And she'd told herself it was enough. But she couldn't smother that need in her to find her birth mother. To know why the woman had given them up.

Eve feared Mary Ellen Small was right, that she wasn't going to like the answer, as she tapped at the motel room door, terrified.

The woman had asked her if she was sure she wanted to know the truth. Without hesitation, she'd said yes.

But now that Eve was this close to it, could she take the truth? What could hurt more than knowing your mother gave you up?

Nothing, she told herself as the door opened and she came face-to-face with a woman who looked so much like her that Eve began to cry.

FAITH FELT AT home right away. The Trails West Ranch house was warm and beautiful inside, the decor keeping with the area and the history of the ranch itself. The walls and floors were rich wood, the fireplace stone and the furnishings Western.

Grayson Corbett was as charming as his son and equally as handsome. He greeted her warmly and then introduced her to his wife, Kate.

She was a striking woman and Faith immediately saw the resemblance between her and Maddie Cavanaugh.

"You brought a date?" asked a male voice as Faith was led into a large family room that looked out over the ranch. It was furnished with soft, deep leather chairs and a bar stocked better than any saloon in town.

"My brother Dalton," Jud said with a sigh. "Meet Faith Bailey. She's a local who's doing stunt work on the film."

Faith shook hands with Dalton and saw three other brothers rise to their feet for introductions, all of them equally gorgeous.

"I heard the other stuntwoman was bitten by a rattlesnake," Kate said. "Is she all right?"

"She's fine. She'll be helping with the stunts," Jud was saying behind her.

"Lantry Corbett. I'm the smart, good brother," he said, shaking Faith's hand. "And this is Shane and Russell."

Faith recognized Shane. Now that she thought about it, she recalled seeing Shane dancing with Maddie Cavanaugh at a rodeo last month at the fairgrounds.

Russell seemed the most reserved of the brothers, as Grayson asked what she'd like to drink and Faith found herself in the middle of all the Corbetts sipping an ice-cold margarita rimmed with salt and laughing at the antics of the "boys," as Grayson called his five sons.

Later, as she was led into dinner, the dining room smelled of corn tortillas and a wonderfully spicy sauce. By then, she'd warmed to all the Corbetts. Her only misgiving was that they did indeed believe she was Jud's date. She felt as if she were auditioning for a role in a Corbett film.

The worst part was that she knew by the end of the evening that she had the role if she wanted it. And that gave her more pleasure than it should have. But it also made her a little sad since she wasn't up for the part.

"I had fun tonight," she said on the drive back toward the movie location. "I like your family."

"They certainly liked you," Jud said, not sounding all that happy about it.

"I'm sorry if that causes you trouble."

He laughed softly. "Maybe I should try to line you up with one of my brothers. Just kidding," he said almost too quickly.

"Want to keep me all for yourself, huh? I don't know if I like that. That one brother of yours…"

"Don't even think about—" He broke off abruptly as he realized somewhat belatedly that she was only joking. "Not that one of them wouldn't *love* you," he said with a shake of his head. "But I'm through playing matchmaker."

They fell into a comfortable silence, the narrow two-lane road seeming endless. Faith felt close to Jud, the cab of his pickup pleasurably intimate. She still couldn't believe the twist of fate that had brought her to this moment in time.

"The stunt early tomorrow is an easy one," Jud said,

as if wanting to get back on more secure footing. It had felt like a date tonight and she was sure that made him uncomfortable.

"I'm not worried," she said of the upcoming stunt and looked out at the night. The stunt was part of the love scene sequence. The heroine tries to outrun the hero on a horse. He catches her, drags her off her horse and into his arms for a passionate kiss. Faith's part would end once her feet touched the ground—just before the kiss.

As Jud pulled into Packy's beside her pickup, he said, "I'll follow you. Just in case you have any problems."

"I don't need you to protect me." Although she was touched.

"Too bad. Until this film is over, I'm stuck to you like glue."

Until the film was over, which wasn't long.

True to his word, he followed her out to the set. As she topped a rise, the lights of Jud's pickup right behind her, she spotted the film's base camp through the now drizzling rain below her and felt disappointed. In a few short minutes, this night would end.

When Jud turned off the charm, he was quite…well, charming, and seeing him with his family, he'd gotten to her tonight.

She drove down the hill and parked. He pulled in beside her and climbed out. They hurried to duck under the awning of her trailer, which was closest to where they'd both parked. She breathed in the damp scent of the rainy summer night as if she could hold on to it and this moment forever.

The night was cool enough that she would have been grateful to be in his arms. But Jud stood away from her, looking out at the dark circle of trailers, the light rain pattering on the awning over their heads.

"If for any reason you need my help, day or night—"

"Don't worry about me," she said, hugging herself. "I'll be fine."

"Just do me one favor," he said, turning toward her, keeping his voice low. "Please don't ask any more questions about the accidents."

The rainy darkness settled around them. Faith hadn't realized how late it was. Not a light glowed in the encampment, not a sound could be heard from any of the other trailers.

"Faith, please. Promise me."

Not wanting to spoil the evening, she said, "Trust me, I'll be good." She didn't say what she'd be good at. Nor did she completely understand why, like her sisters, she'd never been able to turn the other way when there was trouble. Or better yet, run.

"Thank you for a very enjoyable dinner," she said, but didn't move. Nor did Jud.

They stood staring at each other. For one incredibly prolonged moment Faith thought he might kiss her good-night. Her heart was pounding so hard she feared it alone would rouse the whole place.

Jud took a step back, looking nervous, actually awkward, a strange sight considering the grace of the man.

Faith hurriedly opened her trailer door, realizing he was merely waiting until she was safely inside.

Once inside, she peeked out to see Jud walking off through the rain, shaking his head and muttering under his breath. She smiled to herself, touched by his concern for her and pretty sure a kiss had been on his mind, as well.

She hoped he was mentally kicking himself all the way back to his trailer.

EVE STARED THROUGH her tears at the woman standing in the motel-room doorway.

Mary Ellen Small stared back, tears welling in her dark eyes as she said, "You look even more like Constance up close. Please, come in." She stepped back to let Eve enter, her tone businesslike, but Eve saw a tremor in the woman's hands as she closed the door.

The room was like any other motel room, except this one was almost too clean and tidy, making Eve question how long the woman had been staying here.

"How long—"

"I got to town yesterday," Mary Ellen said. "I told myself I only came here to see you from a distance. I had no intention of actually meeting you, let alone talking to you about Constance."

Eve frowned. "What changed your mind?"

"I'm not sure. Won't you have a seat?" She indicated one of the chairs at a small table.

"I think I'm too nervous to sit," Eve admitted.

The woman smiled at that. "I made coffee. I thought we both might need a cup. Please sit down. We have time, don't we?"

"After waiting thirty-four years, what's a few more minutes?" She pulled out a chair and sat down as Mary Ellen Small poured two cups of coffee and using the lid of the plastic ice bucket carried them over to the table. She returned to bring back sugar and creamery packets, napkins and spoons, before she took the other chair.

"You said I look like my mother?" Eve said cradling

the cup of hot coffee in both her hands for the warmth. She was shaking and needed something to anchor her.

Mary Ellen nodded, studying her. "It's quite shocking how much you resemble her. I see nothing of your father—" She broke off and looked away before concentrating on her coffee.

"You knew my father, then."

The woman took a sip of her coffee, then carefully put down the cup. "How much do you really want to know?" she asked, her gaze locking with Eve's for a long moment.

"Everything." It might be her only chance. Eve wasn't about to pass it up, no matter the outcome. "Not knowing is worse than anything."

"Maybe."

Suddenly Eve wanted Bridger here. "My twin brother. He'll want to hear this." She drew out her cell phone.

Mary Ellen covered her hand. "Why don't you decide if you want to tell him after you hear what I'm going to say."

Something in her tone made Eve hesitate. Bridger was so happy right now with his wife and infant son. He'd found peace. Until she knew what this woman had to tell her...

"All right," Eve said and tried to settle back into her chair, afraid Mary Ellen Small might be right. This might be something Bridger wouldn't want to hear. "Please, tell me about my mother and why she isn't the one telling me this."

As FAITH TURNED away from the window and the image of Jud disappearing into the darkness near his trailer, she saw the doll.

It sat on the small kitchen counter, its black-stitched eyes staring blankly at the door—and her.

Faith started at the sight of it, stumbling back, her hand going to her mouth to hold back a scream. Only then did she realize her trailer door hadn't been locked moments ago.

But she'd made sure it was locked when she'd left to go into town. Someone must have the key. Someone who wanted to scare her by leaving one of those horrible rag dolls for her to find.

Her initial shock morphed into anger in an instant. Whoever had done this was wasting her time if she thought she could intimidate her. Nancy Davis. That's who it had to be. She must have spare keys for all the trailers since she seemed to be the director's go-to girl.

Faith was so furious she thought about confronting Nancy tonight, just storming over there with the doll in hand and beating on the assistant director's door.

She took a breath. Probably not the best approach, given that she still had to work with Nancy. No, the best thing to do would be to ignore it. Faith certainly wasn't buying into the dolls being harbingers of disaster.

Stepping to the kitchen counter, she picked up the doll and was surprised by her reaction to the touch. She *was* buying into all this heebie-jeebie stuff. Angry with herself as much as the person who'd left it, she tossed the doll into the trash.

For a few moments, she stood in the kitchen breathing hard, angry and scared. Cursing, she stepped to the door, locked it, then dragged a chair over and levered it under the handle. It wouldn't keep anyone with a key out, but if someone tried to come in, the chair would at least fall and warn her.

She tried to calm down, but her blood still ran hot and her skin clammy and chilled with apprehension.

Knowing she would pay hell getting to sleep after this, Faith decided to take a hot shower. She'd brought along a long white flannel nightgown, a birthday present from her mother that she'd never worn. Usually she slept in a soft, worn T-shirt and nothing else.

Tonight seemed like the perfect night for the old-lady nightgown and the new mystery novel she'd picked up in town. She'd be ready if she had another visitor.

FAITH WOKE WITH a start. She couldn't remember falling asleep, but the mystery novel lay open beside her on the bed. She listened. The rain had stopped. Is that what had awakened her?

Whatever it had been, she knew she wouldn't be able to go back to sleep until she checked the trailer. She hated that the doll had spooked her. It was just a stupid, ugly doll. But it meant that someone on this set was trying to scare her.

Normally, she didn't scare easily, she thought, as she padded through the small trailer. The chair she'd put against the door was right where she'd left it. No one had broken in.

She glanced at her watch. A little after 1:00 a.m. For a moment, she stood in the middle of the living room. The curtains were all closed and she hadn't turned on a light. She moved through the dim darkness to the window that looked out on the other trailers and carefully drew back the curtain.

Low clouds hung over the camp, the moon illuminating them and casting the night in a silver glow. No lights shone in any of the trailers. She stared out into the night and yawned. Nothing moved in the eerie light.

As she started to let the curtain fall back into place, something caught her eye. A dark figure was standing behind one of the equipment trailers.

Faith's breath caught in her throat as she noticed there was what looked like a large bundle at the person's feet. She watched frozen in place as the figure bent down and began to pull on the large object.

A chill streaked up her spine as the two forms melted into the shadows behind the trailer.

The person appeared to be dragging a body.

Chapter Nine

Faith couldn't move, could barely breathe. She wanted to scream, to wake up the entire camp. But reminded herself that she couldn't trust her eyes. The stupid doll had left her jumping at shadows.

But if that wasn't someone dragging a body away from the camp, then what *had* she seen?

She stared out the window. The figure had dropped over a rise. If she just kept standing here... Faith moved quickly to the door, removing the chair, and opening her door to look out.

Seldom in her life had she been unable to make a decision. Better to make a wrong one than do nothing, had always been her motto. She looked down at what she was wearing. No time to change. She looked around for her boots and, giving up, stepped out of the trailer and started across the encampment in her bare feet.

Her instincts told her to go wake up Jud. But she feared that in the amount of time it would take to get him, the person would be gone. Not to mention how she would feel if it turned out she'd only imagined a person pulling a body away from camp.

There was that and the fact that Faith didn't trust herself tonight. Or was it her imagination she mistrusted? Of course it couldn't have been a body. It must have been a bag of equipment.

But why would anyone drag a bag of equipment out toward the prairie in the middle of the night? Maybe someone robbing the set.

Faith needed to be sure she wasn't on a wild-goose chase. If she could just get a good look...

She sprinted barefoot across the open area to the edge of the trailer where she'd last seen the person and worked her way to the back. Squinting through darkness, she saw nothing. No movement. No person. No body.

She was on a fool's errand, she told herself as she slipped around the edge of the trailer into the blackness of the night. The clouds were so low she found herself walking through a foggy mist. This was crazy. Her feet were cold and wet, as was the hem of her nightgown. What was she doing?

Movement. She blinked, took a step and felt something squish between her toes. Mud. That's when she saw the tracks. Drag marks in the mud.

She shuddered. Turn back. Go get help. In the distance, she heard a noise. The distinct clank of a tailgate being dropped. To load whatever the person had been dragging. That meant the person had a vehicle parked out there.

Avoiding walking in the tracks, telling herself they could be evidence, she followed the drag marks through the mist.

As she topped a rise, she saw a light blink on ahead. A dome light in a vehicle parked down in a gully. Faith looked back and saw nothing but mist. She could make out only the tops of the trailers in the distance. If she yelled for help, she doubted anyone would hear her. All it would do is alert the person below her.

Crouching down, she edged her way into the gully. It was an old, dry creek bed, which made her sorry she hadn't at least taken the time to find her boots.

The pickup had been backed into a small bluff. No doubt to make dragging a body into the truck's bed easier. Faith couldn't see anyone around the pickup. The tailgate was still down but from where she was, she couldn't tell if anything had been loaded in the back.

So where had the person gone?

Holding her breath, she moved up the dry creek bed, each step painful barefoot.

The vehicle was one of the trucks rented for the movie crew. The driver's-side door was open, the dome light a dim glow inside the cab. No sign of anyone.

If it hadn't been for the tracks and the pickup, she might have been able to convince herself she'd imagined the whole thing.

But her instincts told her that there was a body in the back of that pickup. Maybe the person who'd dragged it out here had circled back to the camp for something. She had to move fast. Just get a look in the bed of the truck and hightail it back to the camp for help.

Faith edged closer, stepped on a sharp rock and almost cried out. She was within feet of the pickup. Just a little closer. The hair on the back of her neck stood up as she touched the wet, cold metal and leaned over the side to look into the bed of the truck.

The scream rose in her throat, but it didn't get a chance to escape as something hard and solid struck her temple. The night went black and empty.

THE MOTEL ROOM was deathly quiet in the late hour. Eve listened to the hum of the coffeemaker and her own pounding heart. If the woman sitting across from her hadn't looked so much like her, Eve would fear this was all a dream.

Or worse, a hoax.

"You must let me tell you in my own way," Mary Ellen said in her reserved tone. "This is very difficult for me." Her voice broke.

"I'm sorry," Eve said and tried to be patient.

A moment later, Mary Ellen put down her coffee cup and began. "Constance was the sweetest little baby. I was there the night she was born. She was one of those babies that hardly ever cried, smiled all the time. We all loved her and spoiled her. Maybe too much."

Eve waited, saying nothing as Mary Ellen seemed to need time to gain control again.

"Constance began to rebel in high school. I was two years older. I had always been such an obedient child, a straight-A student, the child who never caused any problems. Because of that my parents were at a loss as to what to do about Constance. She became more willful. Looking back, I'm sure she was rebelling because of me. She had always been in my shadow and because of that too much was expected of her. Her grades were never as good nor could she seem to stay out of trouble."

Mary Ellen seemed to brace herself. "I fell in love my senior year. I'd never even dated before that. Paul was—" Her voice broke. "Paul was everything I'd ever dreamed of. Handsome and sweet. We planned to marry after college. My parents adored him. Constance *idolized* him."

Eve felt dread growing inside her.

"Paul gave me an engagement ring on my eighteenth birthday." Mary Ellen smiled in memory. "The diamond was small, but I thought it was the most beautiful thing I'd ever seen."

Eve watched her take a sip of her coffee, aware there were no rings on the woman's slim fingers. Nor apparently had she ever changed her last name.

"For my high school graduation a few months later, my parents threw a party for me at our home. Paul had seemed upset that day. It wasn't until my sister came to me in tears…" Mary Ellen swallowed, her throat constricting for a moment. "She told me she was pregnant. That Paul was the father of her baby."

It felt as if all the air had been sucked out of the room. "You must have been horribly hurt," Eve said, feeling the weight of this woman's pain.

Mary Ellen lifted her gaze to Eve. "I was devastated." She took a breath and let it out. "I vowed to destroy Paul and my sister and the baby she carried."

JUD CORBETT COULDN'T fall asleep. He lay in the dark, thinking about Faith. About dinner. About almost kissing her. It was no wonder he couldn't sleep, given the emotions churning inside him.

What was it about the damned woman? He'd dated his share of beauties, women with talent and intelligence. But he'd never met one like Faith. She was beautiful, talented, intelligent, probably too intelligent, funny, compassionate, passionate and incredibly courageous to the point of concern.

He got up, wearing only his jeans, and padded to the front window to look out at her trailer. It wasn't the first time he'd done this tonight. But he promised himself it was the last. Maybe she couldn't sleep, either. If her light just happened to be on...

It wasn't. He started to let the curtain drop back into place when he saw her. Or at least her ghost.

He hurried to the door and out into the cold night. As he ran to her he saw that her feet were as bare as his own. She wore a long, white nightgown, the hem and back muddy and wet like her feet.

"Faith?"

"Jud?"

"Faith, what are you doing out here in the rain?"

"I..." She looked around, rain running down her face. She shivered. "I was going... I don't know..."

"Were you sleepwalking?"

"I...guess so."

"Faith, you're bleeding."

He swung her up into his arms and carried her toward his trailer. She leaned into him. He listened to her steady breathing, reassured. What if he hadn't gotten up when he did and happened to see her?

Opening his door, he carried her inside to the bathroom. The shower stall was small and he knew from experience that there wouldn't be a lot of hot water in the tank. Setting her down, he saw that her eyes were shut.

"We have to get your wet nightgown off and get you into a hot shower, okay?"

She nodded, still looking confused.

Hurriedly, he turned on the shower and pulled her wet nightgown over her head. Pulling her to her feet, he stepped into the hot water with her still wearing his jeans.

It took the entire tank of hot water to warm her up. When the shower began to run cold, he carried her out to his bed and wrapped her in warm, dry towels, rubbing her skin gently and then covering her with the comforter.

"Feeling better?"

She nodded. "I just don't understand what I was doing out there."

"You must have been sleepwalking." He'd checked to make sure the cut and bump on her head weren't serious enough to have a concussion.

"Don't worry about it. Just rest." She looked exhausted.

She nodded and closed her eyes.

He watched her sleep for a few minutes before he padded back to the bathroom and stripped out of his wet jeans.

Returning to the bedroom, he pulled on a pair of pajama bottoms from a pair he'd gotten for Christmas from one of his brothers. They had scantily clad girl trick riders on them. Appropriate, he thought as he looked down at Faith.

He lay down beside her, pulling her close to keep her warm. She snuggled against him, sighing in her sleep. He listened to her steady breathing, her body warm against his, and fell into a deep sleep.

EVE GASPED, UNABLE to believe what Mary Ellen had just said about wanting to destroy her fiancé and her sister. "You were upset. The two people closest to you had betrayed you. But surely you wouldn't have…" The rest of the words caught in her throat at the look in Mary Ellen Small's dark eyes.

"I wanted to *kill* them," she said in a voice that chilled Eve to her soul. "Constance was crying, pleading with me to forgive her. I knew what she'd done. She'd wanted Paul only because he was mine, just as she coveted everything I'd ever had from my grades to my clothes to my car, all things I'd worked for while she only whined."

The bitterness Eve heard in the woman's voice made her pull away. She picked up her coffee cup, her hands trembling so hard that the now lukewarm coffee splashed onto her jeans.

Mary Ellen handed her a napkin. "You said you wanted to hear this. I can only tell you the truth."

Eve nodded, unable to find her voice, and Mary Ellen continued in that same eerie tone.

"I told Constance I would forgive her if she and Paul did something for me. They owed me. They were to meet me in the trees on the hill behind the house later that night. We agreed on a time and I went back down to my party."

Eve wondered at how the woman could have faced everyone after learning of such a betrayal, but said nothing.

"That night I took all the money I had and packed a suitcase for my sister. Downstairs, I got my father's gun from the cabinet where he hid it, loaded the gun and went into the woods. They were both there waiting for me."

Eve tensed, waiting.

"Paul was as remorseful as my sister. He begged my forgiveness. I told them there was only one way. They both had to leave town, never come back, never contact me or anyone we knew, never tell anyone about the baby. If they broke their part of the agreement, I would kill them. When I pulled out my father's gun, cocked it and pointed the barrel at Constance's head, they believed me." Mary Ellen said the words with such a lack of emotion that Eve shuddered.

"Are you telling me that you never heard from your sister again?" Eve had to ask when Mary Ellen didn't go on.

"I only wish that were true." She took a sip of her coffee her expression as bitter as the brew. "Constance broke the agreement six months later when she called my mother."

Eve waited.

Mary Ellen shook her head, her gaze distant as if lost in the past. "She left me no choice but to do what I had said I would do. I came to Whitehorse. My mother thought I was coming here to save my sister and bring her home. She still believes that. But, of course, that was the last thing I planned to do."

"You didn't *kill* her," Eve said, shaken. Otherwise Eve and her brother wouldn't be here now.

"No, I got there too late."

Eve shook her head. "You were young and hurt, but I don't believe you would have harmed her."

Mary Ellen smiled at that. "I had already harmed her by sending her away at that young age with Paul, who was only a few years older, forcing them to live apart from family and friends with nothing but each other and their shared guilt over what they'd done."

"They weren't entirely innocent."

"No, but I wanted them to suffer the way I suffered. I hoped it would destroy whatever they'd felt for each other and that the pregnancy would make matters worse. I got what I wanted. Constance told my mother she'd been living a nightmare. I took great enjoyment in that."

"I don't know that I wouldn't have done the same thing," Eve said. Her thoughts went to her husband, Carter, and how he had betrayed her when she was a senior in high school. She'd sworn she'd never forgive him. It had taken years. "I have a hard time forgiving."

Mary Ellen glanced at her watch. "There is much more to tell and it's so late. I'm weary. If I promise to tell you the rest tomorrow, will you trust me to do so?"

Eve looked into the woman's eyes, eyes so like her own.

"I can tell you that I never break a promise," Mary Ellen said.

Eve believed her. She nodded and rose.

"Leave your cup. I'll straighten up in the morning."

"What time shall I come back?"

"Ten. It will be good if we both get some rest."

Eve heard the warning in the woman's tone. Eve would need her rest before hearing the conclusion of this story. "I'll be here at ten."

MILES AWAY AT the film encampment, a figure stood in the dark having watched as Jud Corbett took the new stuntwoman into his trailer.

A small faint light was still burning at the front of the trailer, but there hadn't been a sound coming from inside for almost an hour.

What had Faith Bailey told him? She couldn't have been in any shape to tell him much.

I shouldn't have turned my back on her. I thought

she was out cold. Who knew she'd wake up so quickly and head back toward the camp?

It was the last that caused concern. If she'd been able to run away, if she was conscious enough to head in the right direction—back toward the camp, then she might have been cognitive enough to tell Jud what she'd seen.

But wouldn't he have called the sheriff, and wouldn't the sheriff have been here by now?

There was only one thing to do. Wait. Let Faith Bailey spill her guts. But who would believe her if there was nothing to find? Actually, this could be an advantage.

No reason to panic. Everything was going according to plan. This turn of events might work out perfectly.

There was just one fly in the ointment. If Faith Bailey became too much of a problem. Obviously the doll hadn't scared her enough to butt out.

She might need a stronger warning. Or if she became too much of a problem…well, accidents happened all the time on movie sets. She should have learned that with the runaway team.

And if Faith didn't talk…well, no one needed to know about tonight.

But if she continued to hang out with Jud, then she would be jeopardizing Jud Corbett as well as herself. And that would be a shame.

Chapter Ten

Faith woke wrapped in a warm cocoon to the sound of voices outside her trailer. She snuggled deeper, refusing to open her eyes. The room felt cold and she wasn't ready to get up.

For a few moments she couldn't remember where she was. She thought she was at her family's ranch house and that the voices she heard were her sisters downstairs making breakfast. She sniffed the air, hoping against hope for the smell of frying bacon. Pancakes would be good, too. With lots of butter and homemade chokecherry syrup. "Mmmmmm."

Someone stirred next to her.

With a jolt, she shot up in the bed and instantly felt lightheaded, even before she glanced behind her and saw Jud Corbett, where only seconds before he'd been spooned against her.

"What in the—" She was fighting the covers trying to get out of the bed when he grabbed her.

"Easy. I can explain."

She blinked at him, then at the trailer. This wasn't hers. That meant— "What am I doing in your trailer?"

"You were sleepwalking. At least, I think that's what you were doing."

"Sleepwalking?" He had to be kidding. She hadn't sleepwalked since she was a child.

"I found you wandering around the camp in a white nightgown. You were soaked to the skin, muddy and freezing cold."

"And?" she asked, not sure she wanted to hear this part.

"And I put you in the shower, warmed you up—"

"Exactly how did you 'warm me up'?"

"With hot water, then I dried you and put you into my bed and covered you up."

"That's it?"

"What? Did you expect me to take advantage of you?" She narrowed her eyes at him.

"I'm insulted," he said, drawing back from her. "You really don't trust me, do you? No, don't answer that. It's obvious," he said, getting out of bed.

She noted that he wore pajama bottoms- -not that it necessarily proved anything. Glancing down, she saw that she was naked. She pulled the comforter up to her chin. "Where are my clothes?"

"I just told you. All you were wearing was a white nightgown. I hung it up to dry in the bathroom." He moved to the accordion door that separated the living room from the so-called master bedroom/bathroom. "Check if you don't believe me."

She waited until he closed the door all the way before she climbed out of bed and padded into the bathroom. Just the sight of her muddy white nightgown gave her pause. A memory flirted at the edge of her consciousness.

Shivering, she recalled being cold and muddy and… hurt. She stumbled to the mirror over the sink, her fingers going to the bandage on her temple. As she drew back her hand, she realized that Jud might actually be telling the truth.

She'd sworn that he'd never get her into his bed—and he had. But apparently nothing had happened. Unless you considered the fact that he'd stripped her naked and apparently given her a shower, dried her and put her to bed.

She was no prude, but if Jud was going to see her naked, this scenario wouldn't have been her first choice.

"You all right in there?" he called through the thin door.

"Yes." She felt embarrassed for being angry with him, since apparently he'd saved her. Again. Now she was embarrassed on general principle. "Thank you."

"No problem." He sounded gruff. She couldn't really blame him, since she'd questioned his integrity.

"I'm sorry."

"I'm sure it came as shock to wake up next to me."

Something like that.

She could hear people moving around in the camp. She pulled down her nightgown from where he'd hung it to dry. It was still damp. Along with the mud, there was some blood. Her blood, apparently.

"I can't go out like this," she said, glancing down at her naked body and feeling herself flush at the thought of Jud Corbett's hands touching her. Damn, she wished she hadn't missed that.

"I could go to your trailer and get you some clothing. If that's all right. I'll be as discreet as possible."

"That would be nice." She was going to be seen

coming out of his trailer. There would be no getting around that.

As she waited for him to return, she found herself staring again at her nightgown. Bits and pieces of memory played tag in her brain. Just when she thought she could catch hold of one and make sense of it, the darned thing escaped.

She stopped trying so hard, convinced that, given time, it would all come back.

Jud returned and handed her two filled plastic bags through the door. Inside she found a black lace bra and matching panties. Had she been the kind of girl who blushed, she was sure she would have. He'd also brought her a pair of jeans, socks, boots and a Western shirt.

She drew on the clothing, stuffed the soiled nightgown into one plastic bag and opened the door between the rooms. The smell of coffee dragged her like a lasso into the kitchen.

Without a word, Jud handed her a cup. "No reason to go tearing out of here. Everyone's at breakfast." In other words, in plain sight of his trailer.

She nodded, said "thanks" and took the cup. The coffee tasted heavenly. "You're a lifesaver." She meant it because of the coffee, but she realized it covered the situation pretty well.

"How do you feel?" he asked, motioning for her to take the small recliner while he took the couch.

"Fine."

"I just want to make sure there are no ill effects since we have a stunt to do this morning."

"I'm fine and I apologize for jumping to conclusions this morning."

"Not necessary. I suppose I would have been just as suspicious under the circumstances. Have you always sleepwalked?"

"Not since I was a child."

"You don't remember anything?"

"I feel like the memory is just out of my reach. The last thing I recall was going to bed. But apparently I didn't stay there."

"I just want you to know, about last night, I didn't feel anything, you know..."

She feared she did. "You really don't have to—"

"No, I do. It wasn't sexual. I just wanted to get you dry and warm and make sure you were all right. I wasn't turned on. I guess that's what I'm trying to say."

"Please. *Stop*." She felt her face heat.

He looked as flustered as she felt. "It's not that I don't think you're attractive. Or that I wouldn't like to—"

"Jud! Please. *I understand*."

He nodded, looking uncomfortable—something rare for him.

Faith got up to glance outside from behind the curtains. The breakfast crowd was dispersing as the sun rose up out of the prairie, bright and golden. She would be working today after all, since apparently the other thunderstorm the weatherman had called for was nowhere in sight.

As she started to drop the curtain back in place, she saw Nancy Davis headed in the direction of Jud's trailer with the call sheets for the day and groaned.

Dropping the curtain, Faith hightailed it down the hall, motioning to Jud, who just looked confused. An instant later there was a knock at the door. Jud answered it.

"Mornin'," Faith heard him say.

"Have you seen Faith Bailey?" Nancy asked without returning the greeting.

"As a matter of fact, she just stopped over for coffee," Jud said smoothly.

Faith stepped out, holding her coffee cup in both hands. "Good morning." She smiled at Nancy as she took her revised call sheet. Nancy didn't smile back, her eyes darting between her and Jud.

Faith let out a low curse as Jud closed the door. "She thinks we spent the night together."

Jud laughed. "We did."

"You know what I mean."

"So she thinks we spent all night making love," Jud said, his words soft and seductive as a caress. "It doesn't matter if she does."

Faith wasn't so sure about that. There was something about Nancy Davis that bothered her.

FIVE MINUTES BEFORE TEN, Eve Bailey Jackson pulled up in front of motel. She sat for a moment, so relieved to see that the rental car was still there that she was trembling.

She'd slept some. Carter had beaten her home and she'd had to make up an excuse for being so late coming home.

"I wanted to spend time with Faith," she'd said. Not a lie exactly. "I'm worried about her. You heard about the accident on the set."

They talked about that for a while, then went to bed. Eve was glad when her husband pulled her close and began to make love to her. She lost herself in his touch, needing the escape from her thoughts, her fears, her worries about what Mary Ellen Small would tell her come morning. What if the woman changed her mind and left?

After their lovemaking, exhausted and content, Eve surprised herself by falling asleep.

This morning she hadn't had to come up with a plausible story for her need to be in town by ten. Carter had gone off to work. She'd watched him leave, feeling guilty for not telling him about Mary Ellen. But then she would have had to tell him everything, and she wasn't ready to do that yet.

She had to hear the whole story.

As she got out of her car and headed for the motel room door, Eve felt another stab of guilt at the thought of Bridger. She pushed the guilt aside. There would be time to tell him everything.

Knocking on the door, she realized that the truth about their parents might be a secret she would have to keep to protect him. She prayed that that wasn't the case, but she had a bad feeling as the door opened and she saw Mary Ellen's face.

THE RUMORS ABOUT Jud and Faith ran like a wildfire through the film encampment. Brooke overheard someone in props talking about it before breakfast. She tried not to let it bother her, since everyone grew quiet when she walked past.

They thought she and Jud were an item and that she was brokenhearted by this turn of events.

It made her furious. She knew what people were

saying. That first Brooke had lost her job to the bitch and now the bitch was sleeping with Brooke's man.

"Good morning," Jud said, joining her. He sounded too damned cheerful for his own good.

She grunted in response.

"Is there a problem?" he asked.

"You tell me," she snapped.

"None. None at all," he said, meeting her gaze.

Faith showed up then from the makeup and costume trailers, apparently ready for her stunt. Brooke noticed the bandage on her temple. Makeup had tried to hide it behind her hair, but it was still visible up close. The camera wouldn't pick it up since there wouldn't be any close-ups.

Brooke shot a glance to Jud in question.

He shrugged and shot her one of his grins. She began to relax. Everything was fine. This woman couldn't come between the relationship that Brooke had with Jud. She felt better than she had all morning.

Faith Bailey was a nobody. After this film, she would melt back into obscurity. Jud would forget her just as he had all the other women. The only true bond between a man and woman was friendship. And hers and Jud's was stronger than any film affair, Brooke told herself as she watched Jud whisper something into Faith's ear.

"ARE YOU SURE you're up to this today?" Jud whispered to Faith.

"I'm fine," she said under her breath.

"I'm just worried about that knock you took on your head," he whispered, shifting his body so Brooke couldn't read his lips. He'd seen how intently she'd been watching the two of them. No doubt the rumor mill had been running full tilt all morning.

Faith turned so that they were facing each other, so close that he could smell the scent of his soap on her skin. "I can do this. I'm fine."

He shrugged and stepped back, knowing that Brooke probably wasn't the only one watching them. He couldn't have cared less about what people were saying. But Faith cared.

Jud wanted her mind on the stunt they were about to perform—not on what the crew was saying about the two of them.

"Then let's do it," he said and grinned, hoping to relax her. They'd run through this stunt several times, and Faith knew what to do.

Out of the corner of his eye, he saw Brooke's impatient expression. Everyone was standing by. He knew Zander would have another panic attack if this film were delayed any further.

"We're ready!" he called.

The scene would be shot primarily from behind them as they rode along on horseback through the tall grass side by side. When they reached the mark, she would make her horse rear. The rattlesnake would be added later digitally.

Her horse would take off. Jud would chase her down, the film crew racing along beside him. He would ride up next to her horse and pull her over onto his horse, rein in and drop to the ground to take her into his arms.

They hadn't practiced anything, except the exchange from her horse to his and the dismount. Faith had been flawless.

"Ready," Zander echoed across the set.

As stunt coordinator, Jud called "action," and he and Faith started riding across the prairie at a leisurely pace.

He wished that was what they were doing at this moment. Just the two of them riding out across the prairie with no cameras tracking their every move along with a half-dozen members of the film crew.

He tried to concentrate, but he kept thinking about how he'd felt waking up next to her this morning. He hadn't wanted her to wake up just yet. He loved holding her, smelling her, feeling the warmth of her body next to his own. He'd wanted her there always, he thought as they rode along, the cameras rolling behind them. And just the thought scared the hell out of him.

They reached the mark. On cue, Faith reared her horse and took off at a gallop, leaning over the mount as if for dear life.

Jud went after her, his heart suddenly pounding as if this were real, as if Faith really were in trouble and if he didn't catch her he might lose her.

He never had such crazy thoughts before during stunts. It was from seeing her hurt and confused last night, from being afraid for her. He recalled the odd feeling he'd gotten last night at dinner with his family and Faith. She'd felt so right there. Almost as if she belonged.

He caught up to her and reached for her, pulling her over onto his horse as he reined to a stop and dropped to the ground to take her in his arms, relieved to have the stunt over, to have her safe.

"Got it in one!"

He barely heard the director. His heart was thunder in his chest as he pulled Faith to him, holding her as if for dear life as he brushed her hair back from her face and their eyes met.

Zander yelled, "Keep rolling," but Jud didn't comprehend the words.

His mouth dropped to Faith's and he kissed her with a fervor like none he'd ever known—just as the script called for—only he was no hero and this was no longer fiction.

FAITH CAME OUT of the kiss slowly to the sound of applause. She'd completely forgotten about the film crew the moment Jud had pulled her into his arms and kissed her.

"Cut!"

She drew back now, startled to see all the people watching them, smiling and clapping. Even director Erik Zander was smiling—a miracle in itself.

"That's a wrap. Another storm's moving in. We're moving to the covered set for the saloon scene." Zander looked over at Faith. "Good job, Bailey." Then he turned and walked off before Faith could say "Thank you."

Her legs were wobbly, Jud's kiss making her more off balance than any bump on the head could do. Her face fired with embarrassment. She'd been so into the kiss she'd been oblivious of where they were or who was watching.

Now she felt confused, not sure why Jud had kissed her and realizing he'd probably done it because it was part of the script. Or maybe he'd thought that since everyone was already talking about them, he'd give them something to talk about.

They looked at each other. Jud appeared as awkward as she was, as if he regretted the spur-of-the-moment kiss.

"I should get changed," she said when it appeared neither of them wanted to talk about the kiss and that Brooke was nearby watching them.

"You aren't needed for the saloon shoot and aren't scheduled again until tomorrow," he said. "Are you going to hang around here or go home to your ranch?" He glanced past her to where Brooke was packing up the rest of the gear, distracted for a moment.

So it was business as usual? Faith cleared her throat, stalling, wishing Brooke would leave. She wanted to talk to Jud, to understand what that kiss had been about. But she didn't want to say anything in front of Brooke. She couldn't help feeling that the woman resented her for taking her place.

"I don't know yet."

He nodded. "Just be careful," he whispered.

So it was her *safety* he was worried about?

"Jud can lead your horse back," Brooke said to her. "You look pale. Ride with me in the pickup."

"That's a good idea," Jud said before Faith could argue.

Brooke brushed Faith's hair back as if to inspect the small bandage on her temple. "Whatever did you run into?"

"I was just being clumsy," Faith said.

Brooke met her gaze, as if to let her know she knew she was lying.

The last thing Faith wanted to do was ride back to camp with Brooke, but she didn't want to make a fuss, especially after Jud had put in his two cents. Faith figured he just didn't want to ride back to the set with her, just the two of them, after the kiss.

So she climbed into the passenger side of the pickup as Brooke slid behind the wheel. Out the window, she took one last look at Jud, trying to read his expression and failing.

"Nice job," Brooke said. "You really seem to know what you're doing."

"Thanks," she replied, although she suspected Brooke wasn't referring to the stunt.

"CONSTANCE AND PAUL were living in a rambling old house north of town that smelled of cooked cabbage and desperation," Mary Ellen said, resuming her story. "I drove by the spot where it used to be yesterday. It's gone. The building razed. The earth barren."

As she had done the night before, she'd made coffee. Only this time she'd picked up some donuts at the local grocery. Eve had taken a cup of the hot coffee and nibbled at one of the donuts, just to have something to do.

"They had aged during those months. Paul was working at the local tire shop. His body had filled out, and had it not been for the haggard look in his eyes, he would have been even more handsome than when I'd known him. Constance was—" Mary Ellen's eyes filled with tears "—beautiful. The pregnancy, you know. It made her glow. And while she'd told our mother that her life had been a nightmare, her unhappiness didn't show on her. Oh, she cried, of course, and begged again for my forgiveness. She said the pregnancy had been hard on her and that she needed to go home, to be around Mother. All I saw was her selfishness. Even after everything she'd done to me, she was only thinking of herself." Mary Ellen smiled. "I was unable to see my own selfishness in wanting to keep her apart from our mother and the people we had both known at home."

"Surely those same people had noticed that both your sister and your fiancé had disappeared," Eve said.

"I concocted believable stories. Paul was smart, a promising student in high school. Everyone believed that he'd had a chance to go to college early. I was still wearing his ring, still pretending that we would be married the next summer. Mother and I had been making wedding plans when my sister had called her, destroying even that hope."

Eve shook her head. "You couldn't possibly have believed that—"

"That Paul would come back to me?" She laughed softly. "What else did I have to hope for? I told myself that he would realize his mistake. I planned to make him suffer the rest of his life when he came crawling back."

"But what about the babies?" Eve realized even as she said it that she knew what had happened to the babies. She and Bridger would end up being adopted.

"I didn't care what happened to their baby. I didn't know then that she carried twins. I fear that would have made me hate her even more."

Eve said nothing, waiting, thinking she already knew the end of the story. She couldn't have been more wrong.

THE FIRST THING Faith noticed when she entered her trailer was the overturned chair. She stared at it. What was it doing in the middle of the room? She recalled putting it against the door before she'd gone to bed. Obviously at some point, she'd moved it.

But she wouldn't have left it overturned in the middle of the floor unless she'd left the trailer in a hurry.

She stared at it. Had she really been sleepwalking? Maybe she'd knocked it over. But wouldn't the noise have awakened her?

"I'll make you some tea," Brooke said, coming in the trailer behind her.

Faith had just assumed Brooke would leave once she dropped her off. "That isn't necessary, really." She wanted to be left alone so she could try to remember last night. Brooke was distracting her.

"I have my own special blend." Brooke pulled a small bag from her pocket and stepped into the small kitchen.

That's when Faith noticed the small trash can next to the stove. It was empty. Where was the rag doll she'd thrown in it last night? Someone had come in and taken it.

Her heart began to pound wildly. Someone had been in her trailer—*again*. Even if she *had* been sleepwalking, she wouldn't have taken that doll out of the trash.

"Please, I really just want to change and rest," she said to Brooke, who had been searching for something to make tea in. The trailers had come stocked with everything a camper might need, including pots and pans.

"Didn't get much sleep last night, huh?"

"No. I don't mean to be rude, but I don't drink tea. Please."

Brooke appeared to be about to argue, but she must have changed her mind. She pocketed the special blend and with a tight smile said, "I was just trying to help."

Somehow Faith found that hard to believe. "Thank you. I appreciate your concern." She closed the door behind Brooke and locked it. Then she took a step toward her bedroom, the bed coming into view, and stopped again.

The doll sat on the unmade bed, back to her pillow, dark eyes staring down the hallway at her.

It was just a doll. She knew that rationally. But still it sent her heart galloping. The doll on her bed meant someone had come into her trailer last night after she left.

Left for where?

Gingerly she peeled off the bandage and stepped into the bathroom to stare into the mirror. There was a small cut, a bruised bump. What had she stumbled into?

As she touched her sore temple, she had a flash of memory. Her pulse quickened. The memory skidded away but not before she'd had a glimpse of walking past one of the trailers—the equipment trailer.

She'd been following something into the darkness.

Following *someone*.

Chapter Eleven

Faith quickly showered and changed clothes, her mind racing. What had happened last night? Had she ended up confused with a knot on her head because she'd followed the person she'd seen?

There was only one way to know for sure. Dressed in her usual jeans, boots, snap-shirt and Western straw hat, she left her trailer and headed for the back of the equipment trailer.

The camp felt empty. Everyone must have gone to the saloon shoot. She concentrated on last night as she crossed the circle between the trailers. While her memory was still fuzzy, she felt as if she were retracing her footsteps.

But why would she come out into the night barefoot in only a nightgown? What had she seen? Something that had forced her not to take the time to change clothes or at least pull on her boots. It wouldn't have been the first time she'd acted impulsively. Or the last, she thought, as she neared the back of the equipment trailer.

Still, it bothered her that if she'd seen something that had made her rush out of her trailer like that; why hadn't she tried to get help? True, it wasn't in her nature to ask for help. She was mule-headed and probably thought she was more capable of taking care of herself than she was.

The cut and bump on her head—case in point.

At the back of the equipment trailer, she stared down at the ground. Was her memory playing tricks on her? She'd vaguely recalled following tracks.

What tracks there might have been had been washed away by the storm that had blown in later in the night apparently. The top surface of the ground had dried from the morning sun and the breeze that now stirred her hair.

She looked out over the prairie. From a distance the land in this part of Montana appeared flat. Just a huge expanse of grass that ran to the Little Rockies.

It was deceptive, because once you started across the land, you quickly realized it was anything but flat. The terrain rose and fell with gullies and rocky outcroppings. Antelope often appeared on the horizon only to disappear as if by magic when all they did was drop over a rise.

Faith headed in the direction she believed she'd gone last night. She kept getting snatches of memory, the strongest one of being cold and wet and scared. As she walked, she recalled the darkness and something over a rise. A light.

With a start she remembered the pickup parked against the embankment. Last night came back in a rush. The clank of a tailgate being dropped. The tracks in the muddy earth. She'd seen someone dragging what had looked like a body.

Her pulse raced at the thought. It had to have been a dream. If someone was missing from camp, surely by now it would have been noticed. She stopped to glance back. She could just make out the tops of the trailers in the distance. A few more steps and they would disappear entirely.

She shuddered at the realization that no one knew where she'd gone. No one would miss her. Was it possible that she really had seen someone dragging a body out to a truck somewhere near here? If so, that person might not have been missed yet.

Wishing now that she'd told someone where she was going, she dropped over the rise. Ahead she saw what looked like a dry creek bed. She recalled the feel of those rocks on her bare feet. She had to be getting close.

Edging to the top of the next rise, she peered over, half expecting to see the pickup parked where it had been last night. There was nothing in the dry creek bed. No pickup. No body.

She stood looking down. The rain had washed away any boot or drag marks in the earth, but it hadn't been able to wash away truck tracks.

Dropping down the small rise into the creek bed, Faith found where the pickup had been parked against the embankment. She remembered sneaking up to the truck to look into the back, but after that nothing until the memory of being wet and cold and stumbling back toward camp.

Had she seen the body in the bed of the truck? Or had she been hit on the head before she could?

She jumped as a large hand cupped her shoulder, and she swung around ready to put up a fight this time.

"Hey! Easy!" Jud said, taking a step back. "I didn't

mean to scare you. Didn't you hear me? I was calling to you." His look said he was worried.

"I remember what happened last night."

"You remembered your nightmare?"

She shook her head. "I wasn't sleepwalking. I saw someone dragging a large, heavy object into the prairie. I remember thinking I didn't have time to dress."

Jud looked skeptical. "A large object?"

"I followed the person as far as the edge of camp. From there I followed the drag marks in the mud. The person was dragging a body, I'm sure of it."

"A body?"

"Look, you can see where a truck was parked against the embankment. Because the body was too heavy for the person to lift into the back of the pickup." She pointed at the tracks in the earth, then glanced at him and saw his expression. "Don't give me that look. I know what I saw."

"Someone dragging a body away from the camp," he repeated. "And you know it was a body because you saw this dead person?"

"Maybe. I remember sneaking up to the back of the pickup and either looking in the bed or starting to when I must have been hit. That explains the cut and bump on my temple and why when you found me I was confused."

"So you didn't see the body."

Her impatience went straight to anger. "I'm telling you what happened last night. The tracks prove it. There was a pickup parked right there. One of the crew trucks. The dome light was on, the tailgate down. It wasn't a dream, and I wasn't sleepwalking."

"Okay." He held up both hands. "Then we should get back to camp and find out who's missing."

Her relief at his words was at war with the feeling that he was just humoring her. It was as if he were counting on no one being missing from the set.

Just as he seemed to be counting on her forgetting about their earlier kiss.

JUD WASN'T SURE what scared him the most. Faith's conviction that she'd seen someone dragging a body to the dry creek bed last night or this overwhelming need of his to protect this woman.

As they walked back to the camp, neither speaking, he prayed she was wrong. Not because he wanted her to be wrong about anything. But if what she was saying were true, then she'd been in terrible danger last night.

And was still in danger.

She had to have been sleepwalking, and all of this was just part of a nightmare that had seemed so real that...that there were tracks from the pickup she swore she'd seen?

"Let me see what I can find out," he told her as they reached the edge of the camp. "Nancy will know since it's her job to keep track of everyone." He called her on his cell.

Nancy answered impatiently on the second ring.

"When you handed out the call sheets this morning, was anyone missing?"

"No. And you'd better not be missing for your stunt this morning." She hung up on him.

Jud thought about what Faith had asked him. *How well did he know Nancy?* Did *anyone* know Nancy?

He'd gotten few impressions about her, except for one. He thought she had a crush on director Erik Zander.

Not that Zander would have noticed. He was at least twice her age. Not usually a problem for him, but she wasn't his type. While Nancy wasn't bad looking, she came off as frumpy. Odd, he thought, since that impression came only from the way she wore her hair and dressed. Her face, when not hidden behind her mousy brown hair, was quite pretty, and her figure, if not curvaceous, was slim. She would have definitely been Zander's type, if she'd dressed more provocatively. Odd that she hadn't figured that out.

"You said you didn't get to Whitehorse in time to do what you'd planned," Eve reminded Mary Ellen. The wind had kicked up outside the motel room. Another thunderstorm was on the way. The motel room felt too small already.

The older woman nodded. "I had just gotten to their little dreary house in the country when Constance went into labor. She pleaded with me to take her to the hospital. Paul had the car at work. Constance wasn't due for weeks."

"You didn't take her to the hospital," Eve said, knowing that was the only way she and her brother could have come into the world and been adopted illegally through the Whitehorse Sewing Circle.

For years the sewing circle had handled adoptions undercover, so to speak. They would find good homes for the babies and make each a baby quilt. It wasn't until recently that Eve had found out just how important that baby quilt was.

"No, I didn't take her to the hospital." Mary Ellen

said it with a finality, and for the first time, Eve saw how much these decisions had plagued her life ever since. "I let my sister suffer, watched her cry and scream as she brought not one but two babies into the world."

"You must have helped her," Eve said.

"There was a point where I regretted what I'd done, but by then it was too late. We couldn't have reached the hospital in time. I was young. I knew nothing of babies and birth. I wrapped each baby in an old towel. I was scared. I didn't know what to do." She looked up at Eve. "You and your brother were so small, so fragile looking. As much as I hated my sister and Paul, I wanted you and your brother to live."

Eve listened as Mary Ellen told of her decision to take the babies to town. "Constance was too weak to travel. She insisted I just get the babies to the hospital. All she cared about was her babies. She loved you so much." The older woman's voice broke. "It was winter. I hadn't realized it, but a storm had blown in. I didn't get far before I got stuck in a drift. I saw a farmhouse and, taking the babies, I waded through the snow to it."

"I know we were flown to Whitehorse in a small plane two days later, so I assume we never made it to the hospital."

Mary Ellen shook her head. "I told the elderly woman that a runaway girl I'd come across had given birth to the babies and didn't want them. The woman said not to worry, she knew what to do. The storm got worse, though. I ended up being trapped there for two days."

Eve held her breath, knowing the story was about

to end—and end badly. "My mother?" she asked, for the first time saying the words.

"When I found her, she had bled to death."

"SOMEONE *HAS* TO be missing," Faith argued when Jud gave her the news.

"I talked to Nancy. Everyone is accounted for. Look, I don't like leaving you, but I have to get into town for the saloon shoot. Are you sure you're going to be all right? Why don't you come along?"

She shook her head stubbornly. She knew what she'd seen. "Then something large must be missing. If it wasn't a body, then it must have been equipment."

"Nothing appears to be missing," he repeated.

"How do you explain the pickup tracks in the dry creek bed then?"

"Maybe there was a pickup there last night. There are always lookie-loos around a movie set. Please come with me. I don't like leaving you here alone."

She met his gaze. His concern touched her even though she didn't want it to. "You'd better get going. I'll stop by after your shoot. Right now I just need some rest. Don't worry, I'll lock myself in."

His relief was almost palpable. "We'll figure this out, okay? Fortunately, no matter what happened last night, you came out of it just a little worse for wear."

She touched the knot on her temple under her bandage.

"So no real harm was done," he said.

Except for whoever that was who was dragged from the movie set, she thought, but she had the good sense to keep her mouth shut. No one was missing.

She couldn't have seen a body being dragged away. Too bad she didn't believe that.

Jud seemed to think that was end of it. He didn't know her, she thought, as he waited until she'd locked the trailer door behind her before he headed for his pickup and Whitehorse.

FINDING OUT HOW her mother had died, Eve began to cry even though she'd promised herself she wouldn't. Hadn't she known this was the case? Hadn't she known the moment Mary Ellen, instead of her mother, had contacted her?

"And Paul?" Eve asked after a moment.

Mary Ellen went very still. While her gaze appeared to be on the far motel wall, Eve knew it was in the past, thirty-four years ago in some run-down old house north of Whitehorse in the middle of winter.

"In my rush to get the babies to safety, I'd left my father's gun behind. I discovered Paul beside Constance's bed on the floor. Apparently he'd found her and seen the gun and…" She swallowed and looked away. "And thinking the babies lost as well, killed himself. Until that moment, I'd told myself that it was me he truly loved, not my sister."

Eve took a breath and let it out slowly. She knew she should hate this woman. How different hers and Bridger's lives would have been had Mary Ellen Small never lived. This hateful woman had destroyed two lives and changed Eve's and her brother's forever. They would never know their mother or father because of a sister's jealousy and revenge.

"Constance loved you and your brother more than her own life," Mary Ellen said, her hands now folded in her lap. "I have no doubt your father loved you equally as much or he wouldn't have done what he did."

"Where are they buried?" Eve asked.

"In the Whitehorse Cemetery in unmarked graves."

Eve nodded and rose slowly from the table. As a child she'd asked about the two white stones with no names on them.

"No one knows *who* they were," her mother had told her.

"But there are angels on the stones," Eve had said.

"Yes. I think they are both angels now."

Eve felt the full weight of the lies and truths she'd been told her whole life. Her mother had known who was buried in those graves. No doubt the Whitehorse Sewing Circle had purchased the headstones. They'd had to cover up the truth to protect Eve and Bridger.

How Eve wanted to expose them all. But exposing the Whitehorse Sewing Circle would mean exposing her own family. Her mother, her grandmother and grandfather had been some of the ringleaders of the illegal adoption faction. People Eve had known her whole life, good people, now elderly, had been involved. Even today, those people believed they were doing what was right for the babies by finding them homes all those years ago.

Their legacy was now in Eve's hands. She and her brother alone had been told by the sewing circle of the secrets that had been stitched into each quilt. Her own sisters were adopted. Who knew what their circumstances had been at birth? It was no wonder they said they had no desire to track down their birth parents.

But she feared there would be others who would show up one day in Whitehorse searching for the mother who gave them away, and Eve would have to decide whether or not to help them.

Eve looked at Mary Ellen. She didn't know what to say to this woman. Her *aunt*. Mary Ellen had saved hers and Bridger's lives. If she hadn't taken them to a neighbors…

And if she hadn't come to Whitehorse again and shared this painful story, Eve would have gone on looking into strangers' faces hoping to see her own.

"You understand now why I didn't want to tell you," Mary Ellen said without raising her head to look at Eve. "The shame and guilt is something I have carried alone all these years. Not even my own mother knows the truth. My father died believing that Constance simply ran away. I could never bear to tell them the truth, that they had lost one daughter because of the other."

What a terrible burden the woman had carried for thirty-four long years, Eve thought. "I'm glad you told me. I can see how hard it was for you. But if your sister told your mother everything when she called her—"

Mary Ellen shook her head. "All she told my mother was that she was in Whitehorse, Montana, and in terrible trouble and wanted to come home. I offered to go after her. I told my parents that when I got there, Constance was gone. I even offered to hire a private investigator to find her." She nodded. "I had become very good at lying."

Eve could see how those lies had crippled this woman. "You were so young when this happened—"

Mary Ellen swatted the words away. "There is no excuse for what I did. None."

"I'm sorry," Eve said. "I hope that by telling me you might be able to find some peace."

"I am in no place to ask you a favor," Mary Ellen said, her voice thick with emotion. "But I must. My mother, your *grandmother*, I want to tell her about you and your brother. She is innocent in all this. She is a wonderful woman who deserves to know she has two grandchildren."

"And a great-grandchild. Bridger's wife just had a baby boy. They named him Jack."

Mary Ellen's eyes flooded with tears. "It would mean everything to my mother, since I have never married."

A grandmother. A great-grandmother for Bridger's baby. Isn't this what Eve had always hoped for? Family? "I will have to talk to my brother first."

Mary Ellen nodded. "I understand. Please, let him know that my mother is nothing like me."

On impulse, Eve took the woman's hand. A woman who'd done despicable things and paid a high price all these years for them. "I will tell my brother that our mother died in childbirth and her babies were taken away to be given to good homes. That our father loved her so much and, thinking his children were also lost, took his own life. That is all he needs to know. It is time we all let go of the past."

Eve hugged her aunt for a long moment, then left, driving first to see her husband at the sheriff's office, desperately needing to be in his strong arms. Then to see her brother, Bridger.

JUD HAD TROUBLE CONCENTRATING. He hadn't been able to stop worrying about Faith. Fortunately he'd been in more than his fair share of fight scenes and could do them in his sleep. He was just glad when he was done because he was anxious to find Faith. She'd said she would stop by, but she hadn't.

"Where the hell is Chantal?" Zander demanded when all of the stunts were completed and the saloon cleaned up for the interior shots.

Zander had rented the local bar for the day. According to the call sheet, Chantal and Nevada had three scenes to shoot before the day was over.

"I'll try to reach her," Nancy said, snapping open her cell phone. She listened for a few minutes, then left an urgent message. Cell phone coverage was sketchy in this part of the country, but more than likely Chantal just wasn't answering for whatever reason.

"She's probably on her way," Nancy said and gave Nevada a questioning glance.

"Don't look at *me*," he snapped. "I haven't seen her since…wait a minute." His face flushed. "I just remembered. Right before we all left, she said she had to run back to her trailer for something."

Zander swore profusely. "Nancy—"

"I'll go get her," Jud said. He wanted to check on Faith.

He told himself as he drove back out to the camp that she was fine. Probably she'd overslept. Or she could still be mad at him for not believing her about what she thought she'd seen last night and decided she didn't want to stop by.

As he topped the hill and saw the camp below, he felt a fresh wave of anxiety. He'd gotten Faith into this and now he feared that he'd put her in danger. Nearing the parking area, he saw that Faith's pickup was gone.

He felt a stab of disappointment. He'd hoped she

was still sleeping. He wanted to see her, even if for only a few minutes.

Climbing out of his truck, he headed for Chantal's trailer, telling himself that Faith had probably gone to town just as she said she would. There was no cause for concern.

For whatever reason she hadn't stopped by to see him. No big deal. If it had been any other woman, he would have just shrugged it off.

"Grow up," he told himself as he tapped on Chantal's door. He could hear music coming from inside and wasn't surprised when she opened the door smelling of perfume and Scotch.

"I wondered how long it would take someone to realize I wasn't there," she said with a tight smile.

"Nevada just remembered that you'd gone back to your trailer for something."

Her face twisted in anger. "The bastard. I should have known. I told him to tell Nancy. That's the second damned time I've been stood up in two days." Her anger had quickly turned to self-pity. "Tell me, what am I doing wrong?" she asked with a come-hither look.

"I'm sure you're exaggerating," he said, waiting patiently for her, knowing Zander would be losing his mind waiting for her.

She pretended to pout. "I can understand Nevada forgetting me. The man's gorgeous and an idiot. But Keyes Hasting? I mean, the man is *old.* Not to mention ugly as a toad. And to make matters worse, it was *his* idea I meet him last night."

Jud hadn't been listening until then. "You were supposed to meet Keyes Hasting last night and he didn't show up? Is that what you're saying?"

"Yes, haven't you been listening to me?"

"Have you seen him since then?" he demanded.

"Are you serious? After he stood me up?"

Keyes Hasting. Had anyone seen him this morning? When Jud had asked Nancy if everyone was accounted for, she wouldn't have included Hasting.

Jud looked toward the parking area where Hasting's rental SUV had been parked yesterday. It was gone. Maybe he'd changed his mind about meeting with Chantal and had left. Or maybe he hadn't.

Either way, Jud now had to check Faith's trailer. It would probably be locked, and with her pickup gone, he knew rationally that she wouldn't be there. He knew he was probably wasting his time, but he had to try.

She'd been so convinced that she'd seen someone dragging a body away from camp. Why hadn't he listened to her?

He sprinted to the trailer anyway, knocked and tried the door, surprised and suddenly apprehensive to find it wasn't locked.

"Faith?" No answer. He stepped in. *"Faith?"*

Everything looked fine. No sign of a struggle. He glanced down the hall, feeling like a fool. It wasn't like him to panic like this. Or to feel this way about a woman he wasn't even dating—let alone sleeping with.

He was already turning toward the door to leave, when he saw the doll. It was propped up on the bed. He stepped toward it, noticing something strange.

When he was within a few feet of the bed, he saw that the doll had something on it just below the stitched eye. He picked up the doll. Was that dried blood on it?

Faith hadn't left this here. Someone must have put it there after she'd left. At least he hoped that was the case.

To scare her. Or warn her?

A sliver of worry burrowed under his skin at the thought that Brooke might resent Faith. Jealousy was an insidious thing. He'd seen it destroy people in this business.

"I thought we were in a big hurry to get me to the shoot?" Chantal called impatiently from outside the trailer. "Looks like there's another thunderstorm headed this way. Good thing we have a covered shoot this afternoon."

Jud grabbed the doll and stuffed it into his jacket pocket. The last thing he wanted was for Faith to see it. "Let's go," he said, closing the trailer door behind him. Zander would be having a fit.

But that was the least of Jud's worries as he headed for his pickup, dark clouds rolling in.

FAITH HAD LEFT the trailer, the doll on the bed, and driven to the rest home to see her grandmother, Nina Mae. No reason to throw the doll away again so it could show up in the same place again.

She and her sisters stopped by the rest home every day or so to see their grandmother, even though Nina Mae never recognized them anymore. Her grandmother on her mother's side had Alzheimer's. But Nina Mae was always glad to see Faith, even if she didn't have any idea who she was.

After that, Faith had driven out to the ranch, only to find Eve gone. At loose ends, Faith had started back to town just as it had begun to rain.

The rain and dark clouds did nothing to improve her mood. She was still upset with Jud for not believing her about last night. He didn't want to believe her, she thought, as her cell phone rang.

"Hello?" She was hoping it would be him. Now that he'd had time to think about it, he was calling to say he'd changed his mind. He believed her.

It wasn't Jud.

It was Sheriff Carter Jackson, her brother-in-law.

"I got that information you asked for on Erik Zander," Carter said.

She'd completely forgotten she'd asked him for it.

"That car accident twenty-three years ago?" Carter said. "Zander got a DUI and a ticket for leaving the scene of the accident, but he managed to skate on a manslaughter charge. The young woman with him was killed. He swore she was dead when he left the scene to get help, but he didn't call in the accident until two hours later, after he'd sobered up a little."

Faith felt sick. What if the woman had been alive those two hours? She knew people panicked and he'd been young twenty-three years ago, an up-and-coming director who'd already made a name for himself.

But two deaths both involving young women?

"I did discover something I thought you might find interesting," Carter was saying. "The dead woman went by Star Bishop, but her legal name was Angie Harris. She'd just gotten a divorce and moved to California. Her maiden name was Keifer, same as Brooke's before she changed it to Keith. According to birth records, Angie Kiefer gave birth to a daughter twenty-seven years ago. Samantha Brooke."

Brooke Keith was the daughter of the dead woman?

Chapter Twelve

Faith jumped at a tap on her pickup's side window. Her heart lodged in her throat as she looked over to find Brooke Keith staring in at her from the rain.

"I have to go," Faith said into the phone and snapped it shut as she whirred down the window. A gust of cold, wet air rushed in. Just the sight of Brooke standing there had already made her shiver. Now she felt chilled to the bone.

"Brooke." Frantically, Faith tried to remember what she'd been saying on the phone. Had Brooke overheard the conversation from outside the truck?

"I saw you sitting there," Brooke said, her demeanor odd, but probably no odder than usual. "I realized I came on a little too strong earlier. Sorry. It's wet out here. Could we talk in your pickup?"

Before Faith could react, Brooke ran around to the passenger side of the pickup. The door swung open and Brooke slid in, shaking off raindrops as she closed the door behind her.

Faith tried to hide how anxious it made her having Brooke Keith in the cab of her pickup.

What did she want? Clearly, the woman had something on her mind, and given what Brooke might have just overheard, that in itself was cause for concern.

Her instincts told her Brooke didn't like her as it was.

She tried not to think about what the sheriff had discovered. What did it mean, if anything? Hollywood was a small world, kind of like Montana in that everyone seemed related, even though in Montana's case, it was a big state.

Maybe it was no secret that Brooke was this dead woman's daughter. Maybe even Erik Zander was aware of it. Or maybe not.

Either way, could this explain the "accidents" that had been happening on the set?

"AM I MAKING you nervous?" Brooke asked, amused. "You should have seen your face when I tapped on your window. You looked as if you'd seen a ghost."

"You just startled me, that's all," Faith said.

That wasn't all. Faith hadn't wanted her to get into the pickup. Just like back at the trailer when she'd turned down tea. Faith had been almost rude to her. And now she seemed more than nervous. She almost seemed scared.

Brooke remembered Faith's expression when she'd turned from the phone to the window to find her standing just outside. If only she'd been able to hear the phone conversation, but the rain on the pickup had been too noisy. She wondered who Faith had been talking to. Jud?

"You still seem nervous. Is it because I wanted to talk to you?" Brooke asked.

"I guess that depends on what you want to talk to me about," Faith said, her gaze wary.

"I wanted to talk to you about Jud."

"Jud?" Faith looked relieved.

What had Faith thought she wanted to talk to her about? The woman was smiling now, apparently relaxed.

"Look, if this is about last night…"

Brooke waved that off. "Jud gets romantically involved on every movie set."

Faith's eyes narrowed. "Really?"

"He's a good-looking guy. Even intelligent women fall for him. You're new to movie sets so I thought I should warn you. The affair always ends at the end of the movie." She shrugged. "It's just the way Jud is."

"Is that how it was with the two of you?"

Brooke was taken aback. "Jud and I never—" She caught herself. She'd let everyone think she and Jud had been lovers after a big spread in one of the stuntmen magazines. Jud hadn't cared, since it was a normal occurrence for him to be linked with one woman after another, true or not.

"Jud and I are friends. *Good* friends. It's a kind of bond no other woman has ever been able to break."

Faith nodded. She was too calm, taking this better than Brooke had expected. Probably because she thought she was different from all Jud's other lovers. She thought she would be the one who lasted. Maybe she was a bigger fool than Brooke thought.

The woman was headed for heartbreak and refused to believe it. Well, she'd been warned. Faith seemed like a nice enough person. Too bad she'd gotten caught up in something she could neither understand nor get out of at this point.

"It's good that Jud has a friend like you," Faith said, fidgeting with her keys.

Brooke couldn't tell if she was being sincere or facetious. "I'm glad you see it that way."

"What other way is there to see it?"

Brooke didn't know what else to say. "I just want you to know, that no matter what happens, it's nothing personal."

"I never thought it was." Faith smiled. "I'm glad you suggested this talk, because there's something I wanted to ask you."

Brooke braced herself, not sure why she needed to, just something in Faith's moment of hesitation before she leaned forward conspiratorially and asked, "Is there any chance that the accidents on the film set aren't accidents at all?"

MARY ELLEN PACKED up her things at the motel. It shouldn't have taken much time, since she'd brought so little. But she was so exhausted and completely drained that doing anything took all her effort.

Had she done the wrong thing by telling Eve the truth? Eve's husband was the sheriff. Maybe she'd gone to him and any moment Mary Ellen would hear a knock at the door and she would be arrested.

But no knock came. Just another thunderstorm with lightning that flashed behind the curtains and thunder that rattled the windowpanes.

Eve had said she hoped this would bring Mary Ellen some peace, as if that were a possibility. She'd known telling the story to her sister's child would only bring it all back, every horrible, deplorable moment of it. And it had.

There could be no forgiveness. Not from her sister. Not from herself. What she'd done was monstrous. Her repentance had been a life cut off from the world, living simply, suffering alone.

She hadn't told Eve in the hope that she might be forgiven. She'd told the truth because she'd had to. She couldn't let Eve and her brother keep searching for their mother the way her parents had waited for years for Constance to come home.

No matter what Eve and her brother decided to do, Mary Ellen couldn't let her mother spend another day believing that Constance might come home again.

She hadn't told her parents because she'd believed that the truth would kill them. She'd been their perfect daughter, the one they'd always depended on.

After Constance left, her parents had leaned on her even more. "I don't know what we would do without you," they used to say. "We've lost Constance, but if we lost you, Mary Ellen…"

So she hadn't told them the truth, sparing them she told herself while saving herself from their reaction to what she'd done.

As she moved to the door with her suitcase, her cell phone rang. "Hello?" She expected it to be her mother. No matter what she planned to tell her, Mary Ellen wasn't going to tell her over the phone.

"Mary Ellen?" It was Eve.

She had to sit down on the motel bed. Her legs just didn't want to hold her. "Yes?"

"I've spoken to my brother. We want to meet our grandmother."

Mary Ellen began to cry, not softly, quietly, but big gulping sobs. When she could finally get herself under control, she said, "My mother will be so happy. I had already decided to tell her the truth when I got home."

"I don't think that's necessary," Eve said. "Maybe you should tell her what I told my brother. How Constance died giving birth, how the babies were adopted, believing Constance was a runaway, and how our father, finding his wife dead and babies gone, couldn't go on living."

Mary Ellen was silent for a long time. "What about the *truth*?"

"That is the truth," Eve said. "I hope your mother is well enough that the two of you can come to Montana so we can all get to know each other."

Again Mary Ellen couldn't speak for a long moment. "Thank you." Overwhelmed with emotion, she was unable to say more.

When she finally had control again, she loaded her suitcase in the rental car and headed south down the long two-lane highway. Pulling out her cell phone she keyed in her mother's number.

"Mary Ellen?" her mother said anxiously. "Is there something wrong, dear?"

"I'll tell you all about it when I get home from Montana, but I have good news, Mom." She could hear her mother sobbing softly on the other end of the line.

"Constance?"

Mary Ellen felt that pang she always felt. "I didn't want to tell you on the phone, but Constance died giving birth to twins. A son and a daughter. The daughter, Eve Bailey Jackson, looks just like Constance. I haven't seen the son yet. They're thirty-four years old. The son's wife recently gave birth to a baby boy. You're a great-grandmother."

FAITH SAW BROOKE'S REACTION. Surprise, then something more wary.

"What are you talking about?"

"I think someone is purposely trying to sabotage the film," Faith said.

Brooke let out a short, rude laugh. "Why? This film is going to fail all by itself. Sorry to tell you this, but this flick will be lucky if it doesn't go straight to DVD. It's a dog. Bow wow."

"Then why would the director agree to make it? I heard around the set that Erik Zander sunk everything he owned into it."

The stuntwoman shrugged. "Directors and producers make bad movies all the time. What else is he going to do?"

"Still, these so-called accidents—"

"You really are naive about the film industry, aren't you?" Brooke said, her smile laden with sarcasm. "It's a cheap film. We have a fourth of the crew we should have and our props look like they were built by third-graders. Of course there are going to be accidents."

"Like a rattlesnake crawling into your trailer?"

That stopped Brooke for a long moment. "That was more than likely personal. If you stay around this industry long enough, you make enemies. These people play rough."

"It almost killed you."

"What doesn't kill you makes you stronger, right?" Brooke chuckled and started to open the pickup door. "Remember what I said about Jud. In fact, I believe you have only one more stunt. I'd suggest you get off the set as quickly as possible when you're done with it tomorrow. You'll save yourself a lot of pain if you sever ties with Jud Corbett as fast as possible and don't look back."

Faith didn't get a chance to reply before Brooke

opened the door and was gone. Which was probably just as well, considering what Faith might have said.

She watched Brooke head for one of the film's rented trucks parked across the street and thought about the truck she saw last night in the dry creek bed. It could have been the same pickup.

Faith had wanted to ask Brooke about her mother. She wasn't sure why she hadn't. Maybe she didn't want to tip her hand if it was a well-kept secret. Or maybe common sense had overruled.

Even if Brooke had admitted to being the daughter of Angie Keifer, that didn't mean she was behind the accidents on the set. Especially when she'd been the victim of the first accident and had almost died. Even though Brooke had tried to shrug it off, Faith suspected there was more to the story.

She started the engine to let the defroster clear the fogged windshield. She knew she should take both Nancy's and Brooke's advice and leave well enough alone.

If only that were in her nature.

As the windshield started to clear, Faith looked up and saw the dark shape of a person standing in front of the truck. For one heart-stopping moment, she thought it was Brooke again.

"Jud?" Faith asked, rolling down her window partway as he came around to her door.

"We need to talk," he said, and she motioned him around to the passenger side of the car and out of the rain.

Jud slid in, closing the door to the rain and cold, bringing with him his scent of leather and the outdoors. Suddenly the pickup cab felt too confined, too intimate.

Her heart kicked up a beat and she was reminded of being in his arms earlier and that blamed kiss.

"What are you doing?" he demanded.

She stared at him in confusion. "What?"

"I just ran into Brooke. She said you talked to her about the accidents on the set. Now she's worried you won't be able to do your job, and I wouldn't be surprised if she goes to the director with this."

"So you're worried that I might lose my job?" He seemed awfully upset about it. Because he'd gotten her the job to start with? "Look, if you're worried that it might reflect on you since you're the one who suggested me—"

"Hell, no. I'm not thinking about my damned job. I'm worried about you. If we're right about someone purposely causing these incidents, then you've just made yourself a target. And after what happened to you last night, getting fired might be the best thing that could happen to you."

All she heard was the "we're" part. "So you agree with me?"

"That's beside the point," he snapped, pulling off his Stetson to run his fingers through his hair. He had beautiful hair—and fingers, and Faith found herself momentarily distracted by both.

"Brooke was the one who insisted she had to talk to me."

He frowned. "Not about the accidents?"

"No. About *you.*"

That shut him up. "Me?"

"She wanted to warn me about you. She said you had affairs on all the sets and broke them off at the end of the movie, leaving a trail of women behind.

She swears you will break my heart just as you have all the others. Thanks to you, she thinks we're lovers."

"First off, I don't date women I work with. It's the Corbett Code. Dinner with the family the other night was *not* a date. I didn't kiss you when I took you back to your trailer, did I?"

"Nope. But you wanted to."

He smiled at that. "Oh, I wanted to do a lot more than that."

She felt her face heat up, thinking their minds that night had been on the same fast track. Good thing neither of them had acted on it.

"Second, I make no promises to the women I date, and believe me, I have left few broken hearts and dated many less women than my reputation would indicate.

"Third—" his gaze locked with hers across the close expanse of the pickup's cab "—I should never have gotten you into this."

She reached over and pressed a finger to his lips. "You gave me my heart's desire."

At his grin, she quickly removed her finger, realizing too late what she'd said.

"Is that your *only* heart's desire?" he asked softly.

She felt heat rush up from her toes, toes now curling in her boots. This was why Jud Corbett had such a way with women. She held up her hands as if that act alone could ward him off—let alone save her from the way he made her feel.

He took both her hands in his large ones and dragged her to him. The kiss on the set had been passionate enough but impulsive.

But there was nothing impulsive about this kiss. This was one of those I've-wanted-to-do-this-since-the-first-time-I-saw-you kisses. A saved-up, thought-out, dreamed-of and passionately yearned-for kiss.

She felt herself melt into his arms, his mouth warm, his lips strong and sure. It swept her up like an adventure where anything was possible.

Jud pulled her closer, melding their bodies together, as he explored her mouth, his hands tangled in her hair, his body hard and possessive.

When he finally let her come up for air, she was breathing hard, heart racing, traitorous body crying out for more. The pickup's windows were steamed over even though the engine was still running, the heater working as hard as it could to clear the glass.

The outside world appeared to be lost, which was just fine with her. She never wanted to leave this pickup cab or this man's arms.

Rational thought and reality came back slowly. She heard a car drive by, splashing through a puddle. A car door slammed nearby. The blast of the afternoon passenger train whistle as it approached the depot across the tracks from downtown. Brooke's warning, true or not.

"No, oh no," Faith whispered, her voice a croak as she pulled away. What had she been thinking? Even if half the stories about him were lies, there was that other half. She knew all about this man and his women. She wasn't about to become another notch on his six-shooter.

Jud looked surprisingly as shaken as she felt. "Wow. That was—"

"Wrong," she said, finally finding her voice. "What happened to that Corbett Code of yours?" she demanded, angry with him, even angrier with herself for enjoying every nanosecond locked in his kiss.

"To hell with the code. This is different. What I feel with you...what I felt from the first time I laid eyes on you. This is—" He was looking into her eyes, searching for what?

Her to fall for his line? "You say that to every woman." *Tell me it isn't true! Deny it, damn you!*

"You don't believe that. You feel this, too." He frowned, looking suddenly unsure of himself. "Am I wrong?"

She wanted to lie. For her own protection. Jud Corbett scared her. These feelings scared her. She'd never felt anything like what she'd experienced with him from the moment she saw him leaning on the jack fence watching her do her stunts.

"Faith, look at me." He reached over and lifted her chin with his warm fingers. "Tell me you didn't feel anything and I will get out of this pickup right now and never touch you again."

The lie caught in her throat at the thought of never feeling his touch, his lips, his arms around her again.

"That's what I thought." His relief surprised her. He laughed softly, leaned back, sighing as their gazes met. "This scares me as much as it does you, maybe more, and if I did 'date' women I worked with while on a movie, as Brooke said, then I would be making love to you right now, right here, on Whitehorse, Montana's, main street."

"You sure about that?" she teased.

He grinned. "Yeah, and you'd let me." His expression sobered. "I was looking for you for another reason, actually. Isn't your brother-in-law the sheriff?"

"Yes, why?"

"I think we should go talk to him about what you saw last night."

Faith was feeling so many things right at that moment, relief and a whole new wave of tenderness toward this man. "You *believe* me?" She couldn't help grinning. "What changed your mind?"

"Keyes Hasting. Apparently he'd planned to meet Chantal last night but didn't show."

"Hasting? That older man I saw on the set yesterday?"

Jud nodded. "He invests in films occasionally and apparently has mob connections."

"You think he invested in *Death at Lost Creek*?"

"Seems likely, since he showed up," Jud said, frowning. "The word on the street was that Zander tied up every cent he had in the film. But it could be that wasn't enough and he went to Hasting. Either way, I think we'd better find out if Keyes Hasting is missing."

SHERIFF CARTER JACKSON listened as Faith told him what she'd seen the night before. He frowned as she related the part about being struck and wandering back into camp dazed.

"Why didn't you come to me with this sooner?" Carter demanded when she'd finished. "You might have mentioned it earlier when we talked."

"That's my fault," Jud spoke up. "No one was missing from the set this morning, and I was convinced Faith had been sleepwalking." He looked chagrined. "Also, I didn't want to believe it. I'd hoped to get through with the film before there was any more trouble."

Carter motioned for them to wait as he made a few calls. As he finished the last call, he hung up and looked at the two of them.

"Hasting hasn't used his plane ticket back to California," the sheriff said. "Nor has he turned in his rental car, and his family hasn't heard from him since yesterday, but they said he was planning to fly back this afternoon from Billings."

Faith shuddered. Like Jud, she also hadn't wanted to believe it was a body that she'd seen dragged away from the set.

"I don't want you going back out there until I get to the bottom of this," Carter said.

"I have a stunt tomorrow, my last," Faith said.

The sheriff swore. "At least don't stay out there at night."

"I'll stay at the ranch tonight," Faith told him.

"I'll make sure she's safe," Jud said. "I don't think she should be alone."

Faith couldn't believe they were talking about her as if she wasn't in the room. "Excuse me. I have some say in this."

"No," Jud said. "If what you saw last night was someone dragging off Hasting's body and they got close enough to you to smack you in the head, then no, you don't have any say. They will be worried that you can recognize them."

Faith started to argue, but Carter said, "Jud's right. That's exactly what I'm worried about. I don't want you staying alone. Eve will want—"

Faith was just about to say she didn't want Carter bothering Eve with this when Jud spoke up. "I'll stay with Faith. We have a stunt we need to go over, anyway. I won't let her out of my sight."

Faith wanted to object, but this was better than having Eve worrying over her. "So that's settled. Now, are you both happy?" She rose to leave.

"I need to talk to the sheriff for just a minute," Jud said. "Why don't we just take one rig to your ranch? I can bring you back to your pickup in the morning." He started to hand Faith his keys.

"I'll wait for you in *my* truck," she said. She'd always been independent, capable of taking care of herself, and she wasn't about to give that up now when she felt she needed it the most.

If her life was in jeopardy because of what she'd seen last night, then she needed more than ever to keep her wits about her. She'd never liked the fairy tales where the handsome prince saved the princess. She wanted to be the princess who's able to save herself.

Jud had cast himself in the role as her protector. But it was a temporary role, and she wasn't about to kid herself that she could depend on him to always be around when she needed him. Their feelings for each other aside, he would be off to another film after this one. And she...well, she would be staying on the ranch until fall, and then who knew what she would do.

Not that it mattered. In a few days, the movie would be over and that would be the last she saw of Jud Corbett.

JUD WAITED UNTIL he saw Faith cross the street to her pickup. "Mule-headed, isn't she?" he said with a grin.

"Runs in the family," the sheriff agreed. "All three Bailey girls are like that. More spirit than common sense."

Jud turned his attention from the window back to the sheriff. "Don't worry about her. I won't let anything happen to her."

"I appreciate that, but I'm still going to have a deputy near the ranch tonight to keep an eye on things," Carter said. "I didn't want to say anything to Faith because I know what her reaction would be."

Jud nodded. He could well imagine. "Faith's scared but she doesn't want to admit it. Nor does she want to believe that she can't take care of herself. It's one of the things I love about her."

Carter gaze sharpened at the word *love*. "I'm very fond of my sister-in-law."

"So am I." Jud reached into his pocket. "I didn't want her to see this," he said as he reached into his pocket and pulled out the small rag doll he'd found on Faith's bed. "I found it in her trailer where someone had left it. Everyone who's had an 'accident' found one of these beforehand."

Carter took the doll with obvious reluctance. "Are these props for the film?"

"No, these are much cruder made, much uglier. No one seems to know where they came from."

"What's this on the doll?" the sheriff asked.

"That's why I wanted you to see it," Jud said. "I think it's a drop of blood."

Chapter Thirteen

"Why did you want to see my brother-in-law alone?" Faith asked once they were on the road south toward the Bailey Ranch.

"I just wanted to reassure him that I wouldn't let anything happen to you."

"I can take care of myself."

"I know." She could feel his gaze on her. "You're the strongest woman I think I've ever met. And the most stubborn."

"Thank you," she said, and Jud laughed as his gaze took in the country sprawled ahead of them. The land ran south in rolling hills of green to fan out in ridges and deep ravines before falling to the river bottom.

The Missouri cut a deep gorge through the land as it twisted its way east before joining the Mississippi to run to the Gulf of Mexico.

Another thunderstorm had blown through. A breeze swept out the dark clouds, leaving behind a crystalline canopy of blue stretched over their heads from horizon to horizon. The sun hung over the Bear Paw and Little Rocky mountains, painting the scene before them in dramatic golden light.

It had turned into one of those breathtaking Montana afternoons and having Jud Corbett sitting just inches away only intensified the experience.

Faith put down her window partway and breathed in the fresh air. It smelled of rain and grass and promise— and helped cool down her thoughts. She was angry and scared and swamped with emotions she didn't want to be feeling for the man beside her. And now they were driving out to her family ranch for the night. Just the two of them in that big house where she'd grown up.

"You all right?" Jud asked.

"No." She wondered if she would ever be all right again. For sure she would measure every man she met from this moment on against Jud Corbett, and they would come up lacking.

"You can talk to me," he said quietly.

She laughed at that. Talking was the last thing she wanted to do with him.

Suddenly she hit the brakes and brought the pickup to a skidding stop.

"What the—"

Before Jud could finish, she pulled off the road, dropping down into a gully filled with stunted aspens. The leaves rattled in the breeze. Rain droplets on each leaf caught the last of the day's light and sent it back in jeweled prisms.

She brought the pickup to a stop in the stand of aspens and, shutting off the motor, turned in the seat to glare at Jud. "I have to live life on my terms."

He nodded, looking concerned that she'd lost her mind.

She smiled ruefully. "You think I'm crazy. Well, welcome to the club. I think I must be certifiable but even that will be on my terms."

Faith unlatched her seat belt and leaned toward him to brush her lips over his. He froze as if unsure of what was going on. This time, she kissed him softly and pulled back to gaze into his eyes. "Make love to me."

His gaze locked with hers. *"Here? Now?"*

Her smile broadened. "Here. Now."

"And you're sure you want this as much as I do?" he asked, teasing now.

Body, heart and soul. Her rational mind put up a good fight but was out numbered. Faith wanted him, come hell or high water. If this was a mistake, then she was willing to live with it. She was through putting up a fight. She didn't try to make more of this than it was. They wanted each other desperately. Tomorrow she could deal with regrets and recriminations, but today she would give herself freely, surrender to Jud Corbett in a way she'd never surrendered to any man before.

"I want it *more* than you do," she teased back.

He laughed. "Not a chance," he said as he unsnapped his seat belt and dragged her into his arms. His mouth took possession of hers, stealing her breath.

She heard his sharp intake of breath as he peeled off her blouse, his gaze on her rounded breasts, the nipples hard as stones and pressing into the lacy fabric.

He cupped her breasts in his large hands, his thumbs feathering the already aching nipples and making her groan with longing. She dragged off his shirt to bare his muscular chest and the dark fuzz of hair that fell in a V to the waist of his jeans.

She pressed her hands to the warm flesh. His mouth dropped to the points of her breasts. Her head lolled back, mouth open, a sound coming out of her that she'd never heard before.

He shoved her back against the seat. Her body came alive under his lips, his fingers, his body.

Frantically, she fumbled at his Western belt, then the zipper on his jeans. She felt her jeans tugged down, heard her panties tear, and then his fingers were on her, in her, and she was gasping as he entered her.

Locked together in the ancient rhythm of love-making, the pickup rocking, Faith soared to new, rare heights until like a roller-coaster ride that has climbed to its highest point ever, she fell over the edge. Weightless and yet every nerve ending infinitely acute, she clung to Jud until their shared shudders of pleasure ebbed away like the last of the day's light.

He held her until their breathing slowed and heartbeats resumed their normal speed, then they untangled themselves, laughing in the small confines of the pickup's cab.

"That isn't the way I wanted our first time together," he said as he cupped her face in his hands and kissed her tenderly.

She smiled, trying to imagine their first time being any other way as they sorted through their clothing and stepped out into the evening air to finish dressing.

When they got back into the truck, a quiet settled between them. She could hear the soft sound of his breathing and remembered the steady, sure beat of his heart against her breast.

ERIK ZANDER HADN'T realized what an aversion he had to the sight of a police car until the sheriff's car pulled up on the set.

The sheriff was young, and handsome enough that

he could have been in movies. "Sheriff," Zander said, shaking his hand. "I'm Erik Zander, the director here."

"Mr. Zander. Is there somewhere we could have a few words?"

"Sure, let's go to my trailer. But please, call me Zander, everyone does." He walked toward the circle of RVs, studying the sheriff out of the corner of his eye. For days he'd been waiting for the other shoe to drop, unable to sleep, unable to get drunk, unable to enjoy the only thing he ever enjoyed—his Scotch.

Now he wondered if this was the other shoe about to drop.

"Have you ever thought about getting into the movies?" Zander asked the sheriff as they neared the trailer. "I could definitely get you a screen test."

"Thanks, but I'll pass."

Zander reached the trailer and held the door open for the lawman, more worried than ever. What man in his right mind would pass up a chance to be in a movie?

"Can I offer you a drink?" he asked, following the sheriff inside.

"No, thank you. If we could just sit down…"

Zander could feel the sheriff watching him closely and wished he wasn't so nervous. He offered the lawman the couch and he took the recliner. "So, what's up?"

"I wanted to ask you about Mr. Keyes Hasting."

Zander blinked. "Hasting?" He felt him stomach roil. "Why? Has something happened to him?"

The sheriff looked up as he pulled out a tape recorder and set it on the end table between them. "Why would you ask that?"

"Because you're here asking questions about him."

Zander would have killed for a drink. Anything to steady his nerves.

"When was the last time you saw him?"

"Day before yesterday, I guess."

"Mr. Hasting came out here?"

Zander nodded. "He wanted a tour of the set. I gave him one and, as far as I knew, he left."

"You didn't see him leave?"

"No, I was busy trying to get this film finished."

"Mr. Hasting seems to be missing," the sheriff said.

"Missing?"

"Is there anyone who might want to harm Mr. Hasting?"

Zander laughed. "The mob. Anyone who's done business with him. Or met him."

The sheriff wasn't amused. "Have you done business with him?"

"Hell, no. You couldn't get me to borrow money from that man." He realized he was talking too much. Something about a uniform and a badge made him nervous. Could be those other times he'd been questioned and expected to be arrested. "The last person you want to be in debt to is Keyes Hasting."

"Why is that?"

Zander shrugged. "Because the guy is a bastard and plays for keeps. If you owe him money and don't pay, you could get your legs broken or end up in the river wearing cement slippers."

"Was someone on the set in debt to him?"

The question took Zander by surprise. He hadn't considered that. But now that he thought about it, he wasn't sure Hasting had come here to see him. He'd just assumed Hasting had been his benefactor, the person behind this film.

But Hasting hadn't seemed interested in seeing the set or the dailies. He'd seemed distracted.

"Mr. Zander?"

He blinked. "Sorry. I was thinking. I don't know if anyone was in debt to him." He tried to remember who he'd seen Hasting talking to yesterday.

FAITH DROVE THE rest of the way to the ranch with the window down. The evening was a rare one in so many ways, she thought, as she parked in front of the ranch house.

"It's just as I pictured it," Jud said, smiling over at her.

She loved this house, with its white clapboard siding, the sprawling front porch, the old windowpanes that looked out over the ranch.

They were barely through the front door before she was in his arms again. "This time we do it my way," Jud said, grinning and sweeping her up into his arms. "Your room at the top of the stairs?"

"First one on the right," she said, laughing as he carried her up the stairs without even breathing hard and lowered her to her bed.

He made love to her slowly, making her cry out with pleasure again and again until she lay spent in his arms.

Sated, they lay spooned together, his heartbeat in sync with her own, his breath a warm assurance on her neck as darkness crept in, covering them like a warm blanket.

JUD WOKE TO warmth and a sensation for being both content and complete. He lay perfectly still, not wanting to lose that sensation. Faith lay curled next to him, her warm backside snuggled against him, his arm around her, their hands clasped.

He couldn't remember ever waking up with a woman holding his hand. There was something tender about it. Nor could he remember feeling so happy. Dangerous feelings for a man who wasn't interested in anything long term.

And yet he didn't move, didn't want this moment to end. He felt Faith stir. She let out a contented sigh and pressed against him, her hand squeezing his as she brought it closer to her lips.

Jud closed his eyes, fighting the feelings this woman evoked in him. Yesterday and last night were like a dream he never wanted to end. Their lovemaking had been so...natural, as if they could do it every day until the day they died.

Crazy, he knew, but he'd never felt so close to a woman before. The thought of never holding her again was like a blade to his heart. For the first time in his life, he wasn't looking forward to moving on.

FAITH WOKE WITH a start. For a moment she couldn't remember where she was. Her gaze took in the room she'd grown up in, but other than that, this was unfamiliar territory. She'd never made love with a man in this house, in this bed, in this manner. She'd never given herself so completely, felt so safe, knowing all the time that this was temporary.

She let go of Jud's hand and rolled over to face him. He was even more handsome in the morning looking a little sleepy, a little vulnerable. She couldn't help but smile as she touched her fingers to his rough un-shaven jaw.

Her cell phone rang. She glanced at the clock. It was early. The sun had just come up. They weren't expected on the set for hours yet.

"Hello?" She had expected her sister to call last night and check on her. Or at least Carter to call. Neither had, and now that she thought about it, that was odd.

As she answered the phone, she swung out of bed and pulled Jud's shirt on as she stepped to the second-story window. A sheriff's deputy's car was parked in the trees not far from the house.

"Faith." Carter's voice startled her.

"You had a deputy watching the house all night?" she snapped angrily.

"I do what I have to do to protect my family and this community," he said, sounding irritated. "I called because Keyes Hasting has been found."

Her heart flip-flopped. If it wasn't Hasting she'd seen being dragged away from the set—

"He was found murdered in his rental car not far from Lost Creek ghost town."

"Oh, no." Behind her, Jud looked concerned.

"Erik Zander has been taken into custody. I want you to stay put. The assistant director, Nancy Davis, said she will let you and Jud know as to plans regarding finishing the film."

Faith flashed on the memory. Someone dragging away what had looked like a body. It had been Zander?

"Zander confessed?"

Another short silence. "He resisted arrest and, complaining of chest pains, was rushed to the hospital, where he died a few hours ago."

"Then how do you know he—"

"Keyes Hasting had some incriminating photographs taken at Erik Zander's Malibu beach house the night Camille Rush drowned in the hot tub and had apparently been blackmailing Mr. Zander. It would appear that Hasting had blackmailed him into doing the film."

Faith sat down on the edge of the bed. She felt Jud slide in behind her, his hands kneading her shoulder muscles. "He didn't say anything?" she asked dully.

"No. It appears he died of a heart attack," Carter said. "We found more evidence of the blackmail in Mr. Zander's trailer."

Faith was too shocked to think straight. She kept calling up images from the other night, something nagging at her. If only she could remember.

"So that's it." She tried to breathe a sigh of relief as she hung up the phone and told Jud what Carter had told her.

After their initial shock and disbelief passed, he said, "I'm just glad it's over." He pulled her to him.

Whatever had been nagging at her was forgotten the moment Jud kissed her.

NANCY CALLED TO say that shooting would continue. "I know Erik would have wanted us to finish this film."

Jud had his doubts about that, given what the sheriff had told them confidentially. But since Nancy had been in charge of most everything to do with the film before Zander's death, she said finishing the film wouldn't be that hard given that they had only two more days of shooting.

"We'll shoot the rest of the stunts this afternoon," Nancy said. "I left a message on Faith's cell phone. If you see her, let her know."

"Will do," he said as Faith came out of the shower wrapped in a towel.

Jud told her what Nancy had said, still a little surprised. But then again, this was the movies. No time for sentiment.

He and Faith were still in shock over the earlier news about Hasting's murder and Erik Zander's death.

"Blackmail?" he repeated, not for the first time. "I still can't believe it."

"Apparently the photographs Hasting had of the night of the Malibu party where Camille Rush died were incriminating enough that Zander went along with the blackmail," Faith said as he watched her get dressed.

He would never get tired of looking at her. Or touching her. Or making love to her. In fact, right now, all he wanted to do was climb back into the bed with her. He would have been content just to hold her.

"Didn't I hear that you were at that party?"

It took Jud a moment to shift gears. He nodded. "I left before it happened." He frowned. "Keyes Hasting wasn't at the party. So how did he get incriminating photographs?"

"Someone else at the party?" Faith suggested, sitting down on the edge of the bed next to him. "I found out something yesterday. This wasn't the first starlet connected to Erik Zander who died. Over twenty years ago, another one died in a car wreck. Zander was allegedly drunk and driving and left the scene of the accident, but he was never charged for the woman's death. The death mirrors the one in the hot tub in that the woman was allegedly pregnant with his child."

"So you kept digging into things, didn't you?" Jud said.

Faith ignored him. "The woman had a daughter named Samantha Brooke Keifer. The daughter changed her name to Brooke Keith."

He sat up straighter in the bed. "You're telling me it was Brooke's mother?"

"Kind of a coincidence, wouldn't you say, given everything that's been going on?"

"You're not sorry I talked you into doing the stunts for this film even with everything that has happened?" Jud asked.

She shook her head and smiled over at him. "You made my dreams come true. I'll never forget that. Or forget you."

He swallowed, realizing that tomorrow the film would be over. And then what? "What are your plans after the film is over?"

FAITH HAD KNOWN this day was coming and was ready. "Spend the rest of the summer here on the ranch helping my sisters," she said without hesitation. "McKenna has a horse ranch not far from here and Eve always needs help running the cattle ranch my parents left us. There's always plenty to do."

What she hadn't let herself think about was fall. She'd finished college with a liberal arts degree and no plan for the future. Because nothing but trick riding had interested her.

Doing the stunts on *Death at Lost Creek* had only made her more interested in trick riding. She just wasn't so sure she wanted to do movies. She loved Montana. This was home. Unlike Jud, she didn't like the moving-on part after a job was over.

"What about you?" she asked when he fell silent.

"I have another movie, this one being filmed in Wyoming down by Laramie. I was thinking that maybe I could see about getting you a job on the film."

She shook her head. "Thanks, but I don't think so." She couldn't imagine anything worse than trailing after Jud film after film. Better to end it later today after their last stunt, no matter how painful. Make their goodbyes short and sweet.

Faith glanced at the clock. "I suppose we better get going."

Jud seemed to hesitate as if there were something more he wanted to say. Whatever it was, he rose and without another word headed for the shower while she went down to make them something to eat before they left for the set.

THE AFTERNOON SHOOT went off without a hitch. Jud couldn't believe how professional Faith was or how talented. She did all but one of the stunts on the first take. He could tell that Nancy was pleased.

Nancy seemed different without Zander around— more confident, definitely in control. She'd pulled her hair back into a ponytail and, on closer inspection, appeared to be wearing makeup. Jud knew people dealt differently with tragedy, but Nancy seemed to be in awfully good spirits. Either that or she was trying hard to hide her shock and grief.

"You did a great job," Nancy told Faith when they went to Nancy's trailer to collect their pay. "Here you go." Nancy had their checks ready.

"Jud, as always," she said as she handed him an envelope.

She rose to shake their hands. "I added a little extra to both of your checks. Best of luck to you both."

As they stepped out of the trailer, Faith shot him a look. "Was that odd or was it just me?" she whispered.

"Very odd. I've never been paid more than I was contracted for per stunt."

"I meant Nancy," Faith whispered as they walked toward her trailer.

"She does seem to be in a fine mood. I think she likes calling the shots. Zander held her back. I think she's glad he's gone."

Jud realized everything had gone much smoother today than it had when Zander was directing. "Chantal even showed up on time and didn't complain. Nevada didn't scowl at me."

"It's as if a cloud was over this place before," Faith commented as they reached her trailer. "I just have to get my things. Fortunately, I didn't bring much out here." She seemed to hesitate and Jud feared he knew what was coming. "I think we should say goodbye now. Leave it on a high note."

Jud couldn't speak as she held out her hand to shake his. He took her hand and held it. "At least let me take you to dinner tonight to celebrate."

She shook her head. "Thank you, but I think this is best." She smiled then, her blue eyes shining. "See you in the movies." With that she extracted her hand from his and went into her trailer, closing the door behind her.

FAITH STOOD ON the other side of the trailer door, fighting to hold back the tears. She had trouble catching her breath. She couldn't remember ever doing anything as hard as saying goodbye to Jud.

Her heart felt as if it would break into a million pieces. Each beat was a labor. How would she ever get over him?

She'd done the worst thing possible. She'd fallen in love with him. Hadn't she told herself not to? She knew from the get-go that Jud wasn't the staying type, let alone the marrying type. Neither was she, she reminded herself.

And yet now she finally understood what had happened to her friends, why they'd traded their dreams of adventure for a mortgage and diapers when they'd fallen in love.

Love. It changed everything.

She quickly packed up her few things, then, checking to make sure no one was around, she hurried to her pickup. Five miles down the road, she had to pull over, she was crying so hard.

"SO THAT'S THE end of that, huh?"

Jud turned to find Brooke standing behind him. He'd been sitting off by himself on an outcropping of rocks, staring out across the prairie. "Film's over," he said gruffly, wishing she'd leave him alone.

"I can see you're in a good mood," she said sarcastically. She sat down on a rock next to him. "It's not the first heart you've broken. She'll get over it."

He laughed and looked over at her. "What makes you think it's *her* heart that got broken?"

Brooke pulled back in mock surprise. "You have a heart?"

"Funny."

"Come on, Jud, this isn't like you," she said. "Finishing a film is always a letdown. You just need to get on to the next one. You won't even remember that little cowgirl."

He could have argued the point, but didn't. "No one seems very upset by what happened with Zander."

"It was a shock, but it's Hollywood. Maybe we're all cynics or maybe we're just numb to this sort of thing." She shrugged. "You have to admit Nancy seems to be as good a director as Zander was, maybe better because she's sober during the day." Brooke laughed and nudged him. "Come on. I'll let you take me out to dinner tonight. The Corbett Code doesn't apply now that we don't work together."

He shook his head. "I'd make a lousy dinner companion, trust me. Anyway, I need to go out to the ranch. But maybe some other time. Are you heading to Wyoming for the next Western?"

She shook her head. "I'm taking some time off. Regrouping," she said, getting to her feet and brushing off her backside.

"Can I ask you something?" Jud said, looking up to her. "What was your mother's name?"

"Angie. Why?"

"Just curious. Angie Keith?"

"Yeah," she said and lied to his face. "But she changed her last name a lot. I lost count of all the stepfathers I had. Why would you want to know that?" Her eyes filled with suspicion.

"I thought you'd mentioned before that you had stepfathers," he said casually. "I have a stepmother now. It's a little strange. I call her Kate. But it turns out she has a daughter, so now I have a half sister. So what does that make her to me?"

Brooke laughed. "She's just a stepsister by marriage. Kids usually come with stepparents. How old is this stepsister?"

"My age. Instant relatives."

"Been there," Brooke said, seeming to relax. "One day you're an only child and the next day your new daddy's kids are moving in and taking your stuff and telling you what to do. It sucks, but it comes with the territory."

"It must have been hard growing up like that."

She shook it off. "What doesn't kill you makes you strong. Actually, it was okay having stepsisters. There's a bond between sisters. It's hard to explain. Even when you don't share the same blood. Good luck with your next gig. Maybe we'll see each other around."

"Maybe we will," he said, watching her walk away. His first instinct when Brooke was out of earshot was to call Faith. She'd want to know what he'd learned, wouldn't she?

As he keyed in the number, he didn't kid himself. It was just an excuse to hear her voice. Unfortunately, her voice mail picked up.

"Hey, it's me, Jud. I just talked to Brooke. I verified what you found out about her mother. Sounds like she had a rough life, lots of stepfathers and step-siblings. Bet she didn't have sisters like yours." He hesitated, wishing he'd waited to tell her all this. Now what would he use for an excuse to call her later?

JUST OVER THE next rise, Brooke listened to Jud's phone call, balling her hands into fists as she heard him click off.

Who had he called?

Faith.

She quickened her pace, not wanting him to catch up with her. She didn't want him to know she'd overheard his call.

As she reached the camp, she hurried to her trailer to deal with her disappointment.

She'd thought for sure that once the film shoot was over Jud would forget about his little cowgirl and be ready to move on to his next conquest.

Not that Brooke saw herself in that role. But why not? He'd never even asked her out. And what about his stupid Corbett Code? He'd gone out with Faith. She knew for a fact that they'd spent the night together.

Her disappointment with Jud was almost too much to bear. He was acting as if he'd fallen in love with Faith. That wasn't possible, but she'd never seen him this despondent.

Letting out a cleansing breath, she straightened, dried her eyes and readied herself to go see Nancy and collect her money. She'd get over this and move on.

But as she left her trailer, she felt at loose ends. She hadn't expected having this over would be such a letdown, let alone having Jud disappoint her the way he had.

He didn't seem to understand what a good friend she was. Maybe she'd have to tell him, she thought bitterly as she walked through the quickly disappearing camp. But then, that would spoil everything. Better to let it go, right?

By this time tomorrow, no one would ever know they'd been here. That was the way it should be, Brooke thought as she knocked on Nancy's door. Here and gone.

Chapter Fourteen

"They're packing up and leaving," the deputy sheriff said when he reported in. "Looks like a damned carnival—everything loaded on trailers, and pulling out."

Sheriff Carter Jackson swore under his breath. The evidence had been collected. He had no reason to detain the film crew. Just a few loose ends to tie up and this case would be history.

He covered the mouthpiece with his hand and hollered in to the office. "Any word from the coroner on the autopsy or from the crime lab on that DNA test?"

"Not yet," the clerk called back.

"Let them leave. We have no reason to hold them," Carter said.

As he hung up, he told himself that he had Keyes Hasting's killer. All the evidence pointed directly to Erik Zander. Maybe that's what was bothering him. It was all too neat, right down to the director's heart attack.

Carter remembered his sister-in-law's reaction when he'd told her the killer was apparently Zander. She'd sounded doubtful. Something about all this was bothering her, as well. She'd seen the killer dragging the body away to an old pickup. Had she remembered something?

The crime team had gone over the pickups the film crew had rented for the shoot but found nothing. That damned rain had washed away any evidence. Everyone had access to the trucks, including Zander. He had motive and opportunity. He'd tried to make a run for it when they'd gone to arrest him.

What more did Carter want?

He snatched up his phone on the first ring, hoping this was finally some good news. "Sheriff Jackson."

"Bad day?" It was his wife, Eve. His tone changed at just the sound of her voice.

"Not anymore." She'd been through so much lately and he'd missed it. He couldn't believe that she'd finally found her family. The change in her had been dramatic. Now maybe she could move on.

He'd been thinking about that. Sometimes this job got to him and he thought about going back to ranching so he could spend more time with Eve.

"Are you coming home for dinner?"

He groaned, suddenly aware of how late it was getting. "I have to wait for two reports on this Hasting murder. I'm sorry."

"McKenna and Nate have invited me over," Eve said. "Maybe I'll go if it's all right with you. If you get your reports early, you can join us."

"That sounds great. Have you told your sisters yet?"

"Not yet. But I will when the time is right."

He loved the serenity in her voice. Finding out about her mother had been painful but had released her. She now had a family that shared her blood. He knew how much that meant to her.

"I've been thinking," she said. "I know you're busy, but I think I'm ready to start a family."

He wanted to let out a whoop of joy. "Oh, Eve, I wish I could come home right now."

She chuckled. "Maybe after you get your reports..."

He hung up, happier than he could remember being.

FAITH CAME BACK from her ride and saw that Jud had called. She considered erasing the message without listening to it. After saying goodbye to Jud, she'd come straight to the ranch, saddled her horse and ridden deep into the Missouri Breaks.

But nothing would take away the ache inside her. Jud Corbett had broken down all her barriers. She'd opened herself up to him, knowing full well how it would end. At the time, she promised herself there would be no regrets.

But there were plenty of regrets.

Hadn't Brooke tried to warn her? *Don't take anything about movies seriously, especially Jud Corbett.*

Faith hesitated for a moment, then played Jud's message. He sounded odd, she thought. She played the message again, actually listening to his words and not trying to read something into his tone.

"Sisters?" *Bet she didn't have sisters like yours.* As Faith snapped the phone shut, she stood for a moment trying to understand why something was still nagging at her about Hasting's murder.

From where she stood, she could see the dark outline of the Little Rockies against the deepening darkness. Suddenly, she didn't want to be alone tonight. She picked up the phone and tapped in Eve's number. No answer.

"You're just being silly," she told herself as she walked out onto the porch. A breeze stirred the loose ends of her hair that had come free from her ponytail. She breathed in the night air, the familiar scents making her feel a little better.

Carter is convinced he got Hasting's killer. It's over. By now the film crew has packed up and probably left town.

A hawk flew over, the rustle of wings and motion startling her. What was wrong with her? She wasn't usually this jumpy. Faith chuckled at the thought. Why wouldn't she feel vulnerable? She'd seen a murderer, gotten so close he'd not only seen her, he'd struck her. She shivered at the thought.

Zander was dead. She was safe. So why did she feel so anxious? *Because you let yourself fall in love with Jud Corbett.*

That's what she'd done all right. Fallen for the arrogant, handsome, funny, charming stuntman.

Shaking her head, she went back into the house and did something she'd never done before. She locked the door behind her. Whatever had her keyed up tonight, whether it was murder or love, she wasn't taking any chances.

"YOU'RE AWFULLY QUIET TONIGHT," Dalton Corbett said as he joined his brother Jud in the family room at Trails West.

Jud stared out at the growing darkness. The outline of the Little Rockies was etched black against the coming night. He wondered if Faith was looking out at the mountains, as well.

"Jud?" Dalton gave him a nudge.

"Sorry. What?"

Dalton laughed. "I was hoping you were bringing that adorable cowgirl you brought to dinner the other night. You look as if she dumped you."

Jud smiled at that. "She did."

"*Sure* she did."

Juanita called them in to dinner. Jud wasn't hungry, but he rose with the others and wandered into the huge dining room. He could smell the chile verde, warm homemade tortillas, pinto beans and bits of ham simmering in a pot on the table and his stomach growled. *Traitor.*

The conversation around the table was lively, his family in good spirits. Jud knew it was because Maddie was here with Shane. The wedding was on. Maddie and Kate seemed to be working out their differences. His father couldn't have looked happier.

"Finally a wedding," Lantry said and grinned over at Jud. "Let me see, who's next? Oh that's right, wasn't it Jud who drew the shortest straw?"

Everyone laughed but Jud. He looked around the table at all the smiling faces and felt worse than he had earlier. As food was passed to him, he filled his plate, but every bite tasted like cardboard—not that he would tell Juanita that. She'd hit him with the plate of tortillas.

"So where's your next movie?" Kate asked, studying him.

"Wyoming. But I have a few weeks before it begins." He filled a tortilla with chile verde and took a bite.

"Good," his father said. "You can stay with us for a while." Grayson beamed.

"You can help plan Shane and Maddie's wedding," Russell joked.

"I haven't decided what I'm going to do just yet," Jud said and saw his stepmother studying him again with a look of compassion as if she recognized heartbreak and felt for him.

"Tell us about the murder investigation," Lantry said.

Normally Kate would have objected to such a discussion at the dinner table. Jud was glad she didn't, grateful for a change of subject. He told them what he could.

"Faith *saw* the killer?" Kate said, her hand going to her throat.

Jud nodded. "He struck her with something. If she hadn't gotten away…and if I hadn't seen her wandering through the camp…" He didn't want to think about that.

"Well, she must be glad the killer isn't still out there," Kate said.

Jud nodded, remembering how Faith had questioned the sheriff. She hadn't believed the killer was Zander. He felt a tightening in his stomach. He found himself on his feet.

"Jud?" His father's voice.

"Is everything all right?" Kate asked.

"No—that is, I'm not sure. I just have this feeling." He glanced around the table to find them all staring at him. "I have to go. I'm sorry. I don't have time to explain." He threw down his napkin and headed for his pickup.

CORONER RALPH BROWN called just as Carter was about to give up and go join his wife at dinner with her sister and brother-in-law.

"Sorry it took so long, Sheriff," Ralph said. "We've been waiting for the results of the lab tests."

"And?"

"Erik Zander had a drug in his system called metabelazene, which constricts the blood vessels. In large doses it causes labored breathing, dizziness, confusion and death."

"Doc said Zander had been in the emergency room earlier this week with what had appeared to be a panic attack. But he ran lab tests. Wouldn't he have found this metabelazene if that's what it was?"

"Not necessarily. I doubt they tested for it. It's a new drug. It's often given for snakebite victims."

Carter felt his pulse jump. The moment he hung up, he called Doc over at the hospital. "I need to ask you a quick question. Did you give Brooke Keith metabelazene for her rattlesnake bite?"

Doc sighed. "You know I can't—"

"Do you usually prescribe metabelazene for snakebites, just tell me that."

"Yes, it's the most effective new drug we've found, but you have to be careful because of the side effects and too much of it, of course, can kill a person."

Carter hung up and, grabbing his hat, headed for the door.

SHERIFF JACKSON TOPPED the hill overlooking where the film crew had camped. The set was gone and so were all of the equipment trailers and trucks, most of the residential trailers. Only three remained.

His cell phone rang. He stopped his patrol SUV, killing the headlights as he took the call. It was one of the techs at the crime lab, working late.

"The DNA from the doll brought up a name," the tech said. "I thought you'd want to know right away."

"Someone with a record?"

"You guessed it. A small-time crook named John Crane. He's serving time in California for robbery."

"He's in prison. Then how—"

"The DNA wasn't a perfect match, but close enough that it has to be one of his siblings. A sister."

"Sister?" Carter echoed.

"Half sister would be my guess. You know, with all these mixed families anymore…"

A half sister. "So you're saying that the blood on that doll belongs to a half sister of this John Crane. So she probably doesn't share the same last name."

"With the blending of families you end up with lots of different last names unless the stepfather adopts the children. Add to that all the couples who are blending families without the benefit of marriage and there is no record of these relationships."

Which meant Carter was back to square one. Not quite, he reminded himself. He knew Zander had been murdered. He also knew the blood from the doll was a woman's and Brooke Keith had been given the same drug for her snakebite that had been used to murder Zander. He also knew she had a motive for killing the director—her mother's death all those years ago.

"Sorry I couldn't be of more help."

"No, I appreciate you staying on this for me. Thanks." Hanging up, Carter turned on his headlights again and drove down into what was left of the camp.

He wondered why three trailers were still here and noted that there were only two vehicles. He parked and walked toward the first trailer. Voices rose up out of the darkness. As he neared the trailer, he saw a camp-fire blazing in the distance. Two people were standing by it, laughing and drinking.

He unsnapped his holster and moved toward them.

As he drew closer, he saw that the figures standing by the fire were two women. He recognized them from when he'd come out here questioning everyone about Keyes Hasting's possible disappearance.

Chantal Lee must have heard him approach. She turned from the fire to squint into the darkness, then seemed to start as she saw him. Immediately she checked her expression.

"Why, Sheriff, it's so good of you to join us," she said, and laughed as she held up the half-empty bottle of wine in her hand. "I hope you're not here to arrest us for being drunk and disorderly. We're just celebrating the end of the film. It's a tradition."

"You're sure you're not celebrating Erik Zander's death?" Carter asked, directing his question to the other woman standing by the fire.

Brooke Keith raised her gaze slowly. He saw contempt in the stuntwoman's gaze. She said nothing, just seemed to be waiting.

Hadn't Faith mentioned something to Eve about the two women hating each other? And yet here they were.

"I suppose you could say this is a wake for poor Erik, as well," Chantal said. "You know, I was afraid he'd had a heart attack that other time, when the doctor said it was nothing more than a panic attack. The man was under a great deal of stress."

"He didn't die of a heart attack," Carter said.

"Really?" Chantal sounded genuinely surprised.

"He was murdered."

She gasped, covering her mouth as her gaze shifted to Brooke standing across the blaze from her. A look passed between them.

"Do you still have the drugs you were given for your snakebite, Ms. Keith?" he asked.

"I don't. I didn't need them anymore, so I threw the remainder away. Are you telling me someone dug them out of the trash?"

Carter could see how this was going down. Unless he had hard evidence, there would never be a conviction. The problem was, he thought, as he looked back and forth between the two of them, he wasn't sure who had actually killed Hasting—or Zander.

He glanced behind him toward the trailers. Three still left, and only two vehicles. "Who is staying in the third trailer?" he asked, suddenly apprehensive.

"Nancy Davis, the assistant director," Chantal said. "It wouldn't be a celebration without her." They both laughed, clearly an inside joke.

He started to turn back to them, sensing that he'd made a terrible mistake. The blow took his feet out from under him. He heard the crack of the piece of firewood as it connected with his head, felt the repercussions rattle through him and the surprise when he found himself staring up at the stars.

"What the hell did you do that for? Now we're going to have to get rid of him, too," he heard one of them say just before everything went black.

FAITH MADE HERSELF a peanut butter and chokecherry jelly sandwich, eating it standing in the well-lit kitchen. She wasn't hungry, but she knew she had to eat.

She kept thinking about Jud's phone call. She

thought about calling him back on the pretense of wanting to discuss what he'd learned from Brooke.

Erik Zander had been responsible for Brooke's mother's death and now Zander, labeled a murderer for Hasting's death, was dead himself. How just things had turned out after all these years.

Was that what bothered her? She couldn't seem to get out of her head the images from the night she'd seen the killer dragging away Hasting's body. Something was wrong.

And not just with that night. Nancy's reaction when Faith had asked about Ashton, Idaho, and Brooke. Chantal and Brooke's rivalry. The accidents on the set. Nevada and Chantal.

There were always undercurrents on any film, but nothing like on *Death at Lost Creek*. And amazingly as if by magic, they'd all gone away the moment Zander was dead and Nancy took over to finish the film. The only person with a possible grudge against Zander had been Brooke and yet she, of all of them, seemed the least affected by his death.

So what did it all mean, if anything? Faith shook her head, suspecting all her nagging doubts were just her way of diverting her attention away from thinking about Jud. As if that were possible. Every heartbeat reminded her that he was gone.

Faith took a hot bath, hoping to relieve some of her tension. She'd never been afraid in this house, but tonight she'd locked all the doors and had been tempted to check every closet. She couldn't understand her unease.

Filling the tub, she stripped down and slipped into the warm, sudsy water. The water lapped over her naked body. Images of making love with Jud rushed at her. She ducked her head under the water, holding her breath until she couldn't anymore.

Bursting out of the water, she heard something. A creak. Old houses always creaked. But this creak was more like a slow, furtive footstep on a lower stair. After all these years in the house, Faith knew which stairs creaked the loudest.

She brushed her wet hair back from her face and listened. Another creak. Rising out of the bath as quietly as possible, she toweled off and pulled on her robe. She'd left the bathroom door open and now edged toward it. Stopping, she listened.

Another creak below. Someone was sneaking up the stairs.

Frantically, Faith looked around the bathroom for something she could use as a weapon. She'd never used hairspray, didn't keep anything more lethal than an emery board in the medicine cabinet and knew digging out the blow dryer from the bottom cabinet would take too much time—and make too much noise. Also, it didn't make much of a weapon.

Her mind was racing. All her earlier anxiety came back to her. She'd been jumpy because she'd known this wasn't over. It hadn't been Erik Zander who'd dragged Hasting away from the camp. But how did she know that?

It didn't matter now, she told herself. Her cell phone was downstairs in her purse. There was no landline in her bedroom. She had to find a weapon she could use.

Something in the bedroom. Maybe the lamp next to her bed. Or a bookend from the shelf next to it.

She stepped around the door and into her bedroom. And froze.

The only light came from the lamp beside her bed. It cast a golden glow over the bed with its white chenille bedspread and brightly colored pillows.

Faith let out an involuntary gasp at the sight.

The doll sat against one of the pillows, its grotesque face staring out at her. But it wasn't the doll that made her take a step back, stumbling into the wall.

It was the person standing next to her bed.

"Nancy?" Faith said, trying to catch her breath. Her thumping heart threatened to bust out of her chest. All she could think was, *I should have checked the closets.* "What are you…" The rest of her words died on her lips as she saw the gun the woman held.

"You have to come with me," Nancy said calmly, as if there was a stunt that needed to be shot. "Please don't make this more difficult than it has to be."

"Where?"

"To a party," she said.

Faith stared at the woman. Was she insane? "A *party*?" Obviously a party requiring Nancy hold a gun on her to get her to go.

"Your brother-in-law the sheriff is there waiting. Wouldn't it be awful if something happened to him? I know how close you are."

"You're lying."

"Am I? You really want to take that chance? If you want your sister ever to see him again do as I tell you. Get dressed."

Her head was whirling. This was just a bad dream, that's why it didn't make any sense.

"Hurry."

Outside, Faith saw one of the pickups Nancy had rented for the movie. Just like the one she'd seen that night at the dry creek bed.

"I don't understand why you're doing this," Faith said as she slid into the passenger seat.

"Sure you do," Nancy said as she slammed the door and walked around to climb behind the wheel. "You're an eyewitness in Keyes Hasting's murder."

Faith shook her head. "I didn't see Zander, or if I did, I can't remember." She touched the healed cut on her temple.

But hadn't she known Zander didn't kill Hasting? She hadn't seen him that night. But who had she seen? Nancy? Is that what this was about? Nancy was afraid she'd remember?

"What have you done with the sheriff?"

"You'll see," Nancy said. "Just remember, if you try anything, he dies."

Faith stared at the road ahead as Nancy drove, the gun resting on her lap.

She refused to let her earlier fear paralyze her. She had to keep her wits about her if she had any hope of getting out of this.

THE NIGHT WAS unusually dark. Wind blew over the tall green grass beside the road as Jud drove his pickup toward Faith's ranch house. He felt a sense of urgency he couldn't explain. Nothing made sense. All he knew was that he had to get to Faith.

Just this morning he'd awakened in her bed. He smiled at the memory. He wanted to wake in her bed every morning for the rest of their lives.

That thought made him laugh out loud, because it

was one he'd believed he would never give voice to. He *loved* her. He wanted to scream it to the heavens. It was amazing that Jud Corbett had fallen in love. Wait until he told his family.

His fear kicked up a notch at the thought that the woman he loved and wanted to share the rest of his life with was in mortal danger. He felt it as intensely as he felt his love for her.

He was already going too fast, but he sped up. His mind raced as he began to see a pattern. The accidents on the set. Hasting's death. Zander's heart attack.

Was it possible?

Fear seized him as he realized what it was about Faith's story that had nagged at her. The tailgate on the pickup she'd seen in the dry creek bed. The killer had put it down after backing up to the embankment.

Zander wouldn't have had to do that. He was a big man. Hasting was small, a lightweight. Zander could easily have tossed him into the truck bed.

But someone smaller, say a woman...

He took the last curve a little too fast. Ahead he could see the Bailey Ranch house. Faith's pickup was parked out front and a light burned upstairs in one of the windows. Her bedroom window.

There was nothing to fear. She was safe in her bed. She would think him a complete fool for rushing over here, scaring her.

Jud swore as he tore into the ranch yard and jumped out, taking the porch stairs two at a time. To hell with worrying about looking like a fool. The bad feeling he'd felt at dinner was full-blown now.

The front door was unlocked. "Faith!" He charged

up the stairs. "Faith!" He heard nothing over the pounding of his heart and his boots on the stairs. *"Faith!"*

Her bedroom light was on. So was the bathroom light, the door open. The scent of fresh soap and humidity hung in the air. He could see her robe lying in a heap on the bathroom floor as if she'd just dropped it there.

Faith was gone.

It wasn't until that moment that Jud saw the doll. It was propped up against a pillow—just like all the others that had been discovered on the set.

"Son of a—"

The set. If Zander hadn't killed Hasting, then—

He ran down the stairs, the doll clutched in his hand. He tossed it on his pickup seat and took off down the road toward Lost Creek.

"THE LEAST YOU can do is tell me what all this is about," Faith said as they drove through the darkness.

Nancy shot her a disbelieving look. "Come on, girl detective, you spent all that time digging into our lives. Surely you've figured it out by now."

Had she? "I know about Brooke's mother and Zander. But where does Keyes Hasting fit in?"

Nancy smiled, pleased that Faith wasn't as smart as she thought she was. "His goddaughter was Camille Rush."

"The young woman who drowned in Zander's hot tub?"

"He financed the film as a way to get Erik Zander not just to Montana, but to Lost Creek for us. That was his part. I'd read about the legend of Lost Creek in one of my stepfather's real-life mystery magazines.

The setting was perfect. A vengeful father against an entire town."

Or in this case against Hollywood and the establishment in the form of Erik Zander. "Hasting got Zander to do the movie by blackmailing him and picked the cast and crew."

Nancy smiled over at her. "You really are a girl detective, aren't you?"

"So the accidents on the set were for, let me guess, simply setting the stage, building tension so Zander's heart attack wouldn't be questioned?"

"Damn, girl, you are good."

Faith realized where they were headed. Lost Creek. She should have known. *Death at Lost Creek*, and this plot against Zander was all about symbolism.

"Seems like a lot of trouble for a simple case of revenge."

"It was a whole lot more than that," Nancy snapped. "Zander needed to suffer. He thought *Death at Lost Creek* was going to save him. But before he died he came to realize it was his own death he'd been cast in."

"But why kill Hasting?"

"He'd served his purpose and we needed to frame Zander for his murder. Justice had to be done."

She'd said "we." Just as Faith had suspected, Nancy hadn't acted alone.

"You think killing me is just?" Faith demanded.

"You're collateral damage."

"I can understand how Brooke might want revenge against Erik Zander for her mother's death, but what does any of this have to do with you?" Faith asked as Nancy slowed at the top of the hill overlooking what had been the set. Everything was gone but three trailers. Past them a light burned in the dark night. A fire?

As the pickup bumped down the hill to park next to one of the trailers, Faith spotted a vehicle parked beside one of the trailers. Sheriff Jackson's patrol SUV. Nancy hadn't been lying.

Faith knew this was her chance.

She grabbed the gun, slapping away Nancy's hand as she made a grab for it, and bolted out of the pickup at a run.

"Carter!" she cried as she ran toward the light.

Behind her she heard Nancy get out of the truck. She'd expected Nancy to leave, to make a break for it. Why was she following Faith, who had the gun now?

As she ran past the trailers, Faith saw two dark figures standing around a bonfire. Neither was the right size to be Carter. So where was he?

"Faith?" Chantal said, looking surprised to see her. Or maybe she was surprised to see her holding a gun on them.

"Where is the sheriff?"

Faith heard Nancy approaching the fire and turned the pistol on her. "What have you done with Carter?"

"I see you've met my sisters," Nancy said.

"Sisters?" Faith echoed, distracted for a moment too long.

"Stepsisters," Chantal said, shoving something cold and hard into Faith's back. "Isn't that a bitch?"

THE PICKUP BUMPED over the rough terrain, jarring Faith painfully as she lay on the hard metal truck bed. Her wrists and ankles were tied with rope that was cutting off her circulation. Next to her, Carter groaned as he slowly came awake. His hair was caked with blood and when she'd first seen him, she'd thought he was dead and had almost lost it.

"Faith?" He swallowed, licked his lips and looked around.

"They're taking us to the ghost town," she whispered, not sure the three in the front of the pickup couldn't hear them. It could work to their advantage that they didn't know Carter had regained consciousness.

He closed his eyes for a moment as they were both jostled when the pickup hit a bump. "Turn your back to me. Maybe I can get you untied."

She did as he instructed and felt his fingers working at the knots.

"It's all three of them, isn't it?" he said.

"They're stepsisters. They were just fighting over who got to drive the pickup and who got to ride next to the window."

"No wonder it appeared they didn't like each other."

"At least that part wasn't an act. They don't know you're awake yet." She felt the rope binding her wrists loosen and she was able to free one hand, then the other.

Faith swung around and worked frantically to untie Carter's hands.

"Get your ankles free," he said as the pickup began to slow. "There isn't time to untie me. Jump down and run."

She worked faster. "I'm not leaving you."

"You have to. It's our only chance. *Go!*"

The pickup engine groaned as it came to a stop.

Faith scrambled to her feet and leaped off the back

of the pickup, hitting the ground running. The dark night swallowed her as she sprinted down the track, the light of the bonfire flickering in the distance.

If she could get to Carter's patrol SUV, she could call for help. There would also be a shotgun in the patrol car. The shotgun would be loaded.

JUD STOPPED ON the other side of the hill from where the movie camp had been and turned off the engine. Getting out, he took the .22 rifle he carried from behind his pickup seat. Every rancher's kid had one for gopher hunting. Gophers dug holes that horses stepped in. Like most places in these parts, Whitehorse had a yearly gopher hunt to get rid of as many of the varmints as possible in one day.

As Jud started out, he wished he had a more powerful weapon with him. The varmints he was hunting tonight would be much larger, much harder to kill.

He topped the hill, staying low, glad for the darkness. He could see three trailers, all dark inside, below in the prairie and three vehicles. Nearby, a fire burned, but there was no sign of anyone around it.

So where was everyone? He just hoped to hell his instincts were right as he dropped on down the hillside and sneaked along one of the trailers. When he got close enough to the SUV, he was startled to see that it was a sheriff's department vehicle.

His apprehension intensified. Something was very wrong here.

He moved to the next trailer, staying to the dark shadows, listening for any sign of life.

The sound of a gunshot ripped through the air. He heard a cry in the distance, then voices. From the direction of the ghost town, pickup brake lights flashed on as an engine cranked over. As the truck swung around in this direction, he ducked down instinctively.

The glow of the headlights washed over the open prairie between him and the ghost town behind the truck. That's when he saw Faith. She was running toward him, holding her side.

It took him an instant to realize what was happening as the sound of another shot filled the night air. The bullet kicked up earth next to Faith in the pickup's headlights as the truck barreled after her, engine roaring.

Jud raised his .22 rifle and aimed for the pickup's front tire. Like shooting fish in a barrel. The tire blew. The pickup rocked crazily in the rutted dirt track, then veered off, headed for the river.

Jud saw a shape rise from the back of the truck and jump free just an instant before the pickup plunged into the Missouri. And then Jud was on his feet, running toward Faith.

She had stumbled and fallen near the bonfire. He ran to her, dropping to his knees. The firelight caught her beautiful face and he saw at once how pale she was.

"Faith," he cried as he saw that she was still clutching her side, her shirt and hand soaked in blood. "Oh, my God." He swept her up into his arms as Sheriff Jackson came running toward him. "She's been shot."

Faith smiled up at him, then at Carter. "I'm fine. Don't worry about me. Get the stepsisters. You can't let them get away," she said, then passed out in Jud's arms.

Chapter Fifteen

"You have a very tough girl there," the doctor said when he came out to tell everyone how Faith was doing. "Fortunately, the bullet didn't hit any organs. She's awake, if you want to see her now."

"I need to see her first," Jud said as the two families started to get to their feet. *"Alone."* He'd been so afraid he would lose her. The thought that she wouldn't know how he felt about her was unbearable—no matter how she felt about him.

He turned to his family and Eve's. They'd filled the waiting room to overflowing. "I'm in love with Faith and I'm going to marry her," he blurted out.

"As if that wasn't obvious," Eve said, to his surprise.

"Don't you think you'd better ask her first?" his brother Shane said.

"Yeah, she might not want you," Dalton agreed.

"Maybe you should give this a little more thought," Russell suggested. The oldest of the brothers was always the most sensible. The women in the room, Maddie, Kate, Eve, McKenna and Juanita, booed him.

Everyone else laughed, Jud along with them. "Nothing is going to change my mind. There is no one like

Faith. Just give me a minute alone with her. Please? This really can't wait."

Kate and his father were smiling knowingly.

"Make it quick," Eve said, only half joking. "We want to see for ourselves that she's all right."

Jud smiled at his sister-in-law-to-be. "Wish me luck?"

"You don't need luck," Eve said. "You have love."

Faith was lying in the bed. The color had come back into her face. Her eyes were that incredible blue that would always remind him of Montana summer days.

"Hi," he said, feeling strangely awkward. This woman had always thrown him off-kilter, leaving his head spinning, from the first. She would give him a run for his money the rest of his days—just as she had on the dance floor, he realized and grinned at the thought. He was ready for the challenge.

FAITH SMILED AS Jud tugged off his Western hat and sidled into the room, looking shy and sweet. The man took her breath away and had from the first day she'd laid eyes on him.

"You've been making a habit of saving my life," she said, then she turned serious. "Thank you."

Jud moved to her bed to take her hand. She watched him swallow and could feel how nervous he was. "There's something I have to tell you. I love you."

Faith felt her heart swell at his words, knowing these were not words Jud Corbett had ever said to another woman. "I love you, too."

He broke out in a big grin. "I can't tell you how happy I am to hear you say that, because I can't stand the thought of spending another day without you.

Marry me, Faith. Make me the happiest damned cowboy in Montana."

She laughed through her tears. "There is nothing more that I'd rather do, but, Jud, I know how much you love being a stuntman, and I've realized that life really isn't for me."

He nodded. "I gave that a lot of thought while I was waiting out there in the hallway to find out whether you were going to live or die, and I think I have a plan you're going to like."

CARTER STUCK HIS head in the hospital-room door. "Well?" he asked.

Jud gave him a thumbs-up.

Carter stepped in. "I need to talk to Faith for a few minutes, and her sisters are about to start a riot out there."

Jud squeezed Faith's hand. "I need to go buy an engagement ring."

"Make it two simple gold bands," Faith said. "I've never been a diamond kind of girl."

Carter shook Jud's hand as he was leaving. "You saved our lives last night. Thank you."

"What happened to them?" Faith asked her brother-in-law when they were alone. He knew she was talking about Nancy, Chantal and Brooke.

"We found three bodies in the cab of the pickup. They drowned together." He shook his head. "It's crazy. I swear they despised each other, and yet they came up with this scheme to bring down a killer," he said.

"So they really were sisters?"

"Stepsisters. I heard them arguing as they were chasing you. I'm surprised they didn't kill each other.

Brooke knew she was allergic to metabelazene snake antidote and yet she still let that snake bite her so she could get the medicine needed to kill Erik Zander."

"They cooked it up among themselves?" she asked.

"Nancy was the leader, from what I could tell. She planned it, but the others went along with it. It isn't even a case of blood being thicker than water."

Faith was stunned.

"The woman Zander let drown in the car accident twenty-three years ago was Brooke's mother and Chantal's and Nancy's stepmother," Carter said. "When that other young woman drowned in a hot tub at Zander's party earlier this year, they hatched this plot with Camille Rush's godfather. It's crazy, but then revenge is, isn't it? Still, I'm amazed those three women were able to almost pull it off. If you hadn't seen one of them dragging away Hasting's body..."

Faith thought of her own sisters and the bond between them. "What about the dolls?"

"Scraps of material were found in Nancy Davis's place in California, but I suspect the three made the dolls together," Carter said. "They couldn't depend on being able to use the doll props once they got to the location shoot, I guess."

The door opened. "Time's up," Eve said. "You can get her statement later. She isn't going anywhere."

The sisters gathered around Faith's bed as Carter left the room, all three of them crying as they hugged and held hands.

"I'm so glad that you're my sisters," Faith said through her tears.

Eve nodded agreement. "There's something I need to tell the two of you."

Faith thought at once of the woman dressed in green that she'd seen on the movie set. The woman who resembled Eve.

"You know I've been searching for my birth mother," Eve said. "Well, I've found my birth family."

"Oh, sis, I'm so happy for you!" McKenna cried.

Faith echoed her sentiments and listened as Eve told her about her aunt Mary Ellen coming to Whitehorse after a call Eve had made during her search.

"My mother and father are gone, but I have a grandmother and an aunt," Eve said, and they were all three crying again.

"So when do we get to meet them?" McKenna wanted to know.

"Soon," Eve said. "They're coming the first part of August. I can't wait to meet my grandmother and for you to meet them, since we're all family, aren't we?"

"The more the merrier," McKenna said with a laugh. "And on that note, I'd like you two to be the first ones to know... I'm pregnant!"

A cheer rose up in the hospital room.

"I guess while we're all making announcements," Faith said. "Jud and I are getting married and we're going to start our own stunt school here in Whitehorse, and we were wondering—"

Eve laughed. "I thought you would never ask. Of course you can have it on the ranch. One-third of the Bailey Ranch is yours, and I know how you feel about the house. We've always known that you would come back here someday and live in it."

Faith laughed. "Actually, I was going to ask you if you'd be my matrons of honor, but you're right, I want to live in the house. There's so many memories there."

Those memories were in every creaking board of that old house. Good memories stayed in a place just like bad ones, she thought, thinking of Lost Creek.

"This calls for a toast," McKenna said, and poured them each a plastic cup of water. She lifted her cup. "To the Bailey girls."

"To the *wild* Bailey girls," Faith said, and they all three clinked plastic cups.

* * * * *

We hope you enjoyed reading
Rogue Gunslinger

&

Hunting Down the Horseman

by *New York Times* bestselling author

B.J. DANIELS

INTRIGUE

Edge-of-your-seat intrigue, fearless romance

From passionate, suspenseful and dramatic
love stories to inspirational or historical,
Harlequin offers different lines to
satisfy every romance reader.

New books available every month.

HIBJDBPA1018

It all began with a kiss. At least that was the way Chloe
Clementine remembered it. A winter kiss, which is nothing like
a summer one. The cold, icy air around you. Puffs of white
breaths intermingling. Warm lips touching, tingling as they
meet for the very first time.

Chloe thought that kiss would be the last thing she
remembered before she died of old age. It was the kiss—and
the cowboy who'd kissed her—that she'd been dreaming about
when her phone rang. Being in Whitehorse had brought it all
back after all these years.

She groaned, wanting to keep sleeping so she could stay
in that cherished memory longer. Her phone rang again. She
swore that if it was one of her sisters calling this early...

"What?" she demanded into the phone without bothering
to see who was calling. She was so sure that it would be her
youngest sister, Annabelle, the morning person.

"Hello?" The voice was male and familiar. For just a
moment she thought she'd conjured up the cowboy from the
kiss. "It's Justin."

Justin? She sat straight up in bed. Thoughts zipped past at
a hundred miles an hour. How had he gotten her cell phone
number? Why was he calling? Was he in Whitehorse?

"Justin," she said, her voice sounding croaky from sleep. She cleared her throat. "I thought it was Annabelle calling. What's up?" She glanced at the clock. *What's up at seven forty-five in the morning?*

"I know it's early but I got your message."

Now she really was confused. "My message?" She had danced with his best friend at the Christmas dance recently, but she hadn't sent Justin a message.

"That you needed to see me? That it was urgent?"

She had no idea what he was talking about. Had her sister Annabelle done this? She couldn't imagine her sister Tessa Jane doing such a thing. But since her sisters had fallen in love they hadn't been themselves.

"I'm sorry, but I didn't send you a message. You're sure it was from me?"

"The person calling just told me that you were in trouble and needed my help. There was loud music in the background as if whoever it was might have called me from a bar."

He didn't think she'd drunk-dialed him, did he? "Sorry, but it wasn't me." She was more sorry than he knew. "And I can't imagine who would have called you on my behalf." Like the devil, she couldn't. It had to be her sister Annabelle.

"Well, I'm glad to hear that you aren't in trouble and urgently need my help," he said, not sounding like that at all.

She closed her eyes, now wishing she'd made something up. What was she thinking? She didn't need to improvise. She was in trouble, though nothing urgent exactly. At least for the moment.

Don't miss
Rugged Defender *by B.J. Daniels,*
available November 2018 wherever
Harlequin® Intrigue books and ebooks are sold.

www.Harlequin.com

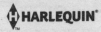

INTRIGUE
EDGE-OF-YOUR-SEAT INTRIGUE, FEARLESS ROMANCE.

Save **$1.00**
on the purchase of ANY Harlequin® Intrigue book.

Available wherever books are sold, including most bookstores, supermarkets, drugstores and discount stores.

- ✂

Save **$1.00**

on the purchase of any Harlequin® Intrigue book.

Coupon valid until December 31, 2018.
Redeemable at participating outlets in the U.S. and Canada only.
Limit one coupon per customer.

52616062

5   65373 00076   2   (8100)0 12394

® and ™ are trademarks owned and used by the trademark owner and/or its licensee.

HICOUP54272

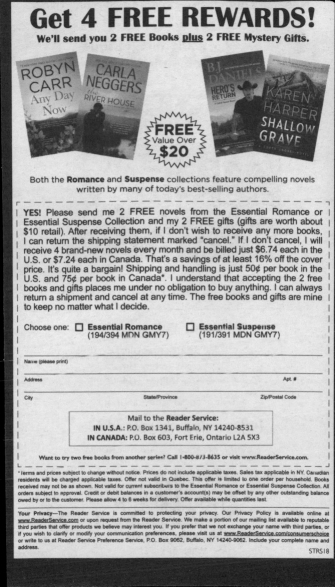